D0338535

CRUX

also by Richard Aellen

REDEYE

CRUX

a novel by

RICHARD AELLEN

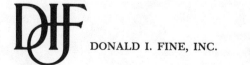

DONALD I. FINE, INC.   NEW YORK

Copyright © 1989 by Richard Aellen
All rights reserved, including the right of reproduction in
whole or in part in any form. Published in the United
States of America by Donald I. Fine, Inc. and in Canada
by General Publishing Company Limited.

Library of Congress Cataloging-in-Publication Data

Aellen, Richard.
    Crux : a novel / by Richard Aellen.
        p.   cm.
    ISBN 1-55611-135-5
    I. Title.
PS3551.E45C78 1989
813'.54—dc19   88-45861
                                    CIP

Manufactured in the United States of America
10 9 8 7 6 5 4 3 2 1

DESIGNED BY IRVING PERKINS ASSOCIATES

This novel is a work of fiction. Names, characters, places
and incidents are either the product of the author's imagination or are used fictitiously. Any resemblance to actual
events, locales, organizations or persons, living or dead, is
entirely coincidental and beyond the intent of either the
author or publisher.

There is a Keith *G.* Johnson whose name is etched in the Vietnam Veterans Memorial in Washington, D.C. Unlike the fictional Keith Everett Johnson of this novel, no combination of accident and event saw him safely home. My lady of Washington Place will understand if I usurp a dedication otherwise hers in favor of the soldier who died on 05 November 1968, a man whose name remains in perpetuity at panel 39 W line 22, the longitude and latitude of loss.

PROLOGUE

According to the wall, he was dead. Keith Johnson stood at the Vietnam Veterans Memorial and saw himself reflected in the polished black granite, a tall, powerfully built man with prematurely gray hair and borderless black eyes. Inscribed in stone was his own name, *Keith Everett Johnson,* one of thousands who died in Vietnam.

But he was not dead.

Keith glanced at his watch and a drop of water fell from his hair to his wrist. The rain had stopped, leaving the sidewalks puddled and the gutters noisy. A low sun peered through layered clouds, painting the white Washington monuments a pale amber. It was five o'clock. Time to settle accounts, time to finish what began a generation ago in Vietnam.

Keith turned and walked up the sloping brick pathway. It was early Spring, the cherry blossoms were out, and the first flood of tourists had descended on Washington. The entrance to the Memorial was marked by a flagpole surrounded by the emblems of the five military services. Waiting for him was Senator Alex Wescott and his wife, Chris. When she saw Keith, Chris ran forward and they embraced. The texture of her hair, the shape of her body, the fragrance of her perfume, all so familiar to him.

◀ 1

"Have you seen him?" Chris asked.

"Not yet."

Over her shoulder, Keith saw the senator watching them, his face stiff. Still a boyish face, still as handsome as he had been in Chim Bai, only today Alex Wescott's blond hair was matted, his eyes were bloodshot and his skin drawn and sallow. At his feet were two blue Hartman suitcases with price tags still attached. Each case contained one million dollars.

They separated and joined him. "If anything happens to her," Alex warned Keith, "I'm holding you responsible."

"If anything happens to her, you'll share the same—"

"Please," Chris said. They said nothing more, turned away, eyes outward, watching, waiting.

Seventy yards away, lying on the roof of an information booth closed for renovation, a man with a rifle peered through a sniper-scope. One by one he brought the crosshairs to bear first on Senator Alex Wescott, then on his wife Chris, then on Keith Johnson, back from the dead. One of them was his special enemy, the target marked for death.

The man with the rifle was not an assassin but a hunter. Money had never been his goal, not in Vietnam, and not now. His objective was to take out the enemy. A bomb or booby trap would have been easier, but these were clumsy, indiscriminate methods with uncertain results. The rifle was the proper tool of the hunter, one which could be used with surgical precision.

He saw Chris Wescott's expression change when she saw a heavy-set man with red hair wearing a raincoat and snap-brim cap. This was his partner, a man named Jerry Burke. Once, Lieutenant Jerry Burke. The hunter despised his partner and would rather have killed him than his target, but just as in Vietnam, adversity and common interest determined his allies.

He took a deep breath and let it out slowly. In the magnified circle of the scope, the men exchanged a few words. Johnson handed Burke one suitcase but not the other. Something was wrong. They were arguing. Then Johnson pulled a gun, and the hunter knew the time was now. He brought the crosshairs to bear

2 ▶

on the target. The squeezing of the trigger was gentle; the crack of the rifle very loud.

The victim never heard the shot. One moment he was facing Jerry Burke, and then the sidewalk slammed into his back and he was staring at clouds framed by trees, a roaring in his ears, and the two people whose lives had brought him here were leaning down, Chris' face coming toward him, a red film covering the world, and the memory of the day they met, the three of them at Travis Air Force Base, in the time of Vietnam . . .

CHAPTER 1

"Dickheads."

"Honey, it's just the army," Chris said.

"No, it's dickheads making dickhead policy."

"That's what I said."

Keith was driving the Bayshore Freeway toward San Francisco. Chris had just met him at the airport. She sat with one arm braced against the dashboard, sunlight caught in her auburn hair.

"Don't make excuses Christie." Keith said. "Don't ever make excuses for stupidity." He swerved to the inside lane and passed a slow car. A Volkswagen behind them beeped a warning. "Eat my shorts!" Keith yelled.

Chris smiled. Loud anger was good anger. The bad anger was when Keith withdrew into himself and watched the world with smoldering eyes. The bad anger scared her because she was helpless to alter his mood and bring him out of it.

"It's not funny," Keith grunted.

She caressed his leg. "I know."

"Then why are you smiling?"

"Because I'm happy to see my husband."

"Your flunky husband."

"You're not a flunky. You didn't have a chance to flunk."

"Thanks a lot."

"You know what I mean."

Keith let his hand drop to hers. Chris would love him whether he was a grunt or a chopper pilot, but Keith hated what happened. Only dickheads had bad luck. While his peers were smoking dope and cruising the Haight-Ashbury, Keith had earned a private pilot license. And when his friends went to college to avoid Vietnam, Keith joined the army to learn to fly helicopters. He went to Basic Training, scored well on his tests and was given orders to Fort Wolters, Texas. When he arrived he found, instead of a cockpit waiting for him, a new set of orders.

"Vacation in 'Nam," the corporal behind the desk told him with a grin. "Sorry 'bout that."

Keith stared dumbly. "But I just got here. I've got orders to begin flight training—"

The corporal was shaking his head. "Cancelled."

"What do you mean, cancelled?"

"I mean cry a little tear, cancelled is cancelled."

"But that's why I joined the Army, to fly helicopters, that's the whole point . . ."

"So?" The corporal, whose chin was dimpled with pimples, put his hands behind his head and leaned back nonchalantly.

From inside the Administration Building Keith could hear the muffled *whump-whump-whump* of helicopters arriving and departing, the sound of his future slipping away.

"But I already know how to fly," Keith said. "I have a private pilot's license. I have fifty-seven hours. All I need is transition training to helicopters."

"You want a medal or a chest to pin it on?"

The corporal was leaning back in his chair, one foot propped against the metal drawer, watching him with a smug smile. Keith leaned down to pick up his dufflebag, put his hand on the desk and pushed hard. The corporal let out a yell as he toppled over, spilling a metal tray of pencils and half a cup of coffee.

"Dickhead floors," Keith said. "Must have been polished by the Viet Cong. . . ."

Now, as they approached San Francisco, Chris gave him directions into the city.

◀ 5

"Where are we going?" Keith asked.

"A surprise. You'll see."

"We've only got seven hours."

"It won't take that long."

She directed him through the heart of the city to the Mark Hopkins Hotel. "Turn here."

"Why?"

"Turn, turn!" She grabbed the steering wheel and they veered into the circular driveway. A uniformed valet came toward them.

"Chris, what are we doing?"

"I made reservations."

"Here? Jesus, this place is too expensive . . ."

She put her hands on his cheeks and stared at him with somber green eyes. "When you get on that plane tonight, I want you to know how special you are."

The valet opened the door. "Checking in, sir?"

They answered in unison, Chris yes and Keith no. Chris got out of the car and turned to the doorman. "I don't know about this gentleman, but I'm going to my room."

She walked into the hotel without a backward glance. The valet raised an eyebrow. "I don't know about you, sir, but I know what I'd do."

"You park the car."

In the bedroom, they drank champagne and stood at the window with their arms around each other. Below them the city of San Francisco dropped away to the windswept bay where white-capped waves marched in rows before a brisk wind. A slate gray aircraft carrier slid beneath the Bay Bridge behind a red and white tour boat pushing its way toward Alcatraz.

"You see this view?" Chris said. "This is where we're going to be one year from now. I've already reserved the room. The day you get back, we're going to stand right here and drink champagne and do everything we do today."

"Everything?"

"Whatever we do today. I'm going to remember every moment."

Keith's smile faded. With their eyes locked on one another, he took her glass and put it on the window ledge beside his own. She stood with her arms slightly akimbo, like a waiting doll, breathing quickly, lips parted, her eyes bright with desire.

"Keith," she whispered.

He unhooked her skirt and blouse and let them slide to the floor. She wore no bra and stood before him dressed only in panties and boots. He pulled her close. Quick fingers reached out and tugged his belt free. He stepped back, pushed off his shoes, and slid out of his clothes. Chris sat down on the bed and began to tug off her boots.

"Don't."

He knelt in front of her and lifted her legs over his shoulders. His cheek was against her inner thigh, the soft skin a delicious contrast to the texture of the boots and the weight of her legs on his back. He kissed her with small, quick kisses, moving upward, pulled her panties aside and ripped them. Chris let out a gasp. Her hands reached for his head, for his hands, and then grabbed the bedspread as her body arched to meet him.

Her passion came in waves, drew her down, swept her dizzy and tumbling and then released her gently and gasping she surfaced to find his eyes on her and his lips close and in their kisses her own scent, the baptism of their love. He entered her and she thought, now. Let it be now. Let me have the anger, the frustration, the pain, let me consume it, overwhelm it and leave him with my love and my love only . . .

His cry, filled with pain and joy, was the catalyst for her own release and their voices mingled in the transcendental moment of love.

Keith and Chris had met in Healdsburg, a small town sixty miles north of San Francisco. Mismatched by birth and temperament, they instantly fell in love. Keith's mother had disappeared when he was four years old, leaving him with a father who worked as an automobile mechanic between bouts of drinking. Like his father, Keith was tall, but his black hair and deepest eyes were his mother's legacy. In repose, there was a hint of truculence in his expression that vanished when he flashed what one girlfriend termed a "wicked smile."

CRUX

Chris was born Christine Szurek, the youngest daughter of Hungarian immigrants. She had about her an air of distinction, a hint of aristocracy which was in contrast to the long hair, short skirts and go-go boots which were the style of the times. She and Keith were married the day after high school graduation. Their marriage remained the way it began—as a love affair . . .

After the afternoon of lovemaking, the reality of Vietnam made them subdued as they drove to Travis Air Force Base. Because family members weren't allowed beyond the main lounge, Keith and Chris stood arm in arm at a long concourse, filling the pre-departure pauses with reassuring words and gestures. Around them flowed sailors, soldiers, and airmen, the returnees laden with gifts and medals, those departing searching their comrades' faces for some clue to their own fate.

A voice said, "Johnson, give me ten on the knuckles!"

Keith turned to find a soldier with golden hair and blue eyes smiling broadly. He recognized the smile before he remembered the name—Alex Wescott. Alex put down his dufflebag and turned his attention to Chris. In a normal voice he said, "And you must be . . ."

"My wife, Chris." Keith slid an arm around her and said, "Honey, this is Alex Wescott. He was in my company at basic."

Alex gave a slight bow as he shook her hand. "Your charms exceed even this guy's wild exaggerations."

The comment annoyed Keith. He was one of the few men who hadn't joined the usual barracks bragging about girlfriends and sexual exploits.

"Are you going to Vietnam?" Chris asked.

"Sadly, yes. Thanks to a father whose motto is *Death before Dishonor,* by which he means my death before his dishonor. Keith may have told you—I'm the one who flunked my sophomore year and this is my punishment. The only Yalie in the Army below the rank of brigade general."

Keith made a point of looking at his watch. "You on Flight 305?"

"That's affirmative."

"I'll catch at the gate."

8 ▶

Alex favored them with a knowing smile. "Nice to meet you, Chris. And don't worry, I'll take care of this guy for you."

Keith noticed that Alex's uniform had been tailored so that it narrowed at the waist to give him a trim, powerful look. Chris' eyes clouded as she watched him walk away. "He's scared," she said.

"Alex Wescott? No way."

"He is."

"He shouldn't be. His dad's a congressman from Connecticut. He could get any duty he— Wait a minute. Maybe his dad could pull some strings and get me into flight school."

"But if he won't even help his own son . . ."

"Christie, listen, it's a chance. I've got to talk to him. Maybe we can call his father right now, before we leave." He wrapped his arms around her and hugged her close. "A year from now, don't forget."

"Keith, don't . . ."

"What?"

Don't let anything happen, she wanted to say, but it was better not to tempt bad luck by mentioning it. "I love you."

Standing behind a class partition at the far end of the terminal, Alex Wescott took a picture of the two of them embracing. Photographing things he wanted for himself was a hobby, and at the moment he wanted the type of trust and intimacy that Keith and Chris shared. Not like his own family, where his father had sent him off to be killed. Alex remembered his shock when he came home after flunking out of Yale to discover that he had been drafted. He showed the notice to his father. The elder Wescott stood with his arms crossed, his back to the fireplace. "What do you want me to do about it?"

"Let's not be coy, father. Make a phone call. Talk to somebody. You're on the Selective Service board."

"That's precisely why you were drafted." His father's voice was deep, resonant, and emotionless. "I've done you a great disservice, Alexander. All your life I've stepped in to remedy your mistakes, to fulfill your obligations, to hold you harmless from the consequences of your actions. I've warned you but you treat my advice with contempt. Since I can't induce you to accept the responsibilities of adulthood, perhaps the Army will succeed where I've failed."

Alex felt a crooked, uncontrollable smile coming on. "You're not serious."

"I have never been more serious in my life."

"I could be killed in Vietnam."

"You could also grow up . . ."

Alex had hoped that after basic training his father would relent and pull strings to get him a stateside assignment but that hadn't happened. Now he was on his way to Vietnam with a bunch of minorities, losers, and misfits who were dumb enough to get drafted. Plus Keith Johnson, who had joined to fly helicopters and gotten screwed.

Enviously he watched as Keith and Chris made their final farewells. Then Keith joined him at the window, where they both turned for one last look at Chris. She raised a finger to her lips and turned it toward them. Alex was struck by the gesture. He let himself imagine that it was for him. Keith returned her gesture, and they began walking toward the boarding gate, Alex barely focusing on what Keith was saying.

"Will you do it?" Keith asked.

"What?"

"Your dad. Get him to help."

"Help what?"

Keith explained again, and Alex responded with a sardonic smile. "The son proposes, the dad disposes. He took positive pleasure in refusing to get me a stateside assignment; he would have no hesitation turning down my favor I asked for a friend. However, I'll be happy to give you our private home number; considering the time difference you at least might wake him out of a sound sleep."

Keith checked his watch. It was seven forty-five P.M.—ten forty-five on the East Coast.

"When does he go to sleep?"

Alex paused. "You'd really call him?"

"Why not?"

Alex wrote down the number and stood watching while Keith made the call. A female voice answered, "Wescott residence."

"Is Mister, uh, Congressman Wescott there?"

"Who's calling please?"

"It's Keith Johnson. A friend of Alex's."

A few moments later a gruff yet cultivated voice said, "This is Congressman Wescott."

Keith explained who he was and where he had met Alex and launched into his explanation of what had happened. The Congressman's impatience made him nervous and he found himself rushing his words. Alex was grinning.

"Wait a minute, wait a minute," the congressman interrupted at one point. "Where do you live, son? Are you a Connecticut resident?"

"I live in California, sir."

"Well, then, my suggestion is you contact the representative from your own district."

"I don't really know him."

"Son, you don't know me but that didn't keep you from calling."

Alex pushed his stomach out, pumped up his cheeks and began shaking his finger in mock admonition.

"No, sir."

"Then that's what you do."

"One last thing, sir," Keith said quickly, "were you by any chance asleep?"

"Not once the damn phone rang. Goodbye."

Keith and Alex sat together on the long flight to Saigon. There were men from all branches of the military and the atmosphere was one of forced gaiety. Stewardesses sported combat ribbons and unit patches and the drinks flowed freely. When the meal was served, Keith's meat was tough so he made a mock attack on it with his survival knife. The knife was a military design with a saw-tooth back and hollow metal handle designed to hold matches and a compass. Chris had wrapped yarn around the handle, creating a colorful design that obscured the part of the pommel that unscrewed. A coat of varnish made a hard, water-proof surface.

"Where'd you get that?" Alex asked,

"I bought it. It's a pilot's knife. Chris did the handle."

Alex inspected it and ran a thumb along the serrated edge. "What's this?"

"For cutting through aluminum. In case you're forced down and the emergency exits are jammed."

"A moot point when your brains are on the ceiling." Alex tipped the knife upside down and heard something rattle. He shook it.

"Is this hollow?"

Keith took it and listened. He unscrewed the top and, blocking Alex's view with his shoulder, stuffed a napkin into it.

"What's in there?"

"Nothing. Personal stuff." He shook it and the handle was quiet. He slid the knife into its scabbard and put it away. "Don't mention it, okay?"

"The soul of discretion."

But if Alex was discreet, he didn't forget. He was captivated by Chris, by Keith, and by the intimacy they seemed to share. His eye kept returning to the knife.

The random elements of disaster were in place.

CHAPTER 2

Lieutenant Jerry Burke had missed out on what he considered the three top attributes—wealth, good looks, and personality—but he made the most of a fourth—his wits. His wits had lifted him from small-town obscurity, had earned him a scholarship to Dartmouth College, and now, in Vietnam, had transformed him from a mere platoon leader to the Military Liaison Officer of the Chim Bai district. The position was largely self-created and loose enough in its interpretation to provide Burke a number of interesting opportunities.

The lieutenant was nominally the leader of the Second Platoon, Company A, which occupied a fortified position on a hill overlooking the village of Chim Bai. At the other end of the village was a crumbling concrete building, the former home and office of the Michelin Rubber representative. A company of Vietnamese Regional Forces occupied this building, and it was here that Lieutenant Burke established his Liaison Office.

The three new men—Donald Minkin, Alex Wescott and Keith Johnson—arrived by helicopter with the daily mail. Corporal Levy brought them to the courtyard. Minkin was short and stocky with wiry black hair and an eager smile. Johnson, tall and skinny, gazed at Burke with straightforward curiosity. The third man, Wescott, had a baby face and watched with cynical amusement as Burke concluded a deal with an old woman and her two sons for a bronze *trimurti,* a small sculpture featuring Buddhist deities seated on a peacock. Supplying temple art to a museum distributor in New York was one of Burke's most lucrative sidelines. He spoke through an interpreter, a girl named Soong Mung, who was also his lover. Sexual prowess, he'd decided, was the fifth great attribute, and Burke gave himself high marks in this area too.

When the woman had gone, Burke began his usual recitation. "This is the village, Chim Bai. It is a vital link in the strategic-hamlet program. It's not very impressive, but by denying Chim Bai to the enemy, we show the viability of democracy in South Vietnam. I know that you men aren't interested in politics, you're interested in doing your duty and getting back home in one piece. We all feel the same way, even I do." He smiled, inviting their confidence. "You men are lucky. This platoon has some very seasoned NCO's, particularly Sergeant Severa. You listen to him, you watch what he does, do what he says, and when you get home, you'll be alive and proud of yourselves. Any question, Levy will fill you in. That's all."

"Excuse me, lieutenant," Alex said. "I'm not supposed to be here. My MOS is three double oh sixteen."

Burke frowned. "What's that?"

"Administrative assistant. I type eighty words per minute. I was assigned here by mistake."

"Who assigned you?"

"A corporal at Brigade. I've got his unit and I.D. number here." Alex pulled a piece of paper from his pocket.

"Didn't you go through processing?"

"Yes, sir, but the man had the I.Q. of a chimpanzee. He obviously didn't look at my MOS."

"Tell you what, private . . ."

"Wescott, sir."

"Wescott, right. Why don't you talk to Sergeant Severa about it and he'll report back to me." He turned to Levy, who was inspecting the *triumurti.* "Take these men to Severa and get their assignments."

14 ▶

"He's on patrol."

"Good, good." Burke blinked away his surprise, his ignorance of what Severa did and when he did it. "Show the men around, get them settled. Severa can see them when he gets back."

Watching the soldiers leave, Burke noticed the way that Wescott walked, shoulders back, patronizing smile, the same way the sons of wealth and privilege walked at Dartmouth. Fatuous prick, he thought. Severa will take care of you.

Second Platoon headquarters consisted of three hooches and two bunkers behind a triangle of concertina wire which formed a defensive perimeter. The sleeping hooch was an open-sided bamboo building with a low thatched roof. Rows of canvas cots with air mattresses ran up one side and down the other. The men wore T-shirts or no shirts at all and rubber shower shoes rather than boots. Helmets were decorated with slogans, peace signs or the names of girlfriends.

Levy introduced the new men to the other members of the platoon: Noyes, the medic, with his cheeks pocked from acne; Epstein, called the Bronx Indian for his skill in walking point; Lorick, an easy-going Mississippi boy; Garrison, a black man from Louisiana who made no effort to hide his disgust with the new arrivals; Tuchman, who sat in a perpetual half-crouch, nervous and edgy; Ito, the Japanese-American from Hawaii; and a round-shouldered man named Worchek who sat on his bunk picking at his forearm with a pin. Worchek's skin was discolored by a row of black marks, and as Keith watched, he replaced the pin with a pencil and began working the lead into the tiny wound.

"These are my dink dots," Worchek told him. "One for every slope I put away."

Garrison said, "He just tryin' to get lead poisoning."

"I'm Charlie's measles, man. The white death from Kansas City."

As the men talked, Keith discovered that the platoon had a fractured chain of command. Lieutenant Burke had abdicated much of his authority to Sergeant Severa. It was Severa who established the offensive posture for the platoon, detailed patrols,

◀ 15

trained the men and made the decisions during enemy contact. Burke was more involved with being liaison officer and rebuilding Chim Bai, which had been partially destroyed in an attack two months earlier.

They met Sergeant Severa late that afternoon in the command bunker. A compact, muscular man, he had a triangular face and sandy brown hair. His lips were flat and unexpressive but his nose flared, giving an impression of perpetual alertness. Severa sat hunched over a desk in front of makeshift shelves filled with books. One of them, Keith noticed, was the *Selected Works,* by Mao Tse-tung.

"Which one of you is Wescott?"

"I am, sergeant."

Severa looked up, and there was something noticeably odd about his gaze. It took a moment before Keith realized that the eyes didn't focus on the same spot.

Severa motioned to Alex, who stepped up to the desk. "The *Trung uy* tells me you want out."

"Who?"

"Lieutenant Burke. He says you want a transfer. Is that right?"

"My MOS is an admin assistant and I want to do the job I'm best qualified for, that's all. I've got a transfer request right here—"

"Climb in there." Severa inclined his head toward a rubber bag that lay on the floor. It was seven feet long with a zipper running up one side. A body bag.

"I beg your pardon?"

"You heard me, Wescott. Into the bag."

"I don't—"

Severa moved in a quick blur, grabbed Alex's right wrist and pulled his hand flat to the table. A knife appeared in his other hand, moving in a broad arc.

"Move your hand."

Alex pulled his hand back just before the knife slammed into the table.

"Good," Severa said. "You know how to follow orders. Now lie down in the bag."

Alex opened his mouth but the words died in his throat. He stepped into the bag.

"Lie down."

"Sergeant—"

"Move your hand!"

"What?"

"I thought you knew how to follow orders."

Slowly Alex sat down, then lay back in the bag. Severa said, "Let me tell you something, Wescott. In this platoon there are two ways to transfer out: vertically and horizontally. You make the end of your tour, you go out walking. You get in a hurry, you ride the rubber limo. This platoon doesn't need a typist, what it needs is killers. You don't want to be a killer, the enemy will make you a corpse. I don't care what you did in the world, I don't care what the Army taught you. This is the two platoon, my platoon, the most effective platoon in Vietnam. A corpse or a killer, that's your choice. Now you tell me, which do you choose?"

Alex's voice was tight. "This is mental harassment—"

"What?" Severa bellowed. "What did you say?"

"My father's a United States congressman and this is mental harassment."

Severa dropped to his knees and grabbed Alex by the ears. "And this—this is physical harassment." Alex grimaced and grabbed at Severa's wrists. "Don't touch me. Put your hands down, Wescott. Put them *down.*" As he spoke his grip tightened. Alex let out a yell and flattened his hands on the floor. Severa's forearms bulged. "I don't give a fuck if your daddy is the President of the United States, nobody yells out on me. A coward is no better than the enemy—worse because he wears the camouflage of a soldier. Now answer my question, do you want to be a corpse or a killer?

Alex's voice was strained. "A killer."

Severa released him and stood up. "Good. Now you're valuable to me. You laid down as a corpse, now get up as a killer." Alex climbed out of the bag and stood massaging his ears. "Now listen up, all of you. You've had the canned speech from the *Trung uy*—honor, duty, country—you believe it if you want but I'm going to tell you the real reason you're here. You're here to pit yourself against the most dangerous adversary in the world. Your job is to kill your fellow man. His job is to kill you. The army has

◀ 17

supposedly turned you into soldiers. Now I'm going to turn you into hunters. Your adversary is strong, cunning, brave, well-motivated and more experienced. He has the advantage of home terrain. You have superior firepower, control of the air, unlimited reinforcements. And you have me. I know the terrain as well as the enemy and I know the enemy better than he knows himself. You listen to me, you follow my orders, and I'll turn you into hunters of men.

"One final note: personal hygiene. I don't give a shit about your teeth but once a week every man takes a bath in the river. If you're wearing jockey shorts, don't. Constrictive clothing makes crotch rot. Sleeping in the compound, at night, you will have your boots on. During daylight hours you will have them off. Report all medical problems to Noyes immediately." Severa paused, his gaze shifted. "Do I worry you, Minkin?"

"Huh?"

"Words twice, do I worry you?"

"Uh, no, I'm proud to be here."

"Then stop picking your hangnail. The Vietnamese are perceptive people. You look nervous and you lose face. All right, you men are in the third squad. Report to Sergeant Lomax."

They left the bunker, and as soon as they were out of earshot Alex said, "Sadistic bastard."

"Did you see the way his eyes went?" Minkin said. "Like you couldn't tell if he was looking at you or what."

"My old man's going to hear about this. You two are witnesses. You saw what he did."

"Write him up," Minkin said happily. "I'll sign. The man is definitely whacko. Sergeant Whacko."

Keith said quietly, "How'd you get a three double oh sixteen, Alex?"

"I'm qualified, that's how. I type, I spell, and I'm as gung-ho dedicated to preserving accurate records as the next man—"

"You never went to admin assistant school."

"I had a little chat with the classifications clerk. A hundred-dollar chat now rendered worthless by the flea-brains at Brigade."

"You *paid* someone?"

18 ▶

"Don't look so shocked. If the Army doesn't have the sense to put people like you and me where our talents can be best utilized, then our job is to save the army from its own stupidity."

"Not with a checkbook."

"At the risk of disillusioning you, money makes the man."

"Yeah?" Minkin said eagerly. "Then what size check do you write to keep the Viet Cong from blowing your balls off?"

Alex didn't respond. He was watching Keith walk away and felt a stab of resentment. Not because Keith probably wouldn't bear witness to Severa's abuse—Alex knew his father wouldn't give a damn anyway—but because Keith seemed so damn sure of what he believed. Alex envied people like that. And he envied Keith Johnson more with each passing day.

CHAPTER 3

The platoon was divided into three squads, each with its own leader. Keith and Alex were assigned to the third squad led by Sergeant Lomax, a huge black man from Detroit who somehow managed to move silently through the thick vegetation that clutched at Keith and tore noisily as he passed. On patrol, the squad assumed an identity all its own. The veterans read one another's body language, knew each other's habits, moods, skills and temperament. The man on point, usually Epstein, would stop, signal with his hand, and Sergeant Lomax would shake his head, nod or make a sweeping gesture to spread the men out. Survival was earned minute by minute, and Keith would discover that he liked that challenge.

During their first week there was little enemy contact. On the seventh day they left at dusk to set up an ambush. Epstein led the way. Behind him came Puma, Sergeant Lomax, the radiotelephone operator Cooper, then Alex, Keith, Tuchman and three others. They left the perimeter and headed east. Two boys from the village ran after them, begging cigarettes, then dropped back and watched as they disappeared into the jungle.

The ambush site overlooked a trail through a narrow valley. Throughout the long night they took turns watching and dozing.

The squad had a sniper-scope, a light intensification device that made details in the dimly lit jungle come alive. It was like watching a television picture of the jungle in shades of green. The first few nights Keith had been skittish, nervous, every sense alert. Now he found himself fighting to stay awake and was relieved to see the sky pale, outlining the hills and bringing detail to a gray world.

On the way back they maintained separation but moved more quickly than going out. Camp was safety. But as the sun touched the tops of the hills, the world in front of Keith exploded. Alex and Cooper disappeared as the earth erupted beneath them. The air was suddenly alive with automatic rifle fire. Keith dove for cover.

"Left flank," Lomax yelled.

Looking from behind a tree, Keith saw that Alex was still on the trail. He had lost his gun and helmet and his pants were bloody. Then on his hands and knees he began to crawl. The wrong way.

"Over here!" Keith yelled.

Alex didn't respond. Keith fired at the enemy and then ran in a low crouch, grabbed Alex by the belt and hauled him off the trail to safety. Gunfire rose to a crescendo and another sound, the thick *whump* of a mortar.

"Incoming!"

Keith shoved Alex down and hugged the earth. An explosion, and dirt, sticks and debris covered them. When Keith looked up, Cooper was only a few inches away, staring at him in mild surprise, eyes glazed, mouth thick with dirt—Keith pulled back in horror. It was Cooper's head, torn from his body.

"My leg, my leg," Alex groaned.

Another *whump* and Keith flattened himself against the earth. This time the explosion was his cue to move. While dust and dirt still filled the air, he ran across the trail and into the jungle. He was at the base of a small hill, heading toward the enemy's position. He moved quickly, pausing every few moments to orient himself to the sound of shots.

Ahead of him the gunfire died, forcing him to move more carefully. Back on the trail he heard Lomax call a cease fire. The morning was suddenly quiet, no sound except Alex calling for a medic. Charlie had broken contact. In a few moments the enemy would be lost in the jungle. Keith took a chance and charged up the hill. When he reached a tree near the peak of the hill, he climbed the lower branches until he had a view of the ridge opposite. At first nothing; then something glimpsed through the trees, moving up the ridge.

Wrapping his leg around the branch, Keith braced the M-16 and waited. Twice he caught a flicker of movement, each time higher, moving toward an open area at the crest. A figure appeared, black clothing, a floppy hat carrying a rifle. Keith hesitated. He had never killed a man . . .

The man disappeared. Behind him came two others, the first with a rifle, the other with a mortar on his back. Keith remembered Cooper, saw him engulfed by dirt, the sightless eyes staring at him . . .

And he squeezed the trigger. The third man's elbows flew wide as he grabbed his neck, then tumbled backward. The first Vietcong fired blindly, covering the second who ran back to help his friend. Keith fired a burst at the rescuer and saw the man stumble. Then the first man spotted Keith's position and sent a stream of bullets so close that branches and leaves flew around him. Keith scrambled, half falling, to the ground.

For the first time he fully realized the danger he was in. He was alone. He had just given away his position. What if there were more of the enemy than the three he had seen? What if someone even now was making his way toward him? The surge of adrenaline that had carried him into battle now urged that he get the hell out of there. He fought to control his panic and moved slowly, quietly, back to the trail.

As he stepped from the trees, Epstein whirled on him, his rifle at the ready.

"Do I look like a V.C. to you?" Keith said.

Epstein jerked the rifle barrel skyward. "You look like a fucking ghost."

Noyes was crouched over Alex, who lay on his back, one leg soaked in blood. "My dick, is my dick—"

"It's okay," Noyes said.

Alex grimaced. "It burns—"

"A little hot shrapnel, is all."

Alex tried to look down, his eyes wide with apprehension. Noyes had torn open the trousers and cleaned the area around groin. Already blood from areas of torn flesh was beginning to clot.

Someone grabbed Keith and pulled him to his feet. Tuchman was glaring at him. "Where were you? Where'd you go?"

"What are you, the new general?"

"You chickened out—"

"I went after them."

"Alone?"

"Three of them going up over the ridge. I hit one maybe two."

Lomax sent Epstein and Tuchman back with Keith to the spot where the Vietcong had fallen. They moved cautiously, aware that a wounded enemy could still be deadly. The clearing was empty, but a blood trail led twenty feet into the jungle, where they found the body propped against a tree. Keith was shocked to see it was a boy, no more than sixteen. The shot had torn away part of his throat, including the jugular vein. Before touching the body, Tuchman used a branch to test for a booby trap.

His rifle and personal effects had been removed, but one of Keith's second shots had evidently hit home. There were drops of blood along the route that the other Vietcong had taken.

"One KIA, one WIA," Epstein said. "That makes us even . . ."

Alex was evacuated along with Cooper's body, and when they returned to the base they reported to Severa. He listened with eyes half-closed, as if imagining the events being described. After a few quick questions he dismissed the others and had Keith lead him back to the body.

Word of the attack had already reached the village. The corpse had been brought to the trail where a woman knelt, crying. When Severa approached, she covered the body with her own. Severa knelt beside her and spoke a few words in Vietnamese. She looked up and he repeated the phrase, this time more harshly. Trembling, she released the body and moved a few feet back. The other villagers watched silently.

Severa placed his hands on the boy's cheeks and let his thumbs rest lightly on the closed eyes. He tilted his head back, closed his own eyes and cocked his head from one side to the other, as if listening for a whispered sound or searching for a distant smell. The villagers stared. Keith wondered what the hell the sergeant was doing.

Severa nodded to himself. His eyes opened, he dropped his gaze to the boy's face and his expression hardened, then he released his grip. With a cry the woman ran forward and threw herself over the body. Ignoring her and the other villagers, Severa led the way back.

"What did you tell her?" Keith asked as soon as they were out of earshot.

"I promised I'd feed the body to the dogs if she didn't move away. The boy was her son. She wants him to have a proper funeral."

"What were you doing?"

"What'd it look like?"

"I don't know."

"Feeling the enemy's thoughts, reading his memory, where he'd been, who his comrades were, troop distribution and strength . . . is that what it looked like?"

"Something like that."

"But you couldn't be sure."

"No."

"Neither could they."

For the first time, Keith realized that much of what Severa did was for effect. They continued in silence until they reached the outskirts of Chim Bai, where Severa stopped and turned. "Is it true that you went after the enemy alone?"

Keith said modestly, "Just instinct. I saw what—"

Severa slammed the butt of his rifle into Keith's solar plexus. A knot of pain exploded in his chest. He doubled over, gasping for breath.

"You left your position," Severa said calmly. "You endangered the squad as well as your own life. Courage without judgment is stupidity. Now you'll remember."

He walked away, leaving Keith on the trail, gasping for breath, thinking, you bastard, you lousy bastard, and knowing that Severa was right.

Keith was made the new radiotelephone operator to replace Cooper. For the next few days he studied the codes, learned how to lash the antenna so that it wouldn't catch on trees and how to take a back-to-back position with the squad leader during firefights. At first he felt tied down by the clumsy twenty-pound radio but gradually he began to appreciate the strategic overview his new position gave him. The RTO stayed close to the platoon leader and provided the vital link to the base and to the local command network.

Alex returned a week later. He was blooded now, no longer a greenie, and the men accorded him a new measure of respect. Although his wound wasn't serious, a change seemed to have taken place in his personality. He was convinced he would die in Vietnam. "I'm here one week and I'm hit. That's a sign."

"It's a sign you're invincible," Keith said without looking up from his book. They were sitting in the lookout tower, a spot normally avoided by the men because of its exposed position. Keith had bought reed mats in Chim Bai and constructed sides to the platform so the enemy couldn't see him when he was sitting on the floor. He enjoyed the bird's-eye-view of the area and the sense of being removed, alone. But the tower made Alex nervous. "You're going to get us shot coming up here."

"I don't remember sending out invitations."

"What's that?" Alex craned his head to see the book. *"Selected Works,* by Mao Tse-Tung? Could this be primitive political consciousness rearing its ugly head or are you deserting to the enemy?"

"I want to learn to think like the enemy. There's a chapter here on guerilla warfare."

"Don't let our beloved sergeant see you reading subversive literature."

"It's his book."

"It is?"

Keith looked up. "I doubt if he plays golf, Alex, and I know you wouldn't take him to that yacht club you belong to. But Severa's going to come out of his war alive, and I am, too."

Alex envied Keith his ability to adapt to the situation and still somehow be his own man. He envied the letters Keith got from Chris, sometimes two or three at once. Rather than rip them open and read them immediately Keith would tuck them away until he could disappear into the lookout tower and read them alone. The only mail Alex got were his mother's occasional letters filled with trivia about their important friends and his father's press clippings.

Alex was haunted by Chris's parting gesture at the airport. And since Keith was unresponsive to questions about his new wife, Alex began sneaking her letters from Keith's dufflebag while he was on patrol. Her words fascinated him

> . . . I went to our secret spot and wondered if you were looking at the same star. The played "Bridge Over Troubled Waters" and I cried. I dreamed we were making love and the taste of your body stayed with me all day . . .

Alex spent hours imagining Chris and Keith togther. He also became obsessed with knowing the contents of the survival knife. Keith wore it on patrol and when he slept kept the knife tucked beneath a rolled towel he used as a pillow. Alex found his opportunity one day when he entered the hooch and saw that the knife had slipped to the floor. Keith was snoring gently. Alex made sure nobody was watching, then quickly picked it up and went outside.

It took only a moment to unscrew the cap and pull out the napkin stuffing. Inside was a rolled photograph. Alex slid it out, removed the rubberband and eased the photo open. It was Chris, stepping out of the shower. She was looking at the camera, lips parted in mild surprise, a towel in one hand, her wet hair lying in streaks across her shoulders. The towel fell between her legs but Alex noted the full breasts with their small, dark nipples.

An innocuous photograph, faintly seductive, but meant for Keith's eyes only and therefore all the more valuable to Alex. He

26 ▶

stared for a long time, committing it to memory. Then he re-placed it carefully, trying not to crack the emulsion any more than it already had been. When the knife was back beneath the cot, he stood and watched Keith sleep, wishing he could climb inside his head and know what it was like making love with Chris. For the first time now but not for the last he wished he was Keith.

CHAPTER 4

A week later Keith's squad was called for a combined forces mission. Led by Severa, they were inserted fifty kilometers to the west, to an area known as the Ia Drang Valley, where Intelligence had located a company of North Vietnamese forces. The operation was named False Dawn and called for two companies to attack from the south while squads pulled from various platoons blocked escape routes to the north.

They marched into the night, stopped to eat and continued until they reached their ambush position at about three in the morning. Severa established a challenge and response signal for the sentries: "Five" would be answered by "ten." Half an hour before the attack was scheduled to begin he went to check sentry positions, and Keith went with him. The first three groups gave the proper challenge but at the fourth position, Keith heard the two men, Minkin and Jacobs, talking in whispers. Suddenly the whispers stopped. Keith expected the challenge, "five," and at first didn't recognize the hollow slide-click of a round being chambered. Severa knew immediately. He shoved Keith aside as he dropped to the ground. "Don't shoot . . ."

His words were drowned in a staccato burst of gunfire. Muzzle flashes fifteen feet in front of them lit the trees. Something tugged Keith's back as he fell.

"Hold fire," Severa yelled.

His words were drowned as the other members of the squad opened up. Keith and Severa were caught in a crossfire, crouching beneath a web of red tracers. Finally Severa was able to make himself heard and the shooting stopped.

"Red tracers, *cease fire.*"

"What happened?"

"Friendly fire. No contact." Severa got to his knees. "Johnson, you all right?"

"Yeah."

"Monitor net and see if anybody heard us." He stood up and called out, "Casualties?"

"Epstein took a hit. Lung shot, sarge. We need a dustoff."

"Johnson, do it."

"I can't. The radio's out."

Severa grabbed the handset and tried it for himself. The tug that Keith had felt at his back had been a bullet shattering the radio. Now they were cut off from the command net and the other False Dawn units. There was no way to evacuate Epstein, who had been shot in the chest. Severa knelt beside the wounded man and put his hand on his forehead.

"Hey, how's the Bronx Indian?"

Epstein gave a tight smile. His eyes were glassy, his skin pale. Severa glanced up at Noyes, who shook his head imperceptibly. A look of determination hardened Severa's features. He turned back to Epstein. "You don't give up. I'm getting you out of here. Got that?"

Epstein barely nodded. Severa leaned close. "You stay with me."

He walked to an area clear of trees and fired a signal flare. A comet's tail rose and burst into a yellow flare. Then without turning he said to Keith, "Can you fix the radio?"

"I tried."

"Try again."

For ten minutes they waited while one flare followed another.

Minkin stood hollow-eyed, staring at Epstein, flinching whenever any of the men questioned him. The truth was, in the darkness he had gotten his direction mixed up. When he heard Severa and Keith he thought they were approaching from outside the perimeter. When asked why he hadn't challenged, he said, "I thought it was Charlie."

The men waited tensely. They had given away their position and now they were advertising it with beacons in the night. When Severa wasn't launching flares, he knelt beside Epstein with an expression of fierce concentration, his fingers on the wounded man's temple.

It was no use. Before the last flare was fired, Epstein died. Severa touched the pink froth at his lips, stood up and went to Minkin, who pulled back as he approached. The sergeant grabbed his arm and applied the tip of his finger to Minkin's forehead, marking it with blood.

"Don't touch it," he said. "Give me your piece."

"What?"

"Give—me—your—rifle."

Minkin handed it over. Severa tossed it to Keith and said to Minkin, "You're taking the body."

Noyes stepped forward. "I'm a noncom, I can take him."

"You're the medic. Your job is to tend to the wounded. Minkin's job is to kill his own men. He takes the body."

Minkin paled. "Sergeant, I didn't—"

Severa grabbed the front of his uniform and twisted it. "Listen, you fat-assed fuckup, don't you say a word to me. Don't you say a word to any of these brave men whose lives you endangered. You listen and do what you're told. Now pick up that body and let's go."

Tuchman replaced Epstein on point. They moved cautiously and at first quietly but it wasn't long before Minkin, who had Epstein's body in a fireman's carry, began to stumble. Severa called a halt and stared at him.

"You killed him but you can't carry him."

Minkin looked at the ground. They made a litter, and Noyes and Minkin carried the body between them.

Just before dawn, the air strikes began. The attack was centered about seven kilometers to the south, and they could hear the low-flying jets interrupted by the hollow crump of explosions.

Severa had been studying his map and Keith assumed that they were on their way to an alternate ambush site. They reached a trail and followed it to a hill overlooking a small village.

"Charlie village," Severa said. "Or once was." He pointed to the side of the trail where a tuft of knotted elephant grass sat between two stones. "It's an old code. They stopped using it about a year ago when Intelligence caught on. Maybe this village didn't get the word. We'll see." He turned to Lomax. "Take Garrison, Levy, Puma and Worchek and work your way to the north side. We'll wait fifteen minutes and go in. You hold anybody who tries to get away. Anyone armed, kill on sight."

The bombing to the south had stopped but the faint throb of rotor blades indicated that the ground assault had begun. After waiting fifteen minutes they entered the village. Children watched wide-eyed but the old people and young women tried to ignore them and go about their business.

"Knew we were coming," Severa said. An old man with a walking stick came forward and offered greetings in Vietnamese. Severa responded in the same language, pointing to the center of town. He fired a shot into the air as a signal to Lomax, and everything stopped.

"Collect them," he told Tuchman. "I want everybody over there."

Lomax and his group arrived without having taken any prisoners. No one had tried to escape. As the villagers clustered uneasily together, Keith and the others checked each hooch. Severa walked slowly around, his eyes bright, nostrils flared, chin thrust forward. He paid no attention to the headman who followed him, asking questions.

The hooches were made of bamboo poles covered with matting, and Severa touched each pole in turn, which seemed to upset the headman, who became louder in his protests. Severa ignored him and continued his inspection, until one pole in particular caught his attention. He touched it, stepped back, stared at the top, then slid a knife from his boot and dug around the base. The old man's objections reached a crescendo.

◀ 31

"Get him out of here," Severa ordered.

Holding his rifle horizontally, Levy herded the old man back with the other villagers as Severa cut a hole in the bamboo and sniffed the opening. He smiled. "The best laid plans of mice and men . . ."

He entered the hooch, kicked aside the rice mats that covered the floor and dug until the knife struck something solid. Lorick brought a portable shovel, scraped aside two inches of dirt to reveal a flat wood cover—a trap door. The villagers were silent now, only a baby wailed.

Severa stepped out of the hooch. "Levy, Puma, McIntire—take these people to the rice paddy we passed on the way in. Put them in water up to their knees and keep them there. Tuchman, you, Garrison and Worchek look around, see if you can spot another entrance. Should be one just into the treeline."

The villagers were led away, eyes opaque with fear. Severa took Keith aside and motioned to the pole in which he'd cut the notch.

"Feel that one compared to the others."

Keith couldn't tell any difference. "What am I looking for?"

"Temperature. Catch it before the sun hits and a breathing tube will be warmer than the others. Especially here in the mountains."

"That goes to a tunnel?"

"Smell it."

Keith put his nose to the hole. A faint hint of sweat mixed with warm, stale air.

Garrison came jogging back. "Found another entrance," he said. "But sloppy, like they already split."

"Set an ambush just in case. Capture if you can, otherwise kill anything that comes out. We'll flush them from this end."

Garrison nodded. "I'll send Worchek back."

"No, Minkin will do it."

Minkin looked up.

"Naw," Garrison said, "he got too much butt on him."

"He wants to make amends. Go on. We'll give you five minutes to get positioned."

Keith and everyone else could see that Minkin was petrified.

Still in shock, ashamed by the blood mark on his forehead, exhausted by the struggle through the jungle carrying Epstein's body. Before Garrison was out of sight Minkin was trying to change Severa's mind.

"Sarge, I . . . I can't go down there."

"You can make amends for your foul-up this morning."

"No, I—"

"Shut up." Severa took his .45 automatic from its holster. "Take this."

Minkin stared at the gun as if it were a cobra.

"Please, I can't—"

Severa grabbed his hand and pressed the gun into it. "Don't you see what I'm offering you, Minkin? You leave the field of battle responsible for Epstein's death and you'll never again hold up your head in the world of men. I'm offering you rehabilitation. Redemption. Do you understand that? Do you?"

Minkin stared into Severa's eyes as if he were hypnotized. He took a deep breath and nodded jerkily. The four of them went into the hooch. Noyes lifted the trap door while the others covered him. Below was a small room, like a root cellar, about four feet by four feet. The room was empty except for two bags of rice and a passageway inclined downward.

"All right, Minkin. Flush them."

Minkin played a flashlight down into the pit. His head began to shake and he stepped back. "I can't—"

"Get *in* there." Severa shoved him forward into the pit.

"Take it easy, sarge," Noyes said.

Minkin started to climb out but Severa shoved a rifle into his face. "You go down that tunnel you fat little coward—"

Minkin was now clawing at the side of the pit, his face a mask of terror. Noyes grabbed Severa's shoulder. "He's lost it. Let him out."

The sergeant jerked free and raised the rifle as if about to smash it into Minkin's face.

Keith jumped into the pit then. "I'll go."

Severa stepped back from the rim, his lips tight with distaste as he watched Noyes help Minkin out. "I gave you a chance to redeem yourself."

"I'm claustrophobic—"

"Shut up."

Minkin stared at the ground, breathing heavily. Severa turned to Keith.

"Johnson, you're too big to get to the main room but see if you can make the first bend. Take the flashlight, take the pistol, make a lot of noise going in, put the light around the corner and we'll see what comes up the other end. Then come back. Don't go any farther. Don't try to be a hero again, you'll get stuck."

Keith had no intention of being a hero. He was already sorry he'd volunteered to go into the tunnel, had been surprised to hear himself volunteer. It was just that Minkin was so damned pitiful . . . He slid the rucksack and broken radio from his back and took off his web belt with its bulky attachments. Armed with only the flashlight and the sergeant's gun he climbed into the pit and knelt at the tunnel's mouth. It angled downward for about fifteen feet, narrowed slightly and then made a sharp left turn. Keith imagined the enemy suddenly appearing when he was a foot from the turn and shooting him in the face. He thrust the thought aside and moved into the tunnel on his hands and knees. In less than five feet he was forced to drop to his stomach and inch his way forward on his toes and elbows. The sides of the tunnel contracted the farther he went, and the roof felt like a giant foot on his back.

As he approached the bend he strained to hear anything that might alert him to danger—the sound of fabric against earth, someone breathing, the metallic click of a bullet being chambered. It was like swimming underground, with the earth closing like water—

A muffled explosion. The ground trembled and the sides of the tunnel squeezed tight. Keith pushed backward, grunting with the effort, but the earth seemed to have collapsed around him . . .

Panic came like a flood. He fought the urge to scream, to twist, turn, claw and elbow. But nothing had changed. The passageway before him was still intact, his feet were still free. He let out a deep breath, the walls drew back. And then he realized: it was

34 ▶

his quick intake of breath that had caused the weird sensation of a cave-in.

He worked his way backward, worried that another explosion might really bury him alive. Was it a bomb? Or had someone dropped a grenade in the far end of the tunnel? The passage widened. He got to his hands and knees and backed out. Daylight and fresh air, a huge relief. As he stood up Severa appeared in the doorway.

"See anything?"

"What happened?"

"Booby trap."

"Where?"

"One of the hooches. We lost Minkin."

Outside, two of the hooches were burning. Keith didn't see Noyes.

"I told him to fire the hooches. That one was booby trapped." Severa pointed to one that was still intact. Keith ran to it. There was a small crater a few feet inside the door. Minkin lay face down in the packed earth, legs, hips and shoulders a mass of shrapnel. Keith knelt and felt for a pulse. There was none. He heard Noyes outside and a moment later the medic came in. He took in the scene at a glance and moved to the body.

"You okay?"

"Yeah," Keith said. But a horrible certainty was already growing in him. He looked for the string, for the cable, for the box, the kerosene lamp, the object that had been booby trapped, the wire that had been tripped. He saw nothing.

"Get his feet," Noyes said.

"Where'd you go?"

"Went to get Worchek."

"Your idea or did he send you?"

"Sarge said we'd need Worchek when you came out. You going to help me or what?" Noyes had his hands under Minkin's shoulders.

"What's the—" Hurry, he was about to say. And then saw the tendril of flame working its way up the wall behind him. Severa had already torched the place.

As they moved Minkin outside, Severa methodically began to fire the other buildings. Keith went to him. "What did you do?"

"The smoke will draw a spotter plane. Get us out of here."

"I don't mean that. I mean Minkin."

"Go tell Tuchman to blow the hole and come back here."

Severa stepped toward the next hooch. Keith grabbed his arm. He was three inches taller than Severa but the sergeant's arm was thick and hard as granite.

"I checked that hooch," Keith said. "I went in there. There was no booby trap."

"You just didn't trip it."

"How'd he get it in the back, sergeant?"

Severa stared at him, one eye boring into him, the other focused somewhere over his shoulder.

"The brave make their own luck." The words were soft and distinct but their warning was clear. Keith could see his own reflection in Severa's dark, ebony eyes. There was threat in those eyes, threat and challenge. Keith hesitated, unable, not wanting to believe what his gut said was true.

"Bird dog," Noyes yelled. He pointed to a single-engine aircraft growing larger in the sky.

Severa relaxed. "See that? I told you they'd spot the smoke."

He pulled away and methodically set fire to the rest of the hooches.

CHAPTER 5

The news spread quickly through the platoon: Epstein bought it. The Bronx Indian was dead. Friendly fire with Severa in charge. Unbelievable. Epstein and the new guy Minkin both gone. Someone heard that it was Minkin's fault, that he screwed up the whole mission. Asshole cherry, it figured, but Epstein, man . . .

Keith found Alex in the lookout tower, staring out over Chim Bai and the nearby rice paddies. At first it bothered him when Alex imitated him by spending his free time in the tower, but today he was glad to have someone to talk to.

"You heard what happened?"

"Epstein and Minkin have gone to Valhalla," Alex said, and then, with a smile, "He who is first shall be last and he who is last shall be first and both shall be dead together."

"Alex, cut it out. Severa killed Minkin."

"What?"

He fragged him, I'm sure of it."

Keith then told him everything that had happened on the mission, from Minkin's tragic confusion on sentry duty to his refusal to enter the tunnel. "Severa was out of his head. He kept telling Minkin he was giving him a chance to prove himself—like it was a big honor or something. And when Minkin wouldn't do it, well, I think he killed him."

"But you were in the tunnel when it happened."

"Yeah, but I inspected that hooch before Minkin went in. There was no booby trap."

"Maybe you were lucky."

"No, I was in the hooch afterward. There was no sign of a trap. Besides, why would anybody go inside a hooch to torch it? It doesn't make sense."

"Unless you're Minkin. After all, he couldn't tell east from west or friend from enemy, so why would he know a booby trap when he saw one?"

"There's something else. Severa was carrying four grenades. That's what he had when I went into the tunnel, but when I came out, there were only three. He did it, Alex, I know damn well he did."

Alex was silent, and Keith turned to the luxurious green valley that wandered toward the distant mountains. The mountains were Minkin died.

Alex said quietly, "He'll kill us all eventually."

"Who?"

"Severa, who else? The war lord of Chim Bai, the one who's going to get us all killed in his hunt for guts and glory. Our guts, his glory. You know what I was going to do last night? Have an accident while cleaning my gun. A bullet in the foot, the million-dollar wound. I got the cleaning kit, got a first-aid kit, and you know what? I couldn't do it. How's that for irony? For lack of a foot wound the body was lost."

"What about Minkin?"

"Minkin's dead. What about us?"

"I'm not going to let it go, I can't. I've got to do something, tell somebody . . ."

"You can tell the mighty L.T. but it won't do any good. He's afraid of Severa."

"Then I'll go to Captain Peterson, I'll go to Brigade. Someone's got to investigate."

"Wait a minute!" Alex turned, grabbed Keith's shoulders. "The keys to the kingdom, old son, you've just given us the keys to the kingdom. We can trade Severa his career for a transfer out of here. This is beautiful. Maybe you can't prove anything, but just the accusation could kill his career. So we make a gentleman's trade—Severa approves our orders to Saigon and you say nothing about what happened. It's perfect."

Keith listened with growing disbelief. Alex raised a hand. "I know it's not exactly Kosher, but it beats the hell out of us going home on stilts or in one of Severa's custom-made body bags."

Keith got up and moved to the ladder. Alex grabbed his leg. "Where are you going?"

"To tell Lieutenant Burke."

"Why? What good—"

"You know why."

"I *don't* know why."

"You should have seen him, Alex. Like he'd been shotgunned in the back. The left side of his face was shredded, his left arm was hanging from a tendon, and you know why? I think he heard it. Maybe even saw it. He was turning around when it blew. No, Severa killed him, and I've got to do something about it—"

"All right then, a piece of advice. Don't let Severa see you talking to Burke. From the way he's been keeping track of us, he's already suspicious."

"What do you mean?"

"He came out of the commo bunker a couple of times while you were talking and each time he looked up here. Then he went into town. Probably on his way to see Burke at the liaison office."

Keith looked toward the village. The hooches and market stalls framed an irregular main street that stretched toward the Michelin building. He saw no sign of Severa.

Alex said, "He's taking the first squad on patrol this afternoon. At least wait until he's gone before making a pilgrimage to Burke. Because I'll tell you something, old son. If Severa calls you for special duty and you don't come back, I'm not as brave as you. I won't say a word."

The last thing Keith wanted was to face Severa before he had a chance to talk to Burke. He decided to wait.

* * *

Each week Jerry Burke plucked the eyebrows from the bridge of his nose. In contrast to his red hair, they were wiry and dark brown and met in a sharp V that Burke thought gave him the appearance of a comic-book villain. When Private Johnson arrived he tucked the mirror and tweezers into his desk before calling for him to enter. "Well, private? What is it?"

"Sir, I wouldn't have come here if I wasn't sure about what happened . . . But I have to report this, there's no other way. I think . . . I'm sure that Sergeant Severa killed Private Minkin."

"Perhaps you'd better explain that."

Keith told him what happened on the patrol. Burke listened carefully, fingering a jade elephant, turning it over in his hands, tracing every curve. The elephant was part of his next shipment to New York, a shipment that, among other things, would be impossible if there was a murder investigation. Burke could just imagine what irregularities someone from CID might discover, not to mention the civilian newsmen who were always looking for ways to discredit the army. Burke preferred to be skeptical of Johnson's story.

"You say you didn't actually see what happened?"

"I didn't see him throw the grenade but I know he did it. Corporal Noyes will back me up."

"He saw it?"

"No, but he saw how angry Severa got when Minkin wouldn't go into the tunnel. He wanted to kill him right there because of what happened to Epstein."

"How long have you been a mind reader, Johnson?"

"I know what happened, sir. If you don't want to investigate I can go to Captain Peterson."

Burke got up and began pacing the room. "You say Severa killed someone. Have you ever seen him save someone? Seen *that* with your own eyes? Because he has, you know."

Keith remembered the push that sent him spinning to one side as Minkin fired blindly into the night. He hesitated.

"Maybe you should consider his record. Four silver stars, in each case for actions that resulted in saving lives. You may want to consider the options before you start something that can't be stopped."

"What options?"

Burke momentarily relaxed. "Well, we could watch him closely and see if anything like this occurs again—"

"Sir, excuse me, he killed Minkin."

"But you say there are no witnesses."

"Sir, someone is going to investigate this. If it's not you, someone else—"

"No, no," Burke cut him off. "Don't misunderstand, we'll investigate. Something liked this can't be, uh, exculpated. I'm not suggesting that. But if I take action against Severa, I have to be absolutely certain that your allegations will stand up during an investigation. You have to be willing to testify under oath."

"I'll swear to what happened."

"Very well. Then what I need first is documentation. A statement. You write down everything you told me, every detail you remember, sign it, and I'll take it from there. Will you do that?"

"Yes, sir."

"The next thing to consider . . . have you mentioned this incident to anyone else?"

"Only Alex—Private Wescott. But he promised not to say anything until I talked to you."

"That's good, let's keep it that way. Considering the gravity of your charges I don't want any premature accusations flying around. That wouldn't be fair to Sergeant Severa or to the Army. It would also undercut our case. You understand?"

"Yes, sir."

"Then we're agreed. You bring me a statement by seventeen hundred and I'll get the ball rolling with Brigade."

After Johnson left, Burke went to the window and watched as he made his way back to the base. A tall, skinny kid who was going to cause a lot of trouble. With a sigh, Burke turned away and opened the door to the adjoining room. "He's gone."

Alex Wescott stepped into the room and folded his arms. "Well?"

The smug, knowing smile infuriated Burke. For a moment he considered backing out of the deal, but then thought better of it. Business was business, and this little puke had just made himself part of doing business.

CRUX

* * *

Keith spent the next three hours writing and recopying his detailed report of Minkin's death. When he returned to the liaison office he found himself following a young Vietnamese woman dressed in a miniskirt that fit like elastic, one of the girls from the bar they called Granny Di-Di's. She marched into the building and spoke briefly with Cao, Burke's secretary. Cao was a polite, middle-aged man whose only qualification for the job seemed to be his limited command of English. He sat at a desk whose top was bare except for a clumsy mechanical typewriter and a pack of cigarettes on a silver tray. The girl tossed her head at Keith and went upstairs. He followed her progress until he had his answer—she wasn't wearing panties.

"She's very nice," Cao said when the girl was gone.

"Number ten dog, Cao."

His face fell. "No, no, number two, maybe. Not ten."

Keith dropped it and asked for Burke.

"He's busy now," Cao said. "He say give you this to leave report." He handed Keith a manila envelope.

"Is he in his office or up there?"

Cao smiled. *"Trung uy* very busy. You leave report with me."

"No, I give it to him in person." Keith stepped around the desk and into Burke's office. As he suspected, it was empty. Through the ceiling, from the room above came a muffled, rhythmic sound. He returned to the foyer and went upstairs.

"Trung uy is wanting privacy," Cao called after him. "You leave papers here."

On the second floor were four doors and a short hallway that opened onto a balcony where a Vietnamese soldier sat dozing, his rifle against the wall. Two of the rooms were behind closed doors, but there was no question which one Burke was in. Keith knocked once and walked in.

It was a large room with tall narrow windows and walls that curved as they met the ceiling. The ceiling fan hung motionless, one of its blades missing. Along one wall was a row of sculptures and two paintings. Burke lay in a narrow bed beneath a drape of mosquito netting that had been pulled against the wall. He was

42 ▶

on his back, naked. One girl lay curled between his legs, head bobbing, her black hair cascading over his stomach. The second girl, the one Keith had seen moments ago, was already free of her clothing and kneeling over Burke's face.

The girls squealed in mock-alarm as Keith crossed the room and put the papers on the dresser. "Sorry to interrupt, lieutenant, but I wanted to deliver the Minkin report in person."

He returned to the door as Burke struggled to a sitting position, covering himself with a sheet. "Johnson?" Keith turned as Burke flicked something from the side of his mouth. His face was red and mottled with anger. "You think you're pretty fucking smart, don't you?"

"No sir. Otherwise I would have thought of using pubic hair for dental floss and saving the Army all that money."

As he went downstairs, he heard the door slam loudly behind him.

That night Keith went on patrol. When he returned the next morning, he discovered he was going to be a father.

CHAPTER 6

Dear Daddy—that was the way Chris's letter began. Keith stared at the salutation. Just back from a night patrol, he was exhausted, his body ached, his mind was fuzzy. Not until he read the first paragraph did he realize what these first words of Chris' really meant.

> "I'm afraid it's true, my sweet one. I didn't say anything before but I just returned from the doctor and he says it's positive. In barely seven months we will be the proud owners of a brand-new baby. You're not angry, are you? I can see you scowling and tapping your teeth the way you do when something bothers you but please don't be mad. I know we planned to wait but that afternoon at the Mark Hopkins I just loved you too much. Tell me it's all right, tell me you're happy to be a father, tell me, tell me, tell me. How I wish we could be together right now . . ."

Keith wanted to sing and cry at the same time. The idea of a child—that they had made a child together—filled him awe and delight. He badly wanted to talk to Chris but there was no phone here. To celebrate, he broke a Hershey bar and handed out pieces to the men in the platoon. "Congratulate me, I'm going to be a father."

"What's the matter, Johnson, you couldn't figure out how to use a rubber?"

"Diaper duty the rest of your life."

The banter continued as he made the rounds. Only Alex seemed uneasy, subdued, with the news. "But I thought . . . you told me you were going to wait to have a family."

"I am. Seven months."

He sat down to write Chris a letter but his hand shook and the words blurred. He had slept only three hours in the last two days. Too exhausted to finish it, he tucked the letter under his pack and fell into a deep sleep.

He was awakened by Severa marching through the hooch yelling, "Gear inspection! Fall in! Let's go, on your feet. Garrison, Lorick, come on. Johnson, wake up. Fall in by your bunk."

The men assembled, incredulous and angry.

"You gotta be kidding."

"What is this Mickey Mouse shit?"

"This is a fuckin' war zone, man. Fuck a goddam gear inspection."

Severa took a position in the doorway, where Lieutenant Burke waited. "Listen up. Lieutenant Burke has called a gear inspection. You will stand—"

A chorus of catcalls and boos rose and fell away. Severa waited until they were silent, waited a moment longer, and went on. "You will stand at the foot of your bunks and empty the contents of your rucks on command." He turned to Burke. "Lieutenant?"

Burke stepped forward. His clean, well-ironed fatigues contrasted sharply with the dirty uniforms of the platoon.

"Men, I know that this is a pain in the ass but—"

"You got that right!" someone called out.

Severa said, "Shut up, Duchesky."

"I'll try to make this brief," Burke said. "We lost two men the other day, Epstein and Minkin. Both were mistakes, both could have been avoided. You know about Epstein. Friendly fire is especially tragic, especially hard to take. Minkin is a different matter. First reports indicated a booby trap but I have new infor-

◄ 45

mation that the hooch in which he was killed had already been inspected."

Keith was instantly alert. What was Burke saying? Was he actually going to accuse Severa? He glanced at the sergeant, but Severa's face showed nothing.

"It's entirely possible," the lieutenant continued, "that there were no booby traps in that hooch, that Minikin was careless and that his own grenade caught on something that pulled the firing pin. Another possibility . . . he might have been on drugs. A man on drugs betrays his buddies and endangers this platoon. Most of you know the score but some of the new men may not. Men like Minikin. That's why I'm instituting gear inspections. These may come anytime, anywhere and will apply to all men E-4 and below. Sergeant, proceed."

"Lorick. Junk on the bunk."

"Come on, sarge—"

"Dump your ruck, Lorick."

Lorick did. A second set of fatigues, letters tied in a bundle, a dog-eared Bible and a Penthouse magazine tumbled to the cot. With Burke watching over his shoulder, Severa rummaged through the belongings, moved to the next man.

Keith was uneasy. He hadn't said anything about drugs. He turned to Alex, but Alex stood stiffly at attention staring straight ahead.

"Johnson. Junk on the bunk."

Keith opened his rucksack and emptied it onto the mattress. Severa pawed through his personal effects, then pointed to the survival knife strapped to his belt.

"Is that regulation?"

"No . . ."

"Where'd you get it?"

"It's mine, I bought it."

Severa held out his hand. "Let's see it."

"Why?"

"Got a hollow handle, right?"

"So what?"

"What's in it?"

"Nothing."

46 ▶

"Let's see."

"No."

"That's an order, Johnson."

Lieutenant Burke moved forward. The hooch had become silent.

"It's a personal photograph of my wife."

"Open the top."

Keith unscrewed the pommel. And stiffened. The photograph was gone. Severa took the knife, tipped it upside down. A plastic baggie filled with yellowish powder fell to the bunk. Keith reached for it but Severa grabbed it first. He touched the powder, lifted his finger to his tongue, and turned to Burke. "Heroin."

That's not mine—"

Burke inspected the packet. "Johnson, you're confined to the command bunker until further notice."

"That's not mine, goddamn it. I never saw that stuff before—"

Burke raised his hand. "We'll see. Sergeant Rayburn, escort Johnson to the command bunker."

"Lieutenant, I swear—"

"I'll talk to you later, Johnson. Right now, go with Sergeant Rayburn."

"This is crazy. It's frame-up . . ."

Rayburn, the leader of the first squad, escorted him out of the hooch. He had sad eyes and a war-weary face. Keith didn't know him very well.

"That shit's not mine," Keith said. "I don't do drugs."

Rayburn let his head fall to one side, a noncommittal gesture. He opened the door to the command bunker and motioned Keith inside.

"It's true," Keith said. "Somebody's trying to frame me, and I know who—"

"Lighten up, Johnson. Ain't up to me, it's up to the L.T."

Left alone, Keith paced back and forth. Severa had planted heroin in his survival knife, no question. But how had he known about the handle? No one else had guessed that Chris' decoration obscured a removable pommel. Well, it was a military design . . . Severa must have seen that before. The knife had always seemed like the one tiny piece of private space he had. He never pulled the picture out when anyone was around—

Except Alex. The name popped into his mind, and he remembered the flight over when he first put the photo in the handle. He remembered how Alex refused to meet his eyes during the inspection and suddenly he was sure—it was Alex who had told. He went outside, intending to hunt down Lieutenant Burke. A soldier named Farmington was on guard at the door. "Hold on, buddy, you're supposed to stay inside."

"I've got to see Lieutenant Burke—"

"No can do."

"It's important—"

"I know, it's chickenshit, man, but you got to wait inside."

Overhead, the sky rumbled as a flight of Navy jets headed inland on their way to bomb the Ho Chi Minh trail. Farmington watched them pass, and Keith almost gave in to an urge to shove him aside and run down to the liaison office. And get shot. And then he had another idea. He brought out a pack of C-ration cigarettes, three to the box.

"I'll give you these if you get a word to the lieutenant. Tell him it's about the dope." But what if Burke was in on it? Never mind, he had to confront him anyway.

Farmington bit his lip. "Ahhhh, I can't, can't leave my post—"

"So grab somebody, anybody. Here." He thrust the pack forward. "Give one to somebody and keep the rest. Come on, Farmington, get word to the lieutenant."

Farmington took the pack. "Okay. But stay inside or my ass is in the sling."

Keith spent the next half an hour pacing back and forth. When the door finally opened it was Rayburn who appeared. "Okay, let's go."

"Where's the lieutenant?"

"The liaison office. Come on."

Keith followed him. Outside, some of the men stood shielding their eyes, watching the sky to the west where a lone parachute drifted downward.

"Navy pilot," Rayburn said. They paused to watch until the parachute disappeared behind the ridge and was lost from sight.

Then they left the compound, but instead of continuing into the village, Rayburn motioned to a Huey helicopter sitting on the landing pad.

"Over there."

"What? Where are we going?"

"I got orders to take you to Brigade."

"Wait a damn minute. Where's Lieutenant Burke?"

"I told you, the liaison office."

"He knows about this?"

"Who do you think gave the orders?"

Burke. First calling the inspection, now sending him to Brigade. It was all three of them, Burke in on it, too.

The door gunner sat in the cargo-passenger door, bare-chested except for a sweat-stained flak jacket. The crew chief, a man with a pug nose and bristling gray hair, came forward. "This the prisoner?"

"Yeah."

"I'm not a *prisoner.*"

The crew chief turned to him. "Hands behind your back."

"Why?"

The co-pilot leaned out of the cockpit and yelled, "Let's go! We got a downed pilot." The electric motor whined, and overhead the long blades began their slow rotation. Cold metal snapped around Keith's left wrist. Handcuffs. He jerked his hand back and the other bracelet, still free, slapped his arm.

"Hands behind your back," the chief ordered.

"Get this off me."

"It's regulations, soldier. As long as we're in the air. Come on."

"No—"

The jet engine caught and the Huey trembled as the blades began to blur. The chief grabbed one of Keith's arms and Rayburn grabbed the other. Keith pulled his elbows close to his chest and struggled to keep his hands in front him. The co-pilot yelled something and motioned them aboard. Dropping his attempt to pull Keith's arms behind his back, the chief snapped the second cuff over his right wrist, pinning his hands in front of him. They tossed him aboard like a sack of potatoes, and the Huey thundered into the air. Angry, humiliated, Keith struggled into a sitting position and leaned against the wall while the wind tugged his clothing and the green hills and furrowed valleys swept past beneath them.

Red smoke rose lazily from beyond a hill. The Huey banked steeply. A dirty asbestos glove hanging on the wall behind the door-gunner swung out and back. They came in low over a shallow valley formed by a sluggish, winding river. The downed pilot was immediately visible in his olive drab flight suit, standing on a narrow sand bar, knee-deep in water, the discarded parachute wrapped like a wet sheet against the rocks.

They circled once and began a quick descent. As they did, tracers rose from the trees near the shore. Rayburn's face tensed as he brought his rifle to the ready. He and the door-gunner, now strapped behind an M-60 machine gun, returned fire. Keith pressed himself against the wall. With his hands cuffed he felt naked, totally vulnerable.

The enemy fire dwindled and stopped. The Huey dropped quickly, flared and hovered with its skids touching the shallow water. The downed pilot ran toward them, water leaping in a silver shower around his knees. Again all hell broke loose with a hail of bullets, this time worse than before. Rayburn grabbed his stomach and sat down heavily, eyes wide with surprise. His rifle clattered to the floor, and Keith grabbed it. The pilot, now ten feet away, spun, fell and began crawling toward them on hands and knees. The Huey vibrated as the door-gunner opened up, pouring suppression fire into the enemy position.

The crew chief jumped out and ran in a low crouch. As he reached the pilot, the door-gunner stopped firing. A muffled curse. The gun had jammed. The gunner yanked back the slide trying to clear it. The crew chief and pilot reached the doorway. Dropping the rifle, Keith grabbed the pilot's collar and hauled him aboard. With the M-60 jammed, a new wave of enemy fire erupted. The chief fell backward, clutching his leg, as the Huey began to lift.

"Wait!" Keith yelled.

He leaped out, grabbed the chief and shoved him toward the door. The skids were already two feet above the water. The gunner grabbed the chief's arms and pulled him aboard. Blood smeared Keith's cheek as the man's leg brushed his cheek. The Huey kept rising and Keith grabbed the skid. His feet swung free and he dangled in the air, expecting at any moment a bullet in his back.

The gunner's head and shoulders appeared in the doorway above him. Keith reached up, forgetting the handcuffs, and almost pulled his other hand from the skid. He swung precariously, singlehanded, and regained his grip just as the Huey swept over the first trees. Something slapped his legs, tangled and wrenched him downward. His fingers tore off the skid and he tumbled, snapping tree limbs, pummeled by leaves and branches as he grabbed wildly, trying to break his fall. A branch caught him beneath the armpit, yanked his shoulder. He grunted, slipped free and landed on his back in a tangle of vines.

Tiny pinwheels of colored light danced before his eyes. Through the trees, the river was visible, its waters still muddy from their rescue. As he gasped for breath Keith saw a dozen figures materialize. Vietcong. They splashed into the river and raised their rifles toward the departing Huey. And something else. A man with a long tube on his shoulder—a Soviet made LAW anti-tank missile.

The man took a widespread stance, aimed, and fired. A puff of smoke and a greedy trail of exhaust traced a chalky trajectory upward, beyond the trees, out of sight and into—

The explosion rocked him. Keith struggled to his feet and caught a flicker of fiery debris through the jungle canopy. A faint shock wave, and then silence. The V.C. cheered, rifles raised above their heads. They hugged the man who had made the shot.

As Keith turned he heard the crack of a twig and gasp of surprise. A man dressed in black with almond eyes and high cheekbones carrying an AK-47. Ten feet away. Too far to disarm him, too close to get away. The Vietcong at the river were silent. As the barrel of the AK-47 swept toward his chest, Keith was aware of many things . . . the pain in his shoulder, the distant sound of an invisible airplane circling somewhere above, the fear in the enemy's eyes, the fear turning to hatred, and in the hatred death.

Christie, he thought, and watched in disbelief.

CHAPTER 7

Major Joyce, the survivors' assistance officer, preferred to arrive just before dinner. That was the best time, really. Family members were gathered, friends and loved ones were available, the house was filled with the comforting smell of food, and the first long, awful night was already at hand. The darkness was like a crucible, containing the pain, intensifying it so that the worst part was over by morning. Usually they dozed, exhausted by grief, at some point during the dark hours before dawn, before the sun came and illuminated a world forever changed.

Major Joyce left the freeway and stopped at a gas station to inspect a map of the city. Healdsburg was a small town, and he found the address quickly. He climbed into the car, a dark green Plymouth with the words "U.S. Army" in small black letters on the door. Sometimes they guessed when they saw the car. Sometimes they knew when they saw the uniform. Joyce wondered if there was something different about the way the bell rang or the sound of his knocking, because sometimes the knowledge was in their eyes when they opened the door.

He parked before a spacious two-story house with a well-tended garden. He parked on the street, not in the driveway, and quickly climbed the steps. Before he sounded the brass knocker he straightened his tunic and took a deep breath.

An elderly man wearing a baggy sweater answered the door. "Yes?"

"Is Mrs. Keith Johnson here?"

A shadow passed over the man's features and the polite smile faded. "What is it?"

"Are you related to Mrs. Johnson?"

"I'm her father. Has something happened to Keith?"

A new voice. "Dad, who is it?"

The girl joined them. She was young and pretty and her green eyes were untempered by tragedy.

"Mrs. Keith Johnson?"

"Yes?"

The father mumbled, "Please, God, nothing has happened."

"I'm sorry, Mrs. Johnson but your husband was killed in action yesterday. The Army deeply regrets his passing."

Her frozen smile tightened. "No," she said brightly.

"Chris . . ."

"No, no, no, no, *no* . . ." She was panting now, her body flinching with each word of denial.

Her father touched her. She pulled away as if scalded, stared at the spot where his fingers met her arm, and realization flooded her face. He caught her as she collapsed and led her sobbing and trembling into the house. Another voice, perhaps the mother's, joined them. Mr. Szurek returned, stepped outside, and closed the door.

"What happened?"

Joyce told him what he knew. That Private Johnson was in a helicopter that had been shot down near the village of Chim Bai. An observation plane had witnessed the explosion. There were no survivors.

"I'm sorry, Mr. Szurek. If there's anything the army can do to be of service, you can call me at this number."

He handed him a business card and returned to the car. He saw a woman watching from a living room window and had to suppress an urge to yell, *It's not my fault.* In the car he breathed deeply for a few moments before checking the list for the next name. Back on the freeway, he turned the radio up loud.

The bullet never came. Someone shouted and Keith's executioner paused. A second man appeared, wearing fatigues and a slouch hat. He spoke quickly in Vietnamese. The first man lowered his rifle.

Keith was surrounded and searched. They took his dog tags, took Chris' last letter and marched him out of the area. When they reached a camp, Keith was questioned by a man who wore the VC checked handkerchief around his neck and spoke broken English. "Why you handscuff?"

"Johnson, Keith, Private First Class, nine nine eight, five one, four six."

"Geneva Convention, never mind. Why you handscuff? You bad, huh? You prisoner, huh?"

They went through the routine a few more times and his interrogator gave up in disgust. The next day three guards escorted Keith out of camp. They marched for five days before the reached a trail busy with a steady stream of men and women burdened with heavy packs, all moving silently, all moving south. They turned against the antlike flow, and Keith knew his destination: North Vietnam.

There was no time for the dead. The men of the platoon heard about the helicopter crash, noted it, and went on with the day-to-day business of survival. Tuchman told Alex, "I had him pegged from day one. The way he took off after them gooks on that ambush, remember? Pow! Off the trail and into the boonies, a fucking space cadet. Shit, I knew."

"What?"

"Johnson. A junkie."

Alex turned away. During the first twenty-four hours after the crash he had been full of guilt. Then he realized that it wasn't his fault, he hadn't meant for anything serious to happen. A reprimand, downgraded in rank, maybe a month in the stockade and afterward a transfer to another unit. Hey, maybe even a safer unit. It might have been the best thing to happen to Keith, reckless like he was . . .

And then Lieutenant Burke sent for him. "I've decided not to write Johnson up. The man's dead, there's no use in, uh, besmirching his memory. Officially, he was being sent to Brigade as a courier. Do you have any problem with that?"

"No."

"Good. A courier. Shot down in the line of duty. That should please his parents."

His father, Alex thought. He only had a father.

Three days later Alex received orders to Saigon and was packing his rucksack when Severa appeared.

"Got your million dollar orders, Wescott?"

Alex shrugged. "Ours is not to reason why, ours is but to say goodbye."

Severa nodded and pulled something from his pocket. "Here's a souvenir for you."

Alex caught the hand grenade before he saw what it was. He flung it away and ducked for cover even as he realized that Severa hadn't pulled the pin. Severa smiled. "Chicom. Deactivated." He walked away and called without looking back, "You're no hunter, Wescott Good thing you're out of here. You'd have never made it."

The journey was endless. They marched by day and night. The people going south stared at Keith curiously or malevolently or indifferently. At night their dim shapes and labored breathing reminded him of some huge animal. Once someone bumped into him, he wasn't sure whether by accident or on purpose, and his guards fell on the man and beat him to the ground. They were actually solicitous of his health, and Keith soon realized why—he was their ticket home. The farther north they went, the more the guards' spirits improved. When they left the trail and began walking openly through villages, Keith knew they were in North Vietnam.

An Army truck met them, mottled green with a red star on

each door and canvas sides that hid Keith from the world. The dirt road gave way to a paved highway, and as they neared their destination traffic increased, the smell of woodsmoke and fish filtered into the truck and at one point he heard a band blaring martial music. They stopped and the driver sounded his horn. A shouted conversation, the clang of metal, and the truck lurched forward. It went about fifty feet, stopped and the engine died. Keith stepped out into a courtyard surrounded by high white walls. The adjoining building, with its ornate doorknobs, arched windows and well-tended garden, was obviously a legacy from the French colonial era.

A diffident man in civilian clothes came out, and after a hurried conversation went back inside. The guards squatted on their heels in the shade and waited. Finally a tall Vietnamese wearing a high-collared black tunic appeared. He wore no military insignia but when when he saw the guards at rest he called the corporal over and had a brief consultation. The corporal nodded, turned and barked a sharp command that brought the guards to attention. The man in black then approached Keith.

"I am Ngo Tran Vinh. You will address me as Comrade Vinh. Before we continue, please tell me, have these men mistreated you in any way?"

The question caught Keith by surprise. He had thought he was going to prison, but this was not a prison and Ngo Tran Vinh didn't look like a camp commander.

"Have they?" Vinh asked. "The cut on your forehead, did one of these men hit you?"

"No."

"Please address me as Comrade Vinh." He stepped back and looked Keith over. "So these are the handcuffs. A badge of shame in your own country but a recommendation here in the Democratic Republic of Vietnam. I think they have served their purpose."

Vinh turned and called to someone in the doorway, and Keith caught a whiff of hair oil or cologne. An old man with a white beard scuttled forward. From a wooden box he pulled out a ring of locksmith's picks. Keith sat on the floor of the courtyard and placed his wrists over the box while the old man worked, nodding and mumbling what might have been apologies. The cuffs clicked open and dropped to the ground. Keith massaged his wrists, which were bruised and swollen and caked with dried blood.

"You are a free man now, Mr. Johnson." Vinh said. "Welcome to Vietnam."

Keith waited for the other shoe to fall.

In the aftermath of Keith's death, Chris lived only for the child inside her. She withdrew from the world, refused to leave the house and spent long hours paging through the wedding album. They had been the near-perfect couple, admired by their peers, favored by the fates, destined to live charmed lives unencumbered by the problems and misfortunes endured by ordinary people. Keith's death not only destroyed her life, it shattered her illusion of special dispensation. If her fate was not preordained by a benevolent universe, then events were mere chance and she was at risk. For the first time she imagined the airplane crashing into the house, the robber coming through the window, the dented can of soup contaminated by botulism.

It was Alex Wescott's letter that first pierced her grief. It arrived with a package mailed from Saigon a month after Keith's death. The letter read:

> Dear Chris:
>
> Forgive me for using your first name but Keith spoke of you so often that I cannot think of you as *Mrs. Johnson.*
>
> First, let me express my condolences for your loss. I knew Keith as a good friend and a brave soldier but for you he was of course so much more. I wish there was something I could say to ease your pain but even the most eloquent are rendered mute by this kind of tragedy. I can only tell you that Keith saved my life the first time we were in enemy contact and I will cherish his memory forever.
>
> Enclosed you will find his camera, which he loaned to me to take some photographs. He gave it to me with a roll

of film half-exposed, and by the time I had it developed the circle of Keith's life had closed. I thought you would like to share some of the sights that greeted him, and they are enclosed, too.

It was signed, "Sincerely, Alex Wescott III."

The photographs showed scenes of Vietnam—a water buffalo pulling a wagon, a group of smiling children, women in conical hats in rice paddies. There were pictures of American soldiers, and one shot of Keith, a self portrait taken in a mirror hanging on a pole. Chris stared at each picture, imagining the exact moment when the shutter clicked, wishing she could turn the clock back to that moment, to be beside him, to warn him of what was coming, to bring him home.

She reread the letter. The phrase about the circle closing brought tears. It made her feel a little better to think that his life was not arbitrarily amputated but had reached at least some kind of preordained conclusion. She wrote asking Alex for details of Keith's last days.

Alex, now at his new duty station in Saigon—courtesy of Lieutenant Burke—responded with a nine-page one of his own. He exaggerated his friendship with Keith, offered a number of anecdotes, some concocted, others embroidered, and praised Keith in a way that reflected favorably on himself. After all, if Keith saved his life, his life must have been worth saving . . . especially to Keith. He went through three drafts before he was satisfied and left just enough unsaid to spark her curiosity. He wanted her to write again, and she did.

Gradually, thanks largely to his manipulation, their letters went beyond reminiscences of Keith to include details of their own lives. Alex told her about his duties in the Public Affairs Office, where he coordinated news conferences and arranged itineraries for visiting congressmen. He wrote about the petty office politics and described the disdain with which most American officers viewed South Vietnam's politically chosen officer corps. He told her about the army's inefficiency with an irony that managed to be clever and amusing even as the accounts outraged Chris.

58 ▶

With Keith gone, Chris found herself with few close friends. Most of her peers were away at college, and on the few occasions that someone stopped to see her, she felt a widening gulf. Gossip about unreasonable professors, newest boyfriends, last week's parties and the latest record albums held nothing for her. She had much more in common with Alex, who seemed to understand *her* concerns, her feelings—the frustration of living at home, her anticipation of having Keith's child, her decision to take a correspondence course to become a court reporter. Prisoners of circumstance, they exchanged letters, and Alex Wescott began his lifelong competition with a ghost.

CHAPTER 8

Keith was given a bedroom with adjoining bath on the second floor. The windows were barred and a guard sat outside his door, but otherwise he might have been in a hotel. Incredible, he thought. An old woman brought a basket of fruit and filled a tub with hot water for a bath. When he questioned her, she shook her head briskly, responded in Vietnamese and left.

He stripped off his dirty clothes and sank into the hot bath. The steam had a metallic smell and the water stung a dozen unknown cuts and scratches. He had leaned his head against the wall and begun to doze when the old woman walked in and, without a glance, swept up his old clothes and replaced them with a clean gray tunic, loose pants and sandals.

As soon as she was gone, Keith got out and put on the clean clothes. The door was locked but through the keyhole he could see the guard sitting on a stool across the hall. Cradled in his lap was a submachine gun, a French-designed MAT-49. Keith lay down on the bed, intending to figure out a plan of escape, but fell instantly asleep.

In the morning a doctor came and applied antiseptic to cuts that had become infected. He spoke a few words of English but his only response to Keith's questions was, "Comrade Vinh speak you later." Not until afternoon was he escorted downstairs to a small library where Vinh was waiting. Floor-to-ceiling bookshelves ringed the room, but Keith's attention was drawn to the ornate frescoed ceiling in which two human figures were surrounded by jungle. It took a moment before he realized that the vine that curled around the woman was a snake and the fresco depicted the Garden of Eden. Strange.

"Good day, Private Johnson," Vinh said. "I hope you are recovered from your journey. The doctor tells me you suffer no serious effects."

"I'm okay . . ."

A faint breeze came through tall, screened windows. Without getting up, Vinh motioned him to a worn velvet chair on the opposite side of an ebony coffee table. "Please, sit. We have much to discuss." He rang a silver bell and a woman entered with a tea tray. A white Burmese cat slid into the room behind her and began a slow exploration. The woman poured tea in delicately patterned porcelain cups and left.

"Will you join me in a toast?" Vinh said. "To peace."

Keith lifted the cup to his lips but didn't drink. Noticing his hesitation, Vinh smiled. "We drink from the same pot, Private Johnson. It's not poison." Vinh sipped his tea and studied Keith. "Let us become acquainted. Tell me about yourself. Where is your home in the United States?"

Keith hesitated. "California. Where are you from?"

"Thanh Hoa. Do you know where that is?"

"No."

"But I know where California is. Sacramento is the capital of California. You see, we know much more about the United States than you know about Vietnam."

"We know enough."

"Unfortunately you know only enough to become involved in our struggle but not enough to realize that you cannot effect the outcome. Just the wrong amount of knowledge, don't you agree?"

"Maybe."

"There is no uncertainty. We will win and America will lose—"

"That's what the Japanese said when they bombed Pearl Harbor."

"Let's not be belligerent, Private Johnson. I am trying to establish friendly relations." He glanced at Keith's hand. "You are married, I see. Would you like to write a letter to your wife? Explain that you are safe. She must be worried, I think. Would you like to write her?"

"No thanks."

"Oh? Are you on unfriendly relations with your wife?"

"No I'm not, but I'm not going to let you twist my words around and use it for your purposes."

"I see. How old are you, Private Johnson?"

"Old enough to pull the trigger if I had a gun."

"But you have no gun, and no need to be provocative. Tell me, what do you think are the chances that the American masses will revolt against the criminal government of President Nixon?"

"What American masses?"

"People such as yourself. The students and peace-seeking people who are massacred in the streets of America when they demonstrate their solidarity with our cause."

"Nobody's massacred in the streets."

"Do you deny the killings at your Kent State University?"

"That was an accident."

"Historical inevitability. The dragon has begun to consume itself. We have seen it happen with the French. Now the process begins in America. You, of all people, should appreciate this."

"Why me of all people?"

"Let me answer a question with a question. You were wearing handcuffs. Why?"

Keith stiffened. "That's my business."

"There is nothing to be ashamed of. Even if you were a deserter—"

"I'm not a deserter."

"A criminal, then?"

"I was framed."

"Framed?"

"Forget it." He'd be damned if he'd give Vinh the satisfaction of hearing him accuse American soldiers.

"Private Johnson, have I not treated you well? I gained your custody from the military authorities. You will understand that life in a prisoner of war camp compares unfavorably with the treatment I offer you here."

"What do you want out of me? Why am I here?"

"I am head of the United States Analysis and Re-education Desk. My job is to interpret aspects of American culture and public sentiment and to design ways and means to accelerate the re-education of Americans. To use a phrase of your own country-men, my job is to win the hearts and minds of the American people. You can help me. We receive much news from Amer-ica—publications, newspapers, magazines, television reports. From all these sources much news is contradictory. I would like you to analyze some meaning behind the events so we can act accordingly. It is an opportunity for you to help bring an end to your nation's suffering."

"No thanks."

"Perhaps you should hear me out."

"Look, I understand the drill. Cooperate, turn traitor, and you let me write Chris. No."

"Cooperation begets cooperation. Do not forget that it was our own country that placed you in handcuffs. It is we who gave you freedom."

Keith got up, went to the door and opened it. The soldier with the submachine gun blocked the way. "You want to tell this guy what you just said?"

"You are free so long as you act responsibly. An American wandering freely the streets of Hanoi would be an irresponsible action . . . I try to be patient with you. I have seen America. I have spent ten years studying your country. Do you think you know everything? Here. Look." He jumped up, grabbed a book from the bookcase, and thrust it into Keith's hands. It was *The Octopus,* by Frank Norris. The pages were yellow and brittle and on the flyleaf was stamped "University of California Library."

"What is your political goal, Private Johnson? To buy a new car? A mechanical toothbrush? A new fur coat for your wife? Do you know why you are here? Why you have invaded—"

There were voices in the hallway and the door opened and a

◀ 63

woman dressed in a pale blue *ao dai* entered. She had an aura of faded beauty despite carelessly applied makeup and a scar that disfigured her left cheek. Without preamble she launched into a diatribe. Vinh's expression hardened. He got up, grabbed her arm and escorted her into the hall, leaving the door slightly ajar behind them.

Keith hesitated, then was up and moving quickly to the window. Outside was a patio surrounded by shrubs. A broad expanse of lawn led to the circular driveway and main gate. As he watched, a man riding a motorcycle arrived. It was a Honda 90, a model Keith had ridden before. The soldier stepped from a small guardhouse to open the iron gate, and Keith thought he saw his opportunity.

Vinh was still in the hallway talking with the woman. He unhooked the screen, climbed through the window, ran across the patio and into the lawn. The motorcyclist had just entered the compound when Keith appeared running full tilt. The man swerved to avoid a collision. Keith lunged in a flying tackle. As they tumbled to the ground he drove his knee into the man's stomach, rolled free, righted the cycle, kicked into first gear and twisted the throttle. On his hands and knees the driver grabbed at Keith's leg and missed. The guard at the gate retrieved his rifle, stepped into the road and was taking aim as Keith smashed into him. The front wheel jerked violently and the gun fired wildly as it flew into the air. The Honda almost spilled and the heel of his right foot tore as Keith fought to keep it upright. And then he was through the gate and on a narrow, tree-lined street.

To his left a group of women had turned at the shot. Hunching his shoulders, Keith turned right, went down one block and then another before reaching a major thoroughfare where he was engulfed in a sea of three-wheeled cyclos, bicycles, motorcycles and people on foot, all dodging one another and weaving their way around the occasional car or truck.

Keith had no idea which direction to go. The streets were chaotic and intersected at odd angles. Keith barely noticed the round-cornered two-story buildings draped in rattan blinds that fronted the street. He turned and followed trolley tracks, hoping they would lead him away from town. Once in the country maybe he would find the coast and work his way south—

A trolley stopped in front of him. Keith maneuvered around it and found himself passing an olive-drab Army truck filled with soldiers crouched beneath a canvas top. Instinctively he accelerated and almost ran into a procession of Buddhist monks chanting and singing, their orange robes billowing in the sun. Keith veered away and ran into a woman carrying two baskets of fruit balanced at either end of a long pole. The cycle jerked and the engine died. And the woman began yelling.

Frantically he kicked the starter.

"Nguoi My!" someone shouted. "American!"

The engine roared to life but now the road ahead was blocked by the procession. He turned around, dodged two young men who were pointing at him and headed back the way he'd come. A soldier from the truck jumped out and grabbed his arm. Keith kicked him away but other soldiers were coming now, blocking his escape. Off to one side was a narrow alley between two buildings. He gunned the engine.

An old man jumped back in surprise as Keith shot past him and down the alley. The alley turned right, continued fifty feet and abruptly ended at a six foot wall. Dumping the Honda, he scrambled over the wall and found himself in an open lot behind brick buildings that looked like warehouses. A flat-bed truck was parked next to a loading dock and a row of bicycles leaned against a wall. He thought of stealing a bike but knew it was no good. Now that the alarm was raised, he would be spotted instantly. He had to hide somewhere until dark . . .

He jumped onto the vacant dock and opened a door leading inside. The whir of machinery and sound of voices reached him even before he saw the two men. They were deep in conversation, one with a clipboard, coming toward him. He shut the door quickly and looked for a hiding place. The stacked boxes? No, that was the first place someone would look. And then he saw the chain hanging from the ceiling. It was a loop that went up to a metal shroud that housed the articulated loading door. The top of the housing, a few feet below the ceiling, was lost in shadow.

◀ 65

Grabbing both sides of the chain, Keith pulled himself hand-over-hand. He was breathing hard by the time he swung one foot up and caught the top of the housing. Below, he heard the soldiers coming. The metal sagged as he rolled on top and pressed himself against the wall. A moment later, half a dozen soldiers appeared and began to search the place. One of them went inside.

Keith tried to breath quietly as the scene unfolded below. And then he saw the chain was still swinging with the momentum of his climb. He could feel the sweat trickle down his forehead. A soldier stooped to tie his boot, his back to the chain.

Don't look up, don't look up . . .

The man with the clipboard came out of the factory. Evidently a foreman or plant manager, he seemed more concerned that the soldiers would damage his inventory than in finding Keith. When the soldiers left he began checking the boxes against the manifest. A drop of sweat tickled Keith's nose and he gritted his teeth to keep from sneezing. The foreman paused directly below, Keith held his breath. The drop of sweat trembled and fell. It shrank in size and then burst, tiny and wet, on the manifest. The foreman's head tilted slowly back. Their eyes met.

Keith rolled off the housing and dropped to the ground. The foreman shouted and ran for the departing soldiers. Keith ran inside. The sound of machinery swelled as he turned the corner and found himself in a huge room where women sat sewing at long tables half-hidden by fabric that shifted and jumped, maneuvered by quick fingers. Each sewing machine was topped by a ten-inch spool of thread. At the opposite end of the room were two sets of doors, one to the left and one to the right. Keith headed for the door on the right, hoping it was an exit. Someone cried an alarm and suddenly all faces turned toward him. Women froze or ducked beneath the tables as he approached. When a man came at him with a broom handle, Keith jumped onto a table and ran the length of it, jumping the crude sewing machines, tripping once over the pointed spindle of an oversize spool of yellow thread. As the workers became aware of him, the machines went silent, replaced by a cacophony of high-pitched voices.

He jumped down, ran to the door, yanked it open and stopped. It was another room, a cutting room, with layers of fabric four inches thick on huge tables where men wearing face masks worked with saws. He reversed course, headed toward the other door in the first room. There was a blur as a broomstick, wielded like a baseball bat, caught him in the throat. Pain cut off his breath, but as his attacker drew back to strike again Keith punched him and sent him skidding across the floor. Something yellow flew past his head and bounced off the wall. One of the oversize spools of thread. Another found its target, caught him in the temple and sent him careening off the wall.

He was running now, the women scattering at his approach. Ten feet from the door, someone pushed a hamper into his path. Too late he tried to dodge, tripped and sprawled. Fighting for breath, he stumbled to his feet, and was met by a barrage of heavy spools, blue, white, yellow, green, black. One broke his nose and another hit him in the groin and sent him writhing to the floor. He tried to take cover but they converged on him, screaming and kicking. Before he lost consciousness, he felt them pull him from beneath the table, and saw through a red haze of blood the angry faces and raised fists and sandled feet that smashed and kicked him into oblivion.

CHAPTER 9

Keith came to his senses coughing, dripping with water. He was lying on a stone floor, bruised and sore, one eye swollen shut.

"Can you hear me, Private Johnson?"

A bright light played over his face. From somewhere came a steady clink, clink of metal striking rock. A shadowy figure stepped forward and threw a bucket of water in his face. Coughing, Keith struggled to a sitting position.

"You are with us now, Private Johnson? Good."

Tran Vinh stood five feet away, his arms crossed, staring down at him. Two soldiers flanked him, one with the bucket, the other holding a pressure lantern that sent jagged shadows dancing against the walls.

"Private Johnson, you are guilty of the murder of Comrade Van Cao Luyen, a citizen of the Democratic Republic of Vietnam. I could have you shot for this. But your crime is even greater. I offered you trust and you abused it. I offered friendship and you betrayed me. Your sentence is a living death. You are a young man, but you will live beneath the ground and grow old in darkness. For the rest of our life, the world of the living will continue without you. Your wife will never know the warmth of the marriage bed, your parents will grow old and die without your comfort, the children you would have had will never be born. Here in the darkness you will see nothing, hear nothing. So you will not forget those you sacrificed, I leave you this."

He stepped aside and for the first time Keith saw the source of the tapping sound. A man working with a hammer and chisel stood facing the wall. It took Keith a moment before he recognized in the moving light the word chiseled in the stone: KRIS.

Shadows leaped and wavered as the men left the cell. Keith stumbled to his feet, one arm clutching his ribs, the pain like a knife with each movement. The squeal of metal hinges filled the cell as he lurched forward and thrust his arm into the doorway, preventing it from closing. When the guard briefly opened the door, Keith tried to lunge past. A dark blur was his only warning before the butt of a rifle sent him reeling backward into unconsciousness.

When Gail was born in June Alex Wescott sent a bouquet of white roses and pink balloons. In December he managed an early discharge from the army to return to Yale for the spring semester. Chris met him at Travis Air Force Base. Her first thought was that he looked more mature than that time she had met him with Keith. There were lines around his eyes that hinted at months of tension. Otherwise he was tan and fit, his blond hair longer than she remembered, and he sported a neatly trimmed moustache.

"Alex," she said.

"Hello, Chris."

He seemed awkward and uncertain. Chris took his outstretched hand in both of hers. "Welcome home." And then her eyes filled with quick tears. "Sorry," she said, brushing them away.

Alex's smile died as he realized who the tears were for. "I know," he said. "I should have been him."

Chris shook her head but they both knew it was true. The last time she had been to Travis had been to say goodbye to Keith. Greeting Alex was like the closing of the last chapter of the life she might have had. Except you didn't close a life the way you did a book . . .

◀ 69

They drove to San Francisco, to the raffish North Beach district, where hippies in bellbottoms and beads mixed with poets and out-of-town tourists and sailors from the U.S.S. *Ticonderoga.* The glass cage where go-go girls danced at night was empty now, but the sidewalk barkers were out in force. A man in a red fez invited passersby to take a free peek at a Turkish love act. Alex was struck by the absence of children. For the past year his every move in Saigon had been shadowed by ragged kids begging money and cigarettes and hustling blackmarket goods.

They ate at Enrico's and sat outside where the sunlight ignited Chris's auburn hair in streaks of glowing copper. She was even more beautiful than Alex remembered or even fantasized. On the plane he had worried that their meeting might undermine the effect of the letters, somehow be a letdown. Greater was the unreasoning fear that Chris might see in his eyes the truth about Keith, and about what he'd done . . . Now, as they chatted, his confidence began to return. He talked about his plans and realized that she seemed really interested, wasn't just being polite, but listened and responded avidly.

"Do it, Alex," she said. "Go into politics if that's what you want. Your background and experience should make you a natural."

"He who competes with his father does so at great peril. At least in our family."

"You wouldn't have to compete with him. He's a congressman, you could run for the Senate."

"Just like that?"

"Why not, if that's what you want?"

The way she looked at him, the confidence she seemed to have in him—something neither he nor his father ever had—made him change his mind about Yale, and decide that his one goal right now was to make Chris Johnson his wife.

Keith regained consciousness in the lap of God. He opened his eyes and saw a pale face haloed by a white hair and beard. The face spoke strange words as cool fingers touched his temple. Keith turned away and the world tilted crazily. He shut his eyes and tried to remember where he was. When he opened them he was looking at a metal door with a pale wash of light seeping beneath it, illuminating a stone floor and a thin, white, bare leg. The leg frightened him. He rolled to one side and struggled to his hands and knees, fighting the nausea and dizziness. As he stumbled forward, God reached out and spoke again, and this time Keith recognized the language. His last thought before darkness came was that God spoke French.

Keith woke up with a start, stiff and sore but the dizziness gone. Touching his head, he felt a rough texture, something alien, not his head, not his hair. It took a moment before he realized he was wearing a bandage. One by one the memories filtered into place: his escape, the sewing factory, his capture. He remembered Vinh and the guards in dancing shadows and God speaking French— No, of course not God. A dream.

He got slowly to his feet. The cell was a small, windowless room about fifteen feet square with walls and floor of stone. The metal door had a small opening at the bottom and a six-inch slit at eye-level. The only light came from outside, through these two openings. Opposite the door, water dripped from a rusted pipe, filled a shallow depression in the floor and then trickled down a small hole in the floor.

The distant clang of a bolt brought him to the door. Through the narrow slot he could see the base of a flight of stairs that led upward and out of sight. Footsteps approached and a shadow stretched across the wall. A young man wearing baggy brown shorts and a shirt with epaulets came into view carrying a bucket and a wood spoon.

"Hey," Keith yelled. "Do you speak English?"

The guard ignored him.

"I want to talk to a representative of the Red Cross. You understand me?"

It was as if he didn't exist. Without even looking at the eye-slot the guard scooped a pale brown mess from the bucket, dumped it at the base of the door and turned away.

"Wait a minute, damn it!" Keith pounded on the door. "I want to talk to somebody. Comrade Vinh. I want to talk to Vinh!"

The footsteps never paused. The man's shadow followed him from view, the door slammed and a bolt slid shut.

"You fucker, I'm an American citizen. I want to speak to the Red Cross, I want to speak to Vinh . . ."

"They never answer."

The voice came close behind him. Keith turned and found himself facing a small, frail man whose deep-set eyes seemed to glow. Dressed in ragged shorts, the man was bald but had a long fringe of white hair and matching beard.

"I shock you. I am sorry, but one cannot ring the stone doorbell, *n'est-ce pas?* Ah, my friend." He threw his arms wide and stepped forward. Keith retreated and the old man stopped. "No, no, no," he muttered to himself. *"Lentement, lentement."* And then, to Keith. "I'm sorry, a prisoner forgets his manners. I should introduce myself. I am Henri Giscard, *professeur d'archeologie.* And you are?"

"You're French."

Henri laughed. "A prisoner has no nationality."

"But how did you . . .?"

"Arrive in your cell? Social discourse can only proceed in a logical and orderly world. You think I am a ghost, yes? But no, I come from the cell adjoining. We have created a tunnel—that is, Truong created the tunnel and I have helped maintain it. Not a ghost, just another unfortunate such as yourself."

"A tunnel? Where?"

"Just there." Henri indicated the back of the cell, where, in the gloom, Keith could barely make out three stones that had been part of the wall now lying on the floor. Keith crossed the room, knelt down and peered into the dark passageway. "Where does this go?"

"To my estate at Elysium. Tell me your name and I shall invite you over. Who are you?"

Henri stood with his head thrust forward like a turtle, eyes bright and eager. Crazy, Keith decided. Without answering he dropped to the floor and crawled on his stomach, pushing his way forward with elbows and toes, gritting his teeth against the pain in his ribs. A moment later he was in a cell that duplicated his own. Henri emerged silently behind him.

"Wait, my friend. Who are you? What is your name?"

"Is this the only tunnel?"

"Such impatience. Has the world changed so much or do not introductions still precede discourse?"

"My name's Keith Johnson. Private, U.S. Army."

"Monsieur Johnson, your catastrophe is my great good fortune. I had thought that no one would replace Truong." Henri extended his hand and Keith was surprised to find the old man's grip firm and hard.

"What you said before, about escape. Is there another tunnel? A way out of here?"

"Tell me first, what is the word in the wall?"

"What word?"

"The word they chiseled in the wall of Xiang Kai. Your cell, I mean. Xiang Kai is what we called it, Truong and I, the land of his imagination. When I first heard the pounding I thought they discovered the tunnel. It is a name, yes? Kris?"

"My wife."

"Your wife? But why—? Ahh, of course. He is a true sadist, Tran Vinh."

"You know Vinh?"

"Who dwells in Hades who does not know Charon? This is the Villa Sedmondante, former home of the French governor, now a police barracks run by Tran Vinh's brother-in-law. This area, before they created a dungeon, was a wine cellar. I once attended a reception here, 1953 it was. We had a burgundy which may have been stored on the very spot we stand. Time and distance, eh, the difference between a guest and a prisoner."

Keith's head ached and it was difficult to keep up with Henri.

"What about a way out?"

Henri touched a finger to his temple. "Up here is the only way out. The ultimate freedom—the imagination. But tell me now, what is the date? What day, what month, what year is it?"

Keith fought an urge to shake some sense out of him. When he told him the date Henri clapped his hands. "Three days! I am only three days incorrect, *formidable*. I congratulate myself. Three days in ten years. *Magnifique*."

"You've been here *ten years?*"

"Fifteen years, eight months, and eleven—no, eight—days. But in the beginning I did not know how to measure time. Then

I developed my water clock, you see?" He pointed to the rock basin half-filled with dripping water. "Three and one quarter times each day it fills. The original computation was based on my heartbeat. Now even my sleeping pattern is synchronized with the overflow of the basin."

Keith was rocked. Just the *idea* of spending even fifteen days in this tiny cell brought a rush of claustrophobia. But years . . .

Henri was saying something about the difference between the time spent alone and that spent with Truong.

"Who's Truong?"

"Truong Dang. My friend. The man who until sixteen months ago occupied your cell. He studied with Ho Chi Minh in Paris and spoke very agreeable French. *Tu ne parle pas francais?*"

"He escaped?"

"Escaped? Ah, yes, the only escape possible from this place. He died. I believe from tetanus. A rat bit him, two weeks later he was in seizures. Be careful of the rats, even if you cover the sewage hole with a stone they will come beneath the door. The food window we dare not block lest the guards realize we have breached the wall. That is our greatest risk, if they discover the tunnel—*mon Dieu*—you must be careful."

Keith scarcely heard him. Spending a lifetime in prison, without sunlight, *without Chris* . . .

He grabbed Henri by his shoulders. "Just tell me—is there a way out? Is there another tunnel?"

"No."

The Frenchman's gaze was calm, steady. Keith felt the stone walls closing against his heart, pressing down, suffocating him. He ran to the walls, picking at the mortar for cracks, exploring for loose stones, some secret passageway. He moved faster, clawed the walls, bloodying his fingers, until he collapsed exhausted, his face pushed against the stones, breathing in hoarse gasps. Henri put a hand on his shoulder.

"The first day is always the worst. From now it will become easier with each passing day."

Chris was living with her parents in Healdsburg. It had been three weeks since Alex had passed through San Francisco on his

way home. She had just fed Gail and put her to sleep when the
doorbell rang.

"There's someone to see you," her mother called.

When she came downstairs and saw Alex, his arms loaded with
presents, Chris' first thought was that her hair was dirty and she
looked terrible. And then a quick pang of guilt. Keith was dead,
what did any of that matter?

Alex had driven cross-country in his Mercedes SL convertible.
He hadn't told her he was coming. She led him into the living
room and for a moment they were alone.

"What are you doing here?"

"I'm transferring to Stanford. California's charms have captivated me—one in particular."

"Alex, you didn't come out here . . . we're friends, but . . ."

"I meant the weather," he said with an Alex grin.

And then her parents returned and she had to drop the subject.
Alex had brought presents for the family. For her mother a bouquet of flowers, her father a bottle of Chivas Regal, and for Gail
a three-foot-high stuffed Panda. Chris' present was last, a five-by-
seven-inch package wrapped in metallic gold and tied with a red
ribbon. Aware of her parents' eyes on her, Chris opened it and
discovered a photograph in an elegant silver frame with a hand-
wrought design. The photo was of Keith and Chris embracing at
the airport.

"This is . . . this was at Travis?" Alex nodded. "But how? Who
took it?"

"I did. You two looked so perfect . . ." No one could tell from
his voice the effort it took him to say this. But he knew when he
saw the tears that he had been right. His arrow had found its
mark.

"Alex . . . thank you." She shook her head, forced a smile. "I'm
sorry."

Her mother put her arm around Chris. "It's a lovely gift. It
helps . . ."

Mr. Szurek adjusted his glasses. "Beautiful workmanship."

It should be, Alex thought. He had paid a steep price for it at
an antique shop in Aspen, Colorado. Now, as he basked in their
approval, he found himself telling them that the frame belonged
to his great-grandmother.

"Alex," Chris said, "I can't take a family heirloom."

"There's no better use it can have than commemorating Keith's life."

A shadow of doubt clouded her eyes, but Mr. and Mrs. Szurek were clearly won over. Alex stayed for supper.

CHAPTER 10

Keith was standing at the door to his cell staring through the narrow slot at the hallway, which represented freedom. Behind him, Henri sat with his back against the wall, eyes closed, describing his imaginary kingdom of Elysium—four rooms built around a turret bordered by a lawn on the east, a greenhouse on the north, a lake on the west and a desert to the south. The old man described the position, shape and color of the furnishings, the doors, windows, Oriental rugs, the walnut desk in the library, even books on the shelves. The more detailed he became, the more uneasy Keith felt. Finally he turned and said, "Okay, *stop.* I'm not listening to that stuff."

"Would you wish your imagination to atrophy?"

"Nothing's going to atrophy, I'm going to get out of here."

"Impossible, my friend. Even for someone young and strong and American."

"Why? You managed to dig through the wall."

"Not me, Truong. He was a political prisoner, once an important man, and he was given a metal cup and bowl he fashioned into tools to scrape away the mortar between the rocks—it took over three years."

"Where are they now? The tools he made?"

Henri held up his finger and showed him an irregular metal band. "This is all I have left of it."

"That's all?"

"You see how thick the wall is. And the floor is equally so. No, we must be patient until Tran Vinh dies or falls from power. Come now, let us exercise our wits with a game of chess."

"You have a chessboard?"

"Of course. Inlaid ivory and ebony. We shall place it here." He spread his hands. "The black square on your left—"

"Forget it. I'm not playing imaginary chess."

"Not imaginary. Where do you think the impression of a concrete chess piece forms? Up here." He tapped his head. "And what does each shape mean? Which moves can be made? How is each scored? All that is up here."

"I don't care, I'm getting out of here—"

"How?"

"I don't know."

"In the meantime . . ." Henri lifted an imaginary chess piece. "King's pawn to king's pawn four."

Keith went to the door and inspected it again. He made his way around the edge of the cell, testing the mortar with his fingernails. The stones were roughly square and the distance between each one was irregular. At one point Keith dislodged a few grains of mortar and clawed stubbornly at the same spot until his fingernail was worn down. Henri, watching him, began to whistle softly *Sur la pont d'Avignon.* After what seemed like the hundredth repetition, Keith said, "Will you *stop* that?"

"One game?"

"I'm not playing games with you, don't you understand?" Keith went to the door and peered through the narrow opening. The metal was worn around the edges, as if someone had pressed close, again and again.

"My headstrong Achilles, better you should be Ulysses in a place like this."

"What do you mean?"

"Think of the *Iliad.* Can you not see the parallel between your own responses and those of Achilles?"

"I never read the *Iliad.*"

78 ▶

"You joke. Homer's *Iliad*? The *Iliad* of Homer? Western civilization's first great masterpiece, and you have not read it?" Henri raised his hands to the ceiling. *"Mon dieu, pourquoi m'avez-vous abandonné?"* Bad enough to be imprisoned by a madman, but this—to have as a cellmate an ignoramus—"

"I'm not ignorant."

"But of course you are. You have only a superficial concept of our own country and none at all of others. You admit a shameful deficiency in your knowledge of the Western civilization from which you spring. You have not much insight into anyone beyond yourself and your mind is unfit for serious philosophical inquiry. I say this without malice, my friend, but merely as a matter—"

"Will you please shut the fuck up!"

"You prove my point. The universal response of the ignorant: *shut up.*"

Keith took two steps and stood with clenched fist glaring down at Henri. "Just leave me alone."

The Frenchman stared up at him like a pale, white leprechaun. Without a word, he got to his feet, went to the passageway and crawled inside. A moment later, his hands reappeared, and one by one he lifted the three stones back into place.

Alone, the quick rush of anger faded and Keith felt more desolate and frustrated than ever. He kicked the door so hard he almost broke a toe. As the pain subsided, he actually did remember a story he read in high school from the *Iliad*. Not up to Henri's level, but . . . "Trojan horse," he muttered. It gave him an idea. If there was no way out of the cell, then he would lure someone into it.

He put his plan into action later that day when the guard came with food. Keith lay in an awkward position and pretended to be unconscious. The man never looked inside the cell but Keith expected this. He would play dead. When they discovered that he wasn't eating, they would open the door to find out what was wrong. That would be his chance to overpower the guard and get away . . .

To where, he didn't think about.

Ignoring the gnawing pangs of hunger, he left the rice where it was. When he woke up, two rats were finishing what was left

◄ 79

of his meal. Keith ran to the door and scared them away but it was too late. Most of the rice was gone. He pressed his fists to his forehead and cursed. Now the guards would think he had eaten the food—the opposite of what he intended.

He scraped together what was left of the rice and ate it. The next time food came, he stayed awake and kept the rats away until, twenty-four hours later, the guard returned. Keith sprawled on the floor and waited to see what the reaction would be. The guard shoved the old rice aside with his foot, dished out a new portion and left. As far as Keith could tell, he hadn't looked inside. He waited anxiously, hoping the man would return with a doctor or another guard. Nothing happened. Nobody came.

He was too sleepy to stay awake for another twenty-four-hour vigil so he memorized the shape of the pile of rice, brought it into the cell and slept on top of it to keep it from the rats. He woke up when something tickled his arm—a rat trying to nose its way to the rice. With a yell, he rolled aside. The rat scurried beneath the door and stopped, watching Keith with dark, greedy eyes. Keith banged the door to scare it away but hunger kept him awake the rest of the night. And when the guard came the next day, the routine was the same. He kicked aside the food Keith had carefully replaced and dumped another batch. After he was gone, Keith stared at the rice scattered across the floor. And then he realized—by leaving an untouched dish of food, he as much as told the guards he was alive. Otherwise the rats would have eaten it during the night.

What a joke. They would keep feeding him even if he died.

He pushed his head to the food slot. Today's rice was mixed with bits of chicken. He took a piece and held it to his nose. To a starved palate, the smell was almost too rich. He smeared the bits of chicken on his lips and face before pushing it into his mouth. And then he realized what he was doing and stopped.

I'm going crazy, he thought.

The idea scared him. Would he end up like the Frenchman, drifting in and out of fantasy, imagining he was somewhere else half the time? Would he think he was back home? With Chris? Would he start hallucinating and carrying on imaginary conversations. Would he see the cell as the home they'd planned on having? And when he slept, would he feel her lying beside him, nestled in the crook of his arm? Oh, God.

He crawled to the opening and placed his head against it. His head was too big to fit through it. He remembered pictures of victims liberated from Nazi concentration camps, how unbelievable it seemed that they could be so thin and still be alive. If he drank only water, he, too, would grow that thin. And if he grew thin enough, he could fit through the food door.

It was a crazy thought, crazy and scary, but he fixed on it, and as the days passed he continued to drink only water. He spent long hours pushing and twisting his head against the opening while chanting Chris' name until his hair was worn off and a crown of raw scalp opened around his head. His hunger faded, replaced by feelings of euphoria. At some deep level he knew he was crazy, but in that knowledge was his security. He courted insanity, that way it wouldn't take him unaware. He would not let the years in prison rob his sanity and turn him, all unaware, into a grotesque parody of himself. So he sat among the rats and spoiled rice determined to will himself to freedom, or starve himself to death.

Henri Giscard expected that loneliness would prompt the young man in the adjoining cell to seek him out, if not to apologize at least to talk. While waiting he imagined himself in Elysium entertaining a group of professors who had been his associates in Paris. He relived an Alpine skiing trip and imagined an affair with a young woman he had seen there. He returned in his memory to Angkor Wat and savored the climax of his career as an archeologist, the Elephant Tomb discovery. He had a good memory and an active imagination but he was bored with his own experiences; he wanted new stimulation. At the end of three weeks, he surrendered his pride, waited until after the guard brought the day's meal, then went to see Keith.

As soon as he set aside the last stone and peered into the cell he knew something was wrong. The American lay curled on his side while outside the door rats were devouring what was left of the day's rice. Henri moved quickly forward, saw the ring of dried blood around Keith's head and thought Keith was dead.

"Fool," he whispered as he knelt over the body. His pride had robbed him of a companion. He should never have left Keith alone. And then he felt the pulse, faint but steady. There was yet a chance.

"Keith? Keith, can you hear me?"

The eyes flickered open. "Chris?"

"It is Henri Giscard."

"Henri?"

"You have not eaten, no?"

Keith looked confused. Henri brought water from the basin. "What has happened to you?"

"She's waiting."

"Who?"

"Chris. Out there."

His eyes slid to the door. Henri jumped up and kicked the door and the rats scattered. He brought back what little remained of the meal. "Here, you must eat."

Ignoring him, Keith crawled to the door and shoved his head against the food slot. Now Henri saw the cause of the abraded scalp. He pulled Keith away. "Stop, stop, my boy. You damage yourself."

"The other side."

"No, no."

"She's waiting."

He tried to crawl to the door again and when Henri pulled him back, he toppled over and lay looking up in confusion . . . "Henri?"

"Yes?"

"Did you see her? See Chris?"

"There's no one there, my boy. Here, you must eat." Henri gathered some of the rice and held it to him but Keith turned away. "Come now, you wish to see your wife again, you must eat."

Again he tried to feed him and again Keith resisted. His eyes remained fixed on the yellow square of light beneath the door. Should he force the food down Keith's throat? The young man's condition was critical; he was hallucinating. Or was he? He had recognized Henri, it was true, but he seemed possessed of the idea that his wife was waiting beyond the door. The doorway to death, Henri thought. But to fight delusion with logic was folly. He remembered Keith's account of how he was captured, how bitter and angry he had been at the men who betrayed him.

"Wait," he said. "I will look and see if she's still there."

He crawled to the door and peered through the food slot. There was only dull reflection of yellow light from the rough stone floor.

"Yes, I see her," he said loudly.

"Chris?"

"But she is not alone, there are three others with her, three men."

"What? What men?"

"Shhhh. I'm listening."

"Who?"

Henri could feel Keith's hand on his leg, tugging weakly. He held his position.

"Who's with her?"

Henri turned to face Keith so that he blocked the way to the door. "They are gone now. But they told Chris some very bad things."

"They told . . . Chris . . .?"

"You know who they were? I think the men who betrayed you. One of them, the officer, what did he look like?"

"Who?"

"Burke was his name, yes?"

"Burke?"

"What did he look like? Do you remember?"

"Red hair, thin lips . . ."

"He was the one. Lieutenant Burke was with Chris. And do you know what he told her? Listen to me, Keith. He told your wife you were using drugs—"

"Not true. Chris!"

Keith moved toward the door but Henri grabbed him.

"Listen. The second one, a sergeant—"

"Severa?"

◀ 83

"Sergeant Severa, yes, the second man. He told Chris that it was you who killed the soldier with the grenade—"

"No!" Keith's grip tightened. His eyes were focused now, their dull glaze gone. "He did it. Severa killed Minkin. I tried to tell—"

"And the third man. Your friend—"

"Alex?"

"Yes, Alex was there, too. And do you know what he told Chris? The worst lie. The worst lie of all. He said that you had deserted, you had run away. From her, he said you ran away from *her!*"

"CHRIS!" With a burst of energy, Keith lurched to his feet and stumbled to the door where he stood with his face pressed against the bars, shrieking out her name.

Henri scrambled up quickly. "She's gone, Keith. She thought you left her."

"No."

"Alex told her."

"Lies. He's lying."

"But how can she know? How can—"

Keith grabbed him by the shoulders. "I'll kill him, Henri. I'll—"

"*Yes,* you will, do that. And your anger, your need for revenge will keep you alive . . ."

"I swear to God I will. I'll kill him, Henri."

"He lied to Chris."

Keith grabbed the bars again and screamed Alex's name. Henri let the sound die away and then moved close and said in a quiet voice, "Live, Keith, live to take revenge."

And God forgive me, he thought as he lifted the food to Keith's lips.

CHAPTER 11

Alex plotted his courtship carefully. He was enrolled at Stanford University but spent each weekend in Healdsburg. Chris told him that she could never love anyone after Keith, which, of course, only increased his need, his determination. He wanted Chris Johnson. But he wouldn't have her while Keith's memory was still strong. He decided to weaken it, tarnish it.

His chance came on a Saturday afternoon when they took Gail, then two years old, to the park. Like Keith the little girl had black hair and dark eyes, but her delicate lips were her mother's. When she was somber Alex saw Keith in her expression and resented it. He wanted to keep her happy and smiling, and so he spoiled her. Anything to take away Keith's memory, to banish the ghost.

When they got to the park, Gail danced ahead of them, chasing squirrels with outstretched arms. They stopped at a bench near the playground while Gail ran to the sandbox. Alex picked up a toy moose that had fallen from the stroller.

"You can't keep doing this," Chris said, tucking the moose into a tote bag. "Spending all your time with us. It's not fair—"

"To you?"

"No, to you. You should be doing things. Dating, going to parties, having a good time—"

"I'm having a good time."

"Alex . . . you're kind, but I'm not naive. I want you to think carefully why you're doing this. And don't say you love me, don't even think it—"

"I *do.*"

"No, you don't. You don't know even yourself well enough to know that feeling."

"All right, then, I *want* you. Is that so bad? The rest can come. I want you more than anyone or anything else in this world." And that much was true.

"Alex, please, think of the real reason—"

"I promised Keith I'd take care of you."

"You did not." She shook her head. "Keith never doubted that he'd come back. He'd never ask anybody to take care of me."

"I didn't say he asked, I just said I promised. Of course I meant it as a sort of joke when I saw your picture, but now that I've gotten to know you . . ."

"What picture?"

"Well . . . as I remember it, you were stepping out of the shower . . ."

Chris looked stunned. "Keith showed you that?"

Alex affected an offhand manner. "Don't worry, the details have long since faded from my memory."

"But *why?* Why did he show you?" She said it out loud but the question was for herself, for Keith . . .

"Oh, just barracks bullshit . . . male bonding, that kind of thing. Showing off your girl to the other guys—"

"What are you *talking* about? *When* did you see that picture?"

He added a hint of reluctance. "Well . . . the platoon had a contest to see who had the prettiest girl. One of those things that comes from boredom, really. Anyway, everyone contributed to the pot—a candy bar, cigarettes, money—and then each man put a picture of his girl on the table. Keith wouldn't do it and the men started kidding him—*Is she that bad, Johnson? Isn't Chris a boy's name? Are you sure you married a woman?*—typical G.I. stuff. Finally Keith got that stubborn look and told them he'd show them if they doubled the pot. By that time everybody had heard about it so the bets went up and Keith brought out the photo. I think it was hidden in a knife, wasn't it?"

Chris was staring at the ground, her face pale. Alex pretended to notice her upset for the first time. "You all right, Chris?"

She took a deep breath and looked up. "I won the bet, didn't I?"

"Hands down."

"Good." She kept her smile as she walked toward the sandbox. "Gail, honey, we've got to go now."

And after that, it was just a matter of time.

In the months following his capture Keith learned how Tran Vinh's animosity led to Henri's imprisonment. The Frenchman's father had owned a rubber plantation east of Hanoi. Tran Vinh's father was a foreman on the plantation. As a young man, Henri studied in Paris and returned to Vietnam an archeologist.

"I took as my mistress Hunyth Thi," he said. "She was Tran Vinh's sister. This was in nineteen thirty-nine. Vinh had become a communist and now hated everything French. When he discovered our relationship he ordered Hunyth Thi to leave me. She refused. Vinh called her a whore and I hit him. You would hardly credit these arms with the power to knock a man down, eh?" Henri patted his thin biceps.

"They locked you up for hitting him?"

"Patience, my young American. This was the beginning of his animosity, not the result. No, after our fight I went to Phnom Penh and took charge of the Angkor Wat excavation. Hunyth Thi accompanied us as our cook. My team discovered the great Elephant Tomb—yes, I was the first one to glimpse treasures hidden from human sight for five hundred years. An archeologist's dream." Henri sighed heavily. "But not to last. The war destroyed everything. The Elephant Tomb treasures—five hundred years of priceless temple art, painstakingly accumulated, cleaned and catalogued—all lost when the Japanese invaded. My life's work. I was in despair, my boy. And so I returned to France and became a perpetual student. Hunyth Thi stayed behind. In

◀ 87

my family, one did not bring an Asian mistress to Paris. Still, I attempted to fulfill my responsibility. When I heard Hunyth Thi was pregnant, I sent money but to no avail. I heard later that she died in childbirth. My only child . . ."

"But how did you end up here?"

"In good conversation, my friend, the art of the listener must match that of the speaker. I still feel guilty, you see, after all these years . . ." He raised a hand. "Yes, yes, how did I end up here? I came back to Vietnam in nineteen fifty-four when my father became ill. A strong man, papa. *Formidable.* I was with him when he died. On the day after his funeral, I was ambushed and taken prisoner. Tran Vinh had waited ten years for me to return."

"He waited ten years?"

"In some people, the passage of time dilutes happiness and fortifies anger. We will see how you feel in ten years about those who betrayed you."

"I won't *be* here in ten years. The war will be over before that. I'll be sent home."

"Yes, of course." But there was something about Henri's expression . . .

"What?"

"Nothing, my boy. Let us have a game of chess." He held out his hands holding the imaginary pieces. "White or black?"

Keith got slowly to his feet and looked around the cell. "Wait a minute. I'm not a prisoner of war, am I?"

"Certainly you must be a prisoner of war. A soldier captured in battle . . ."

"Then why aren't I in a prison camp? Where are the other POWs?"

"A mistake, an oversight," Henri began, but his voice faltered. He looked away. "If only I could lie to you, my boy."

"You should have told me in the beginning."

"I was afraid for your reaction. You are so young, impetuous, the emotions like this." He made a rollercoaster motion with his hand. "I was afraid what you might do to yourself."

Keith felt oddly calm. All these months Henri had known that he would never be repatriated when the war ended. He felt an emotional movement away from the Frenchman and in its place the knowledge that he could trust no one completely.

"Keith?" Henri was watching him.

"I'm all right."

"Perhaps Tran Vinh will die. An accident, an illness, that is what we must hope for."

"No."

"But what then? What are you thinking?"

"I want to be alone now."

The old man was hurt but Keith was firm. He was not going to commit suicide or throw his body against the unyielding walls. He was a different person now than the boy who had awakened in darkness many months ago. He sat down, crossed his legs and placed his palms on his knees. Slowly, deliberately, he began to look around the cell, seeing it with fresh eyes, analyzing his environment from the perspective of a man who had passed through purgatory.

Three days later Keith removed the stones and crawled through the passageway to Henri's cell. The old man was humming to himself, moving around at the far end of the room. He turned at Keith's entrance.

"You are safe. Good. Sit. I am in my greenhouse today tending the gardenias."

Keith sat in the spot where he knew Henri imagined a wrought-iron chair and a round table with a glass top.

"I need your help, Henri."

"Whatever help one man with nothing can give another so situated you will have."

"I want you to grow your fingernails."

Henri blinked. "My fingernails?"

"Don't cut them or tear them, not until they grow at least an inch. I'll do the same. When they get long enough, I'm going to use them to dig the mortar from between the rocks."

"With fingernails? It would take a more generous number of years than I have remaining to accomplish such a task."

"The fingernails are just the handle. I've got something harder for the tip."

"Ah, the puzzle deepens. Now what is harder than fingernails except bones or—" Henri's face lit up. *"Les dents.* The teeth. But surely you cannot mean to take out your teeth."

"I killed a rat. I used the lower jaw with the teeth to scrape away the mortar. It works, Henri. Not very fast but it works. And when it's too deep for the lower jaw, I'll need to attach it to some kind of handle, something so I can reach farther down. That's why I need your fingernails. Will you let them grow?"

"If my fingernails can give you hope, my boy, then you will have them. Of course, fingernails take some time to grow and in the meantime we must not let the mental faculties atrophy." Henri sat down opposite him, clenched his fists and held them out. Keith touched the right fist. Henri opened it and smiled. "Black. I move first."

The two men closed their eyes as Henri said, "King's pawn to King four."

CHAPTER 12

Alex planned a shipboard marriage. It was a way for them to be independent of his parents, whose blessing he neither asked nor wanted, and of Healdsburg, with its memories of Keith. Leaving Gail with her grandparents, they flew to Los Angeles and boarded the *Acapulco Princess* for a two week cruise to Mexico. The first night out they were married by the Captain Lindquist, an austere man who recited the vows with a thick accent. There was one awkward moment when the captain asked, "Do you, Christine Johnson, take this man to be your lawful wedded husband, to love and obey, in good times and bad, in sickness and in health, to have and to hold until death do you part?"

Chris hesitated and then said, "I take Alexander Wescott to be my husband."

A pause, during which Alex felt the blood rush to his head. The captain's eyes flicked to Chris, then to Alex, who forced a smile and said, "She's always been . . . unorthodox."

The captain gave them a certificate, duly signed and witnessed. As soon as they were alone in the passageway, Chris said, "I didn't mean to embarrass you . . ."

Alex wondered if what bothered her was the promise to *obey* or *love* but decided not to push it. They went to the ballroom and had champagne. At one point the social affairs director took the microphone and announced them as newlyweds. Chris found it strange to hear her name linked under the banner, "Mr. and Mrs. Alexander Wescott the Third." They led the next waltz and whether it was the imperceptible motion of the ship or too much champagne, she found herself giddy. Alex took her to the deck, where they stood at the rail and stared down at white-topped waves curling against the hull. He put his arm around her and she leaned back against his shoulder.

"Oh, God, Alex, I haven't felt so dizzy since they gave me Valium when I had Gail."

"You're beautiful when you're dizzy."

Her head was tilted back, lips slightly parted in a half smile. Alex kissed her and for the first time felt the kiss fully returned. His excitement built. They hadn't been intimate yet. Chris just wasn't comfortable making love while she still felt married to Keith.

"Come on, Mrs. Wescott, I want to seduce you."

"You did that already . . . now you just want to have sex."

He wasn't sure how to take that . . . With arms around one another they went down the hallway, Alex nuzzling, touching. His well-tailored white slacks did little to camouflage his arousal, and a matron in mink glanced down and turned quickly away.

The king-size bed had been pulled down. A bouquet of flowers, compliments of the captain, was on the dresser. As soon as they were inside the stateroom, their lips found each other, then their bodies. When they separated, Chris changed clothes in the bathroom and returned wearing a neglige. Alex stood beside the bed. My body is better than his, he found himself thinking, still in competition with a ghost.

They slid beneath the covers but it didn't happen the way he wanted. At one point Chris hesitated. "Alex . . . just a little time . . ."

"You didn't need a little time with him," he mumbled.

"What?"

Kill the ghost. "You went down on Keith, unless he was lying."

Chris was stunned.

"We were buddies, buddies tell each other."

Her body went rigid. Hearing that Keith had shown her picture to the platoon was bad enough, but this . . . that Keith had talked about the most intimate details of their lovemaking . . .

"I'm sorry," Alex said quickly. "I shouldn't have said that." He put an arm around her, felt her tension. "You're right, though, we'll take our time, do whatever's comfortable for you."

But during that night, lying alongside her and getting no encouragement, his anger grew. Son of a bitch Keith . . .

The months turned to years. Keith learned to control the black rages and bleak depressions that periodically came over him. Thoughts of revenge drove him on. To the endless scraping of mortar he plotted the destruction of his three enemies. Death was too quick, too easy. He wanted to strip their lives of any meaning, destroy whatever it was that each valued most, reduce each one to the same state *he* was in—a desolation so complete that consciousness was agony and death would be a gift.

His growing fixation made Henri uncomfortable, even though he had encouraged it at first. "Hatred feeds upon itself," he warned. "He battles the storm who wakes the sleeping wind," he said.

"It was your idea."

"Ah, yes, but that was to keep you alive. Desperation is not a philosophy—"

"It is for me. For every minute of my life in here, each of them owes me a minute. . . ."

Exercise was making Keith physically strong, but Henri decided his mind needed equal attention. "A college of one," he announced one day. "I have your curriculum. We begin each day with French—to be truly civilized one must speak a civilized language—we then proceed to history, philosophy, the classics, social graces—"

"Social graces! Come *on.*"

"And why not? Unless a man feels comfortable in the company of his superiors he cannot aspire to equal or surpass them. You will be my perfect student, my finest creation, a man such as the world rarely sees today, a Renaissance man."

"I don't want to be a Renaissance man."

"But I told you before, my dear boy, your opinions are worthless. You have not the education or background to form a valid conclusion."

"I know what I want, Henri."

"So does a cow. . . ."

Boredom undermined Keith's reluctance and soon they were spending long hours in instruction. Keith was surprised to discover that he enjoyed it. When his mind was engaged time passed more quickly. And their work gave Henri a new lease on life. Time that he wasn't actually teaching he spent reviewing the next day's lessons. Keith discovered that his mentor had a remarkable memory. He could recall dates and information in great detail, a faculty that he had honed to perfection while in prison.

"The mind is a storehouse of information," Henri said. "It is merely a matter of learning to retrieve it."

They exchanged life histories. Keith described his love of flying and discovered that Henri's brother had been a pilot. "Headstrong and impatient, like you," Henri told him. "Claude flew for a company called AeroChine and when he came home to visit he would make *l'entrance grande.* First he came low over the house to attract everyone outside and then he would treat us to a show of aerial tricks loops and rolls and dives, before landing on the road. I admired him until like young Icarus he fell from the sky into the sea."

"He crashed?"

"The engine failed, probably from contaminated gasoline. A bit of rust destroyed my life's work. And I hated my brother for ten years afterward."

"Why?"

"Because on that aircraft was the Elephant Tomb treasure."

And then Henri explained that during the war Indochina was controlled by Vichy France until after the Normandy invasion. Then the Japanese took over. "This was in March of 1945. We knew they planned to confiscate the Elephant Tomb treasure so I prevailed on Claude to take a plane and fly the artifacts to Bangkok. A fateful decision for us all."

"He died?"

"Not in the crash, no. He landed at sea and was picked up by a freighter. But in May he was captured by the Japanese. We learned later that he was working with your O.S.S., flying guns and ammunition to Ho Chi Minh. He died in a prisoner of war camp and after the war the Americans gave him a medal. Papa was proud. Claude has always been the sheep black, you understand? He was captivated by the gambling dens of Macao and the night clubs of Hong Kong and bordellos of Bangkok. But the war matured him, I think, and in death he became a hero."

"In death he became a corpse."

"Perhaps you are right. Heroism is a concept to assuage the guilt of the living. . . ."

The schooling went on. In the darkness of the cell Henri called forth philosophers and poets, kings and religious leaders, scientists and reformers, and introduced each one to Keith. But it didn't stop Keith's bitterness. Over and over he relived the events leading up to his betrayal: Minkin's death, his report to Burke, Severa's gear inspection and the heroin that could have been put there by one man, his friend, Alex Wescott. The memory fed a bitterness that, like a grain of sand caught in an oyster, grew gradually until it lay burnished and luminescent at the center of his being, a hard pearl of hatred.

CHAPTER 13

Years passed and more years and the seasons were all one, all seasons of darkness. The years were divided into time before the tunnel and time after the tunnel. Before the tunnel there was endless scraping of mortar until, like a word repeated over and over until it loses its meaning, the activity lost its connection with escape or freedom and became simply what was *done* every day. The years before the tunnel were long, and then suddenly the first stone was free and after more years another stone and then the earth opened beneath Keith's hands.

It was the time of the tunnel.

There was no light. The earth was seen through the fingertips, rocks pried loose with a surgeon's care and broken to create new digging tools. Rope of braided hair became a tape measure and a crude cradle of sticks set at right angles with a hanging stone provided a plumb line which kept the tunnel straight and level. Haste was the enemy. At one point, the tunnel collapsed only moments after Keith left it. For days they waited to see if the effects had been noticed on the surface but no one came. They began again, bypassing the old tunnel, and proceeded by inches a day until it was time to begin the incline, gently, gradually, slowly upward until—

After twenty years of darkness, the faint, transluscent glow of the test-probe came like an explosion. The probe was three feet long, made of fingernails, reinforced with the leg bones of rats, and carefully bound together with hair. Keith had been driving it gently into the roof of the tunnel. He had done it thousands of times before and always there was resistance and darkness. Again the passageway would be extended another few feet forward, another six inches upward, the contours visible only in his mind. Until suddenly, driving the probe upward into the roof, resistance gave way and light filtered into the probe, illuminating his face, his hands, and the walls of earth.

Keith stared at the tube. The light, so faint that no one who had not lived half his life in darkness could detect it, was more blue and white than the pale yellow that seeped into the cell from the bulb in the hall. It was the sun. Sunlight. For the first time since being imprisoned Keith could be certain that it *was* daytime. Dizzy with excitement, he leaned against the wall, hands still extended, cradling the light.

Bent double, he returned to the cell using a fast, crab-like crawl in which only his hands and feet touched the ground. "Henri, Henri—"

The Frenchman was humming to himself, composing a new song, when Keith burst from the tunnel, his gray hair matted with dirt. For a moment the two men stared at one another.

"Light," Keith said.

"Light?"

"*Allons-y.* Come look."

The two men now spoke only French in deference to Henri's long-standing prejudice in favor of his native language. The Frenchman was like a gnome, frail and bent. Following him into the tunnel, Keith realized how the years had robbed the old man of his agility. The darkness shifted imperceptibly, outlining Henri in faint silhouette.

"*Mon Dieu,*" he murmured.

"Go on, go on."

The illumination was like a magnet, drawing them forward. Henri cupped his hands reverently and pulled the light against his cheek.

"The gift of Prometheus," he whispered.

"Bullshit. *We* did it, Henri. We can get out, we can escape."

But this would not be a haphazard rush to freedom. Keith knew from his first experience all these years ago that it was impossible to blend with the local population. No, they would escape at night and by dawn they would be safe beyond the borders of Vietnam.

Or they would be dead.

They waited until the light grew dim in the probe, indicating sundown, then returned to the cell and emptied the water from the rock basin. It was fall, either October or November, which meant at least ten hours of darkness. They would wait six hours—until the basin was three-quarters full—and in the hours after midnight make their escape.

They were too keyed up to rest. Instead they reviewed their escape plans and talked about food. Each man had a meal he dreamed of. Henri described a five-course dinner which included Vichyssoise, poached salmon, broccoli with cream sauce, a vanilla mousse cake and espresso. Keith wanted a thick steak with horseradish, a baked potato with butter and sour cream, and a chocolate milkshake.

Henri winced. "I thought I had civilized you, my boy. But see—your palate remains that of a truck driver."

More than once Keith got up to check the basin, where the slow drip, drip, drip of the water seemed to take longer than all the years that had led up to this point.

"You know what is surprising?" Henri said. "I have no idea what I shall do after my meal."

"What?"

"When we escape. I had never really believed this day would come."

"I knew it would."

"For you, yes. For me, it is very strange. Leaving Elysium is leaving everything I know."

The imaginary landscape was the only part of Henri's life that Keith had refused to enter. He had no patience for Henri's land of Elysium, nor would he create an imaginary land of his own,

98 ▶

despite the Frenchman's encouragement. His cell remained a cell and he would never pretend otherwise.

The basin was not quite three-quarters full when they went forward to begin digging through to the surface. According to Henri's recollections the tunnel now extended beneath the walls of the Villa Sedomandte, past the street and under the Kai Lo park. At night the park should be deserted but if someone was passing by . . . Keith fingered the dagger he had chipped out of rock. This time nothing would stop him.

It was night, the probe reflected no light and Keith worked by feel. After years of proceeding so cautiously, he felt an exultation in attacking the ceiling without regard to consequences. Dirt showered him as he carved a cone-shaped space around the probe, keeping his head lowered and eyes closed. A root blocked his way and he excavated around it. The texture of the soil changed and became increasingly moist. Suddenly a chunk of earth broke free and bounced off his shoulder, bringing with it a rush of fresh air.

Henri whispered *"Keith?"*

"I'm okay."

There was light now as he chopped at the narrow opening, swiftly enlarging it until he could thrust himself up into the night. A canopy of stars rose above the trees, and the illumination of a quarter-moon was like sunlight to eyes so long accustomed to darkness. From a distant window a faint light shone, and on the other side of the street he saw the gray walls of the Villa Sedmondante.

Only after he helped Henri out of the tunnel did he remember that in the onrush of sensation he had forgotten the danger. Wearing only ragged shorts, their pale skin and haggard appearance would instantly cause alarm.

Henri was staring upward. *"Les etoiles . . ."*

They moved toward the street and took cover behind a concrete planter.

"I'll blink the lights twice," Keith said. "Be ready."

Keith moved along the periphery of the park, looking for a car to steal, but the homes and buildings on the opposite side of the street were, like the Villa Sedmondante, protected by gates or high walls. Henri had given him a mental map of the area and Keith knew that a less affluent area lay to the south along Cham street. His biggest worry was of being spotted before he could find a car.

Leaving the protection of the park he ran across the deserted street and felt an odd mixture of fear of open spaces and exhilaration at the speed, the freedom, of his movements. Shadows seemed as bright as day. He had gone only a block when the twin headlights of a car appeared, and he flattened himself against a tree, moving with the shadow as the car approached. Headlights swept across the tree as the car turned into a circular drive and pulled up to the porch of a three-story home. Using the tree as a shield, he found himself standing with his back to the street. If anyone else drove past he would be immediately visible.

Voices rose in loud commotion. Keith peeked around the corner. Headlights illuminated the ornate front door, and Keith squinted against their brightness. The car was an ancient brown color with tall white numbers on the rear door. Keith recognized it from Henri's description—a Citroen taxi.

The occupants stumbled into the light, the driver leading his disheveled passenger to the door. They argued, lurched forward a few steps, and then the passenger raised a bottle of beer to his mouth, found it empty and flung it high overhead. Keith ducked and the bottle shattered not ten feet away. When he looked again the two men were pounding on the door of the house. The Citroen sat, its motor running, in the driveway.

Keith ran doubled over, keeping the car between himself and the two men. The Citroen was so old that the front door was hinged at the rear and opened into the windstream. Before he got in he peered into the open window and inspected the controls. Not until he had located the clutch, gear shift and, most important, the emergency brake did he slip inside.

The car settled under Keith's weight and the headlights shifted on the building. Someone from the house was helping the drunk inside but the driver turned to look at his taxi. Keith released the brake, put in the clutch and slammed into first gear. The driver let out a yell, took two steps forward and froze as the car came toward him. He took a step back and then Keith was past him, out of the driveway, grinding the gears into second as he raced up the street.

Not until he rounded the corner and headed toward Henri did he realize that he hadn't located the light switch. He fumbled with one knob and then another. A mechanical turn-signal indicator swung out from the body of the car. Keith braked to a stop beside the planter and called the Frenchman's name. Henri promptly stepped forward, shielding his face from the light. Keith jumped out and helped him inside.

"Did you blink the lights?" Henri asked.

"Couldn't find the damn switch."

"I didn't know . . . the lights blinded me."

Keith concentrated now on driving. They had mentally rehearsed this route a thousand times, and the only tense moment came on the Paul Doumer bridge when they had to slow down to let a man walking a goods-laden bicycle pass. Keith hunched low behind the wheel but the man gave them only a cursory glance.

When Henri smelled food, he searched beneath the seat and discovered a portion of rice and six carrots wrapped in a huge plastic trash liner. After he'd eaten, Henri inspected the holes in the plastic bag and was able to laugh.

"The Vietnamese waste nothing, you see?" He slipped the bag over his head and extended his arm and hands through the holes. "A rain coat."

Kam Gai airport was outside the city in an area of small thatched houses. Rather than pass the checkpoint in front of the terminal they parked on a perimeter road. Keith opened the trunk and found a tire iron, then they climbed a dilapidated fence and made their way to the tie-down area behind the terminal where an Aeroflot jet was parked near half-a-dozen smaller aircraft.

"*Merde,*" Keith whispered.

"What's the matter?"

"The smallest one is a twin-engine. I only flew single-engine."

"Are they so different?"

"We'll find out."

◀ 101

The crinkle of Henri's plastic poncho was the only sound as they crossed to the plane, a high-wing Anatopov. Keith undid the tie-downs, removed the pitot tube cover and slid off the control locks. Then using the tire iron, he jimmied open the door.

"I'll need a few minutes," he told Henri. "Stay outside and warn me if anybody comes."

He made his way to the pilot's seat, where the long-forgotten smell of electrical wiring greeted him. The controls and instruments were more complicated than anything he had come into contact with before but after a few minutes he realized that most of what he was looking at were two sets of the same gauges, one for each engine. The original labels in Russian had been overlaid with ones in Vietnamese. He sat there, touching each control as he identified it. Keith had assumed that he would have to hot-wire the ignition, but the Anatopov had an old-fashioned butter-fly switch that required no key.

Henri climbed aboard. "What is taking so long?"

"I have to know what I'm doing before we turn the engines."

"If you cannot fly it, we can drive to the mountains and hike into Laos."

Keith shook his head. He wanted to be out of Vietnam by dawn. Besides, Henri was too frail for hiking. He flicked on the master-switch, and needles and gauges sprang to life. Left engine first: Prime switch on, fuel pressure up, prime off. Throttle positioned. Boost pump on. Ignition to left magneto. And now the tricky part. A single-engine plane could take off as soon as he started the engine. Now he would have to start one and then start the other. Keith took a deep breath, prayed the engines were in good shape and pushed the silver button. The prop began to turn slowly. He inched the left throttle forward.

Start, damn you.

And suddenly with a roar, it did. He switched to both magnetos as Henri instinctively covered his ears. After years of silence, the noise was overwhelming. Quickly Keith repeated the process and the right engine roared into life. In the terminal, lights began to blink on.

He released the brakes and shoved both throttles forward. Instead of moving ahead, the plane began turning to the right, directly toward the Aeroflot jet. Keith pushed the left rudder but nothing happened. He hit both toe brakes and the plane stopped abruptly. Henri looked over. "What is it?"

"I can't steer." Something teased his memory, something to do with steering—

"Keith—" Henri pointed to the terminal where a guard had appeared in the doorway. Keith fought panic as the guard started toward them. Keith released the brakes, gunned the engines and tried again to steer to the left. And again the plane veered toward the Aeroflot. The guard reached for the gun at his waist.

Keith shook his head. "I can't steer, it's like the nosewheel's dis—"

Disconnected. The word echoed in his mind and he remembered something he'd only read about. Some aircraft had nonsteerable nosewheels, freewheeling so that the plane's direction was controlled only by differential braking. Or differential power. He was still thinking like a single-engine pilot.

Holding pressure only on the left brake, he shoved power to the right engine, and the plane swiveled smartly to the left. He added power to the left engine and the plane straightened out and picked up speed while he steered by tapping the right or left brake. The guard began running, gesturing for them to stop. Keith selected a quarter flaps and yelled, "Get down."

He shoved both throttles full-forward. The engines roared and the plane surged forward. Keith did not hear the shots but suddenly a tiny hole appeared in the windshield . . . But they were past the guard, moving swiftly down the taxiway where the white lines blurred and became one. Henri was gripping the control panel, staring at the far end of the taxiway where the darkened trees came rushing toward them. The taxiway wasn't as long as the runway but there was no time and no choice. They were committed. The controls danced beneath Keith's hands, the airplane trembled, and the nose lifted skyward.

And kept lifting. A high-pitched whine startled Keith. The stall-warning. He pushed the wheel forward and spent a frantic moment grabbing at the trim wheel. The plane, which had been mushing through the air on the verge of a stall, increased speed and regained its buoyancy. The trees flashed past beneath as they leaped toward the stars.

"We did it!"

"Like Phoenix, risen from the ashes."

"We're free, Henri, we're *free* . . ."

He retracted the flaps and brought the gear up with a clump. The temperature decreased as they climbed and Keith noticed that Henri was shivering. He found the heat control and a blast of warm air poured over their legs. Banking to the right, he went too far and had to turn back again. The feel of the Anatopov was heavier than the little Cessna 150s he remembered.

"We're heading two five zero," he said. "But that's only approximate. See if you can find a map and we'll plot a course to Chiang Mai."

Chiang Mai, the largest city in northern Thailand, was about four hundred miles from Hanoi. With a speed of one hundred and fifty knots they would be there in less than three hours, Keith figured. A map would give them an accurate compass heading and the frequencies of any radio navigation aids.

A pair of sunglasses dropped to the floor as Henri brought out a sheaf of papers from the pocket next to his seat. He found a map and unfolded it. Keith glanced over. The plane's pilot had drawn lines between a number of cities including Hanoi and Saigon. And he saw something else—a smear of blood that glistened darkly next to one of the lines. Henri gave him a weak smile. "It seems I have had an accident—"

"You're hit?"

"A small-caliber indigestion."

"Where? How bad?"

"It's nothing, nothing."

"Henri, *where?*"

The Frenchman touched his right side. Keith had him lift the poncho and saw a trickle of blood coming from a tiny puncture.

Henri said, "A minor price to pay for the glory of a sunrise."

"We'll go back—"

"Are you mad? To go back is to die. We go forward."

"Henri—"

The Frenchman grabbed his arm. "Listen to me. I will jump

104 ▶

out the door if you dare turn back. We have not come all this way to . . ." He slumped back in his seat. Keith hesitated but Henri waved at the compass. "Go, go. You can find me a doctor at Chiang Mai."

Keith pulled the map onto his lap and found that it didn't include Thailand. Fifteen minutes later, when he discovered that the right gas tank had been punctured, he knew the map didn't matter. They weren't going to make Chiang Mai anyway.

CHAPTER 14

Keith the ghost. That was Alex Wescott's first thought when he saw the wedding photo on Chris' dresser, a wallet-size photo with a thick white border and rippled edges. Chris stood there in her wedding gown, her eyes fixed on Keith so goddamn adoring, her hand nestled in his. All so young and radiant, Keith in a powder-blue tuxedo, tall and skinny, long dark hair the style of a bygone era. He faced the camera with that confident smile that Alex remembered so well, too well. Keith and Chris. The odd link of their names bothered him.

Chris came out of the adjoining bathroom and saw him holding the photo.

"What's this for?"

"I'm going to put it at the memorial."

She disappeared into the closet, her white slip whispering after her.

"Why not the one of him in uniform?"

"That one's better."

"It's a little weird, don't you think? Commemorating a ninety-day marriage instead of his military record."

When she didn't respond Alex turned to the mirror and adjusted his tunic. The junior senator from Connecticut had begun to thicken slightly around the waist, but the custom-tailored Army uniform easily hid this sign of middle age. He wore his Army uniform with mixed emotions. On one hand it reminded him that he had seen combat during a war that, a quarter of a century after its conclusion, had achieved the stature of a rite of passage. The medals he received attested to his service, his bravery, his sacrifice. On the other hand the medals burned his chest in silent accusation, and the uniform reminded him that he was living another man's life. Keith's ghost still hovered like an invisible presence over their marriage.

Chris came out of the closet and began climbing into a knit dress. Still straightening his jacket, Alex said, "People think it's odd, putting up a photo of your first husband."

"You're using him in your speech."

They finished dressing and collected the two boys, Nick and Bobby. It was a blustery autumn day. Fire-colored leaves danced in the gutters and along the edge of the Rock Creek Parkway as they drove to the Vietnam Veterans Memorial where the crowd had already gathered. Stockbrokers and Hell's Angels, drug abusers and doctors, the homeless and heads of corporations, all linked by the common experience of Vietnam. Some wore impeccable full dress uniforms while others looked like a ragged Rebel Army returning from the Civil War. Posters danced above the sea of heads identifying specific army units, and as they made their way through the throng Chris caught words and phrases from another era . . . firefight VC, Bien Hoa, Chargers, number ten, dustoff, Ruff-Puffs, Ia Drang . . .

A platform with chairs on it had been set up facing the Memorial. A large man in a baggy suit greeted Alex, who turned to Chris. "Honey, this is Max Elliot, head of the coordinating committee."

Chris shook hands and introduced the two boys. The wind flipped a strand of Mr. Eliott's hair as he led them to their seats. When he saw an extra chair he pulled out a crumpled list. "We're missing someone."

"Our daughter's meeting us here," Alex said.

Above the crowd the polished black wall was visible, angled toward them like outstretched arms, engraved with the names of those who had died in Vietnam. Chris scanned the faces without finding Gail. Gail . . . daughter of her first love, the daughter Keith had never lived to see . . . Instinctively her eyes sought the panel where she knew Keith's name was engraved.

There was Gail, wearing a green tam o' shanter. She touched a white rose to her lips and placed it at the base of the monument. When she turned, Chris waved, and Gail slipped into the crowd, appearing now and then, moving around and behind, her thin figure causing scarcely a ripple in the human sea. As she approached, Chris noticed that she was wearing a dark Salvation Army cape rather than her red wool coat.

"Hi, guys," Gail greeted them from the foot of the platform. She had Keith's color, along with short black hair and intent dark eyes.

Bobby said, "You're late."

"Who are you, the human Rolex?"

"Come on up," Chris said. "There's a chair for you."

"I'll watch from down here."

"Honey, Alex is making a speech. We want the whole family—"

"I don't do Toyotathon."

Bobby immediately began imitating a car horn. "Beep beep, beep beep."

"All right," Chris warned him. "That's enough."

Toyotathon was Gail's derisive theme for political speeches. When it came to politics, mother and daughter tended to disagree. For Chris, politics had become an exciting process. Her service on a number of national committees gave her a sense of purpose and an identity separate from that of simply a senator's wife. Gail saw only the flaws in the system. To her politics was synonymous with hypocrisy, compromise and duplicity.

Alex left Mr. Elliot and returned to them. "Hello, Duchess. How are things in the city room?"

"I don't know. I'm in research, remember?"

"Right . . . well, here, you can sit beside me."

"I'd rather watch from down here . . ."

"Ahhh." Alex smiled knowingly. "Look, how about you sit up

108 ▶

here and listen to my speech and I'll sit still afterward and listen to your critique."

"You already know it."

"Beep beep," Bobby said in a low voice.

"This isn't what you think," Alex said. "I'm going to talk about Keith, about what he meant to me and how he influenced my life. I need your support on this one, Duchess."

He extended his hand and helped her onto the platform. As they took their seats Chris said, "You could have worn your red coat."

Gail shrugged. "I could have worn my black bikini."

It was the type of flip response that had always been characteristic of Gail but had become more so since she began work at the Washington *Herald.* A literal black sheep in a family of blonds, Gail was a maverick, born with the same stubborn intensity that Chris remembered as attractive in Keith but found troublesome in Gail. Actually the girl was fond enough of Alex. He was, after all, the only father she'd ever known. And Alex had been good to her. Still, down deep, Chris sensed a mutual distrust between the two of them that sometimes puzzled her. . . .

Chris wondered if it wouldn't have been better to prepare her daughter with an advance copy of the speech. Alex had written it himself, polished it with his speech writer, Bert Kreiser, and reviewed it with his campaign manager, Budge Tickman. It was more than a good speech, she thought, it was a dangerous one. Unless he struck just the right chord the speech could do more damage than good. So there were two versions, the second one more general, less personal and impassioned, with only one reference to Keith.

The crowd cheered a welcoming speech given by Jan Scruggs, the man who had initiated the Vietnam Veteran's Memorial, and fell silent for an invocation given by an interfaith minister. By the time his turn came to speak, Alex was confident and ready.

He began with an anecdote about two Saigon beggars, Kam Ji and Kam Jo. "I gave them each a dollar and the next day, there was Kam Ji outside the hotel with four used Playboy magazines for sale. He bought the magazines for a quarter each and was selling them for a dollar each. Kam Jo was waiting, too, and when I asked him where his money went he showed me two Marlboro cigarettes. Every day I bought a dollar's worth of magazines from Kam Ji and gave another dollar to Kam Jo and at the end of the year Kam Ji had opened his own newsstand and Kam Jo had died of lung cancer. I don't take credit for Kam Ji's success and I don't take credit for Kam Jo's failure, but I take credit for this: the *opportunity* I gave both these men to create a better life. And whether the world believes that we invested wisely or foolishly in Vietnam, it is the fact of that investment that we were willing to pay a price for the chance—not a certainty, just a chance—for a better world and a finer future for people beyond our own borders. In that investment lies the full measure of our humanity and of America's greatness."

The ringing tones of his last words brought applause, then like a symphony conductor, Alex held up his hands to orchestrate the silence. Chris watched, impressed as always by his performance. Alex was never more at home, never more sure of himself than when in front of a crowd. The climax began on a quiet note.

"I had a friend named Keith Johnson. Keith earned his private pilot's license in high school but he was a patriot, and so he joined the army to fly helicopters. By the time he finished basic training the helicopter program was no longer open to high school graduates, so Keith Johnson ended up humping the boonies like the rest of us. But he never gave up his dream of flying. He always volunteered for courier duty so he could get up in the Hueys. One day I told him I felt safer on the ground than in the air and I still remember what he said . . . 'I'm not going where it's safest, Alex, I'm going where I can best serve.' Serve. It's what the armed *services* do, and thank God, that word has been restored to its proper place of respect in society."

Applause. But at the mention of Keith's name Gail stiffened and sat with her lips pursed in a tight smile, her dark eyes fixed on Alex's back. When the applause died, Alex let a silent moment pass before continuing.

"Keith Johnson never came back from 'Nam. Like many others, he left behind a family—his wife, Chris, and a baby daughter he never knew, Gail. When I came home, Chris and I met to share our memories of Keith. She had lost her husband, I had lost my best friend. Over time the common sorrow we shared developed into something new, something deeper. In one of those strange coincidences that a war sometimes generates, Chris became my wife, and as I like to say, Gail adopted me as her father. I'd like them to join me now in memory of the man who brought us together—father, friend, husband, hero—Keith Johnson."

Alex turned and motioned to them. Chris got up but Gail remained in her seat. Not until Alex stepped over and took her hand did she stand up. Leaning close to him, she whispered through clenched teeth, "This sucks, dad . . ."

Alex's smile never wavered. "I owe you one, Duchess."

They stood at the podium holding hands, Chris on his right, Gail on his left, the photographers jostling for position while their cameras whirred.

"To best serve," Alex said. "That was Keith's legacy and challenge to me. He saved my life in 'Nam, and I'd like to think it was for a purpose. I think it was for this very day, this very moment, right here standing beside the two people he loved most in this world." Alex tilted his face slightly skyward. "In the name of that friendship and that legacy, I announce my candidacy for the highest office of this land, the greatest opportunity for best service . . . the presidency of the United States."

In the moment of stunned silence that followed, Alex lowered his eyes to the crowd. Without seeming to rush, he continued with only a slight pause, "And whether or not it is me or another who is chosen to lead this country into the twenty-first century, now is the time to fulfill the legacy of those who died in Vietnam, to reaffirm our faith in the ideals for which they sacrificed their lives. I give you the proudest generation this country has ever known, the Vietnam generation!"

The applause all but drowned a few scattered boos and catcalls. Still holding hands with Gail and Chris, he raised hands above his head in a victory salute, then turned and accompanied them to their seats.

Gail left the podium without looking back. Chris caught up to her in the crowd.

"Gail, don't go—"

"You knew, didn't you?"

"I should have told you, I'm sorry."

"I feel used. And Keith. I thought you loved him, I thought he was your husband—"

"He was my first husband, darling. Try to understand." But her gaze faltered before Gails' accusing stare. Keith had been her only love, and deep down she knew, but rarely could acknowledge, the falsity of her life with Alex. . . .

Someone called her name and Chris turned. One of the photographers was waving to her. "Can we get a picture of the whole family over here at the podium, Mrs. Westcott?"

She turned back to her daughter but Gail was gone, lost in the crowd.

CHAPTER 15

They flew southwest, toward the mountains that separated Laos from Vietnam, and Thailand from Laos. Fifteen minutes into the flight, the punctured right fuel tank ran dry. When the engine began missing Keith switched the cross-feed valve to feed-fuel from the left tank. The engine continued to cough and the plane veered toward the right.

Henri looked worried. "Can the aircraft fly on one engine?"

"Sure," Keith said, although the truth was that he didn't know.

Fuel finally reached the right engine and brought it back to cruise power. Henri closed his eyes and leaned against the window while Keith fiddled with the radio, trying unsuccessfully to find a navigation frequency. He decided to keep going until he was certain they were inside Thailand and then land as close as possible to a village. He hoped that he could spot an airstrip; otherwise they would land on a road or an open field. The important thing was to get Henri to a doctor.

After an hour the Frenchman shifted his position and leaned toward Keith. "I have a confession, my boy."

"Don't talk, Henri. Save your strength."

"It takes no strength to sit among the stars. You must listen. I told you that when papa was dying I returned home. Before he

◀ 113

died papa showed me a letter, a letter from Claude written on a small scrap of paper, stained and faded, the letters so tiny you might barely discern the words. It was written in the prison camp where Claude developed gangrene. He asked papa's forgiveness"—Henri's voice became stronger—"although it is *my* forgiveness he should have sought. It is me he betrayed when he stole the Elephant Tomb treasure."

Keith looked over at him in surprise.

"Yes," Henri said. "Stole my discoveries."

"You said he crashed at sea."

"So he did, but without the treasure. He landed first at a deserted airstrip southeast of Bangkok, near Makham. The airstrip was used by an early hydroelectric dam that had been destroyed in the flood of 1942. Claude landed and buried the boxes. The heritage of a forgotten civilization he saw only as the means to becoming a millionaire. A victim of greed. We thought the war had changed him, but no. His was the legacy of Cain. He murdered my work, my reason for living, my—" A coughing spasm forced him to stop.

Keith glanced outside, hoping to see lights, an airport, some place to land, but the terrain below was obscured by low clouds and ragged mist.

Henri took his arm. "Listen carefully to me. The runway at Makham had two sets of stones, each painted white. These stones marked both ends of the runway. The Elephant Tomb treasure is buried at the midpoint between the two stones at the northern end. If I am not with you—"

"Then neither of us will be there. Now lie back, save your breath."

A faint smile creased Henri's features. "We must, after all, consider the possibility that you remember landings with less fidelity than take-offs."

Keith said nothing. The landing would be difficult enough under the best of circumstances, but if it were dark and if the clouds persisted . . .

As they flew on in silence Keith would glance at Henri, who sat now there with eyes closed, his bare arms crossed over his stomach, as if for protection. At one point he said to Keith, "You are not angry with me, are you?"

"About what?"

"For not telling you the truth about the treasure."

"I don't give a damn about the treasure. Right now I just want to get you to a doctor."

Henri sighed. "You were determined to escape at any cost. I was afraid the temptation . . . that you might offer the guards the treasure for our freedom. I do you a disservice, yes? But you must understand that I was afraid. For you and for myself. Tran Vinh would have tortured you—and then me—and even if you had been silent as the Sphinx, I know I would have given in to pain. And after that we could not be friends and I . . . I could not bear that."

Keith said nothing. The needle on the gas gauge was bouncing against zero. Night was fading. Along the eastern horizon the sky was turning a cobalt blue but the earth was still obscured by a low overcast.

Five minutes later, though, Keith spotted a ragged opening in the clouds. A sucker hole. One of those fleeting openings that beckoned a pilot through them and then disappeared, leaving him marooned beneath the overcast.

"Henri," he called. "Seatbelt. We're going down."

He rolled into a tight turn. Ragged tendrils of cloud drifted past as they descended through the opening. The light dimmed as they emerged underneath the overcast where a high plateau stretched more than a mile before it was lost in mist. In the other direction a mountainous ridge touched the base of the clouds. Had the sucker hole been a quarter mile in that direction . . .

The right engine quit and the aircraft veered. Keith added full power to the left engine, jammed the left rudder to hold the heading and looked for an emergency landing spot. The terrain was relatively flat, made up of shrubs and tall grass and dotted with trees. Nowhere was there an open road or cultivated field or enough clearance to land. The left engine stopped, caught again and continued erratically. They began to lose altitude. Keith picked the largest open space he could see and set up an approach.

CRUX

They began a gentle ninety-degree turn, lowered the flaps and dropped the landing gear. The left engine surged, pulling the wing up and forward. Keith grabbed for the throttle, cut the power, brought the plane back under control and silently glided over the first trees, then dropped into the clearing, which suddenly seemed much smaller than it looked from the air.

The plane was ten feet above ground when Keith raised the nose and flared. The speed began to drain away but not fast enough. They would barely touch down before hitting the first tree. Visions of the crash, the plane cartwheeling, breaking into pieces . . . He thrust the thought aside. Do something. Two trees, slightly to the left, caught his attention. Both about the same size, they were twenty feet apart, parallel with one another. Their only chance. He banked slightly and pointed the nose midway between them. A bush slapped one wheel and the plane trembled. A moment later, still traveling sixty miles an hour, they hit. There was an explosion of wood and metal, the wings sheared off and the fuselage skidded sideways, digging a furrow sixty feet long before it bounced off another tree and spun to an abrupt stop.

Abrupt silence. Keith, feeling like he had been shaken by a giant and tossed aside, turned to the Frenchman, slumped forward. Unconscious.

"Henri?"

No reaction. Keith released his seatbelt but when he tried to stand, his feet slipped. The cockpit was canted at an angle. Bracing himself against the throttle quadrant, he put his fingers on Henri's neck and felt a faint pulse.

"You're okay, you're okay," he mumbled.

Moving awkwardly against the tilted deck he managed to open the door and lift Henri through it. Once free of the crumpled fuselage, he carried the frail body to a safe distance. The Frenchman's skin was cold to the touch and the wound had begun to bleed, bright red mingling with the brown clotted blood. He looked about. Had anyone seen them? Heard them?

"Au secours!" he yelled.

The only answer was the sound of birds greeting the dawn.

RICHARD AELLEN

Keith ran back to the plane, tore the rug from the aisle between the seats, brought it back to use as a blanket.

The Frenchman's eyes fluttered. "Keith?"

"We're okay, we made it, just hang on . . ."

Henri gripped his hand tight. "Are you all right?"

"I'm fine."

The old man looked around vacantly. "I can't see you, my boy."

"Here, let me get this around you." Keith freed his arm and began wrapping the rug around Henri.

"After years of darkness," Henri murmured, "I greet a darkened dawn."

"Listen, I've got to go get help—"

"Stay here." He clutched Keith's arm.

"Henri—"

"We have had so many years, you wouldn't leave me now."

"You need a doctor."

"No, no," he said softly.

Keith cradled the old man's head. "I'm sorry, I thought there'd be a town, a village . . ."

"Tell me what you see. There is sun, yes . . .? Silence is darkness, my boy. Come, describe what you see. Is there sun?"

"Not yet, Henri."

"But the clouds. Look to the east. Have they not caught the dawn?"

Keith looked up. A canopy of gray clouds hung low over the land. "Yes," he said unevenly, "the sun's rays on the high clouds. It's . . . it's really beautiful."

"What colors can you see?"

Keith's eyes were on his old friend. "Pink, Henri. The clouds are pink with silver edges. Silver and gold, shifting in different patterns, each shade blending into the other."

"And the sky? It is blue now?"

"Blue, yes. Light blue where the sun is coming up and darker and darker the higher you look. And the stars are fading now, all except the morning star. It's still there."

He gripped Keith's hand tighter and whispered, "What else?"

"The hills are green, Henri, a hundred different shades of

◀ 117

green, some of them wrapped in mist. And lower clouds are catching the light now. They're gold and silver and mother of pearl—"

Suddenly Henri was sitting bolt upright and staring into the distance. "Who is that? Who—?" He turned to Keith, eyes wide. "Oh, my boy."

He died in Keith's arms. Later, when the sun burned away the clouds, Keith had only grief to greet the dawn. He buried his friend in the place where they had found freedom together, and began the long, long trek down the mountain.

CHAPTER 16

The women were working in the rice paddy when Keith appeared. They were knee-deep in water, faces shielded by conical straw hats, and didn't see him until Aporanee straightened up to rest her back. The man was a *farang*, a foreigner, but he also looked like a ghost, naked except for a dark plastic poncho that flapped noisily in the wind as he stumbled toward them across a narrow dike. His gray hair and beard were long and matted, and his bare arms and legs were sunburned a raw pink. As he came forward he shouted something in a strange language.

"Get Prem Chaduvedi," Aporanee called to a young woman who had gone to refill her seed pouch. Smugglers were common in the area and it was wise to have someone who might speak the language of a *farang*. The young woman hurried away.

"*Arretez,*" the man yelled. "*Au secours.*"

He was wearing sunglasses, and as he came closer they saw that his poncho was actually a large plastic trash bag with holes cut for the head and arms. There was blood on the poncho, and like a platoon of soldiers, the women began a slow retreat. The *farang* became frantic and jumped into the paddy to follow them. He slipped and fell and got to his feet, sunglasses gone. With one hand over his eyes, he began searching like a blind man beneath the surface. The women continued moving back until they had regained dry land, then squatted and talked in low voices until Prem Chaduvedi arrived on his Honda motorcycle. Although he was only twenty, Prem had been to Bangkok and Chiang Mai and had met many *farangs*. He took off his shoes, waded into the paddy and approached cautiously.

"Good morning, sir. Are you hurt?"

The man was on his knees, still searching below the water. He had powerful arms and a thick chest and Prem kept his distance. The man peered through his fingers at him. "You speak English?"

"Very modestly, sir. Can I be of help?"

"What . . . country is this?"

"You are in Thailand, sir."

"Thailand? *C'est vrai?*"

"Excuse me, sir. My name is Prem Chaduvedi. Perhaps I can be for your assistance"

"Sunglasses, I lost my damn sunglasses."

"I would be honored to offer my pair, sir."

Prem took off his sunglasses, the ones he had received as a bonus from a British reporter for whom he had acted as a guide. The *farang* put them on eagerly and turned to stare at him.

"If you need a doctor, I know a man not far from here."

"I need the ambassador, the American ambassador. Can you take me to him?"

"The embassy is in Bangkok, sir, many days from here. But in Chiang Mai there is an American consulate—"

"Then take me to the consulate. I'll pay you when we get there. I have to get a passport, have to get home, have to—"

The man's knees buckled and he clutched at Prem for support. "Can I get something to eat?"

"May I ask first your name, sir?"

"Johnson. Keith Johnson."

The American consulate in Chiang Mai was a low two-story concrete building surrounded by a wrought-iron fence. In the lobby Marine Corporal Emilio Lopez sat behind a circular counter reading a copy of Playboy, three months old and dog-eared from having been handed around among the other Marine guards. When the door opened he smoothly slid an open copy of Newsweek over the Playboy, a move designed to forestall complaints from visitors and avoid the eye of the consul. In this case the subterfuge seemed unnecessary. The man coming toward him was clearly a remittance case, sunburned and filthy, long hair and bare feet. His clothes were ragged peasant pants and shirt. Lopez had seen his kind before, Westerners who had gone native and ended up in Chiang Mai because the drugs were cheap and the women easy and because beyond Chiang Mai, there was no place left to go.

The stranger approached slowly, staring around the lobby, his eyes hidden behind sunglasses.

"May I help you . . . sir?"

"I have to see the consul, I need a passport, an airline ticket—"

"Are you an American citizen?"

"I'm in the army. I *was* in the army. I was a prisoner, I escaped last night. I need to see the consul."

Trouble, Lopez thought. The man smelled terrible, was clearly agitated, probably on drugs. He shifted his position closer to the alarm button.

"Your name?"

"Keith . . . Johnson."

"If you'll sign the log, Mr. Johnson, I'll get somebody to help you."

Lopez handed him a pen and indicated the clipboard on the counter. He stepped to the phone and punched a button. A relaxed voice answered, "McKay here."

"Tell Mr. Bravo he's wanted at the front desk."

"I'll be right down."

There was no Mr. Bravo; the name was a code warning of potential trouble. While on the phone, Lopez kept his eye on Johnson. The man inspected the pen as if he'd never seen one before, then leaned forward to sign the log. Something caught his eye and he stiffened. The pen fell to the floor as Johnson reached across the counter and grabbed the Newsweek magazine.

"Excuse me—" Lopez began.

Johnson had torn out the page and the magazine tumbled to the floor.

"*Hey.*" Lopez came around the counter but the man was already running for the door. "You, wait a goddamn minute."

Prem Chaduvedi, waiting beside his mud-spattered Honda, looked up when he heard the door burst open and knew immediately that something was wrong. The *farang's* features were distorted, his teeth were actually bared, and he was screaming something Prem could not understand. Prem grabbed at him. "Sir, you promised to pay my—"

Keith straight-armed him and rushed headlong into the crowded street. A cacophony of horns and squealing brakes. Prem turned in time to see the American bounce off the fender of a bus and tumble to the ground. Something colorful, the size of a fist, flew into the air, and then the bus blocked his view as it squealed to a stop. Prem ran forward, rounded the bus and saw—nothing. Keith Johnson had disappeared. From down the block a street vendor's angry shout. Half a block away, above the crowded stalls, he now glimpsed long white hair disappearing around a corner. Prem started forward and then jumped back as a motorbike swerved in front of him. No matter. He knew he would not catch the American, not the way the man was running.

Prem was angry with himself. He had guessed wrong. He had driven the *farang* almost a hundred miles, given him clothing and food—even his own sunglasses—all in promise of payment when they reached the consulate. Instead, the man had fooled him and run away. Prem cursed himself for not having asked more questions, for not having demanded payment in advance, for having gotten involved at all.

As he turned back to the sidewalk, something caught his eye, something colorful and crumpled lying in the street. Dancing between traffic, Prem grabbed it and stuffed it into his pocket. Passing the consulate, he overheard a Marine talking to a man in a suit.

". . . ripped up the magazine and ran like a son of a bitch."

"Wouldn't give his name."

"Said it was Keith Johnson but he wouldn't write it down."

"And he said he was an American?"

"An American soldier, is what he said. But he talked with an accent and didn't look like no soldier I ever saw. And then he just tore up the magazine and took off."

"Another Lord Jim loony."

"You want me to check the police?"

The civilian shrugged. "If he's real he'll be back. If not . . ."

They went inside and Prem considered his options. He could put in a claim to the American consulate but from what he'd heard he doubted that this would do him any good. Perhaps Keith Johnson was not even American. After all, he had spoken French when they first met. No, if he wanted his money he would have to find the *farang* himself.

Prem pulled out the magazine cover and spread it flat on the seat of the Honda. A headline in large blue letters read "The New Breed," and in smaller type, "Politicians For The Final Decade." A color photograph showed a man and his family standing at a podium. Prem turned it over and found an ad for the Chrysler cars. But there was nothing here that gave a clue to the American's identity.

He tossed the page into the street and mounted the Honda, determined to find the man he had brought to Chiang Mai. There were three things he knew about this Keith Johnson: that the man had no money, that he was blind without sunglasses, and that he would draw attention wherever he went. Sounding his horn, Prem pushed his way into the traffic.

Keith ran blindly through the streets of Chiang Mai, the blood in his temples echoing a single refrain over and over . . . Chris, Chris, Chris. And with each beat of his heart came an image of her, the scent of her hair, the texture of her skin, the sparkle in her eyes when she laughed, the way she whispered his name when they made love. First Henri, now Chris, *both* lost to him now . . .

He found himself outside the wall of a *wat*. He recognized it even though he had never seen a Buddhist temple before. Henri had described the *wats* with such detail that he quickly found the gate and made his way to the *Bo* tree, its trunk wrapped in saffron, the sacred tree under which Buddha had found enlightenment. Two monks walking down a path noted his presence and paid no attention. Keith sat crosslegged and fought to calm himself.

Christie. The nickname mocked him. For twenty horrible long years he had lived on the hope of seeing her again, of taking up their life from where it had been abruptly interrupted. For twenty years he literally had lived on imagined love, her love, but there was no love. There was only Chris on the cover of Newsweek magazine standing beside Alex and both of them smiling . . . He dug his fingernails into his forehead.

"Mr. Johnson?"

Prem Chaduvedi stood staring down at him. Seeing Keith's expression, Prem quickly raised both hands, palms outward. "I wish a gentleman's discussion, please. No police. No problem. This is sacred ground."

Keith said nothing.

"Sir, if you remember our agreement, I am to collect fifteen United States dollars for my transportations and a further ten denominations for those miscellaneous food and clothing expenses."

Keith had not moved. Prem shifted his weight uneasily.

"May I inquire if there is some difficulty at your consulate?"

Keith spoke quietly. A voice from the dead. "Do you know the town of Makham?"

"Makham?"

"Do you *know* it?"

"That town is south of Bangkok, maybe one hundred kilometers."

"Sit down . . . Prem."

"Sir, my indecisive stomach would wish to set beneficial terms for payment of those twenty-five dollars expense."

"How would you like to earn ten percent of a hundred thousand times that much?"

"A hundred thousand times . . .? You are saying two millions and five hundred thousand American dollars?"

"I don't know if it's there and I don't know if we can find it, but if we do, your share is ten percent. All you have to do is take me to Makham."

124 ▶

Prem shook his head. "I am not becoming involved in the drug trades, sir. Although I respect your decision for yourself."

"This has nothing to do with drugs."

"What else can be worth so many millions of dollars at Makham?"

"Sit down and I'll tell you."

This *farang* is trouble, Prem warned himself. I should report him to the police, I should return to my sister's house and mend the fishing nets. Instead, he sat down and listened as Keith Johnson returned down the dark decades to the day when he joined the army to fly helicopters and found instead . . .

CHAPTER 17

As Keith was making his improbable escape from Vietnam, one of the men he had targeted for destruction was on his way to Libya. Ex-Lieutenant Jerry Burke finished his scotch and soda and glanced out the window of the Grumann Gulfstream jet. Below, the Mediterranean glistened in the sun, scalloped in whitecaps that rose and disappeared and returned again. Good, he thought. At least there's wind down there. On his last visit to Tripoli the air conditioning in the hotel broke down and he ended up sleeping on the balcony. Rifles, bayonets, Claymore mines, anti-tank weapons, guided missiles, electronic jamming systems—the Libyans would pay any price for military hardware but they couldn't keep their stupid air conditioning working. All those petrodollars wasted on ragheads and camel drivers.

The bathroom door opened and an Arab woman dressed in the traditional Moslem *chador* came out. Nexli al-Kanuni was Burke's lover. A few minutes earlier she had been wearing blue jeans and a low cut blouse. Now all that was visible were her dark eyes, the bridge of her nose and a portion of her forehead.

"What's that," Burke said. "A joke?"

"I told you I would have to wear the *chador*."

"I didn't even know you owned one of those things."

"What do you think I carry in the suitcase when I go home?"

"Perfume and cigarettes for mommy and daddy."

She lifted the veil and wrinkled her nose. "Now you see why I don't like to go home."

"You didn't have to come."

"You need protection from the wild dogs."

She was referring to a joke he had made after his last trip to Tripoli. A prostitute had scratched his back and Burke had said he was attacked by wild dogs. It was not a joke to Nexli, whose possessiveness was becoming oppressive. They had met in London after Nexli's husband, a Libyan diplomat, died in a skiing accident. Rather than return to Libya and the restricted life of a Moslem widow, she had embarked on a series of carefully designed seductions—fashioned to embarrass prominent members of British society if they ever came to light. When she met Burke, she had just completed a lucrative transaction with her second MP.

Burke said, "You really going to wear that?"

"It will make things easier."

"It makes you look about fifty years old."

"You know better."

He reached for her but Nexli caught his hand at the wrist. As they stared at one another, their eyes reflected a mutual challenge. Nexli pulled his hand between her legs.

"Naughty daddy," she said softly.

Burke glanced toward the cockpit. The door was closed. They were alone in the plush cabin with its leather seats and dark green carpet.

"Turn around."

As she did, he reached beneath the garment and confirmed what he had felt a moment before: beneath the *chardor,* Nexli was naked. When she faced him again her knowing smile mirrored his. Burke dropped to his knees and ducked beneath the garment. In the dim light her legs rose above him to a dusky apex. His fingers slid behind her knees and began circling upward. Nexli murmured and thrust her hips forward. Burke touched her outswelling buttocks, brought his hands forward and thrust his thumbs deep inside her. The scent of love, rich and pungent, excited him.

Burke had begun his relationship with Nexli because her brother, Major Hasnid, was a military procurement officer in the Libyan army. The girl's exotic appearance—her heavy eyebrows, flared nostrils and full arched lips—were of only minor interest. He had made love with Arab women before. By the time he was thirty he had methodically tested his sexual prowess with women of just about every race and national origin. He was, some might say, a sexual predator, which Nexli responded to by challenging him to take risks. And so they made love surreptitiously in public, and privately experimented with drugs to heighten their passions. She was, he knew, a dangerous addiction.

Since leaving the Army, Burke had made his way in the world by using people just like he had in the Army. The threat of blackmail had persuaded Alex Wescott to loan him enough money to start Artex International, a company that specialized in importing artifacts from Asia, the Middle East and Africa. Establishing the company was the same excuse he used with his wife, Leanne, who signed over her family's Virginia farm to fund Artex. Burke maintained offices in Washington and London. The company was mildly profitable, but its real value was as a front for the illegal arms deals that brought in great sums of money overnight. And Burke knew how to spend his profits, playing the role of gentleman farmer in Virginia and international playboy in London. Occasionally the money would run out and Burke would panic until he had put together a new deal. The one he had going now with the Libyans was one of his very biggest.

Major Mahmoud Hasnid was waiting when the Gulfstream touched down in Tripoli. He forced a smile when the clam-shell door unfolded and Jerry Burke stepped out. There was something distasteful about the man. It was more than his obvious greed—it was his appearance, the garish red hair, the invisible lips, and oily white skin that Hasnid found repellant.

He remembered the first time he had met Burke in London, how his sister had hung on the man's arm, obviously infatuated, and in the restaurant how her hand found Burke beneath the table when she thought he wasn't looking. The West had turned his sister into a whore, but at least the whore had found a man who could provide Libya with weapons. In the bloody battle for influence and promotion within the Libyan army, Hasnid's pipeline to the Western areas was a personal coup. He needed Jerry Burke as much as he detested him.

Now Hasnid took one step forward and froze when he saw his sister. Nexli was dressed in a *chador* but she was instantly recognizable. He restrained himself from glancing over his shoulder at the car where his driver waited. If anyone else recognized her . . . He went forward quickly, shook hands with Burke and said in a low voice to Nexli, "What are you doing here?"

"I came home for a visit."

"Are you insane? To arrive like this, in *his* aircraft?"

"Nobody knows I came with him."

"*I* know. That soldier knows."

They had been speaking in Arabic. Now Burke interrupted in English. "What's wrong?"

Hasnid turned to him. "She should not appear with you like this."

"Why not?"

Hasnid had no intention of explaining how his honor would be compromised if Nexli's adulterous relationship with a Christian became public.

"She must get back on the plane."

"What?"

"She must not be recognized." He turned to Nexli. "Go, *go.*"

"No—"

"This is Tripoli, not London. I have enemies. Walk with this man in public and you walk with them. Now get aboard that plane and after we have gone take a taxi to our father's house. Tell him you have returned home for a surprise visit. I will see you this evening. Any communication you have with this man you will make through me. Do you understand?"

"I'm staying with him at the hotel."

She started to push past but Hasnid grabbed her arm.

"Shame me, and blood will wash it away. Do you wish to take that chance?"

Nexli's defiance slipped. She turned to Burke. "I will send word to the hotel." Then she climbed the steps and disappeared into the plane. Burke had never seen Nexli afraid before.

"Come," Hasnid said. He turned and led the way to an official army limousine.

Burke was fascinated. "What did you say to her?"

"I reminded her of the danger she brought on all of us should your relationship become public."

"What danger?"

"You are in a Moslem country, have you no comprehension of what that means?"

"I know enough to stay clear of ayatollahs and take off my shoes before going into mosque."

"Then you should know it is a violation of Islamic law for a Moslem woman, especially the widow of a distinguished diplomat, to have relations with a married Christian."

Burke smiled. Instead of telling Hasnid to join the twentieth century, which was what he thought, he said, "So what'd you say to scare her like that?" For future reference.

"I told her what she already knew—that her blood would wash away any shame she brought on our house."

"You'd *kill* her?"

"That is one option."

"What's the other?"

"I could kill you."

When the driver opened the car door Hasnid ducked inside, but Burke stood for a moment, his smile fading, a trickle of sweat making its way down his back. Goddam Nexli, he thought. She could have gotten him killed. Then he remembered the C-4 shipment and relaxed. Hasnid might kill his sister but he wouldn't touch him. At least not until the shipment of C-4 plastic explosive was delivered. The Libyans had given him one point two million to make the buy and they wouldn't let Hasnid blow that kind of money, not just to avenge his sister's non-existent honor. Not even crazy Arabs were that crazy. He got into the car with Hasnid.

They drove to a nearby Army base where Libyan soldiers were unloading a shipment of arms that had arrived earlier that morning on a Lufthansa cargo jet. The shipment consisted of two thousand M-16 rifles and twelve hundred LAW anti-tank weapons packed in boxes listed as oil-drilling parts. The rifles, which had been broken down for shipment, were being assembled by soldiers who happily brandished the new weapons. A supply officer supervised the inventory while another officer watched imperiously from a reviewing stand still adorned with faded crepe from the last parade. The man on the reviewing stand was Colonel Ibram, a member of the Defense Council, and one of Hasnid's enemies. Ibram's presence was an unpleasant surprise. The man had no reason to be here and hadn't been informed of the shipment. Hasnid pretended not to see him as he greeted the supply officer. But it took only a few minutes for Colonel Ibram's aide to appear.

"Major Hasnid, Colonel Ibram would like a word with you."

Hasnid looked toward the reviewing stand, pretended surprise and excused himself and followed the aide, who stopped at the bottom of the platform and let Hasnid climb the four steps alone.

"Good afternoon, Colonel," Hasnid said. "I didn't know you'd be here."

Ibram was holding one of the new rifles. His only acknowledgment of Hasnid's perfunctory salute was a slight nod. "Had you informed me that the shipment would arrive today I might have enlightened you."

"A standard security precaution, sir. No one on the council was notified—"

"Nor was the council notified of a delay in the C-4 plastic explosive."

Hasnid stared back at Ibram but refused to let his irritation show. Either the man was deliberately needling him or he had forgotten the delays that Hasnid had reported to the council. The C-4 was under strict control and had to be gathered carefully in small amounts from a variety of sources. There had been delays. Too many delays considering the one point two million dollars they had given Jerry Burke to pay for the C-4. Hasnid's sources told him that Colonel Ibram had begun quoting to other members of the Defense Council the amount that the one point two million could have earned in interest had it been placed in a Swiss savings account.

"No, the C-4 was not part of this shipment. It has to come by chartered jet."

"When?"

"Very soon now."

Ibram deliberately leaned over the railing, held one nostril closed and blew his nose. Hasnid stiffened at the obvious insult.

"Before our C-4 arrives," Ibram said. "Perhaps you should insure that it does not undergo the same kind of metamorphosis as have our M-16 rifles."

"What do you mean?"

"These are not up to specification. Look." Ibram slapped the rifle from one hand to the other and pointed to the manufacturer's marking. "These guns are made in Taiwan."

Hasnid fought to control his anger and keep his voice calm. "Are they all . . .?"

"If you wish to inspect them each at a time . . ."

Ibram pushed the gun into his hands, folded his arms and waited. Hasnid forced himself to say, "Thank you for bringing this to my attention. I will see what can be done." As he descended the stairs he imagined a faint smirk on the aide's face as he passed him.

Burke was leaning against a wall in the shade of the warehouse, two half-circles of sweat visible beneath his arms. "Colonel got a bug up his ass?" he asked as Hasnid approached.

"These are not of United States manufacture."

"They're made in Taiwan under license. Exact in every detail—"

"But only three-quarters the price of United States manufacture."

Burke shrugged. "Maybe more, maybe less, supply and demand. You know how it is—when I get the money I shop for price. These were available, the U.S. versions weren't."

"But the agreement was for United States arms."

"The agreement was for M-16's. These are M-16's. Here." He took the rifle and fired a burst at the sky. Soldiers unloading crates looked up, startled. Burke handed the rifle back to Hasnid. "It works just fine. What's the problem?"

"The Defense Council expects arms of United States manufacture, which these are not. Some adjustment of price is necessary."

"Major, I'll be glad to adjust the price if you can show me where in the agreement it specifies the country of manufacture."

"I am talking about the spirit of the agreement."

"Spirits change country to country, that's why I put things in writing. Tell you what I'll do, though. In the C-4 load I'll add a dozen of those chrome-plated Smith and Wessons you like so much. You can give them to your buddies as gifts, or whatever."

"When will the C-4 load arrive?"

"Just a few more weeks—"

"It has *been* a few more weeks for months now. Colonel Ibram is causing trouble with the Defense Council. I would like to tell them an exact date."

"I'll get in touch with my people as soon as I get back to London."

Hasnid returned to Colonel Ibram and lied. "He has agreed to bring three dozen chrome Smith and Wesson handguns to make up for the discrepancy."

"Better than the bite of a camel, I suppose. We will see what the other members of the council say."

Ibram turned and walked away, and Hasnid knew that his credibility with the Defense Council would suffer. He was sorry now that in his eagerness to beat his rivals in finding a source of Western arms he had championed Jerry Burke. Returning to the American, he said that Colonel Ibram wanted six dozen of the handguns. As he expected, Burke objected. And as he planned, they compromised on three dozen. It was one small triumph in a day of dangerous frustrations.

CHAPTER 18

Traveling to Bangkok, Prem proved endlessly inventive. He purchased a handful of rice seeds for a few *baht* and doled them out one by one to pay for gasoline, meals, and a barber for Keith.

"I am a bad man," he said gravely. "I say these are sacred seeds from the Plowing Ceremony. Very valuable to farmers."

The Plowing Ceremony, he told Keith, took place in Bangkok each year to inaugurate the rice-planting season. Sacred oxen drew a gold plow and seeds were tossed to the ground and gathered by onlookers who believed the seeds brought good luck.

The air grew warmer and more humid as they left the mountains and entered the coastal plains, the noise of the motorcycle making Keith's ears ring until he fashioned earplugs from pieces of cloth. When they arrived in Bangkok the kaleidoscope of sights, sounds, movement made him dizzy. For years he had given total concentration to one thing at a time—Henri's teaching, his physical or mental exercises, the work on the tunnel—but now it took three days before he could walk the streets comfortably, filtering the extraneous perceptions and focusing his attention selectively. During this time they stayed with Prem's cousin, a minor official in the Agriculture Ministry who was a bachelor and spent most of his evenings at night clubs.

The cousin had access to a station wagon that Prem borrowed for the trip to Makham. Driving south along the coastal road, Prem stopped to pick up as many riders as he could fit in the car, charging each one five or ten *baht.* Most of them were loaded with baggage that had to be precariously tied to the roof or lashed to the open tailgate. One woman had three live ducks tied to a pole. Since thirteen *baht* were worth only fifty cents, Keith thought it was a waste of time.

"Let's just *get* there," he urged.

"A man has money," Prem said, "he spends money. A man having without money must spend other person's money."

They dropped the last of their passengers at Chanthaburi, a mining town at the mouth of the Chanthaburi River. From there they drove inland, following the river until they reached the site of the old dam, where steep rock walls forced the river into a swift-flowing cataract. All that remained of the dam were jagged concrete ridges and a crumbling, overgrown foundation where the dynamos had once been mounted. Lush vegetation covered a plateau above the dam. There was, though, no evidence of an airstrip as described by Henri. After an hour's searching they drove to Makham, where Prem hunted down an old lady who did remember the airstrip and brought her to Keith.

"This is Mrs. Kultida Rangsit," he said. "She was a young girl when the dam was made. She remembers where the airplanes landed."

Kultida was a short stocky woman whose tiny features were clustered in the center of a melon-shaped face. Her teeth were stained a dark red from chewing beetlenut. They drove back, followed by a dozen children who ran after them and scrambled for room on the open tailgate. At the site Kultida took charge. She motioned the children back and surveyed the area, then waded into the elephant grass with a rolling gait, pausing occasionally to get her bearings. She would eye the ridge to the north and then turn to the south and squint at the rim of the canyon. They made an odd procession, everyone starting and stopping in unison, Keith and Prem following the old woman and the children circling them at a distance.

Reaching the center of the field, Kultida spread her arms,

turned in a slow circle and made a low guttural sound that the children copied. Keith gave Prem a skeptical look.

"What's she doing?"

"She is calling the spirit of the airplane."

The old woman began running heavily, her skirt trailing in the wind. The nasal sound she was making swelled—*eeeow-wow-eeyow-wow*—her imitation of an airplane. She stopped, cocked her head to one side, then began running in a new direction, the kids trailing behind her. It took twenty minutes before she reached an area that satisfied her. She planted herself firmly and, pointing in the general vicinity of where she was standing, called out something.

Prem turned to Keith. "She says this is where the runway started."

Keith could see nothing but trees and grass. He glanced at Kultida, who gave him a broad, red-toothed smile.

"Tell the kids we're looking for two white stones. Give them twenty *baht* for whoever finds the first stone."

"No, no, too much." Prem reached into his pocket, pulled out a handkerchief and slowly unwrapped it. Inside were six rice seeds. Keith knew that in Prem's other pocket was a handful of identical seeds, but Prem handled these six as if they were the last on earth. Hands reached forward eagerly, but Prem held the seeds out of reach. He gave his instructions and the kids began the search. Some crawled on hands and knees, invisible except for the movement of the elephant grass that hid them. Two of the older boys beat the terrain with sticks. It took only minutes before one of the kids let out a yell. They ran forward and Prem cut the bushes and grass aside with a machete to reveal a stone still, remarkably, flecked with white paint.

With one stone discovered, it did not take long to find the others, and when they had located them all they paid the old woman a seed and ten *baht* for her help and gave a seed to each child who had found a stone. Kultida and the children placed their hands together and nodded their thanks, then stood watching.

"Tell them they can go now," Keith said.

"Yes, they know."

136 ▶

"Do they want a ride back?"

Prem put the question to them and heads shook in unison.

Prem said, "They are waiting to see what happens next."

"What happens here?"

"Yes, we are very fascinating to them."

"Tell them we're finished. Tell them we're leaving so we'll take them back to town."

Kultida ignored that and began talking and the children clustered around. From the way she pointed and held her arms outstretched, Keith guessed she was telling stories about the old days. Whatever, it was clear that she and the children were going nowhere, at least not until he and Prem did.

Keith and Prem drove to the next town, where they ate and waited impatiently for night to fall. They returned after dark and with a pick and shovel and tape measure made their way toward the first stone. There was no moon, but Keith had taken off his sunglasses and moved quickly and surely through the dark, Prem stumbling after him. Suddenly Keith stopped.

"It's gone."

"What?"

"The stone. Look."

He pointed but Prem could see nothing. Not until he crouched and felt the hollowed earth with his hand did he realize. "They think if stones are so valuable to discover they must be so valuable to own."

The stones were gone but the depressions where they had been imbedded were not difficult to find. The distance between the two was twenty-three feet. Keith began digging with the pick at the halfway point. He tried to imagine how it would have been for Claude Giscard. The pilot would have been desperate, in a hurry, afraid that someone might see him. Keith guessed that he would have stopped the plane directly over the spot and wouldn't have had time to dig too deeply.

He was right. Just eighteen inches down he discovered the first box. Prem jumped forward with the shovel.

"Careful," Keith warned, "we don't want to damage anything."

The crates were rotted and the wood separated like wet card-

◀ 137

board at their touch. They ended up on their hands and knees, scooping handfuls away. The first artifact they lifted out was wrapped in burlap and tied with twine. Keith unwrapped layer after layer until he was holding a gold statue of a woman riding on an ostrich-like bird. In the flashlight's glare the bird's inset ruby eyes glowed crimson. Prem took the statue, turned it reverently. "We are big time men, now, I think."

The gold ostrich was only the beginning. Eventually they uncovered six crates, each three feet long by two feet square. The artifacts were separated into compartments, some with delicate extensions carefully braced to prevent them from breaking. They packed them all, still wrapped, into the car.

Too excited to sleep, they drove through the night, a permanent smile fixed on Prem's face as he described all the things he would do with the money. Occasionally his enthusiasm spilled over and he pounded on the dashboard, chanting, "Rich man, rich man, rich man."

Keith kept his eyes fixed on the road. He felt oddly removed and distant, not able to share Prem's elation. For him, the treasure was not an end—only a beginning.

Prem was describing the celebration he planned in Bangkok at a particular massage parlor. "Full treatment for millionaires," he said. "First massage, then hot tub, then rolling onto water bed with one girl, six girls, any particular girls you want, everybody warmly happy with suds. I will make the arrangements. A night such as you have dreamed during your many years imprisoned—"

"No thanks."

"On my hospitality, sir. For your including me within millionaire status."

"I don't want a woman, Prem."

"Are you Patpong Three?"

"What's that?"

"In the preference of boys."

"No."

"Then how shall you celebrate?"

"It's not my time to celebrate. Not yet."

Prem looked confused. "I think it is not so good to treat fortune as the enemy."

"How old are you, Prem?"

"I am twenty, sir."

"If I gave you my share of the Elephant Tomb treasure, would you sell me the next twenty years of your life?"

"Sell my years?"

"If you woke up tomorrow forty years old with the whole treasure, everything we have in the back of the car, all yours. I would have nothing. But I would be your age and you would be mine. Would you do it?"

"I think one millions at twenty years is proper balance. A man must not anger the spirits with too much good luck."

"Bad luck doesn't appease them, good luck won't anger them."

"I have sufficient luck for current use. I will make merit at the temple of my father and build a new school and install one blue learning computer."

"I want you to do me a favor, Prem. I want you to deal with the Elephant Tomb treasure alone, without me. Say you somehow recovered it from the sea. You were fishing, you lost an anchor, you dove to retrieve it and found the sunken aircraft. Probably nobody will believe it but it won't matter. As far as the world knows, the treasure was lost at sea, and by the law of salvage it belongs to you."

"But . . . you will not take your credit for such a discovery?"

"I don't want any credit. I don't want any association with the Elephant Tomb treasure."

Prem shook his head. *"Mai sanuk."*

"What's that mean?"

"It means not fun, not joyful. Life without *sanuk* is like the bird without wings. You will believe it is frightening to sit beside a millionaire who is *mai sanuk.*"

Keith didn't answer. Twenty years in prison had changed his priorities. Life was not a matter of fun or joy. His life was dedicated to a purpose . . .

* * *

CRUX

In Bangkok Prem sold the first piece on the black market for enough money to rent a small house hidden behind a wall of shrubs. They would not announce the treasure publicly until they had transferred it out of the country. Prem arranged for a false passport in the name of John Kris and found a Chinese manufacturer of Asian art replicas who, for a substantial fee, agreed to coat the Elephant Tomb artifacts in plaster and ship them to England. With the business arrangements completed, Prem disappeared for two days of massage-parlor celebrations. When he returned he found Keith was sitting in semi-darkness in the living room with the curtains pulled.

"You sleeping so late, sir?"

"I got tired of wearing sunglasses."

Prem had reached for the curtain but now he stopped. "You wish to be in darkness?"

"It's not dark." Keith slipped on the sunglasses. "Go ahead, open them."

Prem wanted to talk about the girls in the massage parlor but Keith had something else on his mind. "I need a partner, Prem. Someone I can trust, someone who knows what I'm doing, and why. If you come with me I'll pay one hundred dollars a day plus expenses from my share for as long as it takes."

"Not for money, sir, but from my gratitude I would help. Only except I cannot take some person's life on a reason which is not my own."

"I'm not going to kill them." He had already told Prem about Burke and Severa and Alex.

"Something bad, I think. Maybe cutting off testicles."

"No, pain destroys objectivity. I want them to see the horror of their fate and know they brought it on themselves. The truth is my knife. I'm going to cut the fancy clothes from the rotting corpse, strip the facade and reveal them for what they are. Lives based on treachery. Whatever they care about most is lost first—family, friends, position, wealth—everything gained at my expense, all of it forfeit . . ."

Prem was unwilling to commit himself on so important a matter until he consulted an astrologer. He went to Sunda Dixit, the famous astrologer who practiced her trade outside the frescoed walls of the Wat Phra Keo. Sunda was an old woman who chewed a huge cheroot as her fingers traced the charts. Her skin had the look of fine parchment, and one tooth was inlaid with an inverted jade heart. Since she rarely smiled, it was said that if you saw jade, good fortune was yours.

Prem waited in line for half an hour before he took his seat on the ground opposite her. Between them a wood box draped in red silk served as a desk. Prem gave the old woman the day, date and time of his birth, and Sunda's fingers flew over her charts. She took a drag from the cheroot and smoke dribbled from her mouth as she assured him that this would be an auspicious time for travel. The serpent and the crow complemented one another. Courage and risk would be rewarded. Sunda had only one warning: "When the locust swarm, danger is near. Beware the locust."

Of course the warning made Prem uneasy, but Sunda would not be more specific, not even for double the usual fee. Afterward he made an offering of a garland of jasmine blossoms at the Golden Buddha and bought two amulets, one to appease the locust and another to ward off air crashes. These he wore around his neck on a gold chain.

One week later Prem and his new partner flew First Class to London, where the announcement of the Elephant Tomb treasure made the front page of the *Daily Mail*. Keith wasn't mentioned in the article, only Prem Chaduvedi, the young treasure hunter from Thailand. And while Prem made arrangements for an auction at Sotheby's, Keith hired a detective agency to locate and assemble dossiers on the men who had betrayed him.

Because he led the most public life, Alex Westcott's file was the largest and the first to arrive. Keith's attention went immediately to the background information on Chris. When he came across his name listed as her first husband, he stared at it a long time. With every day that passed he felt less like Keith Johnson and more like John Kris. All that was left of his former life, which had begun with such optimism and promise, was here, reduced to a few visual statistics.

And then he saw it: *One daughter, Gail Johnson, born June 4th of the following year. Legally adopted by Alexander Wescott at time of second marriage (see below).* The information went on with schools and dates attended, interests and awards, a graduation photo of Gail in the yearbook. He stared at the name. Gail Johnson. *His own daughter.* The physical testimony to what he had been, the love he and Chris had shared . . .

Legally adopted. His eyes fixed on those words and now fury took hold of him. It wasn't enough that Alex took Chris—he'd taken the child of their love too. When her real father's hands should have held her, *Alex* was there. He imagined Alex testing warm milk on his wrist, Alex holding out his hands to catch her when she took her first steps, Alex sitting on the side of her bed reading to her, brushing back a strand of silken hair—

He turned quickly to the photographs of Gail. Black hair. Not blond like Alex, or the two boys. Not auburn like Chris' but jet black, like his had been. The deep-set eyes were like his but, he thought, tinged with a toughness he had never known at her age. The longer he stared at the photo the more certain he became that she was his daughter in spirit as well as in the flesh. She was *his,* not Alex's, not even Chris'. She had been born for a purpose. And when he read in her biography that she had taken a job at the Washington *Herald,* he decided he knew what that purpose was. His daughter would help trap the man who had betrayed them both.

CHAPTER 19

Alex Wescott lay on his stomach while Jenny Jenkins massaged his feet. She sat astride him wearing an orange kaftan, her oiled fingers working their way between his toes. Smoke from incense sticks on the window ledge hovered in gray tendrils and the air smelled rich and sweet. It was the middle of the afternoon and time for Alex to return to his office. He tried to turn over but Jenny didn't move.

"Hey, I've got to go."

She ignored him, moving her cheek in a circle on the soles of his feet. Alex shivered, then with an effort, extricated himself and picked his clothes off the floor. Jenny crossed her legs and sat watching him from the bed. She was tiny and plump. Making love with her, he sometimes thought, was like rolling on a beach ball. As Alex pulled on his shirts she reached out and grabbed his penis. He started to pull back but her grip tightened.

"Hey, hey," he said.

"Leave your friend here."

He bent low to kiss her. When she released him he stepped clear. "No more, honey, until next week."

She pouted for a moment, then got up and opened the bedroom door and a tiny long-haired dog bounded into the room.

"See, you hurt his feelings."

Pascal was her constant companion, banished from the bedroom only while they made love. For Alex, Jenny was a refreshing change from the executive secretaries and occasional Congressional aides who usually became his lovers. She was a costume designer for a local theater. Worried about a rash on her arm that had proved impervious to medication, Jenny had undergone the AIDS test a week before they met at a reception. Alex was cautious. Not until he learned of her clean bill of health did he make her his lover.

In the bathroom Alex washed his face and checked to make sure that no signs of the afternoon's activities were visible. He would stop at the health club in the evening and take a shower after a workout. He was increasingly careful about his extramarital activities, but had long since adjusted to betraying Chris. Their marriage had endured, but they rarely made love. It was her doing, he rationalized. Besides, Alex preferred lovers who were impressed with him, though he would not have put it that way.

Nonetheless, Chris' influence over Alex in political matters was considerable. Her mind worked rapidly and her instincts were uncanny. There were more than a few times when Alex had the uneasy feeling that she had a better grasp of the political situation than he did. I'm glad I'm not running against *her,* he thought, as he left the apartment and headed back toward Capitol Hill.

Before electronic surveillance was declared illegal Lafon Grinki was considered the best wireman in the business. When the new laws came into effect most of the operators changed the name of their services to "counter-surveillance" and continued business as usual. All but Lafon, who prized his peace of mind and had an unreasonable fear of being sodomized in prison. Since he had earned and invested enough money to meet his modest needs, he retired to Key West. His reputation, however, persisted, and it was his reputation which brought Keith and Prem to see him.

They met at Captain Tony's bar, a low rectangular cavern decorated with faded newspaper articles. Lafon, a large man whose flesh hung like soft wax, was dressed in ragged shorts and a stained T-shirt that said: *Don't blame me. I voted for Captain Tony.* He sat in a motorized wheelchair, which surprised Keith. On the phone Lafon's robust voice gave no hint of physical infirmity.

They ordered drinks, and Keith explained that he needed a complete surveillance job on one Jerry Burke. Since Burke's activities made him the most vulnerable, Keith had decided to concentrate on him first. Lafon lit a cigar and waved the smoke away with a pudgy hand. "Told you over the phone, there is no usual rate. I'm retired."

Keith glanced at the wheelchair. "What happened?"

"What always happens? The castration of a great republic. Pink-pantied legislators who need to justify their existence so they pass a law restricting an honest American's freedom to spy on his neighbor."

"I meant your . . . injury."

"Oh, this? This is tourist-repellent. I'm sick of them crowding the sidewalks, but they see a man in a wheelchair, they get out of the way fast enough. Not like twenty years ago when Key West was fishermen, wreckers and conches, toss in a few artists, a handful of precious princes and twelve tourists a day. Raison d'être for Key West was Key West. Now we roll out the red carpet for every white-belly tourist with a dollar bill stuck to his forehead."

Prem frowned. "There is nothing wrong with your legs?"

"Damned if I know." Lafon jammed his cigar into his mouth, stood up and turned to face the barman. "Hey, Dawson, anything wrong with my legs?"

Dawson, a wizened man with a briar-patch beard, was bent over a crossword puzzle behind the bar. Without looking up he said, "Yeah, they're fat."

Lafon sat down. "Dawson the oracle. Never told a lie in his life."

"So you're physically capable of doing a surveillance job."

"As long as it's in Key West. There's no laws against surveillance in the Conch Republic. Hey, Dawson—are there *any* laws in the Conch Republic?"

"Just one."

"What's that?"

"You're not having a good time, point it north and move it out."

Lafon turned back to them. "There you go. Only one law and it doesn't have anything to do with surveillance. You bring the target to Key West and I'll tap his subconscious and tape his dreams."

"Mr. Grinki, I'll pay you a thousand dollars a week, all expenses paid."

"Nope."

"How much do you want?"

"Offer me five."

Keith hesitated. "Okay, five thousand a week."

"Nope."

Prem pointed a finger. "You cannot back up now. You agreed for five thousand."

Lafon grinned. "You got a bad case of tourist ears, kid. I said *offer me five,* and then I said *no.*"

"What's your price?" Keith asked impatiently.

"No price. Like I told you over the phone, I'm retired." Lafon settled back and rolled the bottle of beer slowly between his palms while he let it sink in.

"Then why—?" Prem began. Keith raised his hand and he fell silent.

Lafon noted the non-verbal interchange, nodded and continued. "No, I'm not wasting your time, but I won't leave Key West. Not for all the money in the world. This is the Conch Republic, a land unto itself, the maverick city of anything goes. Only Union port in the Confederacy, only wet port in the Prohibition—"

A young woman entered wearing a maroon tank top, pink shorts and aqua tights. Prem's attention was drawn to her. "You like her, kid?"

Prem shrugged. "Perhaps she has the fun spirit."

"That woman, as we used to say in the Navy, is eminently fuckable. *All* tourists are fuckable. She would probably fuck me but I won't touch her. Tourists carry diseases."

Keith said, "Mr. Grinki, if you won't work with us, who would you recommend? Mac Lowenberg? Rick Crystal?"

Lafon shook his head. "None of them as good as me. And none of them have my gear. Custom made stuff. I design it, build it all right here in Key West. No laws against designing surveillance equipment."

"If you won't help me—"

"Didn't say that. Didn't say I wouldn't help. Get the tourist out of your ears, fella. You think I brought you down here for nothing? What I'm offering is a special course. Five days, I'll teach you everything you need to know about phone taps, wall taps, laser mikes, the whole cheesecake. By the time you leave you'll know more than the average surveillance expert and still less than me. But I'll be available for phone consultations, twenty-four hours a day the first thirty days. You want to keep it confidential, do it yourself, that's my motto."

"Will you sell us the equipment we need?"

"Nope. Selling surveillance equipment is illegal. But if you take the course, each piece of equipment comes as part of your instructional package. I give that to you free, included in the price of the course."

"Which is what?"

"A cheap ten thousand dollars."

Prem said, "For only five days?"

"For five of the most intensive, edifying and instructive days of your life, kid. A week from now you'll be able to bug a bedroom so good that two mosquitoes couldn't commit adultery without your knowing it. You want the best, you pay for the best. Isn't that right, Dawson?"

"What's that?"

"You want the best, you pay for the best."

"No, you pay for the best no matter what you get."

Lafon turned to them. "I leave it to you gentlemen. Give me a week, I'll give you the bedrooms and boardrooms of the world."

Keith nodded and turned to Prem. "You stay and take the course. I'll set things up in Washington."

"Just myself alone?"

"You may not be alone." He indicated the girl in pink shorts. Prem smiled.

"I'm going to keep you busy, Joe Buck," Lafon said with exaggerated relish. Prem's smile faded. "You ever see that? *Midnight Cowboy.* Guy who wrote it used to live in Key West. Everybody used to live in Key West. *I'm going to keep you busy, Joe Prem!* Nah, don't worry. You'll have time to fuck a tourist if that's what you want. Live dangerously, why not? You're a young man. That's what a young man's hormones are designed for . . . fucking tourists."

Despite Prem's expression, Keith had a feeling the two would get along fine.

CHAPTER 20

Keith flew home to Healdsburg and found his father's grave. Frank Johnson had died nine years earlier. The grave was slightly sunken and overgrown with grass and weeds. Keith made arrangements with an agency to have it tended on a regular basis. In filling out the forms, one of the categories was "Relationship to deceased." Keith wrote "None." Frank Johnson no longer felt like his father, Healdsburg no longer felt like home, and Keith Johnson no longer felt like Keith Johnson.

In Washington Keith found the Wescott home in Decatur Street, near Embassy Row. The house, with its rounded corners of red sandstone, turret and scalloped roof, was hidden behind a wrought-iron gate. It was a big house, one that would require live-in help to maintain. Not the kind of house he and Chris would have had . . . Keith sat in the car, half-hoping to catch a glimpse of Chris, and half-afraid he would. Of all the people in the world, only she might recognize him. But he did not see her that day, and would learn that she had been campaigning with Alex in Ohio. Just as well.

Washington exhibited none of the energy or hustle of Bangkok or London, but the sense of understated power that hung over the city was palpable. Washington dealt its clout quietly, playing cards of power and influence behind embassy walls, in committee chambers and briefing rooms. Here were made the quiet decisions that could send a man to the moon or plunge the nation into a war. Washington was a city of indirection, of hidden cause and irrevocable effect.

Keith sought out the Willard Hotel, a Beaux Arts structure on Pennsylvania Avenue not far from the White House. After years of sensory deprivation, Keith enjoyed the rich furnishings—marble floors divided by Oriental rugs, plants overflowing huge hand-painted porcelain vases, chandeliers hanging from frescoed ceilings, the soft sound of chimes marking the hour.

He spoke to the manager, a man who measured his smile according to the importance of his guest.

"You wish the Presidential Suite for an entire month?"

"I want it indefinitely but I'll give you thirty day's notice before I vacate. I pay in advance."

The manager's smile clicked open another millimeter. "Let me check our reservations, Mr. Kris . . . I'm sure we can work out an accommodation."

Which turned out to be the Presidential Suite, with a bedroom that featured an oval window looking out over the Washington Monument and the Mall. The living room became his command center. He had an office-supply store deliver a three-drawer file cabinet and labeled each drawer with a name: WESCOTT, BURKE, SEVERA. Here he filed information, including photographs of his targets, family members, and photos of their homes.

He reviewed the information as he received it from the detective agencies. Alex's career had been characterized by his knack for sensing the timely concerns of the public and making them his own. Just like in Nam . . . He had worked his way upward in state politics to become the youngest attorney general in Connecticut's history. After losing by a narrow margin his first bid for the United States Senate, he had since become the perpetual favorite son, twice elected to the Senate.

A real success story, Keith thought. About to end.

Burke and Severa were less prominent but no less predictable.

Sergeant Severa had left the Army and served as a mercenary in South America and Africa before returning to Los Angeles. He was a bachelor. Five years ago he had formed a security firm that catered to Hollywood celebrities and Beverly Hills socialites. He was arrested once for shooting and killing a man attempting to steal his car. The victim's accomplice maintained that his partner was unarmed, but an unidentified weapon was found at the scene and Severa was acquitted.

The brave make their own luck. The phrase came back to Keith. Remembering Minkin's death, he had no doubt that Severa had again gotten away with murder. His punishment would fit his crimes.

Jerry Burke's file was almost as large as Alex's. Burke had served for ten years in the Army before resigning his commission after an investigation into "misallocation of resources." After an unproductive stint selling real estate in the Washington, D.C., area, he established Artex International. In 1985 he married Leanne Morrison, the only daughter of a prominent Virginia family. No children. A break for the world. In 1986 Burke's name came up in the Iran-Contra investigation. He was rumored to have supplied weapons to the Iranians but no evidence surfaced to back up the charges. His trips to Iran were explained as business trips in pursuit of Persian art. Cover operations, again like Nam.

Glancing through Artex's incorporation papers, a familiar name caught Keith's eye. Listed as vice-president was Alex Wescott. It was the hook he was looking for, the piece that could begin the search backward—Burke to Alex, and back to Chim Bai and the day of his betrayal. Keith would provide the clues, and Gail would follow the trail . . . The daughter Alex had stolen from him would help expose him. He would operate as his three enemies had—with a hidden hand, motives disguised, identity unknown.

He needed time to design his approach to Gail, but he had to see her, if only from a distance, so he waited outside the *Herald* building one Friday afternoon and when she left he followed her. She was smaller than Chris, thin and dark. She walked energetically, crossing streets on an angle to save time. Her clothes confused him—drop-shoulder blouse and baggy pants that tucked in tight at the ankles. He remembered girls in mini-skirts and go-go boots. Now the style seemed to be clothes that didn't fit.

She went to Riggs National Bank, where a number of people stood in line waiting to use a machine—Keith's first glimpse of an automatic teller. Afterward she stopped at a florist and bought a single white rose before continuing down 19th Street to the Mall. Low sunlight lent the grass a particular richness. Heading toward the Lincoln Memorial, the green grass sloped downward toward a dark chevon in the earth. As he got closer Keith saw that it was a wall of black marble, ten feet high at the apex, running fifty feet in either direction, narrowing at the points. People stood singly and in groups before the wall, which was etched with names. On the ground lay various mementos—a photograph of a young sailor, another of a couple holding a baby, a letter, a tiny American flag, a bouquet of flowers, a Purple Heart medal . . .

He had never heard or read about it, but with a shock he realized this was a memorial to the Vietnam war dead.

He watched as Gail went to a particular spot where she stopped and ran her fingers, slowly, along one of the names. *His name.* It had to be his name. She touched the rose to her lips, then knelt down to place it on the ground.

"Gail . . ." It was a whisper full of years . . . And emotions he had not felt in years—tenderness, hope, gratitude—and a dizzying joy. With her simple gesture the dark years, at least momentarily, vanished. The pain, rage and frustration faded, and even the purpose forged in their wake was nearly forgotten. This was his daughter, the child of his love for Chris, and she *remembered* him. He started toward her—

"Gail!"

But it was not his voice. She turned, looked beyond him, and her face broke into a smile. As she waved and started forward Keith turned and saw a young man in a sloppy raincoat coming toward them. He had a camera hanging around his neck. They met, exchanged a quick kiss and went off talking animatedly, bumping shoulders, leaning close. Locking him out.

No, no, it was the lost years that locked him out. He was a father who had never been a father, a friend who had never been a friend, a protector who wasn't there when protection was needed, a provider who had never provided. What did he know about her? About her likes and dislikes, her fears, her dreams? He had played no part in forming her. She was as much a stranger as any of the other people who stood near him, their quiet sorrows reflected in the wall.

He breathed deeply, and the cold-crystal clarity of purpose descended like a cloak. He walked to the spot where Gail had been. Etched in marble, above the rose, lost in the column of names, was the one he knew he would find: *Keith Everett Johnson.* He reached out and traced the letters with his finger. A woman next to him placed a photograph against the base of the wall. Keith let his hand fall and stared at the only evidence that a boy named Keith Johnson had ever been alive. When he stepped back, the woman with the photo glanced at him and said, "Who did you lose?"

Myself, Keith was tempted to say. Except the image that came to mind was of a tall skinny boy, naive, headstrong, self-absorbed, happy and confident. A kid.

"Everyone," Keith said. And he stepped on the rose and pushed it into the earth.

"Stop that!" The lady flew at him like a hawk. "You stop that, who do you think you are?"

Keith knew exactly who he was: John Kris.

CHAPTER 21

Blaine Lowry, the handsome movie star and hero of a thousand daydreams, was sweating fear. He sat in the passenger seat of a modified Mercedes 300, hands gripping the dashboard, jaw clenched as he braced himself. In the driver's seat Mike Severa was aware of his client's discomfort and was enjoying it. Blaine Lowry had wanted a demonstration; now he was getting it. Severa yanked the steering wheel right and left as they weaved through a row of orange cones, then straightened and sped toward a bed of upright nails.

"You may skid," Severa yelled, "but you'll never flip."

Blaine nodded but kept his eyes fixed on the nails as they flashed beneath the car. There was a slight tremor and faint change in sound but otherwise the car continued as if nothing had happened.

"Blow-proof tires. Hardly know they're punctured."

This time Blaine didn't even nod. With tires wailing, they rounded the final corner and raced toward the starting position, where a technician in a dirty T-shirt was waiting. Beside him was a stranger in a trenchcoat. As the car slid to an abrupt stop the stranger stepped forward, lifted an Uzi machine gun and fired. Blaine let out a yell and ducked as far as the seatbelt would allow.

The bullets made tiny chips in the windshield and ricocheted into the air. Severa gritted his teeth to keep from laughing. When the spray of bullets stopped he said, "You can see how effective the bulletproof windows are."

Blaine straightened up, tried to smile. "Do you lose many clients doing that?"

"Never counted."

Severa got out of the car and went into a small office where his salesman, Bobby Necker, was waiting.

"How'd he take it?" Bobby asked in a low voice.

"Better clean the passenger seat."

Bobby winced. "I hope you didn't blow this account . . ."

Severa wasn't worried. Movie stars like Blaine Lowry admired men like him who lived the kind of lives they only could act out on screen. He climbed into a silver Turbo Porche, left the test track in Topanga Canyon and drove the Pacific Coast Highway back to his office . . .

Severa had done well since leaving the army. When the good wars were gone he went back to Los Angeles and opened his own security firm. The intertwined triple-S emblem of Severa Security Services now rivaled Westec as the most popular lawn decoration in Beverly Hills. In fact, triple-S clients enjoyed an added prestige because on one occasion a home was burgled and the stolen merchandise was returned anonymously within a few days. Which led to rumors of Mike Severa's underworld contacts and the legend of invulnerability of triple-S homes.

The truth was that Severa had no underworld contacts but had grown up with the gangs of East L.A. On the occasion that a gang victimized a client's home, he tracked down the members responsible and convinced them that the road to good health lay in returning the merchandise. Since then, professional thieves and independent operators occasionally targeted triple-S homes, but never the gangs of East L.A. The word on the street was that Mike Severa, an ugly dude, took his work personally . . .

It was 11:52 when Severa pulled into his private parking place in an underground garage in Century City. Always alert to his environment, he catalogued the county of origin of the license plates on the adjacent cars and noted the rental plates on a

Dodge mini-van parked three stalls away. In the elevator he checked his appearance in the mirror. A regime of martial-arts training and daily weightlifting gave him a powerful, compact appearance that he accentuated by wearing crisply starched clothes with a distinctly military cut. The hand-tooled Peruvian leather boots were designed to add two inches to his height.

Severa stepped out on the seventeenth floor, walked down a short corridor and around a corner. The receptionist, Grace, buzzed him through double glass doors with the triple-S insignia etched into them. Although he was early, his new client was already waiting.

"Mr. Severa," Grace said. "This is John Kris."

Kris stood up and shook hands. He was a tall, muscular man with a thick mane of gray hair and neatly trimmed beard. If he had been wearing an open pastel shirt with gold chains, Severa might have guessed a record producer. But Kris wore an elegant well-tailored suit and no jewelry at all, not even a watch.

"Sorry to keep you waiting, Mr. Kris."

"Patience is my long suit." There was a peculiar rasp to the voice, as if from a mild case of laryngitis. And something else— the eyes seemed dilated, as if the dark pupils extended beyond the borders of the iris.

Severa ushered Kris into the office, and as he passed Grace's desk she handed him a manila file folder. Clipped to it the usual questionnaire was blank. A note in her handwriting said: "Declined to provide information." A game player, Severa thought as he closed the door behind him.

The office was decorated in shades of khaki, gray and black. A wall of glass looked out over the Hollywood Hills, lost now in a brown haze. On another wall there were framed photographs of Severa, some of them in combat situations, others with famous people in restaurants or outside their homes. Severa's desk was a large, irregular black sheet of slate.

"A drink, Mr. Kris?"

"No."

"I'm having soda water. You're welcome to join me."

Kris inspected the photographs. Severa pressed the intercom

156 ▶

and asked Grace for a soda water and ice, then said deliberately, "Would you like a seat?"

Kris turned. "Do you believe it's a profession?"

"What's that?"

"Killing people."

"The oldest profession, with due respect to prostitutes."

"Contact lenses," Kris said as he sat down.

"What?"

"You were looking at my eyes. I'm wearing full-span neutral density contacts."

"Is that medical or tactical?"

A slight hesitation. Got you that time, Severa thought.

"Retinal hypersensitivity. It makes daylight painful but night is like noon."

"What does a man who sees in the dark need with Severa Security?"

"You protect people as well as property, don't you?"

"That depends on the people."

"I have a client for you, a man with a powerful enemy. The man is successful, resourceful, at the top of his career, but his enemy intends to destroy him. If you had unlimited funds, could you guarantee to protect him?"

Severa wasn't buying. Kris was nobody's errand boy. If he wanted protection, it was for himself.

"It would take more than unlimited funds."

"What else?"

"Total cooperation, for starters. There are some environments that can't be made one hundred percent secure. Personal security is a matter of trade-offs."

"If you had total cooperation as well as unlimited funds, could you offer one hundred percent protection?"

"Your friend wouldn't like the restrictions I'd have to impose."

"He's not my friend." Kris stood up, reached into his pocket, and brought out a cashier's check. "Impose any restrictions you want. Here's a retainer."

He placed it on the desk and turned away. The check, drawn on Bank of America, was made out to Michael Severa in the amount of ten thousand dollars.

"Wait just a minute, Mr. Kris," Severa called. "I need a lot more information before I agree to take the assignment."

Kris turned, his hand on the door. "Like what?"

"Like who it is you want me to protect?"

"His name is on the check."

"No it's not. This is a cashier's check. There's only the bank's name."

"And one more."

"Just my name."

"That's right, Mr. Severa. Protect yourself—if you can." Kris walked out.

Severa sat there, staring at his name on the check. A bad joke. Somebody was jerking his chain. He considered a quick list of possibilities and discarded them. Nobody he knew . . . but if it wasn't a joke—

He got to his feet and went after John Kris. Grace looked up in surprise as he moved past her, his face flushed. Down the hall he turned the corner and stopped. Two men and a woman stood chatting, waiting for the elevator. It had been less than thirty seconds since Kris left his office and a glance at the floor indicators showed that none of the elevators had been there. But John Kris had disappeared.

Maybe a bathroom. As Severa turned, the door to the stairway clicked shut and he had his answer. He opened the door and stepped onto the landing. Echoing from below came the sound of quick footsteps descending. He smiled.

You better run, he thought, before I stuff that check up your ass.

He returned to his office, crumpled the check and tossed it into the wastebasket. Los Angeles. L.-fucking-A. Somebody was always screwing with your mind.

On his way downstairs Keith pulled a walkie-talkie from his coat. "I'm on my way," he said.

"Okey-doke."

He caught the elevator at the fourteenth floor to the parking garage where Prem Chaduvedi waited behind the wheel of the Dodge mini-van.

"Any problems?" Keith asked as he slid into the passenger seat.

"One problem only. A man to whom unnecessary rudeness was required."

"Who was this?"

"A stranger asking what happened. When I told him the leaking transmission fluid, he wanted to help. So I said he should fuck with himself."

"But you got them all?"

"Oh yes. The damage will have equitable distribution. But for the cost of repairs, it will be small I think for a man who owns such a car."

"It's not the car we're after, it's his mental condition. We're going to stretch his nerves so thin that by December, one little Christmas gift will snap them."

"What kind of gift?"

Keith reached into his pocket and pulled out a chrome cigarette lighter shaped like a hand grenade. Prem inspected it. "I think such a gift cannot cause such nerves to snap."

"It might. If it comes with a greeting card from Donald Minkin."

Mike Severa left his office at 4:15. Approaching his car, he pressed a button to deactivate the alarm system. The Porsche emitted a chirping sound in response. Everything was normal. He slid into the driver's seat, turned the ignition and started to back up. An explosion rocked the garage as all four wheels exploded outward and the Porsche dropped flat onto the concrete.

Severa shoved out the door, rolled free and came to his feet in a crouch, a Deutonics automatic pistol in his hand. The only sound was a tire as it rolled into a tight circle and began a wobbling spiral to the floor.

A guard came running as he straightened up. "Are you all right, Mr. Severa?"

The rush of adrenaline turned fear to anger as a crowd gathered. The Porsche sat flat on its belly, as if sunk into the pavement. Severa inspected the stub of an axle that extended from each wheel and recognized the flash marks. Detonation cord. Each axle cut neatly as a saw. If it had been a fire bomb he would be dead.

Ignoring questions from the crowd, he went back to the office, dumped the trash on the floor and found the cashier's check. He smoothed it on his desk and held it to the light. Earlier he had been certain that it was fake; now he was certain that it was real. But who? And why?

Grace had the phone to her ear when he came out of the office. She had just heard the news and looked at him in shock. "Is it true? Someone bombed your car?"

"A practical joke, understand? Anybody wants to know, you tell them it was a practical joke."

After making three Xerox copies of the check, he went to Bobby Necker's office and entered without knocking. Bobby sat with his feet on the desk reviewing ad copy. He had taken his jacket off and loosened his tie. When Severa barged in he looked up in surprise.

"John Kris," Severa said. "K-R-I-S. Maybe a pseudonym. He came in this afternoon, his face is on the videotape. I want a photograph. Then I want him. I want everything about him—who he is, where he comes from, what he does, where I can find him. This might help." He tossed the check down on the desk. "Find out if it's real. I think it is. If so see if you can pick up a paper trail. Get Ramon and T.J. on it. Run the phone book and check D.M.V. for a California license. My hunch is he's out-of-state, so give them the video photo and hit the car rentals, LAX, Burbank, Van Nuys and Orange County. Check all hotels in a twenty-mile radius with rooms over a hundred a night. Meantime call Gottleib's and order a Grade-1 trace. I know," he said, reacting to Bobby's expression. "But I don't care about the cost. I want this guy. I want him here and now. I want John Kris."

CHAPTER 22

In London, Prem enjoyed listening to Jerry Burke and Nexli make love. "This man is like a bull," he told Keith. "Wait, I will play it for you."

"Never mind."

"Even the girl, she makes such joyous sounds, like singing with the gods . . ."

"Just play me the part about the explosives."

Prem frowned, his mood broken by Keith's insistence. They were in an upstairs bedroom, seated at a table piled high with electronic equipment. The tape recorder was on fast forward, its liquid display numbers flashing silently as the tape raced toward a conversation between Jerry Burke and his lover. Keith hadn't heard it yet, but Prem, who eagerly reviewed each day's tapes, told him that there was talk of a shipment of explosives.

They had returned to London and leased a townhouse adjoining Jerry Burke's. Burke lived in Ennismore Gardens Mews, a narrow, truncated sidestreet in the Knightsbridge section. When they moved in, Burke and his lover were out of the country. This gave Prem plenty of time to plant microphones in the common wall. He had returned from Lafon Grinki's with an impressive array of sophisticated electronic equipment and an eagerness to display each piece to Keith: "Drop-in cartridge, infinity transmitter, shotgun mike, hollow-tube mike, carrier switch, radio mike, mini-transmitter . . ."

They drilled through the brick wall separating the two dwellings and attached a number of contact microphones to the back of Burke's interior wall. "Spike mikes," Prem called them. The mikes were long steel needles, pointed at one end and attached to an amplifier at the other. Thick rubber straps held them at right angles with their points imbedded in the target wall. Prem also located a common electrical conduit through which he fed a tube mike. By the time he was finished, their townhouse looked more like a science laboratory with a spiderweb of wires covering the walls and snaking across the floors to amplifiers and voice-activated tape recorders.

Prem punched a button and the flickering numbers froze. He went back and forth until the numbers matched those in his log, then turned the machine to PLAY. Burke's voice filled the room—the same voice that had put Keith under arrest and betrayed him so many years ago.

"Because," Burke was saying. "I've got to kick this deal into high gear. Otherwise your brother's going to shit a brick."

"Let him shit." The girl's voice was high, with a slight accent.

"Easy for you to say."

There was a pause during which Keith heard faint clicking sounds, a tap-tap-tap in the background. Prem put a finger to one nostril and pantomimed snorting cocaine.

Nexli's voice, petulant: "Take me with you this time."

"Baby, that's not possible."

"I can stay in a hotel. No one will know."

"Now you sound like your brother. You get impatient, you screw things up."

"I think you screw things up, Jerry. I think Mahmoud is right—you will never give up your wife and your farm and your fancy friends in America."

"Screw your brother. He's just trying to make trouble. Here."

The clicking had stopped. Now the sound of someone snorting, first one nostril, then another. When Nexli spoke she was straining to hold her breath. "When will you get the divorce?"

"We'll talk about it after the deal comes down."

"Then another deal and another and another. For three years there is always another deal."

"This one's different, believe me."

"Oh, yes, the famous C-4. That's all Mahmoud talks about, his exploding ashtrays and alarm clocks and radios. Everything must blow into pieces to make the colonels feel their manhood."

"That's the way it is, baby. We men like to explode."

The sound of clothes rustling, then Nexli said, "No." Footsteps crossing the room.

"What's the matter? Your brother pushed you around so you're mad at me?"

"Not me he pushed around—you."

"What about this?"

"What?"

"This bruise . . ."

Nexli said something low and unintelligible. Burke replied, "What about here?"

A pause, then Nexli said, "Ow!"

"There," Burke said, "that makes them even."

"You are a bad boy, Jerry."

"I've got your bad boy right here."

Bodies shifting against each other. Burke's voice came low with pleasure. "Umm, yeah, that's it, baby, that's—ouch!"

Nexli's voice, low and hoarse and mocking. "Now you are even, baby."

"I told you—no marks."

"Because she might see? Because she might guess?"

"She *will* see."

"You will tell her you love me."

"Maybe."

The sounds degenerated into the prelude to lovemaking— rustling clothes, exclamations of pain and grunts of release. Keith turned the machine off.

"The next part is very *sanuk*," Prem said.

"Leave it off," Keith said more sharply than he intended.

The doorbell rang. Prem went downstairs to answer it while Keith thought about what they had just heard about C-4, a plastic

◀ 163

explosive with the consistency of putty. It could be formed into any shape or rolled flat into sheets that could be cut and placed between the walls of suitcases or even used as wallpaper and painted over. Its manufacture and dispensation were subject to strict controls. If Burke was involved in a scheme to provide the C-4 to Libya—

"Mr. Prem Chaduvedi?" The voice was Jerry Burke's.

Keith was startled. A dozen thoughts came crowding to mind—Burke had discovered the bugged wall; he had been at the front door and heard the tape; he had seen them through a window . . .

"Yes?" Prem's voice, unsteady.

"My name is Jerry Burke. I live next door."

"Yes, sir, I know."

No, Keith wanted to shout. He got up and moved silently to the door.

"You do?" A dubious note had crept into Burke's voice.

"I mean, I saw your name next door."

"My name's not on the mailbox. Where did you see my name?"

Keith gritted his teeth. Don't blow it, Prem, don't blow it now. He leaned into the hall and peered downstairs. Burke's legs and torso were visible in the open doorway, facing Prem, whose back was to Keith.

"I mean," Prem said, "the postman one day left for me a letter with your name and address. I placed it in your box."

"Yeah, that figures. They've got too many unions running the post office in this country. Listen, can I come in a minute? I've got a business proposition for you."

"For me?"

"You're the guy who's selling the Elephant Tomb treasure, right?"

"Yes."

"Then you're the man I want to talk to." Burke stepped inside.

"Wait, please. The house is too much a mess."

"That's okay. I'll make it quick."

Prem did a neat back-step and closed the living room door before Burke could see the equipment inside.

"This room is better," Prem said, ushering him into the dining room, which didn't share a common wall with next door.

Keith remained at the top of the stairs, listening for any note of threat. He couldn't tell what they were saying but from snatches of conversation he overheard, it all seemed civil. Finally the two men appeared again.

"If you change your mind," Burke said, "you know where to find me."

As soon as Burke was gone, Prem collapsed melodramatically over the bannister.

"Even my shoes are filled with sweat. When I opened the door and saw that man . . ."

"What did he want?"

"He wants to buy a statue from the Elephant Tomb. Yes, you can believe it. For an under-the-table price."

Burke had received the Sotheby's catalogue and seen a statue he wanted. He knew a girl at Sotheby's who gave him Prem's address and phone number, and when he realized they were neighbors he came over hoping to buy the statue before it went up for auction.

"What did you tell him?" Keith asked.

"That I should think about it and let him know."

"Call him tomorrow and tell him the consignment is already committed to Sotheby's. If he wants it he'll have to show up at the auction. Then tell him you're going to be out of the country for a while. We don't want any more surprise visits."

The following day Keith flew to Washington, where he proposed the Henri Giscard Fellowship to Tony and Anne Mahue. They met in the VIP room on the top floor of the Washington *Herald* building. The Mahues were the owners and publishers of the *Herald.* Anne had a thin, chiseled face with patrician nose and blond hair that glowed with artificial lustre. Her restless eyes and fingers evidenced an energy in marked contrast to her husband, a heavyset man whose receding hairline was bordered by a ridge of curly gray hair. As Keith made his proposition, Tony sat with head bowed, eyes focused on the green baize tabletop, one finger tracing the lip of his Limoges coffee cup.

To fund the Henri Giscard Fellowship, Keith would set aside two hundred and fifty thousand dollars to be allocated over the next ten years, twenty-five thousand dollars for each recipient. The purpose of the fellowship was to provide an opportunity for a young reporter under the age of twenty-five to investigate and report on an abuse of the American democratic system.

"There are only two conditions," Keith concluded. "I choose the first recipient and the first subject of investigation."

Their responses overlapped. "No," Tony said without looking up.

"That's not possible," Anne said crisply. "If you had a condition such as this, Mr. Kris, you ought to have mentioned it when we spoke on the phone. We cannot allow the *Herald*'s editorial policy to be determined by anyone other than ourselves and our editor Mr. Stern."

"Don't you want to know the subject of the investigation?"

"It wouldn't matter."

"He may well be someone already on your hit list."

"We don't have a *hit list*, Mr. Kris."

Tony let his head roll to one side and peered at Keith from beneath a wedge of tangled eyebrows. "Ah, just out of idle curiosity, who is it you have in mind to investigate?"

"A man named Jerry Burke. I think he's running arms through a shell firm, an art import-export business."

Anne's face remained closed. "Never heard of him."

Tony said, "And who is the reporter you had in mind?"

"Gail Wescott."

There was a moment of silence.

"The senator's daughter?"

"Why not? She's bright, she's on your staff, and the story she did on Melanie Crowne was excellent."

Keith was referring to an article about a young woman who had grown up with Gail, dropped out of college to work as a topless dancer, became involved in drugs and died of complications arising from AIDS. Gail had chronicled her last months, and the piece was published in the Arlington *Express* with photographs. It was this piece which had earned Gail her job at the *Herald.*

Tony said, "She's hardly more than an intern, Mr. Kris. Why Gail?"

Anne laid a hand on her husband's arm. "Darling, it's a moot point. We're not going to accept a fellowship encumbered by editorial restriction. I'm sorry, Mr. Kris."

"Before you make your final decision you might want to listen to this."

Keith brought out a Sony tape recorder from his briefcase and played them the conversation Prem had taped between Burke and Nexli. The Mahues listened quietly, occasionally exchanging glances. After the pertinent portion, Keith switched the machine off.

"Ah, how did you get that recording?" Tony asked.

"Illegally. It's nothing that you can use in print but it points the way for the investigation."

Anne rose smoothly and said, "Will you excuse us for a moment, Mr. Kris?"

The two of them stepped outside. Keith paced the room, inspecting the various plaques and awards the *Herald* had won. Somewhere in the building his daughter sat at a desk, pursuing a career as a journalist the way he had once sought a pilot's wings. But Keith realized with a shock that at Gail's age he had already been years in prison. It was a perspective that gave him a fresh sense of the magnitude of what he'd lost. He stood gripping the window sill, and not until they called his name a second time did he realize the Mahues had returned.

"Mr. Kris," Tony said, "you gave us two conditions coming in. We'll accept under two conditions. First, Gail Wescott has had no experience as an investigative reporter. If you're determined that she be the first recipient we reserve the right to assign a senior reporter as a mentor. Someone like Arnie Duke or Paul Stafford—people who have contacts, know which shortcuts to take, what's within bounds and what's not. This is a matter of judgment and principle, you understand, and Gail hasn't been here long enough for us to evaluate her judgment or her principles in this kind of assignment. We can't just turn her loose on a story like this. It wouldn't be fair to her or to the paper."

Keith hesitated. "As long as she does the legwork, the actual investigation."

"Under supervision." Anne said. "Don't worry, we won't use the fellowship to give one of our veteran reporters another secretary, Mr. Kris."

"All right. What's the second condition?"

Tony took over again. "That we control the scope of the investigation. We reserve the right to print as much or as little of the Jerry Burke story as we see fit. In short, we determine whether or not there *is* a story, and if there is, how and to what extent we're going to use it."

Keith didn't care what they did with the story. All that mattered was that Gail follow the trail backward, back in time to the beginning of Burke's relationship with Alex, to the betrayal in Vietnam. It was not yet time for him to reveal himself to Alex and the others, much as he would have liked to with Gail and Chris.

"That will be fine," he said.

"One last thing," Anne added. "If we discover this tape is fradulent, we may decide that you're the one worthy of investigation."

Keith smiled. "Maybe I am."

Gail's first thought when she heard that the Mahues wanted to see her was that her father had broken his word. Alex Westcott knew the Mahues socially and several times had offered to "put in a good word" to help her get promoted. Gail made him promise not to interfere but she didn't entirely trust him to keep the promise. He was still trying to win her over with gifts, just as he had from as far back as she could remember.

The Mahues met her in the executive lounge. With them was a tall, heavily built man whose black eyes locked onto hers with an intensity she found disconcerting.

"This is John Kris," Anne said. "Mr. Kris, Gail Wescott."

"Gail."

He pronounced her name carefully in a deep, slightly raspy voice. When they shook hands, his thick, powerful fingers took her hand almost diffidently, as if afraid he might break it.

They sat down and Tony Mahue began. "Gail, when you came to us, you said your goal was to do investigative reporting. Well, you're going to get that opportunity a little ahead of schedule. Mr. Kris has just established a fellowship for investigative reporting and you've been chosen as the first recipient. It's a twenty-five-thousand-dollar fellowship, five thousand an outright grant, the other twenty for expenses in the investigation. Congratulations."

Gail was stunned. She had been working in research, an invisible position.

"But . . . why me?"

"You were suggested by Mr. Kris and . . . we concurred in that choice."

She turned to Kris, who sat leaning forward slightly, watching her closely. "You're not—?" She hesitated.

"What?"

"Mr. Kris, are you working for my father?"

He started. "Your father?"

"If he sent you I want to know it."

Keith chose his words deliberately. "You can be sure that if Senator Wescott was here, he would be more surprised than you."

Gail looked at him, then nodded. "I'm sorry, I just thought . . . I mean, sometimes he tries to help and . . ." She shook her head. "Forget it. I'm very grateful."

Anne Mahue explained to Gail how she first came to Mr. Kris' attention, and then spelled out the details. She would be working under the supervision of Paul Stafford, a two-time Pulitzer Prize-winning journalist. The money would be used for expenses related to the investigation. The subject of the probe was one Jerry Burke and Artex International. When she heard the name, Gail's smile faded.

"That might be a problem," she said.

"Why?"

"Jerry Burke. He's a friend of my father's—a big campaign

supporter, I believe. He used to come to the house when mom gave her Saturday receptions. Does that matter?"

"Not to me," Kris said quietly. Anne and Tony exchanged a look, and Anne said in an undertone, "What do you think? Is it a problem?"

Tony turned to Gail. "You tell us. Do you think knowing Burke would affect your judgment?"

Gail thought back to a time in junior high school . . . she was what? Twelve? . . . she had been putting together a family tree, tracing her real father's ancestors. Burke had suggested that she stop by his office and look for pictures of Keith Johnson in his Vietnam scrapbook. The scrapbook, though, turned out to be a cheap photo album and none of the pictures were of Keith Johnson. While she was paging through it, Jerry Burke came up behind her. He leaned close and identified each photograph and as he did, his voice became more ragged and his words became less connected. She still remembered the horror she felt when she realized he was masturbating. Now, as she recalled the incident, she knew that her feelings about Jerry Burke were still the same. She disliked him, was even a little afraid of him. She should refuse the assignment . . .

"No," she heard herself saying, "that won't present a problem at all."

CHAPTER **23**

Gilt-bronze Vajrabhairava Group stepping to the right in pratyalidhasana over prostrate human figures, the ferocious deity wearing a garland of human skulls, grasping his consort in yab-rum . . .

The description in the Sotheby's catalogue went on and on for a fulsome paragraph. This was the sculpture that Jerry Burke wanted to buy—a carnal tableau depicting a multi-armed god with a bull's head in a standing embrace with a woman who had one leg hooked over his hips, a powerful image, the bull with teeth bared, staring down at his consort with a lascivious expression, his array of secondary arms outstretched like a living cape. The couple stood astride four prostrate human forms, love and death intertwined, creation and destruction in the same act. From Prem's description of Burke's bedroom activities, Keith could see why he was especially attracted to it.

The Elephant Tomb treasure had generated considerable excitement in the art world. Almost half the pieces had originated outside the borders of the ancient Khmer kingdom in India, Burma, China and Tibet. All represented the finest workmanship of the time. Keith arrived early on the day of the auction, filled out a registration form and was given a round gray paddle with a number on it. Prem, wearing a white linen suit, was already there with the Sotheby representative.

The cathedral-like room slowly filled with collectors, art lovers, museum directors and the plain curious. When Burke arrived with Nexli, Keith studied him closely. The lieutenant had put on weight, and his receding hairline accentuated his elongated forehead. Noting the sensuous curve of his razor-thin upper lip and the calculating look reflected in his pale eyes, Keith found it hard to believe that he had ever been naive enough to trust the man. But of course that was over twenty years ago . . .

He motioned to Prem and the two of them went to Burke. Keith let Prem handle the introductions.

"Mr. Burke, you are here to bid on the Vajrabhairava Group. I have another man also interested. This is Mr. John Kris."

Keith forced himself to shake hands . . . Burke's was thick and soft.

"This is Nexli al-Kanuni," Burke said.

The Arab girl looked warily at Keith. "Are you a collector, Mr. Kris?"

"Of particular pieces."

Burke said, "What's your area of interest?"

"What others prize most."

Burke's smile tightened. "And you think the Vajrabhairava Group falls into that category?"

"You tried to buy it, didn't you?"

"I assume Mr. Chaduvedi has already told you that."

"That's right. I know you're interested in Lot 32." Keith referred to the statue's catalogue designation. "So am I. What could I do to tempt you not to bid?"

"Not a thing."

"What about another piece? It would be worth five hundred dollars to me to eliminate you as a competitor."

Burke smiled. "You're a persuasive man, Mr. Kris, but I promised the statue to Miss Kanuni."

From Nexli's look of surprise, Keith doubted it. "In that case I will double the offer. One thousand dollars to ease the disappointment of the lady."

"The lady's not going to be disappointed."

172 ▶

"You're determined to bid?"

"That's why I'm here."

Kris sighed and turned to Nexli. "Then I apologize in advance for denying such a treasure to so beautiful a lady."

At this John Kris moved away, Burke muttered, "arrogant bastard" to Nexli, but loud enough for Keith to hear. Nexli leaned close. "He has the evil eye, that one."

"He has the evil goddamn mouth," Burke said.

The bidding began. The auctioneer, a balding man in a business suit, sat on a raised platform in an ornate wood chair whose back rose throne-like high above him. The objects for sale appeared on a platform that rotated so as to bring each one into view. Above the stage a large illuminated board showed the current bid in six currencies: British pounds, U.S. dollars, French francs, Japanese yen, Swiss francs and Italian lira. One by one the artifacts sold, making millionaires of Keith and Prem. Finally the Vajrabhairava Group appeared and bidding began at twenty thousand pounds. Burke raised his paddle ever so slightly.

"Twenty-two five," the auctioneer said. He spoke into a microphone in a well-modulated, intimate tone of voice. Half a dozen bidders increased the price in twenty-five hundred pound increments until it had doubled. As the price increased the number of bidders decreased until only Burke and Keith remained. When they reached forty-five thousand pounds—nearly seventy-five thousand dollars—Burke knew he was in trouble. This was the limit he could afford.

"It doesn't matter," Nexli whispered.

It mattered to Burke. Especially now that he'd met Kris. He raised his paddle.

"Forty-seven-fifty. Do I have fifty?"

Keith flicked his paddle.

"Fifty thousand pounds, the gentleman in the back row."

Burke moved his paddle and the figure jumped to fifty-two-fifty. The tension heightened as the crowd became aware that a bidding war was underway. At sixty thousand pounds, Nexli tugged Burke's arm and whispered, "It's really too much."

He shook her off and raised his paddle.

"Sixty-two-fifty the bid, Mr. Burke."

◀ 173

Keith flicked his paddle.

"Sixty-five."

Every time Burke raised his paddle, Keith followed a moment later. At seventy-five thousand pounds—over one hundred thousand dollars—Burke knew he would have to drop out. He raged inwardly at the money he had lost gambling in Monte Carlo, the money he had spent on expensive clothes for Nexli, the money he had wasted in currency speculation. The statue, for all its fierce beauty, wasn't worth over fifty thousand dollars. He should quit. Instead, he took a deep breath and moved his paddle again.

"Eighty-thousand pounds, Mr. Burke."

Burke winced as John Kris casually bumped the bid to eighty-two-five. Nexli was pulling at him.

"No, come away now, baby, please . . ."

He pulled his arm free, raising his paddle at the same time. The movement confused the auctioneer.

"Is that a bid, Mr. Burke?"

"*Yes.*" His voice was hoarse.

Keith flicked his paddle and the price escalated again. At one hundred thousand pounds, Burke gave up. Even if he won he would lose everything he owned trying to pay for the statue.

"The bid, one hundred thousand pounds. One hundred thousand against the room." The auctioneer hesitated but Burke kept his paddle in his lap. The gavel hit the table with a sound that made Burke flinch. He was flushed with anger and humiliation. After all the years of work, all the deals he'd made, all the money he'd earned, the sons of wealth and privilege could still take away the things he prized most.

Keith came up to him. "You should have taken my offer. It would have been more profitable for both of us."

Burke felt Nexli's fingers tighten on his arm. Now he saw what she meant by John Kris' eyes—they were obsidian black with no differentiation between the iris and the pupil.

"The market value isn't half what you paid," he said. But obviously the likes of Kris didn't give a damn about such considerations. Born rich, the bastard . . .

Burke hadn't noticed the two men working their way through the crowd until they moved up to Keith. The younger was tall and slightly stooped and wore a business suit, the older had a bony face with cavernous cheeks and wore a sweater vest beneath his sportcoat.

"Mr. John Kris?"

"Yes?"

The man brought out a long wallet and slipped it open. "Inspector Hyams, Scotland Yard. This is Inspector Lessing. Will you come with us, sir."

Keith was cool. "Don't you boys ever give up?"

"Not until the IRA gives up. If you'll come with us, sir."

As Hyams escorted Keith away, Burke said to Lessing, "What happened?"

"Everything's under control, sir. Nothing to worry about."

Bidding on the next article had begun. Few people were aware of what had happened, as Burke watched the departing trio. "I wonder what he did?"

"Stupid police," Nexli said. "They should have been here earlier."

She was right. If the police had shown up five minutes sooner the Vajrabhairava Group would be his. Well, it wouldn't do Kris much good if they stuck him in jail. With that thought in mind Burke hunted down Prem Chaduvedi and left him his business card. If John Kris couldn't pay for his purchase, Burke could maybe pick it up cheap from the front man. Anyway, this Kris was on ice, at least for a while . . .

Outside Sotheby's Keith was handcuffed and put into the back seat of an unmarked car—the handcuffs for show in case Burke was watching. Hyams climbed in beside him and Lessing got behind the wheel. As soon as they turned the corner Hyams began to shake his head.

"Did you hear what the security guard asked me?" he called to Lessing. "Wanted to know if we needed any help."

"I thought he was going to get in the car with us."

"Yeah, we'd all have ended up in the Yard."

Hyams, real name Ian Phillips, unlocked the handcuffs. Keith paid the two actors their fee, left them to catch the subway at Oxford Circus and returned the car to the rental agency. Later that day he and Prem flew to the United States on the Concorde, an extravagance that the two millionaires could well afford. And in his wake, Keith had left an impression with Burke that he was a man of unsavory character. Burke's guard would be down the next time they met . . .

Burke's Artex International was located in a modern, low-lying office complex in Fairfax, Virginia, a suburb ten miles outside Washington, D.C. Keith had hoped to rent an adjoining office, which would have made eavesdropping simple, but none was available. The best they could do was a room in a building across the street that faced Burke's office.

"Not so bad for watching," Prem said as he studied the approach through binoculars. "And good reception for radio microphones if only we have access to the office."

"Access isn't the problem. It's time. How long do you need to wire the place?"

"No wires, just radio microphones. Two maybe, both sides of the room."

"How long will that take?"

"As the cricket jumps. Watch how I do." He opened a case and pulled out a plastic device the size of a domino trailing a thin wire about eight inches long. The wire was encased in a clear plastic sleeve. "Microphone-transmitter and antenna. This one good for maybe ten days before the batteries are asleep. Now say I am coming into your office." Prem dropped the microphone into a briefcase and sat down with it on his lap. He pantomimed looking around innocently. "My hands are busy here"—he peeled off a non-stick backing from the domino and the antenna sleeve—"now I say to you, 'I like that painting,' and when you turn to look—" Prem leaned forward and with both hands plastered the microphone and antenna to the underside of the seat. He sat back and smiled. "By the time you look back, my work is done."

"Not too hard to spot, though."

"Oh, there are many more secret places for this mike, and other mikes for behind walls and inside lamps."

"What about the phone?"

Prem held up what looked like the cover plate to a phone

outlet. "Custom designed by Mr. Grinki. With two screws, we remove the old plate and install the new. No challenge for a master of phone bugging such as myself."

Keith went to Burke's office, knowing he wasn't there, and introduced himself to a secretary with a pink nameplate on her desk that read: "Elsie Flynn." When Keith arrived she slipped a plastic bottle of Diet Pepsi to the floor and greeted him while her bare feet struggled beneath the desk to find their shoes. Keith had a feeling that Artex had very few visitors.

"Good morning, my name is John Kris. Has Mr. Burke returned from London?"

As he placed his briefcase on the floor, a faint click was audible as a hidden switch was thrown and a canister inside the briefcase began emitting gas.

"Not until Monday. If it's important, though, he'll be calling in today. Would you care to leave a number?"

"I'll be on the road. It's probably easier if I stop to see him. You're sure he'll be back Monday?"

"I can't give you an absolute guarantee but that's his itinerary as of this time."

"Fine. Why don't I—That's odd, I thought I smelled gas out there in the hall. Now I smell it in here. Do you smell anything?"

Elsie Flynn pushed her head forward, wrinkled her nose and sniffed. "No, I don't . . ."

"Well, let me leave you my card. If you can just tell Mr. Burke I stopped by about the Vajrabhairava Group."

"The what?"

"Vajrabhairava Group. He'll know what I mean."

Elsie was scribbling. "That's V-A-H . . . ?"

Keith spelled it for her, and as she wrote she began to frown, then looked up. "You know, I *do* smell something."

Prem's cue. He marched in carrying a leather case and dressed in the uniform of a utility man. Waving a plastic identification card he introduced himself as James Kraft. "We have repaired a gas leak in this building and I am checking for residual levels in each room."

Elsie's eyes widened. "I smell something, I was just telling this man . . ."

Prem pulled an official-looking gauge from his bag and took a couple of readings. "Below the danger level. This room is safe. What about in there?"

"No, that's an office."

"I must check it."

"Just a minute." She dug a set of keys from her desk and opened the door to Burke's office. Prem disappeared inside.

"Miss Flynn," Keith called, "if I could just leave this with you. My number's on the back."

He held up his business card but remained by her desk. The woman hesitated, obviously unwilling to leave the doorway. "I'll be with you in just one moment, Mr. Kris."

Her head swiveled back to watch Prem. Keith glanced around, he had to get the woman's attention . . .

A glass of Pepsi, half-full, on the desk. Keith flipped it over and said loudly, "I'll leave my card here on—oh damn. I'm sorry."

Elsie Flynn came running and Prem had time to complete his work while she dried her soggy magazine and sticky desk with pink tissues. In fact, he had so much time he made two installations, one on each side of the room.

"Stereo service," Prem boasted later when they tested the reception by calling Artex and listening to the phone ring. The room was bugged, the trap was baited. They were ready for ex-Lieutenant Jerry Burke.

CHAPTER 24

The Henri Giscard Fellowship was a mixed blessing, Gail discovered. They gave her a cubicle in the City Room on the third floor where it was apparent that some of the junior reporters felt she hadn't paid her dues and that her good fortune was due more to her family name than the work she'd done. Her mentor Paul Stafford seemed to feel that way. A lean man in his mid-forties with quick gray eyes, he was the *Herald's* prestige reporter.

Gail had gone to his office and found him talking on the phone with the door open. He wore a telephone headset, a pale green legal pad filled with notes in front of him. When he saw her in the doorway he waved her in and pointed to a seat.

"Yeah, I know," he was saying, "but it's in tomorrow's edition. Dietweiller knew the test results—what? Yeah, I do. Right here in living black and white." No sooner had Gail sat down than he pointed at the door and motioned for her to close it. She did, and the din of the City Room lessened. Paul's office was separated by a glass wall from the rabbit warren of desks and cubicles where most of the reporters worked. Gail sat down again and waited for her audience with the great man.

"Okay, here's a bounce back. Your words quote *I never saw and I have no knowledge of Bob Dietweiller's July 18th memo*

◄ 179

close quotes. Right? I sure will." He stabbed the disconnect button with a flourish, took off the headset and turned to her. "Gail
Westcott?" She nodded. "So what do you want me to do?"

"I thought you'd tell me."

"Name of subject?"

"What?"

"The guy you're investigating. Breck?"

"Jerry Burke."

"Burke. Okay, so begin with the paper man. Date of birth,
hometown, schooling, friends, wives, kids—all the stuff research
can get you from the public access materials. Your father's a
senator, maybe you've got family connections who can access
police records, military records, FBI, DEA, and CIA files, whatever you can get hold of. Make a list—"

"I can't—" Ask personal friends, she was going to say, but
Stafford didn't stop.

"—list of all significant contacts—business and personal—then
start like a shark, work from the outside in. You're looking for
strong feelings pro and con. Con gives you tips, leads, information. Pro gives you discrepancies. Discrepancies start the ball
rolling so you can—"

Gail fumbled in her purse and took out a minicassette tape
recorder. Stafford stopped. "You're going to *tape* this?"

"Is that okay?"

"Jesus, there's no final exam here." She flushed. "Anyway, discrepancies are your levers. Go back and forth from one person
to another. Look for wedges. If you sense animosity or spot a
contrary interest, see if you can exploit it. You're a woman. Depending on how far you want to push that you might be able to
get information—"

"Do *you* do that?"

"No."

"So why do you assume I would?"

"I don't know you well enough to assume anything, I just cover
the possibilities. You want to show me what you've got on this guy
Burke?"

She gave him the cassette tape and, still seated, he propelled
himself across the room to a recorder. He dropped the tape, hit

the START button and rolled back to the desk. After a couple of seconds of silence, he frowned and said, "Isn't this thing cued up?"

"It was when—"

Burke's voice came from the machine, cutting hers off. As he listened, Paul Stafford wrote something down on his pad. Gail leaned forward to look.

"Lamaze class Thursday," he said without looking up. She sat back, chagrined. When the taped conversation finished, Paul removed the cassette and studied it a moment.

"The guy who set up the fellowship provided this?"

"Mr. Kris. John Kris."

"What's his interest in Burke?"

"He's shipping illegal explosives to Libya."

Stafford shook his head. "*His* interest in Burke. Why him? Why not Vespucci and the heroin connection? The Rockland-Birdwell scandal? The Iran-Contra cover-up? Why did he bug Burke's house in the first place?"

"I don't know." Gail had assumed that Kris wanted to right a wrong, a rich benefactor . . . some might say do-gooder. Now under Paul Stafford's level gaze she felt rather naive, even foolish.

"Might be smart to find out, don't you think? Unless you like being a pawn in someone's personal vendetta."

"Is that what you think?"

"I don't know. But I don't have to know, it's your story. False leads and fake tips are part of the business. If you can't separate bull from shit, go back to human interest stuff like Melanie Crowne."

Actually Gail was pleased that he had read her story but not happy about the way he dismissed it.

"You didn't like it?"

"It was okay."

"What didn't you like?"

"You don't want to know."

"Try me."

"Go to any hospital and you can do a dozen profiles of people dying of AIDS. Agreed, yours was better written than most.

Agreed, you had a better gimmick—go-go dancer with a degree from Radcliffe—but it's still softball journalism. I'm not saying it didn't count but this is investigative reporting, hardball. People's lives and careers and reputations get mixed up with your story. You got to be right and you got to be able to prove it. If Burke is being set up, you could be a party to it. If he's running arms, you could be in trouble. Either way you're at risk in ways you weren't with Melanie Crowne."

"If you don't think I can do it why did you agree to help me?"

A pause, then, "Arnie Duke wasn't available."

He smiled and the cool gray eyes warmed up. For the first time Gail could imagine how charming the man could be if he wanted to be. She wondered how many people who had confided in him regretted it later. But he was right about one thing: there seemed to be as many questions to be asked about John Kris as about Jerry Burke.

Keith stood in the cool, predawn air measuring the wind speed with a hand-held anemometer. He was parked near Mike Severa's home on Mulhulland Drive, a winding road that ran along the ridge of the Santa Monica Mountains. The sky to the east was deep blue, to the west still black. To the south the Los Angeles basin was visible, a vast grid of orange streetlights. A lone newspaper truck rumbled past and disappeared, leaving the street empty.

Keith had spent ten days gathering the materials and practicing what he was about to do. Wind speed and directions were both critical. The two previous nights first one and then the other had been wrong. This morning a land breeze tugged the wind toward the Pacific Ocean at an average of three knots. Conditions were perfect.

Keith returned to the van, where a weather balloon fifteen feet in diameter lay partially inflated on the floor. He adjusted the equipment harness, positioned the balloon and turned the knurled knob on the helium cylinder. With a rush of gas, it began to fill. The weather balloon had cost five hundred dollars; the television camera, transmitter, radio-receiver and mechanical clamp were almost ten times that much. A lot of money for a wicked trick but a small price to pay for upsetting Severa's peace of mind.

Although Keith could see only the top of the roof beyond the wall guarding the house, he knew the layout from aerial photographs. It was a rambling, ranch-style home of Spanish design built around a colorful tiled patio. The house sat on half an acre of well-tended lawn and featured a kidney-shaped swimming pool built by a previous owner. The grounds were surrounded by a stone wall ten feet high, and to this Severa had added a chain-link fence topped by barbed wire. Between the two barriers was a four-foot strip of sand, carefully raked, so that an intruder's footprints would show up. Keith assumed there were infrared or sonic alarms. He hoped so, it would make the effect stronger.

The balloon began, pulling against the ropes that anchored it to the ground. Keith checked the tension meter. Like the other calculations, buoyancy was critical. He stopped when there was just enough positive buoyancy to lift the payload slowly. He turned on the video monitor sitting on the floor of the van, armed the release mechanism holding the canister, and after a final check of the wind, released the balloon.

Lazily it drifted across the road toward Severa's home, but the ascent was too fast. Keith pushed a button that sent a radio signal that released some of the gas. A two-second burst was enough to slow the upward trajectory. When the wind carried the balloon gently over the first wall, Keith turned to the video monitor. Now he had a bird's-eye view as the barbed wire fence slid past, the yard came into view, then the roof. He glanced up—the balloon's height was still good. Then back to the monitor as the roof slid off the screen and the patio passed underneath. When the chaise-lounge reached the center of the screen, Keith held the gas-release button down for five full seconds, and the balloon sank gently toward earth. The edge of the swimming pool had just appeared on the monitor when the transmitter's signal was cut off by the wall. The picture became fuzzy, then turned to hash. From here on, everything would be automatic. Keith looked up to the house and waited.

In the stillness of the back yard the balloon continued its descent, drawn down by the weight of the radio receivers, video camera and by the fifteen-pound canister held in spring-loaded jaws. The sheltering effect of the walls lessened the balloon's forward movement; the canister grazed a cushion on a wrought-iron chair, cleared it and then, continuing downward, reached the pool and graced the water with a mother's touch. Relieved of the weight of the canister, the jaws flipped open, releasing it to the water. The balloon surged, silent as a shadow, toward the stars. Tiny holes in the canister filled with water and it settled slowly to the bottom.

Watching from beyond the wall, Keith saw the balloon with the electronic package pop back into view. A glance at the monitor showed Severa's home shrinking and moving off the screen. He got into the van, released the brake and coasted downhill for a quarter-mile before starting the engine. *Mind-fucking one-oh-one.* Severa's prescription for terror. Now he was the target.

Keith's plan worked better than he had hoped. Mike Severa's home was his sanctuary, the one place he slept soundly and felt completely secure. After all, a security expert knew how insecure the world was. Women he dated were invariably disappointed that he never invited them to stay the night. If they wanted to wake up with him it had to be at their place. Severa employed no maid, no housekeeper, no gardener; he wanted no one pawing through his belongings, spying on him, knowing about him.

Security was shattered at six-thirty the next morning. Severa's bedroom had a sliding glass door that looked out on the back yard. When the radio came on to wake him up he turned over and from the corner of his eye saw a swatch of red in the familiar green of the yard. He jerked upright and stared, heart pounding—the pool was crimson red.

Severa rolled to the floor, grabbing the pistol-handled shotgun he kept beneath the bed. Early morning radio chatter filled the room. He punched the OFF button, moved in a half-crouch to the door and listened. A sound: the refrigerator motor starting. Otherwise the house was silent.

He looked again at the pool. A filter system screw up? Some kind of rust, some kind of chemical reaction? He discarded each explanation as it came to mind. *Someone had breached his secu-*

rity, someone might still be in the house. He moved to each room, spinning around, keeping close to the walls, moving like he had when checking enemy hooches in Vietnam. He caught a glimpse of himself in the bathroom mirror, a tense naked man carrying a gun. When he was certain the house was clean, he checked the grounds. The three-alarm systems were active and armed and hadn't been tripped. The security wall and fence showed no sign of entry, the barbed wire was intact, and the raked sand between the two showed only the tracks of birds.

There was no way in, but someone had gotten in. Someone had put red dye in the pool while he lay sleeping less than fifty feet away. John Kris? John Kris. And for one of the few times in his life he felt the sensation of fear.

When he arrived at his office Severa was in a foul humor. He despised bullet-proof vests but now he wore one. When his secretary offered him a donut, he said, "I don't eat that crap. Get Bobby in my office."

Severa sat down and reviewed what they had learned about John Kris since his first visit. It wasn't much. Kris had purchased the cashier's check, drawn on Bank of America, with cash. He was not a customer and had no account with the bank. Airports and hotels had drawn a blank, as had the driver's license bureau. John Kris was a ghost on paper as well as in person.

Bobby Necker arrived and Severa told him what had happened. Bobby seemed more puzzled than worried. "Red dye in the pool? What's that supposed to mean?"

"It doesn't mean shit, except he's fucking with me, showing me he can get to me any time he wants to."

"Blood, maybe that's what it's supposed to mean. Did he leave any dead chickens or goats' heads?"

Severa gave him a black look. "He's not a nut, the son of a bitch knows what he's doing. The question is, *why* is he doing it?"

"Maybe somebody from your checkered past?"

"What's that supposed to mean?"

"Easy, Mike, I'm just talking possibles. The stories you've told me, I'm surprised you're still alive. Morris the cat—Mr. Nine Lives."

"I never even *met* Kris before."

"Then maybe he's somebody's relative? Somebody who's got a grudge? There's got to be a reason this guy's out to get you. Nobody picks a name out of a phone book and says, Hey, I think I'll give this guy ten thousand dollars and a red swimming pool."

"He was there, Bobby. In my yard last night. Which means if he flew out of L.A., it had to be within the last couple hours. Canvas the airports, show his picture around, see if we can get a line on where he's from."

"Maybe he's local. Maybe he's sticking around. How do you know?"

"Skin's too pale. He's not from this area."

"Maybe he works in an office, hangs out in bars, stays clear of the sun."

"I told you last time—not an office worker. He works out, he's got bulk. We've got his picture from the videotape. We know he was here last night. If he flew out this morning, maybe somebody'll remember him. Maybe we find out where he lives. Maybe *I'll* visit *him* next time."

"Mike, even if we find out he went to New York or someplace, that doesn't mean he lives there. And if he does, you don't think he's calling himself John Kris, do you? What kind of name is that—John Kris? Phoney as a three-dollar bill."

"I'm not so sure. I've got a gut feeling about this guy. Somehow I think he wants to be found."

"Then he should send an invitation: meet me in Griffith Park at dawn, pistols at ten paces, bring your own bullets."

Severa was only half-listening. His notion that Kris might want to be found sparked the edge of a memory of . . . something he couldn't quite get hold of. But it was there, just like in Nam he could sense, smell an enemy even when he couldn't see him . . .

The intercom buzzed, breaking off the thought. Someone had arrived, a prospective employee who needed to be interviewed.

"Tell him I'm busy," Severa said. "Reschedule it for next week." He turned to Bobby. "Get the guys on it. I want every ticket agent, every airline covered by the end of the day."

"Mike, I've got presentations to make—the security committee at Cliffside, the Pollack-Weinstock complex—not to mention the night guy at the Bradbury building who called in sick. And there's the new Beverly Hills ad—"

He stopped. Severa had drawn his Deutonics 9mm pistol from a shoulder holster, cocked it and slowly turned the barrel toward Bobby.

"Hey, come on—"

"You see how it feels?"

"Mike . . ."

"You see how it feels, Bobby? Someone pointing a gun at your head? Here's a bullet with your name on it. Now what's important? The Bradbury building or this bullet with your name on it?"

"Okay. Just put it, you know . . ."

"What? Tell me what's important."

"The bullet, okay?"

Severa released the hammer and guided it with his thumb, keeping the barrel trained on Bobby. They were not equal partners. Severa owned fifty-one per cent of the firm.

"My life is on the line here," he said quietly. "I don't give a flying fuck about the Bradbury building." He pushed the video photo across the desk. "This picture. The airports. However many people it takes. Today."

After Bobby left, Severa went to the window, where he stood looking out at the orange haze that hung over the city. He needed a clue to John Kris. It had almost come to him but slipped away before he could grab onto it. He began to review all the fights he'd been in, the people who might hold a grudge against him, but he'd already been over this ground. All he knew for sure was that somewhere out there was his enemy, a man who one day would come to kill him. Unless he could find him and kill him first.

CHAPTER **25**

The Virginia farm was called Fairoaks. It lay across ten acres of rolling Virginia countryside an hour outside Washington, D.C. There was a main house done in Greco-Roman style, stables and training track with a white three-rail-high fence around it. Fairoaks exuded an atmosphere of grace and charm in spite of its almost too-perfect condition, which prompted one visitor to call it a Confederate Disneyland. For Jerry Burke, the house was his showpiece, the material proof of how far he had come in the world. For his wife, Leanne, Fairoaks had become her prison.

The morning after Burke returned home, Leanne awoke to find the bedroom bathed in sunlight. She had neglected to close the dark drapes as she usually did when she was alone. Her husband lay on his back, arms and legs akimbo, snoring softly. His visits home had become so infrequent that his body seemed more like a stranger's. She noticed something now that had been invisible in the darkness the night before—a purple welt on his chest. She looked more closely. Teeth marks. Not from her.

She lifted the sheet and stared at his body. The bite marks were like tattoos, extending down his abdomen and onto his thighs. Her stomach lurched. She put on a robe, went to the bathroom and took two Darvocets. She also caught a glimpse of her expression in the mirror and looked away. It was not the woman she wanted to see.

She dressed quickly, went to the stable and saddled her favorite horse, a gelding named Saint. The ground was damp, the sunlight suffused and the air heavy with dew. She rode the familiar paths until she reached a spot overlooking an old quarry now filled with water. Once there had been a gazebo on this spot, but the wood had rotted and fallen away, leaving only the stone bench carved by her great-grandfather. Sheer rock walls dropped twenty feet to an opaque surface that mirrored the morning sky. Leanne dismounted and sat down. She had to make a decision . . .

Leanne Mirabel Morrison was the only daughter of an old Virginia family. Her protected existence had been shattered by the death of her father and the subsequent discovery of the family's disastrous financial condition. Her mother's illness added impetus for Leanne to make a good marriage. It was then that Jerry Burke had appeared in her life. He offered money and security and an attentiveness that bordered on the compulsive. Flowers arrived each morning and champagne each night and a white limousine carried them to dinner, to the country club, the hunt club, to opening nights at the Kennedy Center. She was the princess in a whirlwind courtship. Not until they were married did it occur to her that most of their conversation focused on details of the Virginia society she belonged to and most of their dates revolved around prominent public social activities.

Jerry had also been a powerful lover, insistent on doing things his way. "Let me train you," he had said. And in the first rush of passion, she obliged him, had followed him in his search for new forms of titillation—"come on, baby, Leanne, let's put a new spin on the old routine"—until he suggested lovemaking with another couple, and then she balked. Her refusal angered him. "What the cat can't find at home he finds on the rooftops," he told her. His interest in her had decreased as his absences increased. She knew, of course, what was happening but chose to ignore it. Until now. Until it couldn't be ignored . . .

Saint lifted his head and his ears flicked forward, listening. Leanne heard the approaching hoofbeats, turned. It was Jerry.

◀ 189

"You're up early," he said as he dismounted.

"The sun woke me."

"Maggie's got breakfast ready. Wondered where you were." She said nothing. Burke looked over the quarry to the hills and the shredded clouds beyond. "I forget how beautiful it is here." She kept silent. He picked up a piece of grass and began to tickle the back of her neck. She moved away. "Don't."

"You have any idea how sexy you look in jodhpurs?" He tickled her again.

"Stop it, Jerry."

"What's the matter?" She bit her lip and shook her head. "Come on, Leanne, what are you on the rag about?"

She looked at him and didn't know him. A crude stranger.

"I want Fairoaks back, Jerry."

"What the hell brought this on?"

"I think you'll agree it's time. You promised after your business got on its feet—"

"I'm still getting the business on its feet."

"You don't need the farm as collateral any longer. You know that."

"What's the matter, don't you trust me?"

She started to move past him but he grabbed her arm.

"Let go, Jerry."

"What's eating you?"

She pulled free. "I saw the . . . marks."

"What marks?"

"On your chest and . . . and legs."

"Love bites?" He grinned. "So what? We're big boys and girls, here. I don't ask what you do when I'm away, so let's not make a federal case of what I do."

"I don't *do* anything. You know that."

"So maybe you should. Get your tubes cleaned now and then, might loosen you up." He tried to kiss her but she turned her head away.

"Jerry—"

He kissed her neck, nicking the skin with his teeth.

"*Stop.* You're hurting me—"

"Make it work for you," he whispered. "It'll be a turn on."

190 ▶

Revulsion. She pulled free, ran to Saint and swung into the saddle. Burke came after her and grabbed her leg. "We're not finished here."

"Let *go.*"

He reached for her belt but she urged Saint forward and Burke stumbled back. Angry now, he mounted his own horse and went after her. When she saw him coming, she spurred Saint to a gallop and headed off the path across an open meadow. The rougher terrain was more dangerous but Leanne was the better rider. They jumped two hedgerows and he gained ground. Then she took a four-foot-high fence and as Burke followed he leaned too far forward. When his horse landed he pitched headlong to the ground. Leanne stopped. Burke lay stunned for a moment, then started up, saw her coming and fell back, pretending to be unconscious. She knelt beside him.

"Jerry? Jerry? You okay?"

The hint of panic in her voice pleased him. He opened his eyes, put his arms around her. "Hello, baby." She pulled back but he held her tight. "What's your hurry?"

"I thought you were hurt—"

"Maybe I am. Maybe we should test all the equipment." He pulled her down and rolled on top of her.

"Jerry, stop it, you're scaring Saint—"

"On really?" He got up and went to the horse. "Here Saint, come on boy."

Behind him, Leanne got to her feet. "Jerry, for God's sake, leave him alone . . ."

Burke took the reins and moved close. "Your husband can get his leg broken, he can eat cow shit, but we wouldn't want to scare Saint, would we?" He slammed his fist between the horse's nostrils. Leanne screamed as the horse reared and galloped off. Burke caught her arm and swung her around.

"Damn you, Jerry, you shit—"

"I own that horse, you should remember that."

She slapped him then, the first time that had ever happened, and she quickly saw her mistake.

"Jerry, I'm—"

His hand caught her on the side of the head and sent her

sprawling to the ground, ears ringing, specks of color twisting in front of her eyes. And then he was on top of her, yanking at her belt, tearing at her blouse.

"Fucking Blue Ridge cunt . . ."

She turned her face to one side and endured it, knowing finally that she had to leave him, and despising herself for being afraid she never would.

Bobby Necker came to Severa at the end of the day. "Bingo on John Kris. Half a Bingo, anyway. Ticket agent for United Airlines, Barbara Washburn, recognized him from the photo. She saw him in the terminal this morning somewhere around ten o'clock."

"She's sure it was him?"

"Get this—the reason she noticed him was because she thought he was a movie star. Michael Landon with a beard."

"Destination. Did she get it?"

Bobby shook his head. "She was on her break, going to get a cup of coffee. Kris was heading for one of the departure gates, she's got no idea which one. I had Ramon give her a hundred bucks and offer another hundred if she can find Kris on a passenger manifest. She's checking, going to let us know."

Severa felt a rush . . . his analysis of Kris was on the nose. The man was not a local and he was not a ghost. Now if they could just get his name and destination . . .

In Keith's absence Prem had installed a video game called Gunfight in the surveillance room across from Burke's office. Dressed in cowboy boots and blue jeans, he demonstrated how it worked. On a five-foot screen a cowboy appeared in the main street of a Western town. The video image walked toward Prem, who wore a replica of the old Army Colt. When the cowboy stopped and reached for his gun, Prem tried to outdraw him. Prem's Colt fired a laser burst that sensors translated into a video display, a quick streak of light following an automatically computed trajectory. Depending on the player's speed and accuracy, various beeps and zaps and blinking lights resulted in a score.

192 ▶

"I am already a Texas Ranger," Prem said proudly, referring to his gunslinger rating. He twirled the Colt and slipped it into the holster.

"You had this thing delivered here?"

"Only after I have covered up such surveillance equipment as would be visible. My cautions are of excellent order."

Prem insisted that Keith test himself against the video gunfighter. It was like stepping into a television screen. Keith began to understand why he saw so many kids gathered at video arcades.

"What does something like this cost?"

"Seven thousand and five hundred dollars. Chicken food for such millionaires as ourselves."

During Keith's stay in Los Angeles the phone tap had recorded two conversations involving Big Mud, a term Keith associated with the C-4 shipment. Both calls had been instigated by the other party, a man who called himself Jack Jones. The two men were very discreet, their speech full of euphemisms, oblique references and phrases like "Our northern neighbors are running late," and "The natives in T-ville are restless." From what Keith could gather, the C-4 was being assembled by Jack Jones from a number of different sources. The goods were "delicate" and had to be "repacked." Burke complained that it was taking too much time and Jack Jones reminded him that their motto was "safety first." At one point Jones said, "I've found a safe terminal I'll give you over the Watts line." Hearing the phrase, Prem said, "What is the Watts line?"

"Probably a pay phone. Unless he's got a scrambler at home."

"We have unscrambling equipment, types three and four."

"Let's do it. You go out to Burke's farm, see if you can find a remote site to hook up the receiver and tape deck. Meanwhile I'll see if we can put a little direct pressure on Lieutenant Burke."

"You will go to Burke directly?"

"No, but I know who might."

He picked up the phone and, as John Kris, invited Gail to lunch.

* * *

CRUX

In Los Angeles the next morning Bobby Necker delivered the bad news. No one named John Kris had taken a United Airlines flight between the hours of ten and noon. Barbara Washburn had no access to the manifests of other carriers using the terminal.

"Dead end," Bobby said.

Not quite, Severa thought. John Kris would be back. And the next time he would know where to get to him.

Gail met the man she knew as John Kris in the Willard Hotel, an elegantly refurbished Washington landmark. A five-foot-high floral display erupted from the center of a circular couch in the lobby where he was waiting when Gail arrived late and breathless from having jogged the last few blocks. She crossed the lobby with a slightly uneven gait.

"I'm sorry," she said, and held out a thin, dark wedge. "This damn heel came off and I almost broke my ankle."

"You look good to me on one heel."

"Thank you."

The truth was that she felt foolish. Why had she felt compelled to rush home and put on make-up and a black silk dress for the meeting?

Kris led her through the frosted glass doors to a sedate dining room. When they were seated she ordered a glass of white wine and then regretted it when Kris asked for Perrier. They spoke in generalities until the drinks arrived. Kris raised his glass. "To the truth . . . So how is the investigation going?"

"Still doing preliminary stuff, trying to build the paper man."

"When will you talk to him?"

"Not until I know a lot more than I do now. I haven't even begun interviewing his contacts."

"Have you come across anyone named Jack Jones?"

"Not yet. Who is he?"

"I don't know, but I think Burke does. Ask him and see what he says."

It was the kind of eliptical response that would be characteristic of him. When she tried to find out where he was from, he said, "A place called Elysium—you wouldn't know it."

"I might. Give me a clue."

"Sorry. I'll explain it someday when we've got more time. Right now I'm worried that if you don't confront Burke he may succeed in shipping the C-4 to Libya."

"Mr. Kris, I'm a reporter, not a cop. If I find out anything solid about the C-4 shipment I'll certainly report it. But you're the one who can vouch for the tape, why don't you tell the law?"

"We don't have any solid proof yet—"

"*We*, Mr. Kris? Are we going to be working together now?"

"Not together, but toward the same goal, I hope."

"Then let me ask you something—how did you happen to choose Jerry Burke for this investigation?"

"His actions chose him, I didn't."

"But you bugged his house. Why? What's your interest in him?"

He settled back in his chair. "I thought it was Burke who was under investigation."

"It is, but I don't want to be used if this is some sort of personal vendetta." She paused. "Is it?"

"What?"

"A vendetta?"

"Of course."

Gail was taken aback, recovered quickly. "Okay, but why? What did he do to you?"

"He betrayed someone very close to me."

"Who?"

"By the time you finish the investigation, you'll know."

"You won't tell me?"

"Not today."

Should she threaten to quit the investigation, Gail wondered? Refuse the fellowship?

"Is that a problem, Gail?"

"I don't like being used—"

"You're not being used . . . you're being of service—"

"Not if I'm part of a personal vendetta."

"That's why I give the information to you, an impartial observer. You be the judge, you decide."

It sounded like circular logic that Gail didn't quite trust. Still, would it do any good to refuse the assignment? After all, John Kris couldn't decide the scope of her investigation or decide her conclusions for her. *And* he couldn't stop her from investigating him . . .

They ate lunch. Gail had a salad niçoise and Kris steak tartar. She noticed that in contrast to his usual manner, controlled and analytical, he ate quickly and with gusto, leaning forward over the plate. When he ate the parsley she made a face.

He noticed her expression. "What?"

"I tried to eat parsley once, it got stuck in my throat and tickled at the same time. I thought I was going to choke to death laughing. What a way to go."

"When was this?"

"When I was a kid. Dad almost killed me pounding on my back."

Kris' eyes narrowed and his voice seemed oddly strained. "Did he . . . save your life?"

"I doubt it, but he probably saved my funny bone." Kris was still staring at her intently. "Is something wrong?" She glanced down at her dress.

"No, no, sorry . . . Tell me something. You said Jerry Burke was a friend of the family. How long have you known him?"

"I guess he showed up, oh, maybe eight years ago. He'd just left the army and dad brought him home for dinner. Later he came to some of mom's Sunday afternoon receptions until she told dad she didn't want him around. They argued about it, I remember, because dad said he wouldn't give up on a Vietnam buddy."

"But your mother didn't like him?"

Gail shook her head. "Little did she know he was going to end up with the Virginia blueblood crowd. Every year we get these engraved invitations to the Fairoaks hunt breakfast. It's all very posh, they eat eggs Florentine after chasing some poor fox to death."

"You went to one?"

"Not to Burke's, but I had friends who grew up on the farms. You should go in dad's place. You could ask Burke all these questions about the C-4."

"What do you mean go in his place?"

"The Fairoaks breakfast is this Saturday. Mom and dad never go, so you could use the invitation."

"Would you come with me?"

"No *thanks* . . . I had my fill of Burke when I went to talk to him about my real father."

Kris leaned forward. "Who was your real father, Gail?"

"Mom's first husband. He died in Vietnam. I never knew him."

"But you know about him. They told you about him."

"Sure. He was Alex's best friend in Vietnam. And I've read the letters he sent to mom. They wrote every day." She smiled. "I don't think there's anyone in the world I'd want to write every day."

"Sounds like you've never been in love."

"You're right, and I hope it doesn't happen too soon. I doubt I could be in love and work at the same time. Not full-out on both of them."

"What do you think of him? Your real father, I mean, from his letters and what people have told you?" He realized he was pushing but couldn't stop.

"My real father? Oh, I don't know. The letters are sweet. He wrote a lot about being an airline pilot, so when I was a kid I'd make up these stories—real dad stories, I'd call them. He'd land his airplane in the backyard and take me away to this island in the clouds, Chim Bai—"

"Chim Bai?"

"That's where he was in Vietnam. While other kids dreamed of Oz or Never-never Land, there I was dreaming of Chim Bai. His last letter always made me sad, though. Not because of anything he said, but because it was the last one and he never knew it. I always cried over that one.

He turned abruptly then and signaled the waiter, then turned back to her. "Do you want any dessert?"

"Just coffee." The wine had gone to her head. She was babbling on about her childhood. No wonder Kris had gotten bored . . .

The waiter approached.

"Coffee for the lady and bring me the check, please."

The man hurried off and Gail said, "Aren't you having anything?"

"I've got to go. You stay and have your coffee."

"No, that's okay . . ." If Kris wasn't staying, neither would she.

Gail had time for two gulps of coffee while Kris paid the bill. In cash, she noticed. Outside the hotel the doorman flagged a cab that Kris offered to her.

"I'll walk," she said, "it's not that far."

Kris nodded, moved to the cab, but before he got in he turned and said, "The name of the man Burke betrayed was Donald Minkin. Ask him about it."

The doors closed and the cab moved away. Donald Minkin. It was the first piece of new information since the taped conversation. The second piece was waiting for her when she got back to the *Herald.* On her desk was a copy of the incorporation papers for Artex International. The papers had been filed in Delaware eight years ago. The president was listed as Jerry Burke, the treasurer was Neil Rosen, Esq., but the name that caught her eye and caused her to sit down quickly was that of the vice-president —Alexander Wescott III.

CHAPTER 26

Keith arrived at the Fairoaks hunt breakfast with an electric screwdriver strapped in a holster to his ankle and two types of microphone transmitters in his pocket. It was eleven o'clock, the hunt was over and the guests in their brown riding attire were mingling with hunt club staff members in red coats. Half the people were still having breakfast of Belgian waffles and fresh orange juice beneath a huge white-and-yellow tent that billowed gently in the breeze. Children played badminton on the lawn while grooms tended horses gathered near the stables.

Keith meandered through the crowd looking for Burke. He would establish his presence, then slip into the house to plant the microphones. Two pink-cheeked children ran past, one chasing the other, followed by a portly nanny in a white uniform. A woman holding what looked like a Mimosa bumped his arm. "I'm sorry," she said, checking her dress to see if she had spilled anything. Then to Keith, "Are you a Chenley?"

"No, I'm an infiltrator."

She laughed graciously, introduced herself and said, "We're from Twin Oaks, neighbors of the Morrisons. The Burkes, I should say. They've been married for, goodness, years now, but Jerry's still rather a newcomer . . . I suppose that sounds horribly snobbish, doesn't it? But one buys tradition with time, not money. I hope you're not offended."

"I think you're right," said Keith. "Particularly some types of money."

"I beg your pardon?"

"His business. I've heard he's involved in some rather questionable transactions."

"Business?" She blinked as if the idea hadn't occurred to her. "Well, that's beside the point, isn't it? I mean, if a man has to spend time doing business, he ought to do it as inconspicuously as possible. If you'll excuse me." She waved to someone and called "Merideth! Oh, Merideth honey."

Watching her glide into the crowd, Keith found it hard to imagine that these were the descendants of people who fought the revolution that made America.

He walked around the house and saw Burke on the porch smoking a cigar and talking to a group of men. He looked ridiculous to Keith in his tan riding breeches, black coat and white stock tie.

Burke looked up, saw him and did a double take. Keith gave a polite nod. Burke excused himself and came to him.

"Mr. Kris?"

"I should have called, I didn't realize you had something going on this morning."

"No problem, you—you took me by surprise. The last time I saw you I thought they were taking you off to jail."

"A misunderstanding that my lawyer was able to clear up, though not without some expense. I came over to see if you were still interested in the Vajrabhairava Group. But I can see you're busy—"

"No, no, that's all right." Burke waved the cigar expansively. "You want to sell the statue, I'll be glad to oblige. I'll give you twenty-five thousand for it, cash in hand on Monday morning."

"I was thinking more in the range of seventy-five thousand."

"Mr. Kris, let me tell you something, you will never come close to getting seventy-five thousand dollars for the Vajrabhairava on the open market."

"I meant seventy-five thousand pounds."

"Pounds! Now I know you're joking. That or crazy."

"You were willing to pay that much in London."

"The heat of the deal. Besides, I was doing Mr. Chaduvedi a favor. He told me you were hot to trot and asked me to beat up the price."

"Mr. Chaduvedi told you that?"

"I wouldn't mention it except you think you can ream me out on this one, and there just ain't no way."

Burke was so convincing, Keith wondered, did he believe his own lies? "So you think I made a fool of myself?"

"You said it, I didn't. But let me make it up to you with a little old southern hospitality. I'll introduce you around. If America had a king and queen, this is where they'd be right now. If we had a Princess Di, that would be her," and he waved toward a girl in a backless summer dress. "These people are the equivalent of British royalty. There's Leanne, my wife." He lowered his voice. "I assume you'll be discreet about the little lady I was with in London."

"That sort of betrayal doesn't interest me."

Betrayal? It seemed an odd way to put it. Burke's smile wavered, but before he could question Keith's meaning someone caught his eye. He relit the smile and began to introduce Keith to people. Burke's wife, Leanne, was a thin woman whose glassy eyes and effusive greeting Keith suspected were the result of too many Mimosas. She wore a riding outfit that matched Burke's but she looked a lot more natural in it.

"This is John Kris," he said. "A collector of Asian art. We met at Sotheby's where Mr. Kris was, I think he would agree, rash enough to outbid me."

"I'm afraid that meeting your husband turned out to be an expensive proposition."

"Oh yes," Leanne said airily, "meeting Jerry always is."

"I'm just a little old expensive habit," Burke said, trying to cover his irritation with an icy smile.

Leanne was either too careless or too reckless to notice his tone. "Had I but known I would have taken up cigar-smoking rather than husbands."

Burke's eyes narrowed but before he could say anything, a row of firecrackers exploded in the drive and a group of teenagers ran laughing from the spot. A horse reared with fright, almost throwing his rider before she brought him under control. Burke and some of the others headed toward the commotion, giving Keith his opportunity to slip into the house.

He found the study, a walnut-paneled room decorated with an Oriental rug and a number of Asian sculptures, paintings and frescos. There were expensively framed color photographs of Jerry Burke in various guises: in his fox-hunting outfit surrounded by dogs, dressed in white flannels on a lawn tennis court, sporting a captain's hat while at the helm of a yacht, grinning from beneath dark goggles at the crest of a ski trail, wearing a scuba-diving tank over a black wetsuit on the deck of a cabin cruiser. So this was the life he built, Keith thought, while Henri and I suffered in darkness.

In moments he had attached a battery-operated room bug on the underside of a low, inlaid teak coffee table, running a wire along one side to serve as an antenna that would take care of room conversations. The phone required replacement of the wall receptacle with a Grinki special. He took off the cover plate, popped out the female receptacle and fitted the Grinki plate. He was still on hands and knees when the door opened and Burke came in with Leanne.

"Let go of me—"

The door slammed. "You won't humiliate me in public."

Hidden by the desk, Keith hesitated. He could stand up and make some kind of lame excuse or shut up and hope not to be discovered.

"It was a joke, Jerry—"

"It was not a joke, it was a deliberate attempt to undermine me in this community—"

"I wish you could hear yourself, how foolish this sounds."

"I hear fine, Leanne." He imitated his wife's southern accent . . . "You can just put him in the Nautilus room between the snow skis and the scuba tanks and all those other things you never use. Ha-ha-ha." His voice returned to normal. "I know that fake laugh, that fake smile. I know how you people operate—"

"We people?"

202 ▶

"If I want a field hunter, if I want to buy Hobb's Choice it's no business of yours."

"What about Fairoaks, Jerry? How can you justify buying another horse when you can't even pay off the mortgage? When is that going to happen? When do I get Fairoaks back?"

"You don't. Fairoaks is mine."

"It is not—"

"That's what the deed says."

"That was a convenience and you know it. Until the business got on its feet, which has been for some time now."

"That was before I put half a million into the place. If it hadn't been for me Fairoaks would be just so much firewood. It's mine, I own it. Period."

"You do not—"

"Ask any lawyer."

"You get out of here. Go on back to England, why don't you? Go on back to whoever it is you're screwing over there and leave me alone. Get the hell *out.*"

She tried to shove him but Burke grabbed her shoulders and shook her. "Shut up . . ."

"I'll go to court, Jerry. I'll get Fairoaks back."

"Fine, if you think you've got the guts or resources for a long legal fight you're welcome to try. But you won't be living here, and you won't be riding Saint or driving the Mercedes. Maybe you can find a two-room apartment in Fairfax and empty your savings to pay first, last and a security deposit. Who knows? Maybe you can get a job as a check-out clerk at Safeway and earn enough to buy yourself a sofa bed and a pair of white shoes with support arches. But you better plan on working a lot of overtime because a good lawyer's going to cost a lot of money and Neil Rosen can keep the case tied up in court for years. So if that's what you want, go upstairs and start packing. Otherwise, if you want to stay on as mistress of the manor, you keep your mouth shut when I'm talking and you don't put me down in public. Clear?"

"Goddamn you." She left the room, slamming the door after her. Burke stood for a moment, then said in a low voice, "fucking bitch." He came toward the desk. Keith tensed and prepared to

stand up. But instead of walking around the desk, Burke pulled
a cigar from a humidor, lit it and left the room, closing the door
softly behind him.

Keith replaced the cover plate to the phone connection, hands
shaking. When he finished he slipped out of the room, then wandered the grounds, until he saw Leanne. She was talking to a
jockey in white britches and a blue-and-gold tunic. As he
watched she turned and went into the stables. He followed and
found her in a stall brushing a roan horse with a braided mane.

"Nice-looking horse," Keith said.

He startled her. "Mr. Kris, you're quiet as a ghost."

"I'm sorry, I didn't mean to scare you."

"No, I'm just out here . . . forgive me, a hostess should be with
her guests, I know."

"You are with a guest."

"Well, I'm afraid I'm neglecting my duties."

"You are, but not to your guests."

"I beg your pardon?"

"To yourself."

"What? Are you always so . . . outspoken, Mr. Kris, or have you
singled me out for some special occasion?"

"Your husband has singled us both out, Miss Morrison."

"Why do you call me that?"

"Because that's who you are, or ought to be."

"Mr. Kris, you're supposed to be my husband's friend and yet
you come out here—"

"I'm not his friend."

"Oh? What then?"

"His past, his future."

She smiled weakly. "My, but you're very cryptic, Mr. Kris."

"Would you like Fairoaks back, Miss Morrison?"

"What?"

"This place. Would you like it back in your name?"

"Jerry told you . . .?"

"No."

"How then? How do you know?"

"I was in the study. I went to make a phone call and lost a

contact lens. While I was on the floor behind the desk you came in."

"You were *there?*" A few minutes ago?"

"Yes."

"And you think that because you're an eavesdropper you know the truth, is that it?"

"I think you got involved with a man who turned out to be a lot different from what you'd thought. I think that you'd like Fairoaks back, I think you'd like to start over and try again for the dreams you must have had when you married. I also think you're afraid, you don't know where to start or how you'd manage. I'm offering you a chance. I hope you'll take it."

"Mr. Kris, I am not an especially brave person, but please don't think you can come in here and take advantage of—"

"Would you like Fairoaks back? That's the question."

"Can you do that?"

"I can if you help me."

"How?"

"Your husband's business. How much do you know about it?"

"Mr. Kris, my husband and I may not always get along, our marriage isn't exactly perfect—but if you think I would align myself against him with a total stranger—"

"It's your husband who's the stranger, Miss Morrison. I think you know that."

"However, that may be, he is still less a stranger than you."

"Not true. We share more than you know."

"Oh? I see, you and I are soul mates, is that it? We're trapped in bad marriages but can find understanding in each other's arms. For a moment, Mr. Kris, I didn't recognize this as just another come-on. And then for another moment I thought you were some business competitor looking for an unfair advantage, but now I see where this is headed—a room in some motel at five o'clock in the afternoon—"

"That's not true. And I think you know it. I'm not trying to get you into bed—"

A tight smile. "Well, maybe you should, Mr. Kris. If you had approached me as openly as you seemed—no, let me get this out—it's too late, you see. I've either said too much or too little. But it's not going to happen now and if you persist in this matter I will tell my husband everything that happened here. I ask you to leave now."

She ducked beneath Saint's neck and the horse moved against Keith as she pushed her way out of the stall and headed off to the house. Unless he was willing to tell her everything, she would mistrust his motives. The lady was too much on the edge, her emotions too volatile to risk the truth. He would have to operate with a hidden hand and get his information about the C-4 shipment from someone other than Leanne Burke.

CHAPTER 27

Alex Westcott and Chris had returned to Washington late the previous night from a campaign rally in New York. As he feared, coverage of yesterday's rally was sparse. His kickoff speech at the Vietnam Memorial had captured the headlines and propelled him to within two points of the front-runner, Senator Foxhall from Ohio, but since then, despite an energetic campaign schedule, he had slipped to fourth place.

His mood improved some when he got to his office and found Gail waiting. "Hello, Duchess, what brings you to the hallowed halls of hypocrisy?" It was her term, she had coined it in high school. She didn't smile.

"I have to talk to you, it's important."

A switch, he thought. She hadn't asked his advice in a long time now, not since . . . He let the thought fade without following it to its uncomfortable conclusion. Instead, he told his secretary not to disturb him and led her into his office.

"So, what's on your mind? How's the new job?"

"It's tricky . . . I'm investigating a friend of yours. Jerry Burke."

"I wouldn't call him a friend."

"What then?"

"Just someone I knew in the army. Why investigate him?"

"It seems he may be involved in shipping arms illegally overseas."

A quick, patented smile. "That's yesterday's news, Duchess. His name came up in the Iran-Contra investigation but nothing ever came of that either—"

"I have to ask you—are you involved with Jerry Burke?"

"Of course not. Did he say I was?"

"I haven't talked to him. But I found this."

She put down a sheaf of legal papers on his desk: the incorporation papers for Artex International. Alex scanned them. "Your name is on page six . . ."

He looked up. "This is what you wanted to talk about?"

"You were the vice-president. I wondered why."

"To protect my investment, Duchess. Jerry Burke came to me out of the army and I loaned him start-up money."

"How much?"

"I don't know, I think we were partners, maybe fifty-fifty. After a few months or so he was on his feet and I bowed out."

"A year-and-a-half."

"Was it that long? Maybe so. It was just a favor to an old army buddy. Why in the world are you going into all this?"

"I have evidence that Jerry Burke is involved in a shipment of C-4 plastic explosive to Libya."

Alex raised an eyebrow. "You have evidence?"

"Yes."

"What is it, Duchess?"

"It's confidential."

"From your own father?"

"From a former vice-president of Artex."

"Gail, I told you, my involvement was strictly ceremonial—"

"Is it over? Your involvement, I mean?"

Alex looked disappointed, wounded. "Is that what you really think? That I'm involved with something like running guns to a proscribed country?"

"I just don't know what you're doing, that's why I'm asking."

There it was again, he thought, that damned reserve, that distrust that had grown between them accompanied by the intense expression that reminded him so much of Keith.

"Duchess, I'm running for President, do you really think I'd be skulking around circumventing export laws."

"Your answer is no?"

"Do you really have to ask? I'm your father. You know me. We spent eighteen years in the same house. How can you consider the possibility that I'd be involved in such a thing? If you can— my daughter—then I might as well call off the campaign right now. If you don't believe in me as a father, who can believe in me as a President?"

He stood with arms spread, awaiting her verdict.

"I'm sorry . . . I . . ." She moved forward and hugged him. Alex held his breath. It was a moment that hadn't happened in a long time. Not since the "incident" with Jerry Burke when she had come to him in tears and told him how Burke had exposed himself in his office. And what had Alex done? Comforted her and told her to forget about it. And then, afraid that a confrontation between Burke and Chris might somehow bring out the truth about Keith, he cautioned her not to tell her mother, saying that it would upset her. Gail did as he said but he paid a high cost. Since that day things had never been the same between them.

She picked up the incorporation papers. "I should let you get back to work."

"This investigation, this exposé of Jerry Burke . . . how many people are working on it?"

"Just me. It's my story."

"Is publication soon?"

"Why?"

"You're a politician's daughter, Duchess. I won't insult you by trying to get any promises, but I'd appreciate knowing in advance if you get close to publication. That's fair."

"To who, dad?"

"To me. If you publish a story that Jerry Burke is using Artex to ship explosives to Libya, somebody else is going to publicize that I was once an officer of the company. I can explain, of course, but a man running for office automatically loses credibility every time he stops to defend himself." He took her hands in his. "You can give me advance notice without compromising your principles, can't you, Duchess?"

She hesitated, then nodded. "Advance notice. But please don't try to talk me out of it."

"I wouldn't think of it."

After she left, Alex sat staring at the papers on his desk without seeing them. Jerry Burke again . . . he remembered him appearing in Washington eight years ago looking for a loan to start a new company. At first he'd refused but Burke made it clear he might tell Chris about Keith. He remembered how he had to keep up the fiction that they were army buddies when Burke began showing up at the house. Then after the business with Gail he'd cut off their relationship, foregoing the balance of the loan in exchange for Burke's promise never to contact him again. Except for a wedding announcement and the annual invitations to the Fairoaks hunt breakfast, Burke had kept his word. And now this . . . his daughter investigating Burke at the worst possible time. If only there was a way to delay things at least until after the elections . . .

Rick poked his head in the door and waved a notebook. "I've got tomorrow's itinerary, Senator."

"A few minutes, Rick."

"More than five and we'll have to cancel the schoolteachers."

"Five minutes."

When Rick was gone Alex ducked out the private entrance, went down the hall to the front of the building, where, surrounded by tourists, he went into a phone booth and made the call Keith had been waiting for.

Video games held an endless fascination for Prem. In addition to Gunfight, the surveillance post now boasted three less sophisticated games, each of which had its own litany of zooms, zeeps, pings, pops and electronic victory chatter. While Keith spent his mornings at the townhouse, Prem's routine was to arrive early at the surveillance post, check the surveillance equipment and replace the tape. He was free to play video games until Burke arrived, after which he had only to log phone calls and photograph the occasional visitor. At noon Keith arrived and took over while Prem drove to Fairoaks and exchanged the tape and the batteries at the remote site. When he got back the two of them logged the Fairoaks conversations from the day before.

Alex's phone call came during the afternoon. Keith was at a table listening to conversations of the day before when the phone rang in Burke's office. After a moment the secretary's voice, filtered through the intercom, came to them: "Excuse me, Mr. Burke. There's a man on the line who won't give his name. He says to tell you that your former V.P. is on the line and it's urgent."

"Quiet!" Keith told Prem, who had just scored five hundred points on the Star Wars game.

The familiar voice said, "This is Jerry Burke."

"Jerry, it's me. No names, just tell me yes or no, you know who this is?"

Prem gave him an inquisitive look and Keith whispered, "Alex Wescott."

"My illustrious friend; glad to hear from you."

"You won't be when I tell you why I called. The little deal you're involved in right now is in danger of going public. I'm talking about a certain nasty substance and a certain nasty dictator. I called to warn you not to go through with it. Do we understand one another?" There was a pause. "Are you there?"

Burke's voice was strained. "I . . . where did you get such information?"

"I can't tell you that. I can't have any more contact with you. Just take my word for it and drop it . . ."

"Wait, wait a minute—"

But Westcott had hung up.

Prem was at the window with the binoculars. "He is looking very upset, you can believe it."

"Don't let him see you."

Prem stepped back quickly and put his back against the wall. "More suspicious now, yes. I think some shit has finally struck upon the fan."

The green light on one of the consoles lit up: Burke had picked up the phone. The tones came through clearly, five of them, and the liquid display read-out: 81889. Then a pause and Burke hung up. Keith glanced at Prem, who was peering cautiously through the binoculars. "He is putting down the phone. Thinking now. He is worried. Oh oh." He lowered the binoculars. "Leaving the office."

Keith had hoped that Gail would approach Burke; instead, she had evidently gone to Alex. And it had almost worked. He was willing to bet that Burke was about to contact Jack Jones. 818-89. There were two digits—no, five digits missing. The 818 could be an area code.

"There he comes."

Keith joined Prem at the window. Below them, Burke walked quickly across the plaza to a pay phone.

"That's it. Have you got anything that'll pick up the conversation?"

"Shotgun mike, maybe." Prem jumped to a suitcase and began to pull out equipment. "But we must get outside and find some place hidden."

"No time. He's already—"

Burke was searching his pockets, the phone clenched between his shoulder and ear. The receiver slipped free, fell, and dangled.

"Out of change. He's heading for the snack shop. What about a phone mike?"

"Drop-in mike. Yes, I have one here."

Prem began rummaging through the equipment, mumbling to himself. Keith glanced out the window. Burke had disappeared into the shop.

"Come on, come on."

"The other case. Now I remember." In his haste to open it, Prem dumped the contents onto the floor.

"Jesus, Prem."

"Coming soon."

"I'm going out there, keep him away from the phone. You just get something in that booth."

He ran to the elevator, it wasn't there so he raced down the stairs. Burke was coming out of the snack bar as Keith reached the plaza. He intercepted him, blocking the path to the phone.

"Mr. Burke, just the man I was coming to see."

Burke frowned. He was obviously worried and just as obviously in a hurry.

"Mr. Kris, I'm a little busy right now—"

"Just a word about your farm. About Fairoaks. I'd like to buy it."

"What?"

"You have as good a taste in property as you do in art, Mr. Burke. I've decided that I want Fairoaks. How much will you take for the property?"

"It's not for sale, now if you'll excuse me."

He tried to move past but Keith side-stepped and cut him off. From the corner of his eye he could see the phone booth still empty. Where was Prem?

"Wait a minute now. We haven't even discussed a price."

"There is no price. It's not for sale—"

"There's always a price. If your life depended on it, I'm sure you'd sell. If you needed cancer treatments—"

"I *don't.*"

Again he tried to pass and again Keith blocked his way. "There must be something you value more than Fairoaks. What would that be?"

"I told you, there's nothing. Now if you—" Keith glanced at the phone and suppressed a smile. Prem was there with his back to them, his head obscured by the huge cowboy hat that he had bought in California.

"What about other farms? Are there any others in the area for sale? What do they usually get for that kind of acreage?"

He kept at Burke until Prem vacated the booth, then he let Burke go and went back to the surveillance room, where Prem already had a tape running.

"There is the number," Prem said, pointing to a ten digit phone number he had written down.

A female voice answered. "Nelson Mowrer Associates."

"Jack Jones calling for Mr. Mowrer."

"One moment, Mr. Jones."

Prem frowned. "I thought he was calling Jack Jones."

"Fake name. A cover name for whoever calls."

A deep voice said, "Mowrer here."

Burke rattled off seven numbers and Mowrer said, "Five minutes." They hung up.

Prem gave Keith a look. "All so much work and they are using code numbers."

"I don't think so."

"Then what?"

Keith went to the window and looked down to where Burke waited restlessly beside the phone. Minutes later the phone rang. Mowrer, probably from a phone booth. Now the two men spoke freely . . . Burke wanted to expedite the shipment, he wanted to know how soon it would be ready.

"It's the repacking, Jerry. Eight hundred and forty-two cans it's going to come out. Takes a lot of time."

"How close are you?"

"We'll be done Thursday. I've got Jaeger Independent arriving Friday morning. Take an hour to load and they're gone. The stuff will be in Dallas late Saturday."

"Saturday's a lock?"

"If there are no breakdowns on the road. What about the plane?"

"Ready and waiting. You get it to Dallas and I'll get it to T-ville. As long as customs goes like you say."

"No problem."

"Better not be."

"Like I told you, they ship tons of Bentonite out of Dallas every week, use it like a French whore uses perfume."

"Just keep the lid on it at your end, okay? There's talk, you know what I mean?"

"What kind?"

"That something like this is going down. It's just . . . it's in the woodwork, but I want to expedite."

"You're too much in a hurry, Jerry. Should never get in a hurry with explosives. Ask me. I lost two fingers the last time I was in a hurry—"

"Yeah, right. Listen, unless there's a change in plans no more communication, okay?"

The men confirmed their arrangements and hung up. Prem was grinning. "The cat is out of the bed, I think."

Keith glanced at his notes. Eight hundred and forty-two cans of Bentonite picked up at Nelson Mowrer Associates Friday morning for transport by Jaeger Independent to Dallas. It took only a few phone calls to fill in the missing pieces: Nelson Mowrer Associates was a reputable explosives dealer located in Van Nuys, California; Bentonite was a brand name for drilling mud, a compound used in oil drilling operations; and Jaeger Independent Trucking was a California firm that specialized in fast, door-to-door frieght transport.

Prem was right. The cat was out of the bed.

CHAPTER 28

Keith and Prem moved quickly in Los Angeles. Posing as Jerry Burke of Artex International, Keith leased a small warehouse on Saticoy Boulevard just three blocks from Nelson Mowrer Associates. He had a rush job-printing of Artex business cards and checks using the new address. Meanwhile Prem hunted down the manufacturer of Bentonite drilling compound and ordered eight hundred and forty-two cans, duplicating the Burke-Mowrer load. Again the transaction was made in the name of Artex and again Keith signed the certified check with Jerry Burke's name.

The next step was a visit to Jaeger Independent Trucking, a firm that specialized in round-the-clock team transport service. Keith visited the office in person so that he could get a look at the trailers. As he anticipated, they all looked the same—long white vans of varying length with the Jaeger name in a blue rectangle on the front and rear. Keith spoke to a bald salesman whose few strands of hair lay combed across the top of his head like dark fissures. He arranged for Jaeger to pick up the drilling mud from the manufacturer in Denver and deliver it no later than Thursday to the Saticoy warehouse.

"After we unload the Bentonite," Keith told him, "we've got

another load to ship back to Denver on Monday. Is there any problem leaving the trailer so we can load it over the weekend?"

"Nope, no problem. We'll spot the trailer at your warehouse and you give us a time when you want the driver to pick it up."

Again a check from Artex paid for the service. Keith's original thought had been to reveal the C-4 shipment to the FBI, but now he had a new plan, one which required the services of the Aaao-kay Driving School. The school occupied a narrow office sandwiched between a laundromat and a liquor store. A pink neon sign read DRIVE and below it the words CARS, TRUCKS, and CYCLES lit alternately. Inside there was a framed poster featuring a gleaming tractor-trailer rig titled "California Dreamin" and near it a sign warning students that all cancellations had to be made one day in advance. The salesman, a young Hispanic, was the only one of the staff wearing a tie. When he heard that Keith and Prem wanted to learn to drive a truck in three days he turned them over to one of the instructors, a huge, sad-faced man named Bud Mahoney.

"The course normally takes six to ten days," Mahoney told them. "If you want to cut it in half, we could run private lessons, three hours to practice, three hours to rest, then three hours in the afternoon depending if your left leg holds out. You'll be running through thirteen gears, up and down, with a clutch that's stiff as a dead man's dick. It's up to you."

Most of the instructors were heavyset men with gray hair who looked like they'd seen better days. When not giving lessons they sat around the office drinking coffee, kidding one another in dour fashion and grumbling about the stupidity of their students. Keith discovered that some of them owned their own rigs but because of the deregulation of the trucking industry and changes in I.C.C. regulations, they found it tough to make a profit. Hiring out to the Aaaokay Driving School was at least a way of making ends meet.

The pace was exhausting but they learned quickly. For Keith it was a matter of necessity, for Prem, it was fun. He loved sitting high in the cab and powering the big rig through the streets of Van Nuys. Because he was small, he used two cushions, one to sit on, another behind his back. Bud Mahoney's cab was a Mack

◀ 217

R-686 ST, known to the drivers as a "Bulldog." Prem visited a Western clothing store and came back wearing snakeskin boots, a hand-tooled leather belt, a fringed leather vest and huge Stetson hat. "I am Bulldog cowboy," he said.

Keith approached Mahoney about renting his cab for the weekend but it was already committed to the school. He had a daughter and son-in-law who were independent truckers, a husband-and-wife team who owned a Peterbuilt. Keith made them an offer of five thousand dollars for a five day rental. They were eager for the money but reluctant to let the "Pete" go without them. It was in immaculate shape with its classic rectangular lines, polished black cab with red pinstriping and chrome mud guards.

"Why can't you hire us to drive?" the boy asked. "We'll take anything anywhere you want to go."

"I want to drive myself, but I'm willing to meet any terms you want to protect your equipment."

They were in front of a tiny stucco house in San Fernando, one of many communities whose individualities had been submerged in the featureless Greater Los Angeles area. Aluminum window awnings hung haphazardly, the house needed painting and a Chevrolet without wheels or an engine sat on cinderblocks above a discolored patch of front lawn. They settled on seventy-five hundred dollars for the five day rental and a cashier's check for twenty-five thousand dollars as a security deposit in case anything was damaged.

The Bentonite arrived from Denver on Thursday afternoon. The driver backed the trailer to the loading dock, lowered the landing gear and left it to be unloaded. As soon as he was gone, Prem called Keith's attention to a metal security band looped through the handle of the loading door. It had the initials J.I.T. followed by a seven digit number. There was no way to open the truck without destroying the band.

"This number will not match the C-4 load," Prem pointed out.

"It will when we're done."

"How?"

"Take guess."

Prem made a face. "Guessing is like a cat pursuing its tail—too much exhaustion leading nowhere."

"Then you'll be surprised."

The next morning they were watching when the Jaeger truck arrived at Nelson Mowrer Associates. It spent an hour and a half at the loading dock, then rolled onto the highway and headed east on Interstate 10. Keith and Prem followed in the Peterbuilt. They kept well back, sometimes losing contact with the Jaeger but never for too long. They knew the route and the destination; it would be difficult to lose their target.

Beyond the San Bernadino Mountains the air grew clear and the earth turned stark and sculpted in shades of brown, ocher and desert red. Prem tuned the radio to a country-western station and sat with one elbow cocked out the open window, a breeze tugging strands of hair from beneath his Stetson.

"Now we are in the real cowboy country," he said with relish. "I will make a nickname: Prem 'Tex' Chaduvedi. 'Tex' for my friends. After we conclude the unhappiness of these men, I will move to Arizona and buy a ranch. Then I will learn to broke horses and wrestle cows and with a pistol shoot bottles in the air."

The dry heat of the desert filled the cab and the land was awash in sunlight. Even with his tinted contact lenses, Keith needed sunglasses to cut the glare. Sitting high in the cab, he could see down into the cars below, the knees of the adults in front, the kids twisting against each other in back, families surrounded by maps and toys and Kleenex boxes and soda cans. People on vacation living the life he and Chris had planned . . . He wondered what he would do when it was over, when he'd destroyed what *they* valued most. The thought made him uncomfortable, irritated him, and he pushed it quickly aside and lost himself in the hypnosis of the road, the endless ribbon of asphalt.

The cab pulling the Jaeger was a K.W. cab-over—a Kenworth-White with a sleeping compartment. Since it was a rush load, there were two drivers. They stopped briefly in Indio and picked up McDonald's hamburgers, but it wasn't until dusk, when they pulled into a sprawling roadside complex, that Keith found the opportunity he was looking for. Here were facilities for both truckers and tourists—a gas station with multiple bays and two restaurants linked by a hall with toilet facilities, phones and a video game room. Cars parked in areas along both sides of the complex while trucks, many with their motors running, were in the rear, out of sight of the diners.

They parked near the perimeter of the lot, apart from the C-4 load. Keith followed the two drivers into the restaurant, watched as they settled into a booth, then returned to the parking lot, where Prem had disconnected their trailer and removed its license plate. He took a deep breath and approached the K.W. Unlike many of the truckers, the C-4 drivers had shut down the engine and taken the keys. The cab, however, was unlocked. Keith slid into the driver's seat as if he owned it.

A quick survey of the parking lot to make sure nobody was watching, then he ducked beneath the dashboard and used the electric screwdriver to remove a metal panel. After locating the ignition leads, he took a short wire with two needle-sharp pincers at either end and hot-wired the ignition. Prem stood with his arms folded, the signal that everything was ready. Keith took another deep breath and pushed the starter button.

Working the K.W.'s unfamiliar clutch, Keith lurched forward a couple of times before he adjusted to it. A mother on her way to the Howard Johnson's restaurant grabbed her child by the arm and scowled as he passed. Keith waved that he was sorry, then turned in a large arc and maneuvered the rig behind their own trailer, partially hiding it from view. Prem then removed the license plate while Keith lowered the landing gear and disconnected the two air hoses and electrical connection. While Prem exchanged license plates, he pulled free of the C-4 load and hooked onto the Bentonite load. Hose connections and landing gear took less than ninety seconds. Keith returned the K.W. with its new trailer to its parking place. The whole operation had taken six minutes.

Lying on his back, he removed the hot wire and replaced the cover plate. But his exhilaration was short-lived. When he sat up, he saw one of the K.W. drivers coming around the corner of the restaurant. Keith saw him at the same moment the man turned to watch two girls heading the other way. In another moment the man would turn back to the cab and see him leaving. Unless . . .

He vaulted into the sleeping compartment above the seat. Moments passed, slowly, slowly . . . Had the driver seen him? It was dusk now. Even if they didn't discover him immediately, one of them was bound to use the sleeping compartment on the next leg of the trip. He needed a plausible story . . .

The cab rocked as the driver mounted the step and opened the door. From beneath the curtain Keith caught a glimpse of the man's head and shoulders as he leaned into the cab, fumbled beneath the seat and brought out a silver thermos. Then the door slammed and Keith was alone again. He waited a long minute, then cautiously checked to see if the coast was clear. As he climbed down from the cab, he became aware of his shirt, damp with sweat and clinging to his back.

He returned to the Peterbuilt, where Prem stared at him. "How did he not see you?"

"Must be blind, I guess."

Keith went to the rear of the C-4 trailer, now hooked behind the Peterbuilt grabbed the security band and yanked it free. Returning to the Bentonite trailer, he tossed the broken seal beneath the loading door and went into the restaurant. "Who's hauling a Jaeger on a K.W.?" he asked.

The driver who had been within a few feet of him just moments earlier turned around. "That's me."

"Some little creep was trying to get your load. Took off in a Ford pick-up when I yelled at him."

The men bolted up and ran outside. Keith followed them, adding a few details about the thief. "I had a load stolen once," he went on, "made up my mind I'd kill the next sonofabitch I found trying it."

The two men thanked him and offered to buy him a beer but Keith begged off, saying he was running late and had just stopped to get gas and make a phone call. One man stayed with the truck while the other went inside to pay the bill. Keith went to a phone booth and pretended a conversation until they left. No need to draw their attention to Prem and the other Jaeger trailer.

Once the K.W. was gone, Keith and Prem pulled onto the

freeway and headed in the opposite direction. Prem turned up the volume to a cassette tape of a Marty Robbins western tune, "El Paso," and sat behind the wheel singing his head off all night long as they drove back to L.A.

In less than twenty-four hours, the C-4 shipment had returned to within three blocks of its departure point.

Keith left Prem to oversee the unloading and return of the Peterbuilt and took a United flight back to Washington. He was so tired that he didn't notice a short, dark-haired ticket agent staring at him from a nearby check-in counter. The agent was Barbara Washburn. After Keith had gone she hurried over and got his name and destination from the flight coupon, then called the number she had been given, but it was Saturday and nobody was in the office. She left a message with the answering service and spent the rest of the day wondering what the mysterious man who reminded her of Michael Landon might have done to generate such intense interest on the part of the people at Severa Security Systems.

CHAPTER 29

When Nexli wasn't with him Jerry Burke sometimes sat in the cockpit and flew the Grumman Gulfstream under the direction of his pilot, a Dutchman named Udo Lauer. Lauer had given him enough instruction so that Burke felt he could take over and land in case of an emergency. To prove it, he negotiated all but the last few moments of the landing in Tripoli.

"Good job," Lauer said.

"Damn right."

Burke was in a good mood. When the C-4 load left Mowrer's warehouse he had flown to London, where Nexli was waiting with cocaine and pornographic videotapes. After a twenty-four hour drug-induced sexual marathon, they fell into an exhausted sleep that ended with a phone call. "The chicken has flown the coop," Nelson Mowrer said. The chartered Boeing cargo plane was on its way.

Even Major Hasnid seemed happy when he greeted Burke and drove him to the hotel. The four-lane freeway which led from Idris Airport to Tripoli was flanked by huge banners that had long ago faded in the desert sun.

"So when's the parade, major?"

"Parade?"

"All those flags. Maybe you'll have a chance to use them now that you've got the C-4."

Hasnid smiled. "Perhaps." And then, indicating the bandage at the base of Burke's neck, said, "You had an accident?"

"Cut myself shaving."

Burke wondered what Hasnid would say if he knew the wound had been caused by Nexli's teeth or that she wore a similar bandage on her neck? It had been an incredible experience—the greater the pain, the greater the high, until the taste of blood during their climax had driven them both to a near-frenzy. The memory of it scared him a little. She was a dangerous addiction.

At the Beach Hotel, a dull brick building with a cavernous dining hall, Burke demanded and got a room with a working air conditioner. When he was alone he brought out a bottle of whiskey and poured himself a shot, then stripped to his shorts and took a nap until four, when one of Hasnid's drivers picked him up and drove him to the Hajazzi Army Base on the outskirts of town.

As soon as he arrived, Burke sensed that something was wrong. Some of the C-4 cans were still on the truck while others had been moved into a new concrete bunker, leaving behind a stack of wooden pallets. Major Hasnid stood with Colonel Ibram and a group of the soldiers gathered around a dozen cans that had been opened and upturned. A heavyset man with gray hair and a purple beret knelt and pushed his knife through the brownish-gray substance that lay glistening on the sand. Burke recognized him as Walid Fahmy, the Libyan's explosive expert.

Hasnid turned to him, face set in stone. "We have a problem, Mr. Burke. These cans contain a drilling compound, Bentonite."

"Only the top layer."

"Perhaps you can show us where the top layer ends and the C-4 begins?" He nodded to one of the soldiers, who opened another can. Walid Fahmy dipped his knife in the contents, smelled it and shook his head.

"Not C-4."

The soldier let the contents spill slowly to the ground. There was absolutely no difference in the color or consistency. Walid stood up. "Bentonite."

"You see?" Hasnid said. "Beneath the drilling mud there is
. . . *more* drilling mud."

"That's not possible—"

"Do you accuse me of falsifying the contents of this shipment?"

"No, but—"

"You accuse Colonel Ibram?"

The colonel stood with his chest outthrust like a hawk, watching him from beneath heavy-lidded eyes.

Burke's mouth felt dry. "I need to make a phone call."

Hasnid took him to a private office whose only decoration was
an oriental rug spread over a concrete floor. There were flies and
an air conditioner wheezed fitfully. It took ten minutes to get
through to Nelson Mowrer.

"It's me," Burke said. "We have a problem here."

"I know." Mowrer's voice was strained.

"You know?"

"A can of Big Mud was just delivered. Along with a note offering to sell us the rest. What happened?"

"You have the Big Mud?"

"One can, Jerry. Just one can. The rest of it . . . what happened
to the shipment? Didn't the plane get through?"

"The plane arrived but they say it's regular mud. It looks the
same inside."

"Brown or gray?"

"Kind of brown."

"All of it?"

"They've spot-checked a whole bunch of cans. It's all the
same."

"Shit."

"What about the note? Who sent it?"

"I don't know. It just says, you know . . . I've got the stuff and
you can buy it back. Typewritten note, that's all. No name, no
phone number. Delivered by cab. Some Oriental guy grabbed a
cab at a bus station and paid the driver two hundred dollars to
deliver it."

"Oriental?"

"That's what the cabbie said. Dressed like a cowboy. Driver

◀ 225

thought he was nuts but for two hundred bucks he wasn't going to argue. Jesus, Jerry, if this thing comes apart . . ."

Burke's mind was racing. An Oriental. Who? Someone inside the organization? A list of culprits came to mind—the truck-driver, the pilot, the forklift operator . . . He became aware of Hasnid's eyes on him, the man's anger apparent. He turned his back to get a little privacy. "How much do they want?"

"They want Fairoaks."

"What?"

"That's what it says. They want your farm."

"Read the goddam note. Just read it."

There was a moment's pause, then Mowrer returned. "Okay, here it is. *I have the Big Mud. If you want it back, tell Jerry Burke the price is Fairoaks. Tomorrow morning at ten o'clock in the lobby of the Willard Hotel.* That's it."

"*Tell Jerry Burke?* It says that? My name?"

"Just like I read it."

Burke's hands grew cold. Someone knew his name, knew his involvement with the shipment. He remembered Alex West-cott's warning. Was it someone in the government? Fairoaks . . . Leanne had been hot to get the farm back. Could she actually have hired someone to hijack the load? He dismissed the thought, Leanne didn't have the imagination or the resources. Whoever did this was tough, and knew too much.

John Kris. The name popped into his head. Kris had offered to buy Fairoaks just last week. Was it possible . . .

Mowrer's voice was tense. "You said everything was taken care of, Jerry. What the hell's coming down?"

"Take it easy. It's not my end that fucked up."

"Meaning what? You think I did?"

"No, no. Listen, I think I know who did it."

"Who?"

"A guy named Kris. You don't know him but—never mind, I'll deal with it."

"Someone from *your* end."

"He's not one of mine."

"Is he with the government? FBI?"

"I don't know."

"Shit, Jerry, I could lose my license. I could go to jail—"

"Fuck your license. I've got half a dozen camel-humpers waving guns over here—" He was yelling. Remembering Hasnid, he lowered his voice and said as calmly as he could, "I'll be back, I'll take care of it."

"When?"

"I'm leaving right away. Be in Washington in twelve hours."

"So what do I tell this guy if he contacts me?"

"Tell him he's got a deal, what else?"

He put down the phone and stood for a moment, staring at his hand resting on the receiver. Freckles and well-manicured nails. Like somebody else's hand.

Hasnid said, "Someone stole the shipment?"

"I'll get it back."

"When?"

"Right away."

He started toward the door but Hasnid blocked it with his arm. "You are going back to the United States?"

"That's the only way you're going to get your C-4, Major."

"Then you will wait here until I get permission from the Defense Council."

"Permission for what? I don't need anybody's permission."

"To leave the country you need permission."

"Bullshit. I'm an American citizen."

"We have no diplomatic relations with America, or had you forgotten? You will wait." Hasnid called out in Arabic and a soldier appeared in the doorway. After giving him instructions, Hasnid said to Burke, "If you try to leave, this man has orders to shoot you."

Hasnid left. The guard stood in the doorway eyeing him like he'd welcome an excuse to shoot him. Burke considered trying to overpower him but knew he couldn't do it. He was an operator not a fighter. He had to use his wits. He paced nervously, cursing the Arabs, cursing the man who stole the shipment. *John Kris.* Who the fuck was he, anyway? An Asian art collector? Bull. Burke had never heard of him or his collection. The more he thought about it, the more convinced he was that John Kris was responsible. *Whoever he was.*

An hour later Colonel Ibram returned with Major Hasnid and a soldier toting an Uzi submachine gun. This time it was Ibram who gave the orders and Hasnid interpreted. "The colonel says come with us."

"What's the problem?"

Ibram gestured with his head. The soldier jammed the Uzi into Burke's back.

"Look," Burke said as he followed them, "I know who took the C-4. I'm going to get it back, *okay?*"

A half dozen men stood in the courtyard. They were unarmed but that didn't reassure Burke when the guard pushed him up against the wall. His legs turned to butter. Jesus . . . they were going to shoot him . . . ?

"Hey, come *on*. People know where I am. It's not you guys who got ripped off. It was me. You think I'd show up here if I was pulling something?"

The guards stepped back and a young man with a motorized Nikon stepped forward. Burke flinched at the sound of the shutter: Ka-zip, ka-zip, ka-zip, ka-zip.

The photographer paused, and Hasnid said, "Turn to the side."

"Why?"

Before Hasnid could answer, Ibram barked a command. One of the guards grabbed his head and turned it to one side. More photographs.

"Head to front," Hasnid called.

This time Burke obeyed without help. Colonel Ibram turned to the group of men and made a short speech, occasionally pointing toward Burke. All eyes focused on him, then, one by one, the men walked around him, inspecting him from every angle. When the last man had completed his circuit, Ibram had one final word and then everyone left except Hasnid. Burke brought out a handkerchief and wiped his neck and face.

"Your own fault," Hasnid said. "I could intervene no longer in your behalf."

"What the hell was that all about?"

"The Defense Council will give you exactly three days to replace the C-4 cargo or return to them the one point two million dollars plus interest in the amount of two hundred and forty thousand dollars."

"I told you I'd get the stuff. I told you that. Don't you people understand civilized negotiating?"

"What do you expect from camel-humpers?"

"I didn't mean you," Burke said quickly. "You're okay. I mean all that stuff with the pictures and those guys giving me the evil eye. Who are they supposed to be?"

"Those men are members of our Special Operations Director-ate for Overseas Action. If we do not received the C-4 or the return of the money in three days, they will be sent to assassinate you. They are not, as you say, civilized."

CHAPTER 30

Mike Severa divided the women he dated according to their specialties. Mandy Zanrano was a scuba diver. A bronze-skinned would-be movie actress, she made a living doing something called "crystal healing." Her apartment was a gemologist's delight, filled with rock crystals of varying shapes, sizes, and hues, each of which had its own particular healing properties. Severa considered it all a crock, but Mandy was a real good diver in more ways than one and loved making love on the boat. Which was all he asked of her.

After making sure that he wasn't being followed, Severa picked up Mandy at her apartment. She wore heavy cotton shorts and a roughly pleated cotton top that left her midriff bare. They drove to the Bamboo Reef, a dive shop in Marina del Rey where Severa stored his tanks and had them filled. The tanks were yellow U.S. Divers, twin seventy-twos in a backpack, which gave the diver an hour under water at thirty feet. The boat was a twenty-four-foot Chris-Craft. Before they left, Severa inspected it so thoroughly that Mandy asked what he was looking for.

"Checking for gas leaks."

A plausible enough excuse when he had his head in the engine compartment but made less sense when he checked the wiring beneath the control panel and poked a flashlight into all the storage compartments. Mandy didn't really care. She sat on the bow and applied suntan lotion while Severa went over the boat like he'd once done with the barracks in Nam. He even slipped on a face mask and went overboard to check the hull. Just the usual marine growth, no sign of tampering.

They moved slowly out of the harbor, past endless rows of gleaming yachts, down a channel bordered by insistently nautical restaurants and multilevel pastel condominiums. Once past the breakwater, the Christ-Craft accelerated with a full-throated roar. Mandy gripped a handrail as the bow plunged and split the waves. Sheets of silver spray arced over the boat, flung backward by a brisk wind. A half hour later they anchored over the kelp beds off the Palisades and put on their equipment—wetsuit, weightbelt, tanks, regulator, fins and mask. Severa gripped the mouthpiece between his teeth and jumped, legs spread, into the water.

Weeks of constant vigilance had taken their toll on Severa's nerves, and he now welcomed the ocean's embrace. At least in this environment no enemy could approach unseen. Like a giant fish, he rose and fell with the waves, then ducked beneath the surface and followed the anchor line until he could see that the hook was secure. For some reason he felt more buoyant than usual. And slightly dizzy. He swam back to the boat, grabbed the boarding ladder and let the mouthpiece fall as he called for another weight.

"Mandy, give me . . ." A high-pitched Donald Duck voice spoke his words.

Mandy came to the side and grinned down. "What did you say, Mike?" she squeaked, imitating him.

"Shut up." Again the cartoon voice. Severa repeated the words without meaning, testing them, analyzing what was happening. "Shut up, shut up, shut up."

"Are you doing that on purpose?"

Severa took a couple of deep breaths. "How's that? How's that?" His voice had returned to normal. Mandy was watching him, puzzled. "Did you screw around with the tanks?" he said.

"What do you mean?"

Her blank expression told him she knew nothing. Severa put the regulator in his mouth, took a deep breath and said, "Testing, testing," again in a high squeaky voice. "Son of a bitch!"

Mandy laughed. "Do that again, say something dirty."

"Test your tanks, take a breath and say something."

She turned on the air and put the regulator to her mouth. "My name is Mandy." It came out a high, reedy squeak. "That sounds so weird."

"It's helium."

"You think they made a mistake when they filled the tanks?"

Severa climbed aboard and slipped off the scuba gear. He was in no mood to explain. The taps on scuba tanks and a helium bottle were different. To fill an air tank with helium would require a custom-made adapter. It wasn't a mistake . . . It was John Kris.

He started the engines and ran full speed back to the marina. The Chris-Craft leaped and pounded, yanking them from side to side, and it took all his self-control to slow to five knots when they entered the harbor. Having given up trying to talk to him, Mandy sat in the stern, face hidden behind dark glasses and a baseball cap.

They took the tanks back to the Bamboo Reef, where Severa confronted the manager, a young man in an oversize T-shirt and shorts.

"Who filled these tanks, Luis?"

"I did. What's wrong?"

"You take a breath and tell me."

One of the assistants who worked in the shop and two customers stopped to watch as Luis took a breath and said, "Now what?" His face betrayed his surprise. "Holy shit," he squeaked. "This helium?"

"An inert gas, Luis. I could have gone down and everything felt fine until all of a sudden I'm dizzy and a second later I black out. I could have been dead."

"These are the tanks you picked up this morning?"

"You saw us. And you filled them." He grabbed Luis by the shirt. "How'd you do it, Luis? How much did he pay you?"

"Cut it out, man."

"It was Kris, right?"

"I don't know what you're talking about."

The assistant moved forward. "Hey, be cool, Mr. Severa. Come on."

Severa released Luis. "If I find out you had anything to do with it—"

"I filled the tanks, sure, the same as always. But not with helium, man. We don't even carry the stuff."

"It's like a birthday party," Mandy said. "You know, like when they have helium in balloons."

Luis tugged at the the wrinkles in his shirt. His confusion was real, Severa decided. Around them, other customers were talking and pointing.

"I'm sure. You had any break-ins the last month?"

"No."

"New customers? A guy in his forties, gray hair and beard, pale skin, looks like a body builder?"

Luis's face brightened. "Yeah, a guy brought in tanks last week. Already filled but he wanted a place to store them. I forget his name but I got it right here . . ."

"John Kris?"

Luis pulled out the registration card. "Yeah, that's it. Kris."

Severa looked at the card and knew that the address and phone number would be fake—it turned out they were *his*. Luis told him that Kris had taken his tanks out a couple of times but had never had them filled.

"He said something like the boat's engine wouldn't start the first time and another time he got the tanks and somebody was sick. Never did need no air."

"He switched them," Severa said. "My tanks for his."

"Your name is on yours and so was his."

All tanks left at the Bamboo Reef were identified, but Severa knew that his name, black-stenciled letters on the yellow tanks, could easily have been duplicated. Or Kris might have done a temporary exchange, taken his tanks and had them filled with helium, then brought them back.

"His tanks, I want to see them."

"Yeah, okay."

"Wait a minute," said the assistant. "They're not here. If it's that guy you're talking about, he came Wednesday and took his tanks. Never came back that I know about."

The tanks were gone and Kris was gone. Severa nursed his anger all afternoon, first in a Mexican bar where they drank Margaritas and later in Mandy's apartment, where he attempted to lose himself in her. But his performance was perfunctory and he left early, still tense and irritable, his mind on John Kris.

When he got home he found a message from Bobby on his answering machine. The ticket agent, Barbara Washburn, had seen John Kris again. And this time she knew his name and destination.

Thirteen hours after leaving Tripoli an exhausted Jerry Burke walked into the lobby of the Willard Hotel. He was early. He stood restlessly, eyeing those around him, looking for John Kris, the man who he was certain had caused twenty tons of C-4 explosives to disappear into thin air. Not into thin air, he corrected himself. Nelson Mowrer had discovered an incident at a truck stop—an attempted theft of the C-4 that had evidently been successful. But how Kris had found out about the shipment and how he had managed to switch the cargo remained a mystery.

A bellhop sauntered through the lobby paging Mr. Burke. He went to the concierge, who told him that his party was waiting in the Willard Room, a dining room done in shades of gold and gray and powder blue.

"I'm Mr. Burke," he told the young woman who stood behind a white podium. "Here to meet someone."

"Right this way, sir."

As they crossed the room Burke was uncomfortably aware of his disheveled condition. He had been in such a hurry to get out of Libya that he had gone directly to the Gulfstream without bothering to retrieve his bags from the hotel. During a brief fuel stop in London he'd called Nexli and told her what had happened. She offered to come with him but he said no. "If you want to help," he told her, "get your brother to call off the hit squad."

Too worried to do more than doze fitfully on the fold-out bed in the Gulfstream, Burke had arrived an hour earlier at National Airport. He was able to shave on the plane but there wasn't time to return to Fairoaks for a change of clothes. He looked out of place and knew it.

As they moved past a planter the young woman motioned toward a table. "Here you are, sir."

John Kris sat reading the Washington *Herald* over a glass of orange juice and cup of coffee. He glanced up and put the paper aside. "Good morning, Mr. Burke."

"I thought so, I thought it was you."

"Damn clever of you."

"As soon as I heard you wanted Fairoaks I knew—"

"Have a seat, join me for breakfast."

As Burke sat down, the linen tablecloth caught and tugged.

"You look tired," Kris said. "Have a rough flight?"

"This isn't going to work. It's extortion . . ."

"How about a cup of coffee?"

"Never mind that. I want my shipment back."

"Of Bentonite?"

"You know what I mean."

"You mean an illegal shipment of C-4 plastic explosive." Kris said it without lowering his voice and Burke instinctively hunched down in the chair. Kris raised a finger and signaled the waiter.

"Have you decided what you want?"

"Nothing."

"It's on me."

Burke waited impatiently while Kris ordered eggs Benedict and blueberry muffins. When the waiter was gone Burke said in a low voice, "It's illegal what *you're* doing."

"That's pretty funny coming from you."

Burke leaned forward. "I paid for that cargo, you fucking stole it from me."

"Such talk. What would the hunt club say?" Kris reached into his jacket, pulled out a small envelope and slid it across the table. Burke opened it. On a card embossed with the hotel's logo were written three sets of numbers, two digits each.

"What's this?"

"The combination that opens the padlock to the warehouse where your C-4 is stored." He pulled another envelope from his jacket and placed it beside his plate. "This is the location of that warehouse. I give this to you when you sign Fairoaks over to me."

"How do I now you'll give me the shipment even if I do?"

"If I wanted the C-4, I wouldn't have contacted you. What I want is Fairoaks. I told you that last week."

"It doesn't belong to me. It belongs to my wife."

"It *used* to belong to your wife. She signed it over to you six years ago and you mortgaged it to First Virginia Federal Bank that currently holds the title."

"How do you know all that?"

"The C-4 was a challenge, these transactions are matters of record."

The waiter approached with the muffins in a silver basket. When Kris turned to ask for honey, the envelope beside his plate lay unguarded. Burke lunged across the table and grabbed it. Coffee and orange juice sloshed and stained the tablecloth. Burke jumped to his feet, chair thumping to the carpet behind him. Stepping back, he tore open the envelope and pulled out the card.

Never trust a thief.

The waiter was staring. Burke felt people's eyes on him. Red-faced, he picked up his chair and sat down.

Kris said, "It was worth it to see the look on your face."

"Fuck you."

"Anger. Frustration. Good." He turned to the waiter and finished his order. Burke wanted to hit Kris, but there was something threatening about the man—the power inherent in his physique, the intensity reflected in the borderless black eyes. When the waiter was gone he said, "How did you find out about the shipment?"

"When you know as much about me as I know about you, you'll know how."

Kris was jerking him around. "All right, play the mystery man. But I'm going to tell you something . . . you didn't steal the Big Mud from me, you stole it from the Libyans. They paid for it, they own it. And if they don't get it back they're coming after you because I already gave them your name."

"You threaten the dead, Mr. Burke?"

"What?"

"You heard me."

"What kind of question is that?"

"It's a practical question. Even if I believed you, which I don't, I'm beyond threats."

"You'll sing a different tune when the Libyans have your balls in a vise."

"But I'll have the satisfaction of knowing that your balls were there first."

Burke's genitals contracted at the thought. Kris was crazy, or he was bluffing. Burke decided to find out which. "All right, we're both in trouble. The difference is, I don't have the Big Mud and you do. This is your last chance. Either I get them what they want or I tell them you've got it and I'm out of the picture."

"The price is still Fairoaks."

He shook his head. "You just don't know who you're dealing with."

"Neither do you."

Burke stood up. "I almost pity you, Kris." He walked out of the Willard Room without looking back, but in the lobby he slowed his pace to give Kris a chance to catch up. He reached the door and stepped outside. Still no Kris.

"Cab, sir?"

Burke shook his head. "I'm waiting for someone."

Kris wasn't coming. The son of a bitch knew too much, had read him too well, had called his bluff. He glanced at his watch. With every passing minute the death threat came closer. Sick at the thought of giving up Fairoaks, he returned to the Willard Room, where he found Kris eating his goddamn eggs Benedict.

"I just talked to my people," Burke said. "They'll reimburse me so . . . all right, you've got a deal."

Kris didn't even bother to acknowledge the obvious capitulation. "At two o'clock this afternoon, you and your lawyer will appear at the Fairfax branch of First Virginia Federal. The manager will—"

"Wait, I don't know if my lawyer can make it on such short notice."

"Mr. Rosen has already agreed to be there."

"You talked to him?"

"I told him I was leaving the country tomorrow. He became very accommodating when I mentioned the premium I was willing to pay for his inconvenience."

There was something really weird about the man, Burke decided. The C-4 heist infuriated him, but he understood it. It was Kris' absolute assurance and apparent control of every detail that really got to him. He decided to ask Mowrer to hold back enough C-4 to put in a Federal Express envelope with John Kris' name on it.

"Eureka," Bobby Necker said when Severa called him. "You remember the ticket agent at the airport . . . Barbara? The one who saw your buddy? Well, she saw him again Saturday morning. Only this time she found out where he was going. Washington, D.C. Better yet, she found out his real name."

"Who is he?"

"Donald Minkin."

For a moment, nothing. Then the name exploded in his memory. Minkin. Vietnam. Epstein's death, Minkin's cowardice, the grenade tossed into the hooch—but Minkin was dead. Could this John Kris be his father? Too young. Maybe a brother or a relative, somebody who had discovered what no one but that kid knew, the soldier who tried to blow the whistle on him . . . Johnson . . . That was his name, *Keith Johnson . . . John Kris . . .* The two names crisscrossed in his mind and then merged into one. Except Johnson had died in a chopper crash. There were witnesses. He remembered when Lieutenant Burke told him the news. But he hadn't *seen* the explosion. Had Johnson somehow escaped . . . ?

In his mind he stripped John Kris of the beard, the years, the bulk, and there it was, there emerged the vague outline of a face dimly remembered from the past. *John Kris was Keith Johnson.* Somehow he had survived the crash and come back, come back to kill him. But why? Because of Minkin? Had they been such buddies? No. The gear inspection. The heroin in the knife handle. That was it. Johnson didn't realize that Westcott and Burke—or did he? Was that why he went to Washington? Sure . . . *he was after all three of them . . .*

Severa reached for the phone, paused. What did he owe Westcott or Burke? If they were in trouble, so much the better. They would be the bait that would draw Johnson out of hiding. Severa smiled. At least the ghost had been given a name, a face—and a motive.

"You made a mistake, my friend," he said softly. "You made me the enemy."

He went to the gun cabinet and pulled out a Mauser 66SP Match Rifle, a weapon whose boxy silhouette belied its accuracy. Severa had won eight national sharpshooting matches with the Mauser. It was a bolt-action rifle with a three-shot magazine and an adjustable trigger, made for accuracy rather than rapid fire. Fitted with a Schmidt & Bender 1.5-6 × 42 sniper scope, he could hit a three-inch target at two thousand feet.

Severa put the rifle in its reinforced shipping case and tucked the Deutonics pistol in beside it. Then he called American Airlines and ordered a ticket to Washington. It was time to finish what should have been finished in Nam. When the agent asked him the name of the party traveling, he smiled and said, "Donald Minkin."

The hunter had become the hunted.

CHAPTER 31

First Virginia Federal Bank occupied a gracious brick building in downtown Fairfax. Burke arrived with his lawyer, Neil Rosen, a wiry, dark-haired man with the fastidious manner of a cat. Dianne Nash, the manager of the bank, led them to the conference room, where a painting of the bank's founder stared down on an oval table of bleached wood and matching chairs with purple upholstery. When he entered the room Burke stopped in surprise: Leanne, wearing a pale blue dress, sat beside Edwin Graybar, an avuncular silver-haired lawyer who for years had handled the legal affairs of the Morrison family until Burke replaced him with Neil Rosen.

"Leanne? What are you doing here?"

John Kris, seated at the head of the table, stood up. "I asked Miss Morrison to be here. She'll be part of this transaction."

"That was unnecessary," Neil Rosen said. "Fairoaks is solely in Mr. Burke's name."

"That's what we're here to remedy."

Burke frowned. "What do you mean, remedy? What's going on?"

"You're going to sell Fairoaks to me and I'm going to pay off the mortgage and assign title to your wife in exchange for life-time riding privileges."

"For *what?*"

"A horse to ride any time I want to go fox hunting. My favorite sport."

"Oh no, this won't work, the two of you, I see it now . . ."

"Is there some problem here?" Dianne Nash asked.

"The two of them, they stole some property of mine and now they're trying to blackmail me into giving up Fairoaks to get it back. I see it now."

"You see nothing," Kris snapped. "This is the second time I've met your wife. The first was at the hunt breakfast and she ordered me off the property when I asked about your business affairs. It was only after I talked to Mr. Graybar that she agreed to come to this meeting. Miss Morrison doesn't trust me any more than you do."

"Then why are you giving her Fairoaks?"

"I don't give a damn who gets Fairoaks as long as *you* don't have it. Clear?"

Burke blinked in surprise, taken aback by Kris' naked hostility.

"I don't know what's going on here," Dianne Nash said, "but if this transaction is some form of blackmail, the bank will not be involved."

"In that case I'll find another buyer for my merchandise." Kris started toward the door.

"Wait, wait," Burke called after him. "Okay, okay . . . we have a deal."

The undertone of tension remained as the lawyers brought various documents from their briefcases and copies were passed around. Fairoaks was being sold "for value received," without specifying what it was. Tight-lipped, Burke signed the papers which stripped him of the estate he considered his own. Kris gave him an envelope that he opened, and when he saw the address, thought he'd been tricked again.

"What is this? You're telling me Mowrer still has the shipment?"

"Look again. It's the same street but three blocks away."

◀ 241

Burke excused himself, left the bank and went immediately to a pay phone, from which he called Nelson Mowrer with the address of the shipment and then waited impatiently for the return call confirming that it was there.

"All but the one can they sent to me," Mowrer reported.

"Okay, now listen. I've got the plane and pilot—the same guys as before. This time we load out of L.A. so all you have to do is get the stuff to the South Terminal by midnight tonight."

"Not L.A., Jerry. Dallas is better."

"We don't have time for Dallas. I want the stuff on that plane tomorrow morning."

"There's not much oil drilling equipment shipped out of L.A. We want it to look like a normal shipment so we ship it normal routes, normal channels."

"I don't have time for normal routes, normal channels. I've got my balls in a vice with the ragheads. They want to start blowing up enemies and they want the Big Mud yesterday—"

"L.A.'s too dangerous."

"Why should it be dangerous? What the fuck did we spend weeks repacking if it can't pass inspection? You think the customs guy is going to open the cans and check? You think he's going to know the difference between Big Mud and Bentonite? It's all silly putty, Mowrer, it all looks the same. You get the stuff to LAX, I'll do the rest."

"No, I don't want to take the chance."

"You should have thought of that before you took the money."

"Don't pressure me, Jerry. I came through with my part of the bargain. The shipment was complete when it left the gate."

"And got how far? Three blocks? You owe me, buddy."

"The leak came from your end. If you want my help, you wait a few weeks and run it through Dallas."

"We go tomorrow."

"Then count me out."

"No, I'm counting you in. If that load doesn't make T-ville tomorrow, I'm a dead man. Anything happens to me, I've got a full confession, including phone calls I taped in case you tried something like this. *All* our phone calls, buddy, you and me. Three copies of everything, one to the ATF, one to FBI and one

242 ▶

to the Attorney General's office. You think it's dangerous shipping through LAX, let me tell you something—it's your ass if you don't. So you make sure the Big Mud gets to the South Terminal and onto that plane when it arrives at six tomorrow morning or we both go down, you got it? Whatever happens to me is going to happen to you."

He slammed the phone down. The whole fucking world was against him—John Kris, Major Hasnid, Leanne, and now Mowrer. He banged the receiver as hard as he could against its cradle, again and again until it broke. He left it hanging. As he stepped out of the booth a woman moved back in alarm. "Out of order," Burke snarled.

Walking away, she gave him the finger. Burke laughed. He felt a little better now.

While Burke called Nelson Mowrer, the others completed the transfer of Fairoaks from John Kris to Leanne Morrison Burke. When they were finished, Leanne and her attorney accompanied Kris to the lobby of the bank, where Leanne said, "I must thank you for what you've done today, Mr. Kris. I only wish I trusted your motives as much as I appreciate the consequences of them."

"It's a wise idea to trust no one's motives, Miss Morrison."

"Why do you call me that?"

"For the same reason I return Fairoaks to you—I don't accept *anything* Jerry Burke has done during the past twenty years."

"Twenty years? Why twenty years?"

"Ask me again in twenty days."

"You certainly are one for mysteries."

"I need them. Remember, Miss Morrison, I can return Fairoaks to you but I can't keep you from making the same mistake again. By the way, keep a saddle for me. I may actually want to go fox hunting someday."

Watching him leave, Leanne said to Graybar, "That man has the saddest eyes of anyone I've ever known."

"Don't trust him, Leanne."

"Edwin, do you think I've taken leave of my senses?"

"When it comes to mysterious strangers, your senses have been known to take a vacation. The expression on your face a moment ago reminded me of the way you used to look at Jerry."

"And you warned me then, too, didn't you?"

"I tried."

She patted his arm. "All right, I've learned my lesson. If I'm to be a lonely old spinster, so be it."

"That's not likely. You're too much woman to live alone, if you don't mind me saying so."

He said it quickly and with conviction. Edwin Graybar's wife had died three years before, and Leanne suddenly saw him not as a fatherly friend but as a man with his own problems and loneliness to deal with. Her hand, which had been resting on his arm, assumed an awkward intimacy. She moved it and patted her hair. "Well, I thank you for that, Edwin."

Graybar cleared his throat. "Do you want me to be there when you ask for the divorce?"

She shook her head. "No, if I'm ever going to grow up, the time is now."

Among the messages waiting for Alex Wescott when he returned from lunch was one from Gail. Normally he would have been happy to hear from her but after their recent conversation he worried that the Jerry Burke story was about to break. He hoped Burke had taken his warning. While he scanned the day's mail his secretary got Gail on the line and transferred the call to him.

"Sorry to bother you, but I have one quick question . . . when you were in Vietnam did you know a soldier named Donald Minkin?"

He was instantly alert. "Sounds familiar, Duchess. What did Burke say about him?"

"I haven't talked to Burke. Was Minkin in the same platoon with you and Keith?"

"That's right. How'd you know?"

"I had a tip that Jerry Burke somehow betrayed Minkin but I couldn't come up with anything until this morning when I remembered where I'd seen the name before—it's on the Vietnam memorial, a few places above Keith's. So I put two and two together and figured if Burke betrayed him, he was probably in the platoon. Do you remember how he died?"

"A booby trap, I think. I didn't really know him."

"Were he and Burke enemies? Did they ever argue? Was there something between them?"

"I have no idea, Duchess. I was in the hospital part of the time and Minkin died not long after I rejoined the platoon. Is this something you're going to ask Burke about?"

"Not until I know a lot more than I do now. If you remember anything else, I know you're busy, but . . ."

"I'll let you know."

"Thanks. And congratulations on the Harris poll."

"What?"

"You're up two points. Talk to you later."

"Wait. Where'd it come from, that . . . tip about Donald Minkin?"

"My benefactor."

"Who?"

"Mr. Kris. I told you about him. The man who set up the Giscard Fellowship. I think he knows more about Burke than he's telling."

"Was he in Vietnam?"

"Not according to army records. Maybe he's a relative of Minkin's, I don't know yet."

"You want me to call him?"

"What for?"

"Maybe I can find out something. After all, I was over there, I knew Minkin."

"No, that's all right."

"I'd like to talk to him."

"Dad, it's my story, okay? Just let me handle it. I'll be in touch."

They said goodbye and Alex looked down at the word he had scribbled in the margin of the letter he was about to read. *Minkin.* He blackened the name and called Tony Mahue at the *Herald,* who gave him Kris' phone number. He called Kris at the Willard Hotel. The switchboard patched him through. "Yes?"

"Mr. John Kris?"

"Speaking."

"This is Senator Alexander Wescott. My daughter, Gail, is the recipient of the fellowship you set up."

"Your step-daughter, as I understand it."

Alex was surprised that Gail had made this distinction to Kris. "Technically speaking, yes. She was adopted at an early age . . . The reason I called is that Gail says you knew a boy—a soldier—named Donald Minkin."

"That's right."

"So did I. He was in my platoon in Vietnam." Alex waited but there was no response. "Are you related to Don Minkin?"

"I'm sure that Gail will tell you the answer as soon as she knows it."

"But you won't?"

"I will, but not over the phone. If you're interested in talking about Donald Minkin you can meet me at the Vietnam War Memorial. I'll be there at six this evening to lay a commemorative wreath."

"Wait a minute, why don't we meet for a drink, say the Yale Club at five-thirty?"

"I don't drink, senator. The War Memorial at six, in front of Donald Minkin's name. I'll be wearing a white carnation in my lapel."

Keith hung up without waiting for a response. Events were moving more quickly now than he'd anticipated. He waited a moment to see if Alex would call back and smiled when the phone kept silent. Alex was worried. Good. He would be at the memorial. A glance at his watch told Keith that he had two hours to get ready. He called Prem at the surveillance room across from Burke's office.

"How's our boy doing?"

"Very busy this afternoon with calling to lawyers and art dealers. He is trying to sell many of these artifacts in his inventory."

"All right, let machines monitor him for a while. I'm going to need you this evening." And Keith gave Prem a list of equipment to pick up. Then he went to a barber shop and got a haircut and a shave. When the steaming towel was lifted and the barber turned him to the mirror, Keith saw a face he hadn't seen in twenty years. The cheeks were lean now that he remembered as full, the skin was white instead of bronze, and a faint scar tugged at his lip and traced a jagged pattern across his cheek, a legacy of the long-ago beating in the garment factory.

A fierce joy gripped him. The time of John Kris was at an end; it was time for Keith Johnson to step out of the shadows and into the sunlight. He felt lightheaded and strong at the same time.

He was ready for confrontation.

CHAPTER 32

Alex arrived by taxi five minutes before the appointed time. As he approached the memorial his eyes scanned the crowd for a man wearing a white carnation. There were families and tourists and Vietnam veterans looking at the long long list of names. A young man with a video camera was filming a framed photograph at the base of the wall. Alex continued toward the panel Donald Minkin's name was engraved on and saw a man in army fatigues place a wreath on the ground. Coincidence, he thought. And then the man turned, and for a moment it was almost like he saw Gail's face, altered but strikingly similar, before he noticed the white flower tucked into the row of ribbons. "Mr. Kris?"

"Wrong, Alex."

Now the face shifted, blurred, no longer Gail's but the man who still haunted his nightmares . . . He stepped back, a cry strangled in his throat.

"That's right, *old son.*"

"*Keith? . . . Johnson?*"

"You remembered the name."

"You're *alive?*"

"No thanks to you."

"But the Huey . . . The report said no survivors—"

"I was knocked out of the chopper before it crashed. I spent three months walking to North Vietnam and twenty years digging my way out of prison with my fingernails. Thanks to you, old son."

Now Alex looked like the ghost. A dozen different emotions played across his features.

"Whatever you say," Keith said, "don't deny what you did. Don't tell me now you didn't substitute Chris' photograph with that heroin—"

"Keith, I—" He glanced around, lowered his voice. "I swear to God, I never meant for it to happen, I never meant to hurt you—"

"Just a practical joke?"

"No, no I . . . let's go somewhere were we can talk—"

"We can talk here, in front of Minkin, in front of Johnson."

Alex looked at the two names and saw himself and Keith reflected in the polished surface like black ghosts. He shook his head. The glib senator had no words.

"It won't matter, whatever you say."

Alex looked at him. "I owe you, Keith, God knows I owe you . . . I realize nothing can make up for your . . . for what happened to you, but if it helps at all, believe me when I tell you there hasn't been a single moment of a single day during the last twenty years that I haven't carried the burden of what happened at Chim Bai—"

"Must have made the honeymoon a real ordeal."

"That . . . Chris and I, it just happened, Keith. When I got back to the States I felt awful. I at least wanted to help Chris and we just . . . well, neither one of us planned it. I know it seems unfair but—"

"Unfair?"

"I'm just trying to tell you that there was no intent, no planning that it would turn out this way—"

"The heroin. Why?"

Alex looked away. "You know why."

"Tell me."

"I was a kid, we all were kids. I was stupid, scared. It's no excuse but it's the truth. Severa knew I was scared. He smelled the fear on me that first day when he made me lie down in the body bag. He was out to get me. Look what he did to Minkin. I had to get out of that platoon, Keith, I had to get a transfer. I told you but you wouldn't listen. And then when Severa killed Minkin I saw the leverage, except you wouldn't use it. Remember? I was sure I would die if I didn't get out of there."

"So you planted the heroin."

"That was Burke's idea. Christ, I was weak and scared, he insisted on it. He figured nobody would believe anything you said if you'd been busted for dope. And I told myself all that would happen to you was a little disciplinary action, Article 15, a week in the stockade. I was going to make it up to you. I was going to pull some strings and get you a good billet in Saigon for the rest of your tour. Once I was safe I wouldn't have let them bury you—"

"Once you were safe . . ."

"Look, I can make it up to you now. As much as I can, anyway. Whatever you need. You still want to be a pilot I've got contacts in the airlines, the president of T.W.A. was at my house for dinner two weeks ago. Anything, just say the word."

"The word is no."

"Let me make it up to you, let me help—"

"I'm not here for your help, Alex."

Alex's eyes went to Keith's hands and he took a step back.

"I'm not going to hit you, and I don't have a gun, senator. There's no gasoline to burn you, no iron bars to break your bones, no brass knuckles to crack your jaw. I've imagined all that and more. Much more. Those fantasies kept me alive during the early years, until I realized physical pain was easy compared to what I wanted for you. No, the worst fate for you will be having the truth known. To *everybody.*"

"Oh God . . . you've told Chris?"

"No."

"Gail?"

"She'll find out on her own. She's getting closer to the truth every day."

Alex licked his lips, obviously shifting gears. From contrition to the offensive. "Well that's . . . that's a little shortsighted, don't you think? I mean, when it comes down to it, Keith, it's my word against yours—a United States senator's against a man who's prison ordeal is enough to unbalance even the strongest mind. Don't forget, Burke will back me up, not to mention other witnesses—the men in the platoon—who will testify that you *were* discovered with heroin. Think about it, Keith. It would be more . . . productive for all of us to concentrate on the future and let the past be the past."

"Except for one thing, Alex. *Your* past cost me twenty years of my life, years in which I thought about this moment a thousand times and imagined a thousand different reactions, including this one. That's why I'm wired for sound." He pulled the carnation aside to reveal a tiny microphone. "And that's why my cameraman over there has recorded this conversation on videotape. Wave to the senator, Prem."

Alex turned abruptly. The man he had noticed earlier with a videocamera waved. Alex instinctively put his hand up. Too late. Keith had positioned him so that while they talked the camera had a full view of his face. He turned his back to the camera.

"Uncomfortable, old son?"

"You're going to ruin me—"

"The truth of you is going to ruin you, Alex. Everything you've built, loved and worked for the last twenty years—you're going to lose it *all.*"

"Don't do this to me, please—"

"You built your house on my grave, Alex, your life based on my death. Now pay the price of betrayal." He turned and walked away. Alex ran after him, grabbed hold of his arm. "Wait, we'll work something out . . ." He stepped back at the expression on Keith's face.

"Touch me again and I'll break your hand."

"Keith, believe me, I've . . . I've been a good father, a good husband . . ."

The cameraman joined Keith. Neither of them looked back.

For Jerry Burke, Fairoaks was, as it had been from the start, substance and symbol of his *place* in the world that had put him down most of his life. It spoke of his worth, at least to him, and he was determined to get it back, *had* to get it back . . .

He arrived that evening with a huge bouquet of roses. Leanne was in the living room reviewing a shopping list with Maggie, the cook, a short, heavy woman in her late sixties who wore thick-soled white support shoes and kept her hair tucked in a bun. She and Lucas, her husband, were live-in domestics at Fairoaks. Each Wednesday they drove to Warrenton, where they attended a "movie matinee" and did the shopping for the coming week. They had been with the Morrison family since Leanne was born.

Burke presented the roses and said, "Congratulations on your coup this afternoon."

Leanne scarcely reacted but Maggie was delighted. "Now here's a sight would make a bulldog smile. Let's find these children some water and a fancy vase." Holding the bouquet like a baby, she left the room. Leanne stayed on the couch.

"So, you've got Fairoaks. That's good," Burke said.

"Is it, Jerry?"

"Keeps it in the family, although I've got to admit, I still don't understand why Kris would do something like that."

"I am not sleeping with him, if that's what you're suggesting." She stood and went to the fireplace.

"You're a little prickly this evening . . ."

"You were about to sell Fairoaks without even telling me."

"No, now that's where you're wrong. You don't know what's going on, honey." He moved toward her. "This John Kris is a thief, he flat out stole something of mine—merchandise that other people have already bought and paid for—and Fairoaks was the price of getting it back. It was blackmail but I'd already talked with Neil Rosen about suing to void the contract on the grounds that it was signed under duress. I had a plan to get it back, you see?"

"Do you still intend to sue?"

"Well, we don't need to now, do we? After all, it's still in the family." He touched her arm but she moved away. "Leanne, you really don't understand what's going on . . . The people I'm dealing with can be very dangerous."

"Then you must be very brave or very foolish."

"I was doing it for us, for Fairoaks—"

"You know, Jerry, there was a time when I would have believed you. I don't know if that thought amazes me or saddens me."

"What's gotten into you? Have you been drinking?"

"Yes, I'm drunk on independence, on the feeling that I can exist on my own. A very heady feeling, I assure you. After all these years of waiting for your approval or disapproval, waiting to find out when you were coming home, trying to make everything comfortable and pleasant for you . . . all these years living in a mirror, seeing myself only through other people's eyes, first daddy's, then yours. I think this is the first time in my life I'm looking at myself through my own eyes. It's not a perfect picture, but at least it's me, and I don't need to worry if it's not going to please somebody. I've run out of pleasing people, Jerry. Even you. Especially you."

"Is this confessional leading somewhere?"

She looked at him. "Yes. To a divorce."

It was a kick in the stomach. She seemed to have changed in a single day from the insecure, acquiescent woman he'd known to a selfish blue-blood bitch . . . "And where did this idea come from?"

"Jerry, you don't love me, I don't know if you ever did."

"Don't say that, honey. Maybe I've been preoccupied recently—"

"*Don't*, Jerry. Don't insult me or demean yourself with lies."

From the dining room came the sound of the dinner bell. Burke ignored it. "You think I'm lying? Fine, you've got all the answers. What do you want me to do? Move out so John Kris can move in?"

"That's not it and you know it."

"What I know is that Kris gave you Fairoaks. Now why would he do that if you're not screwing him—?"

She winced. "I believe he hates your guts—"

"Why? I've only met the man twice in my life."

"Perhaps you should ask him that."

"Perhaps I should ask him if he likes the way your toes twitch when you come."

She pointed her finger at him. "That's why, Jerry. Why I want a divorce. Not just because you've been unfaithful . . . but you're so selfish and *unkind.* Because you don't love me and I don't love you. I can't even care for you any longer. You destroyed any chance of that when you raped me—"

"What rape? What are you talking—"

"Out at the quarry. You hit me and raped me."

"I'm your husband, it's not rape—"

"It *was.*"

"Fuck your feminist shit. Besides, that happened weeks ago, this divorce thing came up *today,* and only after Mr. Mysterious Sugar Daddy handed you Fairoaks on a silver platter. Otherwise you'd still be on your knees with your mouth on my cock and your fingers so far up my ass I could talk sign language—"

She started toward the door, body rigid.

"You want the truth, look at the truth." Burke yelled. "Where were all these big deal declarations of freedom yesterday or the day before or the day before that or last week or last year? No, I was good enough while I was pumping money into this place, but now that Fairoaks is in A-1 mint condition I can go fuck myself."

She paused. "All right, Jerry, I've been weak. I admit it. I should have left long ago but without Fairoaks I felt I had no place to go—"

"Without me you wouldn't have Fairoaks. It's all my money. What's yours?"

"It's all mine, Jerry. You got your money back when you mortgaged Fairoaks. Now it's back where it belongs and I'll have to ask you to leave."

They faced each other from across the room, Leanne with her shoulders stiff, fingers tugging one another behind her back, Burke haggard and unshaven, the hatred in his eyes undisguised. He wanted to put his hands around her neck and squeeze until she was on her knees again—

Maggie appeared then in the doorway. "Dinner's served, Miss Leanne, Mr. Burke."

"I'm not feeling well, Maggie," Leanne said. "I'll have it in my room."

The two women left Burke alone in a room no longer his. He was actually trembling with anger. Above the mantle was a gilt-framed portrait of Leanne's great-great-grandfather in the uniform of a Confederate officer. Burke grabbed a crystal ashtray and turned to throw it, but stopped at the last moment.

Easy, easy now. He had to use his head. He wasn't going to get Fairoaks back by making an enemy of Leanne. And he couldn't sue her. In spite of what he'd said about going to court to have the contract voided, doing so would mean revealing the C-4 shipment, which would land him in jail. He had to seduce Fairoaks away from her, just as he had done before. The problem was that once burned she wasn't likely to trust him again. Plus she no longer loved him.

He pulled the bell cord, and Lucas entered. The old man greeted him and stood at attention, eyes focused at a spot just above Burke's head.

"Bring me a scotch and soda, Lucas."

"I believe dinner is served, sir."

"I'm not hungry. Just bring me a drink. Make it a double."

Lucas left. Burke stood at the window and looked out over the land. The light, he noted, was on in the barn manager's cottage. How did Leanne think she was going to pay Reed Cunningham's salary? For that matter, how would she pay the taxes, the insurance, the maintenance, the upkeep? She couldn't get along without him. As soon as his checks weren't there to pay the bills she'd come crawling back . . .

Unless she found a new husband.

Kris. If he and Leanne weren't already lovers, they soon would be. Fairoaks was the biggest box of candy Kris could have given her. If she fucked him from now until the turn of the century she'd still owe him. And if there was a divorce, he would never get Fairoaks back.

Lucas brought the scotch and soda on a silver tray. "Will you be wanting me to pick up anything in Warrenton, Mr. Burke?"

"No."

"Maggie's keeping the supper warm in case you get hungry."

"Thank you, Lucas."

Surprised, the old man momentarily dropped his eyes to

Burke's. "Why yes sir," he said. "And a pleasant evening to you." And he left, wondering at Mr. Burke's sudden change in attitude.

Burke sat on the couch and kicked off his shoes. Warrenton. Maggie and Lucas were going to Warrenton tomorrow. Only Reed Cunningham would be here. Unless he had somewhere to go, something to do tomorrow afternoon. In which case, Leanne would be alone.

The drink helped him begin to imagine all kinds of terrible things he knew he couldn't do sober. Exhausted, he fell asleep and didn't wake up until nine-thirty the next morning, when a phone call from Nelson Mowrer wiped all thoughts of Leanne and Fairoaks from his mind.

Customs agents and police were waiting at the airport. The C-4 load was busted. And Jerry Burke was a dead man.

CHAPTER 33

Alex Wescott spent a long night hunting for the courage to kill himself. He canceled a campaign staff meeting and returned home, where, except for the housekeeper, he was alone. Gail had her own apartment, Chris was in Boston at an Amnesty International symposium, the two boys had left boarding school and were with Alex's parents in Connecticut for the Easter weekend. He was supposed to join them on Saturday but the thought of facing his family made him sick.

He went to his office, where he paced the floor, thoughts running like rats up one tunnel and down another. He considered a dozen possible courses of action. He would deny everything, claim the tape was false, a fake, sue Keith. He would call a press conference, confess everything and resign. He would tell only Chris, beg her forgiveness and ask her to intervene. He would kill himself. He would kill Keith.

He went downstairs and poured himself a shot of Jack Daniels, downed it, poured another. The more he drank, the more unfair it all seemed . . . a youthful mistake ruining his life now at the peak of his career. Taking the bottle with him, he made his way to the bedroom, where he put on his old uniform and stood in front of a mirror. Keith had looked hard and all business in his uniform, but the man Alex saw in the mirror looked like he was wearing a costume. A fake. But he couldn't stand the thought of facing the truth. Chris would leave him, Gail would hate him and the boys would despise him. He would lose everything—the election, his seat in the Senate, his wife, his children . . .

He returned to his study and took a chrome-plated custom-engraved Smith & Wesson .38 Police Special from a wall safe. The gun had been presented to him by the Hartford Police Benevolent Association in recognition of his support of tougher penalties for cop-killers. He hefted it and sighted at the door. He imagined Keith opening the door, the look of surprise before Alex pulled the trigger. He would have to disguise himself, wear a wig, wear gloves to avoid fingerprints and destroy the gun afterward . . .

The imaginary scenario collapsed. He was afraid of Keith. The son of a bitch seemed immortal, an avenging ghost. And what about the cameraman? How many others were involved with Keith's plot? How many others knew? How many copies of the videotape were there?

Only one solution: kill himself. Alive he would be despised, dead at least he would become a martyr, victim of a bloodthirsty, vengeful, Keith Johnson. His suicide would turn the tables. Shaken yet exalted by this booze-enhanced vision, Alex composed a letter on his IBM computer. He adopted the elegiac, melancholy tone of a man too long burdened by a secret shame. He wrote that his life of public service had been motivated by his desire to make up for what he had done in Chim Bai. He prayed that his children would be absolved of their father's sin and that his family would understand and forgive him.

When he was done he printed the letter on stationery embossed with his initials in silver letters, slipped it into an envelope, addressed it to Chris, Gail, Nick, and Bobby. He gathered photographs of the family, arranged them in a semicircle on his desk, and kissed each one. He loaded the gun slowly, aware of himself as if watching from a great distance. Tears flowed. With trembling hands he put the barrel of the gun into his mouth, flinched at the touch of cold metal. The thought of the bullet ripping through his upper palate, breaking the skull and disgorging a wet, mutilated brain tissue made him shudder.

He put the gun down and sat there shaking, his skin clammy with sweat. He went unsteadily downstairs and returned with a bottle of Johnny Walker Red. Half an hour later, his mind reeling from liquor and recrimination, he decided to let God decide. He removed every other bullet from the cylinder, giving himself a fifty-fifty chance of survival. Perhaps God would take pity on him. He took a deep breath, spun the cylinder, and again placed the barrel in his mouth. As he did so he could not help noticing through the crack between the cylinder and the frame the sharp gleam of brass, the metal casing of the bullet in the chamber which would rotate into position as soon as he cocked the trigger.

He slammed the gun back onto the desk. He could not do it if he knew the outcome. Next time he would close his eyes. He set arbitrary deadlines—when the clock reached three, then four, then five—and each time his nerve failed him.

Dawn caught up to him. Emotionally drained, dizzy from drinking, he stared at the outline of trees against a lightening sky. A night of deadlines had slipped past and he hadn't found the courage to pull the trigger. Now reckless with genuine self-disgust, he downed the remainder of the whiskey, raising the bottle overhead, sending it spilling over his chin and into his eyes, where it burned.

"Coward," he whispered. He grabbed the gun, shut his eyes and as the coward inside him screamed in terror, jammed it into his mouth and pulled the trigger.

Although he had been expecting it, the frantic knocking at the door made Keith start. Outside he could hear Burke's voice. "I know you're in there, Kris. I know you're there."

No, Keith thought. Not John Kris anymore. He opened the door to a Jerry Burke who blinked in confusion when he saw Keith without a beard. He quickly looked past him. "Where's John Kris?"

"Gone."

Burke recognized the voice. "*You* . . . you tipped off customs. You told them—"

"That's right."

"You admit it."

"I *planned* it from the beginning."

"Why? *Why?*" Obviously, even without the beard Burke didn't recognize Keith.

"Come on in, lieutenant. And close the door."

As Keith crossed the room he kept an eye on Burke in the mirror. He didn't know if the man was armed but if he was, this was the way he would do it, from behind, where he didn't have to face a man, eye-to-eye.

Burke stepped inside and looked around. The chairs and coffee table had been moved against the wall and an army cot, stretched canvas over a wood frame, sat in the middle of the room. A set of camouflage clothing lay neatly folded on top of a wool blanket stretched tight over an air mattress. Keith said, "You look a little edgy, lieutenant. How about a beer?"

"Fuck your beer. You blew the whistle on that shipment—"

"That's affirmative."

"But why? We had a deal—"

"Haven't you figured it out, lieutenant?"

"Stop calling me that. I'm not a fucking lieutenant."

"You were in Chim Bai."

Burke's expression slowly changed. He eyed Keith. "Do I know you from the army?"

"I don't know. Do you?"

Keith held out a beer, a Xien Lo, a Vietnamese brand. Burke stared at it, then over to the cot. "What's all that?"

"Gear inspection, lieutenant. Junk on the bunk. You remember how it goes."

"What the hell are you, some kind of Vietnam nut?"

"I'm your past, lieutenant. And your future. Don't you recognize me? We were in Chim Bai when you made a decision with a terrible consequence. I'm your consequence, your worst nightmare come to life. And you don't recognize me."

Burke had been backing away. Now he jumped as his leg struck the edge of the cot. He glanced down, saw a survival knife and grabbed it. "Keep your distance."

"You can't kill a man twice, lieutenant. Didn't they teach you that in R.O.T.C.?"

"What the hell are you talking about? Who are you?"

"You've got the answer in your hands. Unscrew the top, let's see what's inside. Maybe a photograph of somebody's wife, maybe a relic from a Buddhist temple, maybe heroin . . . But you already know, don't you, lieutenant? You know it's heroin because you put it there."

Burke's eyes widened. "You . . . you can't be . . ."

"Oh, yes. I can. I am."

Burke's mouth moved, no words came out.

"You built your life on my bones, lieutenant. Now everything you built is mine."

". . . *Johnson?*"

"Am I still under arrest, lieutenant?"

"It's *you?*"

"Shall I go to the command bunker and wait for a chopper?"

"The chopper . . . it went down . . ."

"I wasn't on it."

". . . but . . ."

Keith stepped to the left and grabbed Burke's wrist with his left hand. At the same time, he slammed his right palm against his knuckles, snapping the fingers open, knocking the knife free. As Burke raised his hands to defend himself, Keith yanked his jacket down around his elbows, pinning his arms.

"Sit down, lieutenant."

He shoved him back into the cot, which overturned and sent him sprawling to the floor. Keith scooped up the knife, a moment later had it at Burke's throat.

"You armed, lieutenant?"

"No, no, don't—"

"I'm not going to kill you, lieutenant. Unless you make me."

Burke stopped moving but kept talking as Keith checked for weapons. "No, I—listen, people know I'm here. I told my secretary, I told my lawyer, my wife, they'll find you if anything happens. They'll tell the police."

Keith stood up and moved away. "On your feet."

"Take it easy, take it easy, we can work this out." He got up, keeping his eye on Keith. "So . . . you made it back. That's great, that's really great . . ."

CRUX

"I can see you're thrilled to death," Keith said, blocking the door. Burke began edging toward the far end of the room.

"That's the bedroom," Keith told him. "You go in there and I'll stuff a pillow in your face. That door's the bathroom. Go in there and I'll drown you in the toilet. Out the window it's a five-second drop to Pennsylvania Avenue. The only way out is behind me."

Burke opened his mouth, then shut it. In a low voice he said, "What are you going to do?"

"You owe me twenty years of darkness. Everything you got while I was in prison is forfeit. I'm going to strip you of everything you value, everything you want, have wanted. From this point on, even if you survive your Libyan pals, every plan will fail, every dream will die, every hope vanish before your eyes. You are screwed, lieutenant, and now you know why."

"No, listen, what happened in Chim Bai, that was an accident. Jesus . . . nobody knew that chopper would go down. But this . . . that C-4 shipment was bought and paid for. It doesn't belong to me, I told you that yesterday. It belongs to the Libyans, and if they don't get their money back—one point five million— they're sending a hit team. These people are crazy. They'll kill us *both*."

"But you first."

"For God's sake, man, what do you *want?* You want an apology? All right, I'm on my hands and knees. But you've got to help me to help yourself now. Give me the money and we'll go into business. That's it, that's fair. Every desert kingdom and coconut empire in the world is on the warpath and they all want guns, explosives, missiles, the latest technology. This C-4 deal is peanuts. Once we get going you'll have anything you want, the best hotels, the most beautiful women, five-star restaurants, a château on the Riviera, you name it. The one point five, that'll be your investment. You'll live like a king the rest of your life, I guarantee it. Come on, man, what do you say?"

Keith stepped away from the door. "Goodbye, lieutenant."

"You'd let them kill me? A bunch of crazy Arabs?"

"Why not?"

"Johnson, I'm begging you—what do I have to do to make you understand?"

"Pee in your pants."

"What?"

"I want you to pee in your pants. Maybe then I'll loan you the one point five."

Burke's smile twitched. "Hey, come on."

"Goodbye, lieutenant."

Burke moved to the door, hesitated. "You . . . are you serious? If I piss my pants . . . ?"

"One point five million to show your true colors."

"Right here?"

Keith glanced at the floor. "Step into the hall so you don't ruin the rug." He opened the door.

"You're really serious?"

"You know I am."

"Okay, okay." Burke stepped outside and glanced up and down the hallway. It was empty. Keith folded his arms and watched.

"Can you get the money right away? By tomorrow?"

"Whenever you want it."

"Okay, then, this'll make up for—"

Keith glanced at his watch. "I'm expecting a call . . ."

"Yeah, okay." A sick look came over Burke's face and his eyes wrinkled in concentration. After a moment, his lips bent in a nervous smile. "Harder than you think."

Keith said nothing. Burke cringed as his pants dampened and a dark stain seeped slowly down his legs.

"Okay," Burke said. "I did it. Noon tomorrow, okay?"

"Don't bother."

"What?"

"I wouldn't give a nickel to a man who pees in his pants."

Keith slammed the door in his face, then stood and listened to the stream of obscenities that erupted in the hallway.

CHAPTER 34

Chris ate breakfast in the hotel dining room with other members of the Amnesty International symposium. When she went back to her room for a sweater the message light on her phone was blinking. Budge Tickman had called and left an urgent message that she call back as soon as possible. Budge was Alex's campaign manager, and the number he left surprised her: it was her own. A vague premonition gripped her and she found herself twisting her hair nervously as she waited for someone to answer.

"Wescott residence."

"Irene, it's me."

Irene was their housekeeper. As soon as she heard Chris, her professional demeanor disappeared. "Mrs. Wescott, it's terrible. I heard the noise and I came inside and saw him at the bottom of the stairs. I called the doctor and then—wait a minute, here's Mr. Tickman."

"Irene, is Alex all right?"

A man's voice came on the line. "Chris?"

"Budge, what happened? Where's Alex?"

"An accident, Chris. Fell down the stairs this morning. Doc Lambert has him in bed but it I think we need you back here."

"Is he all right? Can I talk to him?"

"He's asleep now." Budge's voice lowered. "Actually, he passed out. Last night he cancelled a staff meeting and from the looks of things here, he spent all night drinking. Apparently that's why he fell down the stairs."

Chris found her voice lowering to match his. "You mean he's drunk?"

"About three whisky bottles worth of drunk. Irene called the doc before anybody else so I think we're in the clear on newspapers. Lee's canceling his appointments and the official word is a mild case of food poisoning. Doc'll go along with it."

"What happened last night?"

"I thought maybe you'd know."

"No, I don't. Alex has never been that much of a drinker, I can't imagine why . . ."

"Has he seemed depressed to you recently?"

She hesitated. "Did something else happen?"

"Nothing else happened but . . . well, in the study, where he'd been drinking, I found a loaded gun."

"Where was the gun?"

"On his desk. And the strange thing, every other chamber is loaded. You know—a fifty-fifty chance if you pull the trigger."

"Who knows about the gun?"

"Irene might, but I got here before the doctor arrived."

"Tell Irene to say nothing. I'll talk to her when I get back. Is that everything?"

She sensed a slight hesitation. "Yeah."

"Budge?"

"He's fine, just sleeping it off. But we're going to have to make some quick decisions, you know?"

"We'll talk about it when I get there. The shuttle leaves every hour. I'll be on the next one."

When he left the Willard Hotel, Burke took the stairway rather than the elevator. His pants were damp and clammy against his crotch and legs. He took off his Pierre Cardin jacket and held it in front of him as he made his way through the lobby and waited for the valet to bring the Rolls-Royce. In his pocket were folded dollar bills he kept for tips but they were damp now so he slid into the driver's seat without offering the valet anything.

He stopped at a Woodward-Lothrop department store, where he purchased underwear and a pair of corduroy slacks. While he was paying, a mother with a little boy of about four joined the line behind him. After a moment he heard the little boy say, "Mommy look."

"Shhh."

"He made tinkles."

Burke went rigid. He imagined everyone in the store staring at him. As soon as he had his receipt he rushed to the nearest bathroom and changed clothes, leaving the underwear and slacks behind.

He reviewed his financial holdings as he drove back to the Artex office. He could raise a hundred, maybe two hundred thousand cash, but that was it. He had fifty thousand dollars tied up in Asian and African art, some of it his personal collection. He could realize twenty-five thousand if he sold the Rolls, fifteen thousand in his checking account, and from the Artex account he could pull another twenty. The Gulfstream jet and the Ennismore Gardens Mews townhouse were leased but he could sell his show hunter, Dandy Jim, for six or seven thousand. But even if he sold everything he owned, liquidated every asset, he'd be lucky to come up with a quarter million dollars.

He placed an international call to Major Hasnid. There was difficulty in getting through and a long wait before Hasnid came to the phone. Probably screwing a sheep in the backyard, Burke thought. When the Libyan came to the line, Burke launched into his explanation, coloring the facts so that Keith came out an employee of Mossad, the Israeli intelligence organization, who scuttled the shipment on orders from Tel Aviv.

"My contacts in the CIA confirm this man's association with the Mossad," Burke said. "In fact, they tell me there's a contract out on my life for all the supplies I've sent you guys. But I'm not going to be intimidated. I've got another source for your merchandise up in Canada. You work with me and we'll negotiate a rock-bottom price—I won't take a penny in commission—and we'll make up for the loss, we'll double the next load. Forty tons. You just give me some time to set things up, how's that? Is that fair?"

In the slight pause that followed while his voice bounced into space and back, the words seemed to lose their vitality and hang hollow in the air. Evidently they sounded the same way to Hasnid.

"You amaze me, Mr. Burke. Your capacity to assume ignorance in other men is limitless."

"I'm just telling you what's going on. I've got the goddam Mossad on my back, the entire state of Israel, I could use a little help. What I'm saying is, please be patient, let's be partners—"

"Unfortunately, Colonel Ibram has discovered a partner in Czechoslovakia who will supply a comparable product and for somewhat a cheaper price."

"No, that's not fair, I had your merchandise all ready to go. It's not my fault, a nut, *Keith Johnson,* tipped off the government."

"How sad that you must die for someone else's dishonesty."

"You want money? Fine, I'll give you a hundred thousand now and you give me a month to raise the rest."

"I am sorry, Mr. Burke, but our terms were clear. If you have not the merchandise, you must return one million four hundred and forty thousands of dollars by tomorrow sundown."

"Come off it. What good does it do killing me? You'll never get your money back."

"It is not the money. A single day's oil revenue brings more in earnings than the sum we are discussing. It is the principle of the transaction. You have led us like a caravan of blind camels, always moving, arriving nowhere. Now we will have satisfaction, of one form or another."

"At least bring it up to the Defense Council—"

"I no longer have my seat on the Defense Council. Thanks to your ineptitude, Colonel Ibram is the ascendant star whose course we follow and he has long wished you dead. With the loss of my high hopes I am inclined to agree."

"Yeah? Well this is America, major, not some African sandbox on a pile of petroleum. My CIA contacts know all about your death threats. So you want to take me out, you're going to have to take out the whole CIA—"

Burke slammed down the phone. He cursed Hasnid and Ibram

◀ 267

and all camel-humping raghead Arabs. They should kill Johnson, not him. He wished he'd never heard of Johnson, he wished he'd kicked Wescott out of the office that day—

Wescott. The name rang like a gong. The answer to his problem? He'd gotten money from the senator once before, and now the man had even more to lose if the truth about Chim Bai leaked out. He picked up the phone and dialed Alex Wescott's office.

Budge Tickman was there to meet her when Chris arrived home. He was a short, thin man who darted his head like a prizefighter when he spoke. Their relationship was one of mutual respect rather than friendship.

"How is he?"

"Still sleeping. The doctor left an hour ago."

He accompanied her upstairs to the bedroom where Alex lay with a small bandage on his forehead. His skin was pale and drawn, his hair matted, breathing heavy. Budge reviewed the circumstances in which he'd found Alex, gave her the gun and left. Chris had Irene make a cup of tea, then she returned to the bedroom and pulled a chair with embroidered upholstery next to the bed. When she placed a hand on Alex's forehead, his eyes opened.

"Chris?"

"How do you feel?"

He moved his head and winced. "What happened?"

"You fell down the stairs."

"I thought you were in—" He let out a groan and closed his eyes. It all came back to him, including the suicide note. Chris had read it—now she knew.

"Alex, what happened?"

For a moment she thought he had lost consciousness, then his eyes opened and he looked at her. He mumbled something unintelligible.

"What?" She leaned close.

"Are you going to leave me?"

"Why would I leave you?"

"For him."

268 ▶

"Who?"

"Keith."

He's lost his mind, she thought. Maybe a concussion. "Shhh. Try to rest."

"What about Gail? Does she know?"

"Budge called me. I haven't told the children."

Alex sat up, caught his breath. There was a plastic bucket beside the bed. He gagged, leaned over, then fell back and lay breathing deeply, his skin like wax. It seemed as though Alex had aged ten years in moments.

"Can I get you anything?"

"Do you hate me?"

"Of course not. Just rest."

"Have to tell Gail before he does."

"Before who? Doctor Lambert?"

"Keith. She has to understand."

"Alex, please, you're not making sense. What happened last night? Why did you have the pistol out?"

"Didn't you read the letter?"

"What letter?"

"*You don't know?* Oh, God . . ." He closed his eyes again.

"What letter, Alex?"

"The study, on my desk. I wrote it last night when . . ."

Chris went to find it. The sight of the family photographs arranged in a semicircle brought a reminder of what Alex had apparently intended to do. She looked through the papers and beneath a silver pencil tray but found no letter. On her way out she checked the wastebasket but it was empty. And then she saw it, lying on the floor behind the wastebasket next to the wall: a crumpled envelope. She smoothed it out, uncrumpled it, and began to read . . .

Twenty minutes later, she returned to the bedroom. Alex opened his eyes, saw her face, saw that she had read it. She knew. He closed his eyes. She crossed the room and sat on her own side of the bed, back straight, the letter clutched in her hand, her eyes vacant. The measured ticktock of a Tiffany alarm clock grew loud. In the kitchen the faint stutter of a water pipe as Irene

◀ 269

turned on a faucet. The sounds of their life together, the heart-beat of their home, attenuated, and now unreal.

After a while she said, "Where is he?"

"The Willard." Alex's voice was low, lifeless. They were silent again until he took a ragged breath. "Are you leaving me?"

"I don't know."

"Do you hate me?"

She turned to look at him and knew that he would never again look the same. "Twenty years . . ."

His mouth worked as he struggled to control himself. "I'm sorry, Chris, I'm . . ." She made no move to reach for his hand, stretched toward her across the bed. He withdrew it and after a moment, in a low voice, said, "I have to tell Gail."

"Let me talk to . . . him first."

The doorbell rang and they could hear Irene's footsteps down-stairs as she went to answer it. Alex's army tunic was lying on the bed. Chris fingered the red-and-gold Vietnam medal. Watching her, he said, "I thought, last night, I could at least finish it like a—"

A man's voice, angry, from the foyer. Then Irene calling, "You can't go up there, sir, the senator is resting, please—"

Chris reached the door as Jerry Burke appeared. Behind him came Irene. "I told him he couldn't come up here . . ."

"What do you want, Mr. Burke?"

"I'm sorry to insist, Mrs. Wescott, but I have to see the senator immediately." He tried to move into the room but Chris blocked his way.

"He's not feeling well—"

"Sorry. I have to talk to him. It's a matter of life and death, I mean it."

Alex called out, "It's all right, Chris."

She held her ground for a moment, then dismissed Irene and stood aside. Burke went into the bedroom.

"This is something that won't wait, not even twenty-four hours. If I could just have a word with you, senator. Privately."

"Anything you've got to say you can say in front of my wife—"

"No, I have to talk to you alone."

"If it's about Keith," Chris said, "I already know what happened, Mr. Burke, including the despicable part *you* played in his frame-up and betrayal. So if you've come to blackmail Alex with that particular piece of information you're too late."

Burke's eyes narrowed. "All right, great, you know already. Then you better know this. Keith Johnson screwed up a very important overseas transaction, screwed it up so bad that if I don't come up with one point five million dollars by tomorrow night the people at the other end of the line are going to kill me." He turned to Alex. "I'm a dead man, senator, and all because of *you*. It was *your* idea back in Chim Bai. You were the one who wanted a transfer. You were the one who started all the trouble, so you owe it to me to help me out of trouble now. I need a loan, I need one million five hundred thousand dollars by tomorrow, and I'd better get it—"

Alex shook his head. "It's over, Jerry. It's all out. There's no reason for us to have any more to do with each other."

Burke turned on Chris. "What about you, then? What about your children, Mrs. Wescott? Does your daughter know this man sent her real father to prison for twenty years? Do your two boys know that they're illegitimate? Do they know you're a bigamist?"

Alex said, "Shut up, Jerry."

"What about that, Mrs. Wescott? His career doesn't matter? Your family, your name? Want to wash it all down the drain?"

"I don't think people will take the word of an illegal arms dealer against a United States senator—"

"It's not just my word—*it's Keith Johnson's word.*"

"What makes you think Keith will help a man like you blackmail his former wife?" Burke looked stunned. Obviously the thought hadn't occurred to him. "Now *get out.*"

Burke felt suffocated. The walls of his life were closing in, wherever he went people turned against him. "You people think you shit roses but I've got news for you . . . whatever happens to me happens to you. Both of you. I didn't start this and I'm not going down alone. Remember *that.*"

He went down the stairs two at a time, slammed the front door open, didn't bother closing it.

"Keith won't help me," Alex said. "You know that, don't you?"

CRUX

She glanced at him, then went to the mirror and studied herself. Putting her fingers on her cheeks, she pushed back gently, tightening the skin around her nose and mouth, smoothing away the wrinkles, as though trying to imagine away the years.

CHAPTER 35

Driving back to his office Burke got the shakes. He left the high-way and pulled into the parking lot of the Burning Tree Country Club. Taped to the back of the ashtray was a small packet of cocaine. He climbed into the back seat, where the Rolls-Royce had a drop-down "picnic table." Using his American Express card, he cut and laid out the lines on the polished burl surface. What a joke, he thought. Sitting in a Rolls snorting coke through a tubed hundred dollar bill without enough money to pay the men who wanted to kill him. And dope was where it all started . . .

As the shakes disappeared, he settled back with an induced sense of well-being. He was not beaten yet. He could liquidate his assets and disappear. Maybe he would take Nexli and they could live off her money. He liked the idea of the sister of the man who wanted to kill him keeping him alive. Nexli was the only person in the world he could count on. Not like Leanne, the witch bitch of Fairoaks.

Fairoaks.

The farm was worth a million five, easy. And John Kris—*Keith Johnson*—had just paid off the mortgage. It would be perfect if he could use Johnson's money to pay back the Arabs. The terrible scenarios that he imagined the night before returned. Yes, there was a way. A way to get Fairoaks back and find the money he needed. If he could first find the courage . . .

He did two more lines of coke and then returned to the front seat, where he used the cellular telephone to call Edna O'Brien, a trainer who often boarded horses and worked with them at her own stables. He had sent Dandy Jim, his show hunter, to her once before. Now he explained that he was leaving for England right away and would like her to work with Dandy Jim while he was gone. Could she take the horse this afternoon?

Edna agreed. Burke's second call was to Fairoaks, where he arranged for Reed Cunningham to take Dandy Jim to Edna at three that afternoon. The last thing he asked was "Is Leanne home?"

"Yes, sir," Reed said. "Shall I ring her?"

"No, I'll talk to her later."

More than talk, he thought as he hung up. This time it would be more than talk.

Prem Chaduvedi had returned from Los Angeles the complete cowboy. In addition to boots and Stetson hat he wore jeans and a leather vest over a flannel shirt. His belt buckle and watch band were custom designed silver inlaid with turquoise; around his neck he wore a colorful bandanna that obscured the gold chain with its amulets, the last vestige of his Asian background. He was polishing the silver decorations on the heel and toe of his boots when Keith arrived at the observation post across from the Artex offices.

"Not arriving yet," Prem said, referring to Jerry Burke. "Much quiet in the office today."

"He's probably in a laundromat waiting for his pants to dry."

Keith filled him in on Burke's visit. Prem made a face. "This man today is *mai sanuk.*"

"He's also desperate, so stay on your toes."

"My Cochise will protect me."

He was talking about a cigar store Indian he had found the day before at an antique store on the way to Fairoaks. It was a monstrous seven-foot carved wood figure holding a cigar box and tomahawk. Keith had seen only a polaroid picture of it. The statue had been too large to fit in the Toyota Celica so today Prem was taking the Ford Aerostar, a van with plenty of room and wide loading doors.

Prem stopped at Blue Ridge Collectibles on his way to Fairoaks. The proprietor was a barnlike man who smoked continually as he helped Prem load the Indian into the truck. "A museum classic," he growled as he jammed the figure through the sliding side door. "You got a great buy, buddy."

"Careful, be careful."

The Indian's paint was peeling, his nose was chipped and the head of the tomahawk he clutched in one hand was missing. Prem knew a craftsman in Bangkok, Harka Gurung, who carved Buddhist images and could repair the missing pieces.

With the Indian lying in the van behind him, he drove to the remote site near Fairoaks to change the tape on the recorder and check the batteries. He parked on the country road that bordered the farm and hiked two hundred yards to a stone structure that had once been a curing barn for tobacco. Less than a mile away, the house and stables were visible across an undulating landscape crisscrossed with hedgerows.

Prem pushed past weathered, half-rotten wooden doors as he stepped inside. Streaks of light from a multitude of cracks between wood planks stabbed the gloom. Inside were what remained of an early tractor and a few pieces of obsolete and rusting farm machinery. He moved a crate against the wall and stood on it as he hoisted himself into the rafters. The air near the ceiling was warm and smelled of mice and creosote. When Prem lifted the tape recorder into view the tape was running and the bouncing needle told him that a conversation was in progress. In case the conversation was important, he plugged in an earphone and listened. Jerry Burke was having an argument with his wife.

"Leanne, I'm asking you in a civilized way . . ."

"Just stop. Put the papers back in your briefcase."

"All right, I'm begging you. Are you satisfied? I'm begging you, just what you always wanted."

"I never wanted you to beg—"

CRUX

"Then sign the papers, help me out. I'll give you an I.O.U. It's for your own good too."

"I can't do that."

"You mean you won't."

"Have it your own way, but I'm never giving up Fairoaks again."

Burke's voice was low and tense. "You're going to sentence me to death, is that it?"

"Aren't you being a little melodramatic?"

"No I'm not being fucking melodramatic. They're going to cut my balls off—don't you understand that?"

"I don't have to listen to this—"

"Leanne—"

A pause, then a cry of alarm. Something heavy smashed against the wall along with the sounds of a struggle. Now a woman's scream and a table overturned. Prem tore the earphone free and ran back to the car.

Burke had arrived with two plans, one to cajole the money from Leanne, the second to kill her. He began by telling her the danger he was in, giving her a chance to cooperate. He even brought her into his study and showed her some of the secret documents he kept locked in his safe, documents outlining his arms transactions with the Libyans. Leanne shook her head. "Jerry, what have you done?" she said.

But her sympathy was short-lived. Every time he urged her to mortgage Fairoaks and give him the money, she got that stubborn tilt to her chin and stopped listening. When she turned to walk out of the study, he was ready. On his desk was an ashtray made from a horse's hoof, complete with metal shoe. It was an awkward object to use as a weapon but it would inflict the kind of wound that would make Leanne's death look like an accident.

Leanne was walking away from him when he moved. At the last moment she saw him in the mirror above the fireplace and just managed to duck the blow, which glanced off her shoulder. Burke grabbed her and the ashtray fell to the floor. She screamed as they careened against the wall, but Burke knew that it was too late to turn back. He put his hands around her throat and pinned her against the wall. She flailed at him, striking him in the eye. When he grabbed her wrists she tried to lunge away. Off balance, they tripped over a magazine rack and fell to the floor amid copies of Architectural Digest. Her elbow struck him in the solar plexus and stunned him long enough for her to break free, but Burke grabbed her ankle and for a moment, neither had the advantage. Leanne hopped on one foot, trying to keep her balance, the hem of her dress brushing Burke's face. He brought his knee to his chest and kicked upward. The blow lifted her off her feet and she collapsed with a cry of pain. Burke was on her then, jamming his knee into her, knocking the wind out of her. While she gasped for breath he grabbed her hair and began slamming her head against the floor. Her lips moved, she tried to speak, and along with panic Burke saw in her eyes disbelief and then pain and pain again as he pounded her head until the eyes were no longer hers but glazed like a doll's and one canted crazily to one side.

He stopped. She was not dead, but her pulse was faint and her breathing shallow. He was afraid that Lucas and Maggie might come home early or Reed Cunningham might return. Keeping his face as far from hers as possible, he lifted her over his shoulder. He grunted as he started across the room and almost dropped her when the smack of her leather sandal falling to the floor took him by surprise. He tried to retrieve it but couldn't manage it, burdened as he was. He'd get it later.

On the porch he dumped her into a wicker chair and picked her back up in a fireman's carry. Panting with the effort, he made it to the stable, where he stumbled against the wall and sent a rake, shovel and pitchfork clattering to the ground. In one of the stalls, a horse neighed. And then another sound—a car approaching. He put her down on the straw-covered floor and moved to the doorway in time to see a car he did not recognize, a white van arrive and disappear as it parked in front of the house.

He decided to hide in the barn until whoever it was left. Most of the farms had more cars than people so it would not seem unusual that his Rolls was parked in front and Leanne's Mercedes was in the garage. Although it would have been better, he realized, had he parked out of sight. Then he could have told the police that he hadn't been home all day. As the minutes passed he became more and more agitated. How long did it take to ring the doorbell a couple of times? What was going on?

And then, with a shock, he saw through the French doors that the visitor was in his house, in his study. The image of the over-turned table flashed in his mind. Whoever it was would see something was wrong. Now there was no choice—he had to make an appearance and offer an explanation. Caught between fear of discovery and anger at the intrusion, he smoothed his jacket and left the barn. As he did, the visitor opened the French doors and called out, "Mrs. Burke?"

Leanne must have invited someone over. The man on the porch wore a Stetson, jeans and cowboy boots. Weird. Burke did not recognize him.

"Can I help you?" Burke called.

The stranger leaped down the steps and came toward him. Burke could see now that he was a foreigner, an Asian . . .

"Where is your wife?" And with a shock Burke recognized—"Mr. Chaduvedi?"

"What have you done? Where is she?"

"What are you doing here?"

Prem looked past him and called again. "Mrs. Burke?"

"What the hell are you doing here?"

"You have had a fight with your wife. Where is she?"

Burke was stunned. Prem Chaduvedi, the art collector from England, suddenly here at Fairoaks dressed up like a damn cowboy and knowing more than he ought to know . . .

Prem pushed past him and headed toward the stables. Burke took two quick steps and grabbed his arm. "Just a minute now—"

"I will look in the stable."

"No you won't."

"Where is your wife?"

"She went to town, not that it's any of your business."

"You are lying."

He tried to push past but now Burke had recovered his wits. He shoved him back toward the car.

"You're trespassing, get off my property."

278 ▶

"Sure, partner."

Prem pivoted on his left foot, bending from the waist. His right leg shot out and struck Burke in the stomach. Before he could recover, Prem's cartwheel movement carried him onto his right foot, freeing the left, which whipped in an upward arc and caught Burke on the temple, knocking him off his feet. He fell heavily and lay groaning on the ground.

The centrifugal force of his maneuver had flung Prem's hat to the ground but for once he abandoned it and ran into the stable, where it took a moment before his eyes adjusted to the dim light and he saw Leanne. Kneeling beside her, he immediately realized she needed a hospital. This was more than a beating, Burke had nearly killed her. He rocked her up and over his shoulder and carried her out of the barn. He had gone almost ten feet before he realized that Burke had disappeared—

The crunch of gravel was his only warning. Before he could turn, something struck his ankles, tripping him. He pitched forward, aware of the sharp pain in one ankle, aware that in his concern for the woman he had miscalculated his danger. Leanne landed on top of him. Prem rolled free and was in a crouch when he was hit from behind. Now a searing pain and two sharp spines burst from his stomach. Prem stared in disbelief. A pitchfork.

The weapon was pulled free and blood came quickly. Still on his knees, Prem turned in time to parry the next thrust, but the tine pierced his arm. He grabbed the neck with his free hand. Burke dropped the handle and jumped back. Prem got unsteadily to his feet. A stomach wound.

Holding the pitchfork like a weapon, he started forward. Pain shot up one ankle and his foot almost buckled. He kept going. Burke watched, moving back at his approach. Prem felt his legs growing weak, the pain in his stomach moving outward, upward, making the world spin. I will kill you, he thought as he sank to the ground, I will kill you, as he fell forward. His eyes were open and he saw the grasshopper land on his forearm and then he knew.

Too late. The locust had come too late.

Jerry Burke's face became distorted, leaning down, red haze thickening, Burke's hand reaching forward, tugging the pitchfork out of his grip, Burke watching fearfully because Prem was staring at him, but the eyes were glazed. Prem was dead.

"Looks like you fucked up, L.T."

The voice came from behind. Burke whirled around. There was no one.

"Up here."

Shielding his eyes, he squinted against the sun. Above the door to the barn, in the hayloft, Mike Severa stood looking down at him, a piece of straw dangling from his mouth.

CHAPTER 36

Keith first grew impatient and then worried when Prem didn't come back. It was a forty-five-minute drive each way to Fairoaks, and maybe half an hour to pick up the cigar store Indian. At first he suspected that Prem might have gone looking for more antiques, but the longer he waited the more worried he became. He called the Willard but Prem hadn't appeared and there were no messages. After putting the tape recorder on automatic, he drove to the remote site, half-afraid that he would come on a traffic accident and find the Aerostar wrapped around a tree.

Once in the curing barn Keith hoisted himself up to the rafters and saw that the cassette had yesterday's date on it. Prem hadn't been here. He took the cassette and returned to the Celica, wishing he knew the name of the antique store where Prem had bought the Indian. As it was, all he could do was call the Highway Patrol and wait. As he pulled onto the road, an ambulance turned out of the Fairoaks property and drove away. It left without flashing lights or siren. Keith made a quick U-turn and went to the house, where he found a police officer wearing a wide-brimmed hat filling out a report.

"What happened?"

"An accident. The lady of the house was trampled by her horse."

"The lady of the house?"

"Mrs. Burke. Are you a friend of the family?"

"I knew her . . . What about a man name Prem Chaduvedi. Was he here?"

The office frowned. "That's a new one on me. Never heard a name like that before."

"He's a Thai, dressed up like a cowboy. He was coming out here to . . . to go riding. Have you seen him?"

"You can ask Sergeant McGillin. He's inside interviewing witnesses."

A silver-gray Mercedes pulled up and Edwin Graybar got out. He greeted the officer by his first name and then turned to Keith. "You heard what happened?"

"Just now."

The officer took them to the stall where Leanne was found. According to Burke, he returned home to find his wife away and her horse, Saint, wandering loose wearing a bridle but no saddle. When he went to the stable, he discovered her body.

"Looks like she was getting ready to ride," the officer said, "and something spooked the animal. Mrs. Burke suffered a fatal blow to the head. That's not official, of course, but that's the sense of it."

The stall she was found in was empty now, but blood was visible on the hay covering the cement floor. Graybar studied the area, not saying a word.

"Who was here when it happened?" Keith asked.

"Nobody. The house staff was gone and the barn manager was delivering a horse to a trainer."

Sergeant McGillin appeared in the doorway. "Frank, you ready to roll?"

Burke was behind him. He was not pleased to see Keith. "What are you doing here?"

"I had some business with your wife."

"Now you've got business with nobody. Get off my property."

"Have you seen Prem Chaduvedi?"

Burke's eyes began blinking. "Who?"

282 ▶

"Prem Chaduvedi. It's not an easy name to forget."

Burke turned to the officer beside him. "Sergeant, this man is an imposter. He's been calling himself John Kris and his real name is Keith Johnson. The FBI is investigating his background right now and I want him off my property or else I want him arrested for trespassing."

The sergeant raised a hand. "Wait a minute. Who's Prem Chakaveki?"

"Chaduvedi," Keith said. "An art dealer from Thailand. Mr. Burke and I met him in London and I invited him to go riding with me this afternoon."

The sergeant turned to Burke. "Have you seen the fellow he's talking about?"

"No. And now I want this man off my property or I want him arrested for trespassing—"

"All right, simmer down. I'm sure he'll leave of his own accord."

"You better take his license number," Burke said. "He may have stolen the car."

"Got something in your eye, lieutenant?" Keith said as he passed.

Looking after him, Burke wanted to tell him he wouldn't live long once Severa found him. He remembered the ex-sergeant's eyes as they stood over Leanne's body. He remembered the questions.

"How did you intend to get rid of her?" Severa had asked.

"Put her in the stall and toss this inside." He pulled out a band of firecrackers the kids had left behind after the Fairoaks hunt breakfast.

"Why would your wife light a firecracker in a stall with a horse?"

"Nobody would know that's what happened."

"They would after they found shreds of rolled paper with powder burns all over the floor."

Severa had stood there with his thick forearms crossed, wearing the same disdainful expression he had shown in Vietnam when Burke tried to devise military strategy for the platoon.

"I could clean up the pieces," Burke had said, and then, reacting to Severa's expression, "All right, so what would you do?"

The ex-sergeant lifted Leanne by the shoulders and nodded to Burke to take her feet. They moved her into the stall and put her beneath the horse, which shied away, trying in the tight quarters to avoid stepping on her. They shut the stable door and Severa slid an automatic pistol from a shoulder holster. He pointed the gun at the ceiling and fired three times. In the stall, Saint reared and slammed against the door.

Next they had disposed of Prem Chaduvedi's body. Ever since Severa had realized who Kris was, he had been tracking him, knew his contact with Burke, with Leanne. He had positioned himself at Fairoaks, watching, waiting. He knew where to find the plastic groundcloth they used to wrap around Chaduvedi's body before lifting it into the van. He knew where to get the shovel they used to scoop the bloodied dirt and toss it into the van on top of the wooden Indian figure. And he knew just where to take the body where it would never be found. When they returned to the house Severa took a beer from the refrigerator and insisted on a tour. He seemed to take special pleasure in questioning Burke about the sports room, a hundred-thousand-dollar addition to the house that featured expensive Nautilus equipment, a punching bag, sauna and all sorts of sporting equipment. Severa ran a hand along a pair of custom-designed Lacroix snow skis.

"You ski?"

"When I get a chance."

Severa moved to a Prince Thunderstick tennis racquet, hefted it, looked at three others hanging next to it. "In case you want to play doubles, right?"

"Leanne has friends who like to play—"

"Had friends."

He moved to a set of golf clubs, picked up one and inspected it. "It's signed?"

"The man who carved it. It's a St. Andrews putter."

"No shit."

"Come on, Severa. Somebody's going to come back and see you."

"Relax, *Trung uy*. Nobody sees me if I don't want to be seen."

He opened a door to a small room and smiled. The floor was lined with yellow scuba-diving tanks. Regulators, face masks, fins, weight belts and wetsuits were stacked neatly on shelves. "You dive, too."

"The local diving club uses our pool for their classes."

"Impressive. You've done well, *Trung uy.*"

Burke worried that Severa would blackmail him to keep quiet about the murders. He was relieved to discover that the ex-sergeant had a killing of his own in mind. Keith Johnson. He had come to kill Keith Johnson. Burke was glad to be of help, gave him the address of the Willard Hotel, and Severa had slipped out the back as Lucas and Maggie arrived . . .

Burke turned his attention to Edwin Graybar, who was still inspecting the stall after the police left. He made Burke nervous.

"What are you looking for?"

"Leanne was very good with horses . . . with animals of any kind. I just can't see how it happened."

"A freak accident, all right. Come on up to the house, we both could use a drink."

"I don't believe I will."

"What's the matter, Edwin?"

"Now that Leanne is gone, I doubt there's need for us to maintain a pretense of friendship."

"You mean I'm not good enough for you."

"I mean you weren't good enough for her. I knew Leanne when she was a child, a sensitive, awkward little girl who cared more about animals than anything else in the world. Especially horses. If there was a mare about to foal, she'd stay up all night. She loved animals more than people. She trusted them more. In your case, she made a bad exception."

"Why don't you cut the crap, Ed. You wanted her and I got her, that's what's bothering you. That sensitive little girl—you wanted to fuck her brains out."

Graybar went rigid. "I may or may not have been in love with her—I never just wanted to *fuck* her. That was *your* specialty, Burke. In more ways than one."

"I've got a few videotapes that would show just how much your sensitive little girl loved to put her heels behind her head."

"You're disgusting." Graybar turned and walked to his car. Burke followed, calling after him. "You had no problem coming to my disgusting home and eating my disgusting food and drinking my disgusting liquor all these years."

"It was Leanne's home. It always was."

"Not any more. Now it's mine and you can keep out of it." Graybar turned. "What did you say?"

"You heard me. This is the last time you'll see Fairoaks."

He shook his head. "You don't know?"

"Know what?"

"She didn't tell you . . . she—oh, my God, you think you're going to inherit Fairoaks—"

"That's what our wills say—we left everything to each other."

Graybar whispered it. *"You killed her . . ."*

"What?"

"She changed her will, and you didn't know."

"That's bullshit. I've got her will in my desk drawer."

Graybar shook his head. "Two weeks ago she came to my office. Something had happened between you, she wouldn't say what but she was in tears. She made out a new will, left everything she owned to the S.P.C.A."

"You're lying—"

"I have a copy in my safe, signed, dated, witnessed by my secretary and notarized."

Burke felt the ground turn to quicksand. "You have a copy?"

"Leanne knew horses too well to be trampled to death. You killed her, Jerry, and if it's the last thing I do, I'll prove it."

"What are you saying? I wasn't even here."

Graybar walked quickly to his car, Burke behind him, his voice rising in panic. "You dare make that accusation and I'll have you in court, I'll sue you for slander, for defamation of character, I don't care what it costs I'll ruin you . . ."

Burke stood watching the car disappear, Graybar's threat echoing. But in spite of the threat he was more worried about the loss of Fairoaks than someone proving Leanne had been murdered. Graybar would go to the police, the police might suspect, but no one could *prove* anything. Even the murder weapon had been disposed of, gone with Prem Chaduvedi and the van, disappeared from the face of the earth.

But now he knew it had all been for nothing if he had lost Fairoaks.

He went back to the house and savaged her belongings until he found the will. Leanne had tucked it in the drawer of an old treadle sewing machine that once belonged to her great-grand-mother, and, like Graybar had said, it left all her worldly possessions to the S.P.C.A. Burke ripped it into pieces, burned it in the fireplace, aware as he did that the gesture was empty. Graybar's copy would make Leanne's earlier will obsolete.

A formal portrait of Leanne hung on the wall, painted at the time of her coming-out party. Her eyes seemed to be watching from wherever he went in the room. He picked up a Chinese porcelain vase and threw it, shattering the vase and tilting the portrait to one side. Lucas came quickly and took in the situation.

"Are you all right, sir?"

"Leave me alone. Just get out."

"I'll get a broom."

"I said, leave me alone."

Lucas closed the door softly behind him, a subtle reproof. Burke unlocked the desk drawer and brought out his cocaine. After snorting four lines, the panic subsided. He was still alive and he would stay alive. He would empty his bank account, take Leanne's jewels, disappear. The Gulfstream was waiting at National Airport. He would have Udo Lauer fly him to Belize or Costa Rica—some place where he could spot an Arab a mile away. Better yet, Lauer would drop him in Hong Kong and he would make his way to Australia or New Zealand.

He picked up the phone to call the pilot but there was no dial tone. And then a woman's voice said, "Hello?"

"Hello?"

"Is Mr. Burke there?"

"Who's this?"

"Gail Wescott from the Washington *Herald.* Is that you, Mr. Burke?"

"What do you want, Gail?"

"An illegal shipment of C-4 plastic explosive was seized in Los Angeles this morning. Mr. Nelson Mowrer has been arrested. My sources tell me that you're responsible for that shipment. Do you have any comment?"

"Mowrer said I was responsible?"

"Do you deny the charge?"

"Of course, I deny it. And if Mowrer—did Mowrer really say that?"

"I'm not prepared to reveal my sources, Mr. Burke."

"Oh, you're not? Well how about this. You want a story? It goes like this. Back in Vietnam—"

He cut himself off just in time, dazzled by a new idea, a plan which would solve all his cash-flow problems and give him enough money to bury himself so deep the Arabs would never find him.

"Listen, if you want a real exposé you meet me at my office in one hour and I'll give you copies of files that will blow the whistle on a lot bigger fish than Nelson Mowrer. And you'll thank me twice over."

"What are you saying?"

"Mowrer is only the tip of the iceberg. Come to my office and I'll show you."

"The last time I came to your office you promised one thing and showed me another."

"Okay, kid. I'll send the files to the *Post*. Goodnight."

"Wait. We're talking about files involving Nelson Mowrer, and who else? A member of the government?"

"That's right."

"How high up?"

"Higher than you'd think. That's all I'm going to say over the phone. Do you want the files or not?"

"You're going to make them public? Why?"

"Because I'm not safe while I'm the only one who has them. Do I have to spell it out?"

"All right then, your office in an hour."

Burke hung up and called the Travel Lodge where Severa was staying under the name of Donald Minkin. There was no answer. He was uneasy operating alone. What if Gail brought someone with her? But if he couldn't find Severa . . . one more possibility. He dialed the Willard Hotel and asked them to page Mike Severa. After a moment, a familiar voice said, "You are one fucking asshole, *Trung uy.* Wescott's wife met the target not more than two minutes ago."

"Chris Wescott is there?"

"They went up to his room, lucky for you."

"Listen, I need your help. How would you like to go home with a million dollars in your pocket?"

No answer.

"Gail Wescott. Johnson's daughter, adopted by Alex Wescott. She's coming to see me in my office. I want you to help me grab her, I want to hold her for ransom."

"Ransom is not the objective—"

"It is for me." Burke told him then how Leanne had cheated him out of Fairoaks and how Edwin Graybar had sworn to prove he killed her. He was leaving the country, going underground and he needed money. "Two million dollars, one for you, one for me. You kidnap her and I'll handle the negotiations. We split the money, I disappear to Timbucktoo and you go back to L.A. with nobody the wiser."

"Except Gail Wescott."

"Well . . . you can handle that, right? Just like Charlie, a white gook, another Minkin."

"The job is to take out Johnson, no one else—"

"So wear a fucking ski mask. I'll be the only one she sees. I'll be the only one they identify. You'll be listed as unidentified accomplice. Hell, if we decide to send her back safe and sound, Wescott probably won't even report it to the police, he'll be so glad to have Johnson out of the way. You choose the place and I'll have Johnson there, with the money. Put him wherever you want. Right between the crosshairs, there's your objective. What do you say? You help me get the girl, I'll deliver Johnson, and we're both a million on the high side of the shitpile."

A pause, then: "All right, *Trung uy,* it's your mission, but we *do* it my way."

CHAPTER 37

Returning to the Willard Hotel Keith's one thought was to find Prem. He went to the front desk and asked if there were any messages. The clerk in his pale gold jacket turned and ran his finger down the boxes. "No, sir, nothing."

Chris' voice. "Keith?"

He turned. She was right there, in front of him, the sudden reality of a thousand fantasies. She wore a skirt and jacket of pale green with a cream blouse. Around her neck was the jade tear-drop necklace *he* had given her on her eighteenth birthday, but the Tiffany watch was unfamiliar and the wedding ring . . .

"It's you," she said. "Oh God, it's you . . ."

"Hello, Christie."

A nickname she hadn't heard in twenty years. For a moment she felt like the sixteen-year-old girl who blushed the day Keith Johnson, waded into the Russian River still wearing his shoes, to help her and a girlfriend launch a canoe. She took a deep breath. "Is there somewhere we can talk?"

They were silent in the elevator but fiercely aware of each other. Keith noticed the tiny lines around her eyes, the subtle eye makeup, the well-coifed hair, all so different than he remembered. An elegant, sophisticated woman had replaced the casual

California girl. When he led her into the suite she looked around. "This is very grand."

"Would you like a drink?" So inadequate. But how breach twenty years with words?

"A glass of wine. Keith, you're alive—"

"So is a cockroach."

It startled her. Its bitterness. But what did she expect? "You look . . . different," she said. "You sound different."

"I had throat surgery with a foot."

"What?"

"Kicked in the face and throat."

"Don't. How can you joke about it?"

"It's how you survive. If I had escaped after the first year I would have killed Alex on sight."

"He told me what happened, what he did . . ."

"Because he knew you would have found out."

"He said you were in prison, you just got out."

"I escaped three months ago."

"You broke out of prison?"

Keith held up his hand, the fingers thick and muscular. "Not the hands of a concert pianist, are they?"

"But why did they do it? Why did they keep you all this time? And how did you get all this?" She indicated the room.

"I inherited some money." He handed her the glass of wine and held up his own. "To the truth."

"To your return . . ."

"Til death do us part." Chris remained motionless. "What's the matter?"

She put down the glass.

"Keith, Jerry Burke came to us yesterday. He's going to tell the world what happened at Chim Bai, how Alex betrayed you. It will destroy Alex. He'll kill himself."

"He hasn't got the guts."

"He already tried." She told what happened.

"A failed suicide, a coward's blackmail. He's trying to hold onto you by playing for your sympathy."

"He never had my love, Keith. You know that."

"I know nothing. I've been in prison for twenty years."

"Keith, please, they told me you were dead. A man from the government came to the house . . . he said you were shot down in a helicopter. And then they sent back a box of your things, your clothes, shaving kit, letters. I didn't want to believe it. For years I *didn't* believe it, but there was no word, no clue, nothing. And after a while . . ."

"Two years, eight months and eleven days."

"What?"

"That's how long you waited before you married Alex."

"I should have died, is that what you think? I almost did, you know. I stopped eating, I wanted to die. If it hadn't been for Gail I wouldn't have made it through that first year."

"And missed your chance to be First Lady—"

"Don't be cruel, that's not like you."

"You don't know what's like me. You left me long ago—"

"That's not true."

"You married Alex."

"I married a father for Gail."

"All right, I understand that. But why *him?* Why Alex?"

"Mostly because he was my only, my closest link to *you.* I never meant to marry again, I never planned it. But at least Alex could tell me about you, what it was like in the platoon, how you spent your days, what you thought and talked about . . . it was a way of keeping you alive. That was how it started."

"And then you fell in love . . ."

"No, I *didn't* fall in love. For a long time I kept that separate. Then I *learned* to love what was there, life went on. And Gail, Gail needed a father . . ."

"She had a father," he said stiffly.

"Two fathers . . . that's what she tells people. She reveres your memory, Keith. She has every photograph, all your letters, your medals, your service record in a scrapbook—"

"You gave her my letters?"

"Except a few that were too personal. They're taped where they began to fall apart. I must have read each of them a thousand times. Not recently, no, but after you died—" She stopped. "Oh, God, Keith . . ."

She was smiling and trying not to smile at the same time. And

292 ▶

RICHARD AELLEN

Keith actually found himself smiling, and he felt a strange sensation—the long-forgotten warmth, humanity, of humor.

Chris said, "I didn't mean it that way."

"The description's mostly accurate. Dead. I was, and in a way
I still am."

"It's just that for years I couldn't come to terms with your being
gone and now, after twenty years, it's hard to believe you're
really here."

She drank her wine in quick gulps. When she lowered the glass,
his face was hard again.

"The letters in the scrapbook. I assume *he's* read them?"

"Alex?"

"Did he?"

"Yes . . . but they're sweet letters, Keith. Gail is very proud of
them."

"You should have burned them. They were meant for you, no
one else."

"So was that picture."

"What?"

"The one you took of me on our honeymoon. You showed that
to the men in the platoon."

"I never showed that to anybody."

"Not even to Alex?"

"Especially not to him. If he saw it, it was after he stole it from
the survival knife." He saw in her eyes the pain of this revelation.
"He told you that? He said I showed the men in the platoon?"

"It doesn't matter . . ."

"That bastard."

Keith moved to the phone and Chris followed him. "What are
you doing?"

"I'm going to call him."

"No, please don't."

"He's going to tell you the truth."

She put her hand on the receiver, breaking the connection. "I
know the truth, I already know it. I lost the only man I ever loved,
I lost the life I dreamed of living. That life died when I thought
you died, and what I built in its place was a way to survive. Yes,
I had to survive too. Except it was so much easier for me . . . I

◀ 293

had Gail. She helped me carry your memory into the long nights even after Alex. I cried when I married him, cried for you, for Gail, for us, for what we had lost . . ."

She stopped, eyes glistening. The changes he had noticed earlier faded. He saw her again the way he had on the first day, a sixteen-year-old girl wading in the Russian River, blue jeans rolled to her knees, the sunlight turning copper in her hair. He put his hands on her temples, a half-forgotten gesture, and smoothed her hair as he drew her to him. Her body melded into his, familiar and foreign, her fragrance a dizzying reminder of an early first love.

"Keith, oh, Keith . . ."

And the years rushed backward, down a long dark tunnel, swept back by what had never died, and then exploding into the light, the passion of their reunion transcending time . . .

Much as she disliked him, Gail was excited as she drove to her meeting with Jerry Burke. The story promised to be bigger than anyone had anticipated. John Kris had known about the C-4 shipment, but no one had mentioned a prominent member of the government. Who knew how big the story might be?

As she got out of the car, a white Rolls-Royce pulled into the stall next to her. The passenger window rolled down and Burke called her name. He was leaning across the front seat, tilting his head to see her.

"Change of plans," he said. "The U.S. Marshal is on his way to secure the office but I got the files out."

"Where are they?"

"The back seat." He reached to the console and pushed a button. With a click, the rear doors unlocked.

"I thought we were going to talk."

"I'm leaving the country tonight. I'll call you once I'm safe."

Gail opened the door. Two cardboard boxes, bulging with manila files, sat on the floor. They were wedged tight, and she was already half in the car, bracing herself on the seat, when there was a crunch of gravel outside and someone shoved her forward. The door slammed. As she turned, trying to get up, a blow on the head stunned her. Rough hands pulled her arms back and a pair of handcuffs snapped around her wrists.

She screamed once before her attacker slapped a wide piece of duct tape over her mouth. The car began to back up. Gail rolled to her back and found herself staring up at a man in a white ski mask, his eyes, mouth, and nose outlined in red.

"Listen to me, little lady. Your life depends on your following instructions. Be quiet and you won't be hurt. Scream, try to escape and I'll kill you."

The words made no sense. This was crazy.

"You understand?" A gun jabbed into her ribs. She nodded, at the moment more frightened of being unable to talk than she was of being kidnapped. She tried to sit up but the man in the mask put his foot on her chest.

"Down."

The man in the ski mask pulled off another piece of tape hanging from the edge of the seat and pressed it over her eyes. At the last minute she tried to turn her head and the tape bridged her nose slightly on one side, leaving a tiny space through which she had a pinhole view of the world.

Burke's voice was strained. "Anybody behind us?"

"There will be if you don't slow down."

She tried to place that voice, couldn't. There were two smells now, the rubber adhesive of the duct tape and the smell of fine leather from the car's interior. They hadn't gone far before the car stopped and Skimask . . . she could only think of him that way . . . took her by the arm and pulled her into another vehicle. The handcuffs were pulled above her head and roped to the ceiling, higher than a normal car . . . a van? When she tried to pull away, Skimask said, "Take it easy, little lady. We don't want you opening the door on the freeway."

Her hands were close to the roof, too high for her to sit down. She knelt on a blanket and braced herself as the van headed back to the highway. Now that she had recovered from her initial shock, she was plain angry. Burke had kidnapped her. A reporter. Why would he go to this extreme?

She explored the rope with her fingers, trying to find a knot. Skimask stabbed the brakes hard and set her swinging.

"Leave the rope alone."

Gail scrambled to get her knees beneath her. The exertion left her breathing so heavily she was afraid she might suffocate. She tilted her head back and through the gap between the tape and her cheek had a view of Burke's accomplice, the back of his head like a white knit doll, his eyes visible in the rear-view mirror, monitoring her. There was something odd about the eyes. It took her a moment before she realized that one stayed focused on the road while the other was fixed on her. Fear replaced anger.

Burke followed the van in the Rolls-Royce. He was high, exhilarated by Gail's kidnapping. They drove to Fairoaks, where Severa had chosen the spot to park—a grove of trees near a creek reached by a dirt road used so rarely it was covered by grass. Severa directed Burke twenty feet to one side of the van, where it was out of Gail's sight and hearing. The Rolls-Royce looked incongruous beneath the trees. Severa slid into the passenger's seat and removed his skimask.

"So what do we do now?" Burke asked. "Call Wescott?"

"Poor psychology, *Trung uy*. We call him at twenty-one hundred and tell him we want two million dollars, what can he do? Can he get the money? Negative. The banks are closed. So for twelve hours all he can do is worry or call the police. If we call tomorrow morning and give him ten hours to deliver, suddenly he's got focus, motivation, and he doesn't have time to get clever."

Burke was nodding impatiently. "Fine, you can sit out here all night. I'm going home. Unless . . . maybe we take turns doing a little close guarding of the girl."

Severa gave him a look, tilted his head back and closed his eyes.

"This isn't Chim Bai, *Trung uy*."

"So what? She's lucky we—"

Severa interrupted, running over Burke's words as if he wasn't there. "The problem is that once our adversary knows you've kidnapped his daughter, he knows that she'll be alone when you collect the money. This might tempt him to a false sense of his daughter's safety. It might tempt him to call the police. We need a fail-safe mechanism, assurance that if anything goes wrong, the little lady will die. I don't suppose you have any of the C-4 shipment at Fairoaks?"

"No."

Severa kept his head back and eyes closed.

"Are you looking for enlightenment or something?"

"Strategy, *Trung uy*. Terrain, symmetry, psychology, karma, poetic justice."

California, Burke thought. Either Severa had been there too long or not long enough. He shifted his weight and pulled out a cigarette.

"Don't do that," Severa said quietly.

"Hey, it's my car."

He brought out a lighter. Severa slammed the side of his hand into the windshield karate-style. A spider-web pattern of cracks burst forth.

"Are you *crazy?* What was that for?"

Several fixed him with his wall-eyed stare and motioned with his forefinger for him to get rid of the cigarette.

"What, this? Okay, fine. You don't want the fucking cigarette." Burke smashed the cigarette against his side of the windshield, grinding it against the glass as if it were an ashtray. "There, no cigarette. What about my windshield?"

"Are you taking the car when you deploy out of the country?"

"So what? I'm not burning down the house just because I can't take it with me."

Severa wasn't listening. He traced the pattern in the cracked glass and a smile spread over his features. "How many scuba tanks did I see up there at your house?"

"Who knows? They belong to the club."

"Six, anyway, right?"

"So what?"

"Here's your mission, *Trung uy*. You go to the house. You bring six air tanks and regulators back here. Make sure you have full ones and don't let anybody see you loading them. Report back by zero six hundred for further orders. That's dawn. Can you handle that?"

"Why don't you cut the military crap and tell me what's on your mind?"

"An eye for an eye, a tooth for a tooth, a tank for a tank."

Mr. Mysterious, Burke thought as he drove back to the house. He hated Severa's condescending attitude. A wild card, unpredictable and dangerous, Severa seemed more interested in killing Johnson than getting the money, a reversal of priorities that made Burke uneasy.

And then an ominous thought that made more sense . . . What if Severa decided to kill him and take the two million for himself? It was the sort of double-cross Burke found tempting, so he could assume Severa did too. No wonder the man wanted to remain anonymous. Now if Severa killed him there would be no witnesses, no loose ends. "Bastard would do it, too," he muttered.

Now Burke began to make his own plans. Severa wanted to keep secrets, fine, two could play that game. When he reached the house he began making phone calls. He told his pilot, Udo Lauer, to be ready to leave the next day. He made plane and hotel reservations. The last call was to London. From Nexli's voice he could tell that she was either stoned or half-asleep or both.

"Jerrr-ree, where you are?"

"You whacked, baby? You on ludes or what?"

"Mmmmm."

"Focus now. This is important. Leanne's dead. You listening?"

"She's dead? Really?"

He explained how Leanne had screwed him out of Fairoaks and then told her the plan.

"Tomorrow morning you get up early, you move fast. Stay straight tomorrow, you understand? Empty your bank account, collect all your valuables, everything you need for the rest of your life and catch British Airways Flight 217. I got you a first class seat. It leaves eleven forty-five, gets you to Dulles Airport at three-ten. You get there, take a taxi to the Holiday Inn—you can see it from the terminal. You wait until I come for you. You get hungry, order room service, but don't leave the room no matter what. You got that?"

"What about Colonel Ibram? He will send those men to kill you."

"We're going to disappear. Start a new life . . . fake names, fake passports, we're on vacation the rest of our lives."

"How Jerry? With no money—"

"Don't worry about it. By tomorrow this time Mister Jerry's going to be a millionaire. And with a little help from Miss Nexli, he'll be a double millionaire."

He made her write it down and had her set the alarm clock. The rest of the night Burke spent gathering Leanne's jewels and packing everything valuable into five suitcases. He was nervous, on a natural high. He didn't need any coke until just before dawn the next morning.

CHAPTER 38

The slow return to consciousness. Keith and Chris lay wrapped in each other's arms. After a while she spoke his name. There was no response.

"Keith?"

He let out a deep breath and opened his eyes. "Christie."

"Are you all right?"

"No."

She touched his cheek. "What's the matter?"

"I still love you."

"I'm glad."

They dozed, woke up and without speaking made love again, bodies moving over and around each other. It was long after midnight when they began to talk, reviewing their lives, leaping from one subject to another, sudden intimacies interspersed with awkward silences and overlapping revelation. Keith told her about his years in prison, Henri's teachings, their escape, and the Frenchman's death.

"He sounds like a wonderful man," Chris said. "You must miss him."

"I don't think about him. Not as a separate person. He's a part of me, part of everything I do and think and feel. When love couldn't keep me alive, he focused my hatred and gave me reason to live."

"That's odd. From the way you describe him, he doesn't sound like a man who would promote hatred—"

"It helped me live for the day I could confront the three who betrayed me."

"Three?"

"Alex, Burke and Severa."

"Severa?" She frowned. "You mean the sergeant who killed Minkin?"

"The one who found the heroin. He knew just where to look."

"But I thought . . . I mean, from what Alex said it was just the two of them."

"What do you mean?"

"Alex said Burke didn't want Severa to know. He was afraid he'd use the information against him."

Keith sat up. "Severa didn't know?"

"He didn't mention him in the suicide note, either. Why? Have you—"

Keith got out of bed. "Where's the note? Do you have it?"

"In my purse."

She got it for him and watched as he read Alex's story. When he was through he closed his eyes. "He battles the storm who wakes the sleeping wind."

"What?"

"Something Henri once said."

According to the note, when Burke called the gear inspection he told Severa to check the knife handle because he had a tip from one of the men. That was all. And that had been enough.

Keith went to the phone. It was eleven o'clock in Los Angeles. He dialed Severa's home number and left a message on the answering machine: "Mr. Severa, this is John Kris. It seems I owe you an explanation, maybe even an apology. I'll call you tomorrow but in the meantime be advised that your scuba tanks at the Bamboo Reef are filled with helium rather than air."

* * *

Gail spent the night lying on a blanket in the back of the van. When morning came, Burke returned and they drove to a public phone booth at a gas station outside Middleburg. It had rained during the night and the sun glistened silver between low clouds that hung heavy over multi-hued hills. Grazing cattle breathed a fine mist that settled slowly in the moisture-laden air. They parked in such a way that the van hid the phone booth from view. Severa held Gail while Burke made the call. A sleepy-sounding maid quickly became attentive when Burke told her that it was an emergency about Gail. A moment later Alex was on the line.

"Senator Wescott speaking."

"Jerry Burke here, *senator.* I told you yesterday my life was on the line but you didn't give a shit. Maybe this will change your mind: I've got Gail, and unless you come up with two million dollars by five o'clock today she's going to meet with a fatal accident. Do you understand that?"

"What?"

"Get the wax out of your ears. I've kidnapped your darling daughter. Here."

He held out the phone and Severa pushed Gail forward. She was still blindfolded and handcuffed. Severa stripped the tape from her mouth.

"Dad?"

"Duchess, are you all right?"

"There's two of them, they kidnapped me—"

Severa pulled her away and shoved the tape over her mouth.

"Gail? Gail?"

"She's all right," Burke said.

"If you hurt her, Jerry, I'll kill you."

"You can shit green bricks for all I care, senator. But you better have two million in cash by five o'clock. Two suitcases, a million in each, I'll tell you at five where to deliver it."

"Are you crazy? You'll spend the rest of your life in prison—"

"I'll spend the rest of my life dead if I don't get that money. Ten hours. If you call the police, the FBI or anybody else, Gail dies. I mean that, any dumb move, any at all, and the girl is dead."

"All right, all right, I'll get you the money—"

"I know you will. And when you do, I want Keith Johnson to deliver it. You two to answer for."

A gray dawn found Keith and Chris at the oval window overlooking the Mall. He was behind her, his arms around her waist, her hands covering his.

"I can't let you go again, you know that, don't you?"

"I know, but . . ."

"But what?"

"What about my other life, other responsibilities?"

"Not to Alex."

"*No,* but to Nick and Bobby. I can't just walk away."

"Take the boys and come with me. I have money, Chris. We can go anywhere, live anywhere, do anything we want. *I can't lose you again.*"

She spoke softly. "If I do . . . if I divorce Alex and take the boys—will you be willing to pay the price?"

"What price?"

"Not tell the truth about what happened at Chim Bai." He drew back and she went on quickly. "When Burke tells the world that Alex planted heroin in the knife, you have to deny it. I don't know, blame somebody else, somebody gone . . ."

"Have you got any idea what you're asking?"

"I know how it sounds—"

"It sounds like you want *me* to protect Alex?"

"Not *him,* Keith, the children. The boys. Like it or not, Alex is their father. How can they live with the man who destroys their father? Don't you see?"

He looked away, shaking his head.

"Listen to me. Please. Alex built his life by destroying yours. I can't begin a life with you by destroying his. His children are mine too. If you want us for more than this one night, you have to decide—hate or love, Alex or me . . ."

The ringing phone was a reprieve. For a moment they stayed as they were, eyes on each other. Then Keith turned away, crossed the room and picked up the phone. "Hello?"

"Is my wife there?" It was Alex.

"No, *my* wife is here."

A slight pause, and then the words came like bullets. "All right then, Keith. Tell *your* wife he has your daughter. He has Gail and he's going to kill her if he doesn't get two million dollars."

"Who? Who has Gail?"

"Jerry Burke. Satisfied?"

After making the call Severa and Burke returned to the Rolls-Royce, where they transferred the scuba tanks to the van. When they were finished Severa held out his hand.

"Give me the key to the trunk."

"I'll open it."

"I don't want you to open it, I want the key."

"Why?"

"Orders, *Trung uy*. We need discipline in the ranks. The key."

Burke gave it to him and Severa opened the trunk. With a pocket knife, he began gouging out the rubber seal from around the lid.

"What are you doing?"

"I want to make sure our little lady has enough air. She's going to wait in here while I do a little reconnaissance."

"You don't have to put her in there, I can handle her."

"That's what I don't want—you handling her."

Severa put a blanket on the floor and forced Gail, still bound and gagged, inside. "You'll be uncomfortable but safe. Just don't move around much and you'll have plenty of air."

He shut the lid and turned to Burke. "Anybody comes, you can drive away. Just be back here by fifteen hundred—you remember fifteen hundred don't you, *Trung uy?*"

"I don't need your fucking condescension, Severa."

"Sure you do. It's good for you."

Severa drove back to Washington and parked hear the Vietnam Veterans Memorial. What began in Chim Bai should finish here, on the last patch of ground that remained of America's presence in Vietnam. Johnson was the link. He had made himself the enemy. Severa quickly reviewed options. He could walk up behind Johnson and put a pistol to his head, but that was risky. Too many witnesses might give his description to the police, and there were always a few Vietnam veterans around who might interfere. There was also the risk that Johnson would spot him approaching. There had to be other options.

He performed his usual ritual at the wall. He stopped before the names of men he had known and saluted each in turn. Then he turned his attention to the surrounding terrain. Two days earlier he had noticed an information booth under construction. At that time it was swarming with workmen; now it was deserted.

The booth was fifty yards from the entrance to the memorial. It was surrounded by a temporary wall made up of plywood sheets supported by metal poles. The door was a hinged plywood panel secured by a chain and padlock. Signs on each side read: "YOUR NATIONAL PARK SERVICE WORKING FOR YOU." Peering through the cracks, Severa saw a small, octagonal building in the final stages of construction. The walls and roof were in place, and on the ground were a stack of windows ready to be installed. Boxes of electrical equipment and tubing were visible inside.

Severa went to a nearby table, where vendors sold MIA T-shirts and Vietnam memorabilia. He struck up a conversation and indicated the information booth. "Nobody working today?"

"Good Friday and a government contract, what do you expect?"

Severa spent the next two hours tracking down the items he needed. From a hardware store he bought padlocks, bolt cutters, and items he needed for the scuba equipment. A uniform shop provided him with a National Park Ranger's outfit—green pants and gray tunic and a brown Smokey Bear hat with matching raincoat. He changed clothes in the van and returned to the memorial. After waiting until a policeman patrolling the area had disappeared over an embankment separating the memorial from the reflecting pool, he adopted an official air and marched up to the booth. Beneath the raincoat, bolt cutters dangled from a cord looped over his shoulder. He fixed his own padlock before cutting the links holding the old one, which he slipped into his pocket. The bolt cutters disappeared beneath the raincoat.

"Excuse me," someone called. He turned to find a man and his wife coming toward him. "What day is the Easter Egg hunt on the White House lawn? Sunday or Monday?"

"Monday," Severa said. He didn't know and didn't give a damn. The couple went away satisfied. In his park ranger uniform, Severa felt like a fox in the henhouse. He glanced back once as he left the area and smiled. The killing ground was secure.

CHAPTER 39

Burke's voice: "You're going to sentence me to death, is that it?"
Leanne answering: "Aren't you being a little melodrama-
tic?" . . .

Keith was listening to the tape he had retrieved from Fairoaks the day before. He had eight hours before the four o'clock phone call when Burke would tell them where to meet—eight hours to track down Burke and rescue Gail. He listened with a growing sense of foreboding as the argument between Burke and Leanne escalated to an attack. Screams, grunts of pain, something pounding on the floor, and then quiet. Now Burke breathing heavily, grunting with exertion, stumbling once as he left the room. The sequence ended.

The next sequence was the last. It was triggered by the sound of a vacuum cleaner, Burke cleaning up, straightening the tables and chairs. He left the room and the sound-activated recorder shut off. The rest of the tape was blank. Although there was no indication that Prem had been present, a terrible certainty took hold of Keith. Prem must have discovered Leanne's body or interrupted her murder and . . .

And Burke killed him.

Keith closed his eyes. Something Henri once said came to

mind: In its death throes, no animal is predictable. Now Keith realized that he had misjudged Burke, figured him a coward, afraid to use violence. But the threat of a Libyan death squad had made him desperate, unpredictable.

And now he had Gail.

Keith went to Prem's room, filled with Western gear. A feathered Indian war bonnet hung on one wall, a Navajo blanket on the other, and along the floor were a row of boots and one pair of beaded moccasins. A hand-tooled saddle was spread over the back of a chair and every drawer was filled with Western wear—embroidered snap-button shirts, chaps, fringed leather jackets, spurs, hats, buckles, and the gun—a double action Army Colt that Prem had bought at a California gun show. Keith took it out of the holster, loaded it and dropped it into the pocket of his overcoat.

Driving to Fairoaks, the low clouds that hung over the Virginia countryside reminded him of the day Henri died. A bad omen? When he arrived, he found the front door draped in black. He went in and went to the base of the stairs.

"Burke!"

A servant appeared, a stooped black man.

"May I help you, sir?"

"Where is he?"

"Mister Burke? He left early this morning."

"What's your name?"

"Lucas."

"Where is he, Lucas?"

"I don't know, sir."

"Then you won't mind if I look around."

Keith went into every room of the house, opened every closet, looked down every stairway. He expected Lucas to protest or try to stop him, but the man waited in the foyer and watched with a somber expression, as if he somehow expected this. A woman joined him and the two stood there silently, arms around each other, until Keith left.

He went to the stable and found the barn manager, Reed Cunningham, in the tackroom. Hanging on the wall were winner's ribbons, pedigrees and framed photographs of riders and horses. Reed was a lanky man with sleepy eyes and crewcut hair who spoke with a backwoods drawl.

"Heard the car this morning," Reed told him. "But haven't seen the man."

"Do you know where he is?"

"Told me yesterday he was going to England. But that was before what happened to Miss Leanne."

A single question got a single response. Eventually Keith pieced together the scenario—how Burke's instructions to board the horse came at the last minute and Reed was gone when Leanne was supposedly trampled.

"Did you see a stranger around here last night, or today? A girl in her early twenties, small, thin, dark eyes and black hair?"

"Nope."

"Was there anyone in the car with Burke this morning?"

"Just heard him, didn't see him."

"Who lives in the house down the hill?"

"I do."

"You married, Mr. Cunningham?"

"You taking a census?"

Keith pulled out the gun and Reed's sleepy eyes snapped open. "Wait a minute . . ."

"I'd explain but there's no time. Are you married?"

"No."

"Fine. Where's your tool kit?"

They found a large screwdriver, and Keith led Cunningham to a horse van parked beside the stable. The van had high windows, too narrow for a man to escape. Once Reed was inside, Keith closed the door and slid the screwdriver through the hasp. It was a quick job that would not last long and didn't need to.

"I'm going to check your house, Mr. Cunningham. I'm not going to take anything so don't you do anything foolish."

"I'll find you, Mister, when you don't have the gun."

Keith doubted that Burke's accomplice was Reed Cunningham, but he needed to be absolutely sure, so he searched his house. When he was done he returned to the main house and told Lucas where to find Reed. As he left Fairoaks he wished that he had replaced the tape in the remote site. Now it was too late. He was sure that Burke wouldn't be back.

Keith returned to Fairfax, to the observation post opposite Artex International, from which he could see across the plaza that Burke's office was empty. He listened to the recent telephone conversations and heard Burke's unsuccessful attempt to get a reprieve from Hasnid. None of the other calls had anything to do with the C-4 or with Gail.

He then went to the Artex office, where Mrs. Flynn told him the same thing that Lucas had: Burke wasn't there.

"Has he been in this morning?"

"Mr. Burke's hours are his own business."

"I'm sure they are, Mrs. Flynn. And your car payments are your business." He put a hundred dollar bill on the desk. "Has Mr. Burke been in this morning?"

Her eyes fixed on the bill. "Well, no, actually he hasn't."

Keith described Gail but Mrs. Flynn hadn't seen her. The secretary's eyes remained on the money. Keith took a pen from the desk and wrote his phone number on the border of the bill.

"If Mr. Burke calls or comes in today, I'll have another car payment waiting if you call me at this number, Mrs. Flynn."

Her fingers raced across the desk like a tarantula after its prey. "Well, I can't promise anything, of course . . ."

"Of course."

He returned to the Willard. Mrs. Flynn was watching for Burke. Chris and Alex were gathering the money, and the clock was ticking. There was nothing else he could do.

While Keith waited for word of Jerry Burke, Gail was lying in the trunk of the Rolls-Royce. She tried to work the blindfold and gag free, but the tape was wrapped around her head and all she managed to do was tangle it in her hair. Outside, she could hear the birds, a frog croaking, and the occasional distant jet. Then came the drumming of rain, which drowned all other sounds until Burke turned on the radio. Hours later, she heard a car return. Hoping that it was a stranger, she kicked the trunk and tried to scream. A few moments later the trunk opened. Fresh air washed over her and faint light filtered beneath the blindfold.

"Something bothering you, little lady?"

It was Skimask's voice. He helped her out of the car and pulled the tape from her mouth.

"Water," she gasped.

For some reason she couldn't understand, the men found the request funny. Skimask and Burke took her to the van, and after a ten minute drive over rough terrain, let her out and took off the blindfold. The day was overcast but the first rush of light nearly blinded her. They stood near a gazebo on a cliff overlooking a body of water a quarter mile in diameter.

"You said you wanted water," Burke said. He stood on her left. On her right, Skimask remained inscrutable behind the red-rimmed lip and eye holes.

"Have you ever been scuba diving, little lady?"

"Yes."

"Good." He tossed a wetsuit at her feet. "Put it on."

"Why?"

"You're going to spend a couple of hours in the water and you'll die of hyperthermia without a wetsuit. Put it on."

"No."

Skimask drew an automatic pistol and cocked it. "No time to argue, little lady. You're going into the water, alive or dead, your choice."

"Then take off the handcuffs."

"It's got velcro shoulder straps. Do the long johns first. We'll take off the cuffs for the hood and jacket."

Burke was watching her, lips half-parted.

"Pervert," she said. She pulled off her shoes and slacks and pulled on the lower half of the wetsuit that was designed like overalls. Skimask stood behind her and flipped the straps over her shoulders. Not until they were attached did he remove the handcuffs.

"Now the jacket."

Gail massaged her wrists. Ignoring their eyes, she took off her parka and slid out of her blouse. The wind, damp and chilly, brought goosebumps to her skin. She picked up the top of the suit.

"Take off the bra," Burke said suddenly.

"Go to hell."

Burke took two steps forward and ripped the bra away. Gail hit him, losing her balance in the process. Burke stumbled back, touched his nose and looked at his hand. Blood. He started toward her as she was scrambling to her feet.

"You little bitch—"

The gun went off. Grass and wet dirt sprayed Burke's knees. The bullet had landed inches in front of his feet.

"That's enough, *Trung uy.*"

"She gave me a bloody nose—"

"Put in for the Purple Heart." Skimask glanced at Gail, on her feet now. "The jacket and the hood. Let's move."

She tugged it on and stood there, wet hair drawn tight by the neck of the suit. Burke led them past the gazebo and down steep stone steps cut into the side of the quarry to a floating dock on which there were six yellow scuba tanks and two large metal wheel rims with iron spokes. Skimask took her to the end of the dock, which was swaying now beneath their weight. He lifted one of the scuba tanks.

"Put this on."

She slipped her arms through the harness and took the weight on her back. After fastening the straps, Skimask handcuffed her again, her arms in front of her. He ran a chain over the cuffs, threaded it through the spokes of the iron wheel and padlocked it.

"You're going to drown me?"

"Not if your father pays on time. You're going to stay at the bottom until he rescues you."

"On a single seventy-two? You might as well shoot me."

"Those tanks go with you."

For the first time she noticed that the five remaining tanks each had regulators attached. Around their valves were padlocks through which another chain was threaded and fastened to a second iron wheel rim. A necklace of scuba tanks.

"Listen up," Skimask said. "The depth here is between twenty and thirty feet. With any luck the six tanks should last you three hours. Have you used a J-valve before?"

"No."

"There's no pressure gauge. You run out of air, pull that lever and you'll get an extra five minutes. An hour from now we meet with your father, who pays to find out where you are. He'll have two hours to get here. You'll be alive if you don't panic. Breathe fast and cut your time in half. Breathe slow, you live twice as long."

"Why can't you just chain me to a tree or something?"

"I like to know that if I die, you die. Besides, a good mission utilizes the resources at hand. Are you ready?"

"No—"

He shoved her off the dock. There was the shock of cold water on her face and a sharp pain as the handcuffs were brought up short by the chain running to the wheel. Breathing in short quick gasps, she grabbed the dock with both hands. Skimask pushed the other tanks into the water so they dangled below her. Only the two metal rims were left on the dock. Burke squatted at one of them, balancing it on the edge, waiting. Skimask knelt above her. He followed her air hose to the mouthpiece and put it to her lips. "Let's go."

"I hope they do kill—"

He shoved the mouthpiece between her teeth, cutting off her words. Then he pushed the other rim to the edge and called to Burke, "On my count. One, two, three—"

As the heavy wheels splashed into the water, Gail pulled and kicked upward. At the top of her lunge she made a reach for the ski mask and nearly managed to rip it off. Severa pulled back so quickly that one foot slipped off the dock into the water. When he looked up, Jerry Burke was laughing.

As the waters closed over her, Gail almost lost her grip on the chain holding the five supplemental tanks. She sank to the bottom, where the tanks clanked and the wheel skidded a few feet down a crevice before coming to rest. The neopreme suit was buoyant, and since she wasn't wearing a weight belt, she floated upside down, anchored by her wrists to the wheel. She saw her legs above her silhouetted by a silver gray surface and the dark bulk of the dock. Without a mask, the icy water clutched at her face.

Gail grabbed the wheel, pivoted her body until she could tuck her legs beneath it. Silt, dead leaves and debris swirled off the bottom. She sat with the wheel partially on her lap, the five supplemental tanks floating nearby like thick balloons, bumping against one another when disturbed.

She was alone with the sound of her breathing, and three hours left to live.

CHAPTER 40

Severa dropped Burke at the Rolls-Royce. His instructions were simple: "Arrive at the wall no earlier than five. When you get the money, give this to Wescott." He handed him a sealed envelope. "It's the location of a phone booth at Lafayette Square. As soon as I confirm you're free of surveillance and check the money, we call and give directions to the girl. Exiting the area, leave the Rolls and take a taxi to the Key Bridge Marriott—not the downtown Marriott, not Tyson's Corner—the Key Bridge Marriott, where you wait for me in the lobby. Clear?"

"Yeah."

"One last thing: when you meet Johnson, face north or south, not east or west."

"Why?"

"If it goes wrong and I have to move early, you don't want to be in the line of fire."

"Where will you be?"

"There."

That was all he would say. Burke did not much like the idea of Severa hiding with a gun trained a few feet from his head, but there wasn't much he could do about it. He drove to the Holiday Inn at Dulles and found Nexli waiting nervously in the lobby. She was wearing a red knit suit adorned with enough gold jewelry to fill a display window. From her dialated eyes and exaggerated movements Burke knew she was high. She kissed him greedily.

"I thought I told you to wait in the room."

"Jerry, I'm afraid." She took hold of his arm. "I talked to Mahmoud. He says the death squad is already sent to kill you."

"Screw the death squad. By the time they get here we'll be on our way to the Bahamas. Where are your bags?"

She pointed to a stack of luggage that took up one whole corner of the lobby. It took ten minutes and a twenty dollar bill to the doorman to get the car loaded. As they drove to Washington Burke told her how he killed Leanne and Prem. She shivered as she listened, turned on, and also impressed. He exaggerated the danger and left out Severa and his role in disposing of the bodies and planning the kidnapping. He didn't mention Severa at all. No need to share the credit.

Nexli's eyes were wide, glowing as she listened. Her fingers found his leg and she leaned close to whisper, "You put that girl in the water, Jerry? I think you are a very bad boy."

"I needed a fail-safe. If they don't deliver, she's in the river."

"You are very, very bad."

She tugged at his pants. He lifted his hips so that she could get at the zipper. She leaned down and her lips closed around him.

"Yeah, yeah," he murmured. But in his mind he saw the Wescott girl half-dressed in the wetsuit with her breasts bare to the breeze.

Weighted down at the bottom of the quarry, Gail had no intention of leaving her fate in Jerry Burke's hands, or Skimask's. Freedom, fresh air waited twenty feet above. Slipping on the mud, she moved in stages, first the wheel and then her feet, across the bottom to the side of the quarry. She hadn't far to go but progress was difficult with the buoyancy of the wetsuit. Unless the weight of the wheel was balanced just right, her feet and lower body floated upward and she had to struggle to regain her footing. By the time she reached the sheer rock wall she was breathing heavily, using up air at too fast a rate.

The side of the quarry was broken by small crevices and narrow ledges. She slid her arms through the spokes of the wheel and let it rest on her upper arms against her chest. Then she found a crevice just above her head and stepped up on a narrow ledge some eighteen inches above the bottom. The mud on the underside of her boot made her slip. She struggled to regain her footing, wiped the mud free, and the next time succeeded in making the first step.

Clinging to the wall, she faced a new problem. The handcuffs prevented her from keeping a grip with one hand while searching for the next crevice with the other. Every time she tried to move, the wheel threatened to push her away. She tried to lunge upward with both hands at once. The result was a slow-motion tumble backward, with the wheel landing on her face, knocking the regulator from her mouth.

She held her breath, remembered her training and recovered the regulator. A tendril of blood dissipated like smoke. The wheel had cut her lip. Breathing heavily, she was seized with an unreasonable fear that the air in the tank was almost gone. Now she wished the tank had a pressure gauge. How long had she been down? Fifteen, twenty minutes?

She moved clumsily back to the five tanks, pulled the wheel onto her lap and exchanged regulators with one of the fresh tanks. Deliberately she calmed herself and slowed her breathing. If there was no way to escape, she would do best to conserve what air she had. Would anyone visit the quarry at this time of year? In this kind of weather? If so, would they see her? And if they did, how would they know something was wrong?

She forced her eyes away from the surface and began to consider her resources. Could she cut the chain? Ten minutes scraping it against a rock only increased her breathing and had no effect on the chain. She was anchored to the bottom. Only the bubbles rose carelessly to the surface. Only the air was free to rise.

The air.

And then it came to her how to do it, how at least to try to get to the surface. She pulled off the rubber boots and began to wriggle out of the bottom of the wetsuit . . .

CRUX

* * *

The Vietnam Veterans Memorial was situated on the north side of the Mall near Constitution Avenue. The opposite side of the street was bordered by government and private buildings. One of them, a small neo-Grecian design with a windowless facade housed the American Pharmaceutical Association. On each side were narrow parking lots, both shrouded by trees, both untended. It was four forty-five on Good Friday and the building was closed. Jerry Burke pulled into the lot facing 22nd Street. Using Nexli's mirror as a base, he laid out four lines of coke.

"Energy time, baby."

The faint prickling in the nasal passage gave way to a heightened sense of well-being and renewed confidence. They walked a wide stone patio to the front of the building, where a low wall topped by Grecian urns overlooked Constitution Avenue. Beyond it, a grassy slope dotted with trees led to the crest of the Vietnam Memorial. Sunk into the earth, the memorial itself was invisible from their position. Burke handed Nexli a pair of binoculars.

"You're going to keep watch. That sidewalk up there, that's the entrance. You see me come out with two suitcases, bring the car down to the intersection. Keep the doors unlocked. Anybody follows me, you pay no attention, just turn right on Constitution and head over there."

He pointed to the Roosevelt Bridge, which crossed the Potomac. Beyond it was Virginia and a five minute drive to National Airport. He had Nexli repeat the instructions and then gave her the car keys. "Going to be rich, baby."

Nexli rubbed her hands to keep them warm while Burke crossed Constitution Avenue and headed up the sidewalk. Her gloves were in the car but she was too excited to go back and get them. As Burke reappeared between trees she took out the binoculars and followed his progress past a souvenir table, past an information booth under construction—

A movement caught her eye and she turned back to the information booth. At first, nothing. Then she rotated the focus ring and saw him—a man lying on the roof. He seemed to be watching

318 ▶

Jerry, turning with him as he disappeared down the path to the Memorial. And then she saw the rifle.

"*Jerry . . .*"

The distance was too great, the traffic between them too loud for him to hear. Dropping the binoculars, she ran to the car. It never occurred to her that the gunman might not be Libyan, or that the target might not be Jerry Burke.

Keith was at the wall before Chris and Alex arrived. It had stopped raining but puddles hugged the sidewalk and the surface of the wall was beaded with drops. Too edgy to stand still, he walked to the apex of the wall, the Army Colt in the pocket of his overcoat bumping his leg. There were less people now than the day he had first followed Gail. As he passed two parents and their children, Keith heard the oldest boy ask, "Was he a really good friend, daddy?"

"Like you and Stewart . . ."

A really good friend. How good a friend was he to Prem? How good a father to Gail? The innocent were suffering for the sins of the guilty. In a perverse way Keith felt that he was responsible. The vendetta, the desire for revenge at any cost—He thrust the thought aside and glanced at his watch. A drop of water fell from his hair to his wrist. It was five o'clock. He returned up the sloping path and saw Chris and Alex waiting at the flagpole, two suitcases at their feet, as instructed. When she saw him, Chris came forward and they quickly embraced. "Keith, Keith . . ."

"Shh."

Over her shoulder he could see Alex staring at them, his face stiff.

Chris said, "Have you seen Burke?"

"Not yet."

Alex came forward then. His eyes were bloodshot, his skin sallow, tiny welts were on his neck where he had cut himself shaving. "If anything happens to her," he said to Keith, "I'm holding *you* responsible."

"If anything happens to her, you'll share the same—"

"Please," Chris said.

◀ 319

They stopped talking, eyes outward, watching, waiting. Chris took a quick breath. "There he is."

Alex turned to look, and Keith picked up the suitcases. Jerry Burke wore a fixed smile, eyes bright-glassy. "Well, well, like old home week."

"Where's Gail?"

"She's okay."

"Where is she?"

"First things first. I believe those are mine." Burke reached awkwardly for the suitcases, keeping his head back. Keith's hands stayed locked around the handles. Burke's smile died.

"What are you doing?" Alex said nervously. "Give them to him."

Keeping his eyes on Burke, Keith put one suitcase on the ground and shoved it forward with his foot. "Where's Gail?"

Burke put the suitcase between his legs, then pulled an envelope from his pocket and waved it. "I've got directions right here. First, give me that other one."

"For this one you tell me where Prem is."

"Keith . . ."

"I don't know what you're talking about."

"Prem Chaduvedi was at Fairoaks yesterday. I want to know where he is, what happened to him?"

Alex said, "Who's Prem?"

Burke glanced around. "That wasn't the deal—"

"I'm making it part of the deal."

"It's my damned money," Alex said. He tried to grab the suitcase. Keith drew the revolver and put the barrel to Alex's forehead. *"My* deal, old son."

Alex stepped back.

"Keith, please." Chris put her hand on his arm. "Let's get Gail first."

"Two million for two answers. Where's Gail and what happened to Prem?"

From the street, a car horn sounded and a pedestrian called a warning. Burke turned to see his own Rolls-Royce careen up over the curb, race across the sidewalk toward the information booth. Nexli at the wheel. It burst through the plywood wall and

320 ▶

smashed headlong into the side of the booth. Amid the crunch of metal and splintering wood, another sound, a sharp crack. Burke's overcoat brightened with a spray of blood as Alex spun and fell.

"Down!" Keith yelled. He shoved Chris aside, turned and saw someone climbing from the roof of the booth. He fired three quick shots as the figure dropped behind the splintered wall. The horn on the Rolls-Royce was a continuous blare. Keeping his eyes on the booth, Keith moved to Alex. Chris knelt beside him, her raincoat staining with his blood. Alex was staring at her, his face white, mouth working soundlessly. Chris looked up. "Get an ambulance."

Jerry Burke was running, moving toward Constitution Avenue, the two suitcases bouncing off his legs. Keith pointed the gun at the sky. "Hold it!"

He fired a warning shot but Burke just hunched his shoulders and moved faster. Keith pivoted to the information booth, gun ready. A woman stumbled out of the car, her face bloody, hands searching the air, blinded by glass or blood. A cloud of concrete dust drifted over the area. There was no sign of the shooter.

Keith ran after Burke. Someone yelled, "He's got a gun . . ." Visitors and tourists scattered as Keith caught up to Burke, grabbed him by the collar and pulled him around with such force that one of the suitcases flew out of his hand. He pushed the gun against Burke's temple. "Where is she? Where's Gail—?"

A blur of khaki in the corner of his eye, someone tackled him and a moment later he was on the ground wrestling for the gun. The attacker was heavyset, shaggy-haired, wearing a camouflage jacket adorned with unit designations and MIA patches—one of the Vietnam veterans. They rolled across the ground, over a bouquet of flowers and into the wall. Keith got a forearm across the man's throat and pinned him to the black granite. About to suffocate, the man released the gun and grabbed at Keith's arm while from behind a dozen more veterans converged on them. They dragged Keith away and twisted the gun out of his hand. Pain shot up his arm as he yelled at them, trying to explain.

"It's not me," he began, but a fist caught him in the mouth. "Get the gun, get the gun."

"I got it."

"That's enough, stop it."

They pulled Keith to his feet and held him spread-eagled against the wall. All around people were yelling . . .

"Somebody's down near the flag."

"Medic, get a medic."

"Get the goddam police."

Beyond the crowd of angry men, Keith saw Burke getting into a taxi. "He's the one, he's getting away . . ."

"You shut up, man."

He turned to look for Chris. Maybe she could convince them . . .

A park ranger stood ten feet beyond the crowd, staring at him calmly, one eye on Keith, the other focused somewhere over his shoulder.

"You," Keith said.

Severa smiled and turned away. Keith shoved forward, momentarily broke free, but then the veterans carried him back. A tiny American flag broke and fell to the ground. Pinned against the wall, Keith watched helplessly as Mike Severa walked away.

The lower half of the wetsuit, designed like overalls, was called a farmer john. When it was free of her body, Gail felt the shock of icy water. She had to act quickly now. After shoving one of the legs of the suit into the other, she clamped them together by tying them with the shoulder strap. Holding it upside down, she had an air-tight bag, shaped like a human torso, open on the bottom where it fit around the chest and shoulders. Now what she had to do was fill it with air.

How heavy was the wheel chained to her handcuffs? She didn't know. She would have to leave behind the five tanks chained to the second wheel. No extra weight. If it worked, she wouldn't need any more air than what remained in the tank on her back. She was still breathing from one of the auxilliary tanks. Now she switched regulators and began using her own tank. After closing the valve on another auxilliary tank she removed the regulator and pulled the tank between her knees. She positioned the farmer john directly above it, held tight, and opened the valve.

An explosion of bubbles. The farmer john shook as air surged into it, displacing the water, pulling upward, pulling harder, threatening to slip through her arms—she grabbed the lower edge where the shoulder straps were attached and struggled to hold the opening over the bubbles. The wheel was lifting, its weight causing the handcuffs to bite painfully against her wrists. She gritted her teeth and kept her legs beneath the second wheel, the one that held down the five tanks. She would need as much buoyancy as possible. When the strain was great, she kicked free of the second wheel. The tank slipped from between her knees and bubbles pummeled her legs as the bloated farmer john pulled her upward.

Gail felt like an underwater balloonist, dangling beneath the inverted wetsuit, holding tight as the rusty wheel pressed her chest and the chain rubbed against her face. When the farmer john broke the surface, it floated low in the water, leaving her hanging below. She could see the dock, a blurred dark shape ten feet away. Kicking gently so as not to overturn the wetsuit, she tried to move to safety. But instead of getting closer, the dock moved farther away. She kicked harder, the motion causing a bubble to escape the suit. She stopped moving and looked at the surface, just a few feet above her, rippled by the wind—

The wind. That was the force that was pushing the distended wetsuit away from the dock. She remembered the outline of the quarry. The wall opposite the dock was a tumbled mass of rock where the sheer walls had caved in on themselves. What she had to do was hold on and let the wind take her to a safe shore. She kicked again, this time with the wind, using it. The dock faded from sight, the shoreline faded, and with each passing moment the warmth drained from her body. How far was it? A quarter of a mile? Hold tight, kick gently, keep moving . . .

And then her fingers began to cramp. No, she thought. Not yet. I can't let go. She willed her hands to life, willed her fingers to tighten. How far had she gone? Was it her imagination or was she drifting more quickly? Kick out, help the wind. The neopreme suit slipped half an inch through cramped hands. She tightened her grip. She could no longer feel the fabric, no longer feel her fingers. Her hands were numb. Turning her head, she searched for a sign of shore.

It happened so fast, first her left hand, fabric slipping away, then her right—and she was free. The wheel pulled her gently downward, pulled her eyes away from the retreating wetsuit, now drifting more quickly, black against the shimmering gray surface. The pressure grew and she cleared her ears. The light faded. It was deeper here, much deeper. What little air she had left wouldn't last long.

A rectangular boulder rose to meet her. The wheel touched first with a metallic clink. On her hands and knees, she slipped on something too smooth to be rock, slid over the edge and felt a metal seam, a window, a side-view mirror—a vehicle. Someone had driven a van over the cliff. Air. Perhaps there was air trapped inside. Her fingers found the door, found the window already open. Even as she realized that there would be no air, her fingers slid over teeth bordered by cold, soft lips—someone's mouth.

No sound came when she screamed. The mouthpiece fell free and when she recovered it, breathing became a struggle. Panic and disbelief and then she realized—she was out of air. She pulled the reserve lever and breathed again.

A five minute reprieve. Not enough. She was going to die.

CHAPTER 41

Paint me a word picture—how many times had Henri said that? Words to capture the past and plan the future, words to describe worlds both real and imaginary. Keith needed words now. He had to paint a picture for the men who held him. A word picture of the truth before Severa disappeared for good.

"You see that phony park ranger? Listen to me . . . he just shot Senator Wescott and you're letting him get away—"

"No, man, you had the gun."

"I had a handgun. The first shot was a *rifle*. You were in Nam, you know the difference. Who heard the first shot?"

"There were three shots."

"That was return fire. That was the revolver. But the first shot—when the car hit the building—who heard it?"

"Yeah, I did. Sounded like a three oh eight."

"Sniper bullet," Keith said, "and the gunman's the guy in the ranger outfit."

"According to you."

"According to me and I'm one of you. I was in 'Nam, in the Chargers, hundred and ninety-sixth Brigade, Company A, the three twenty-one, Quang Tin province. Who served there? Anybody know that province?

A black man stepped forward wearing a frayed nylon flight jacket. "I was Company B of the three twenty-one."

"What's your name?"

"Walt Higgins."

"I'm Keith Johnson. You guys were ten klicks on the other side of Hill 510. Remember the old rubber plantation in Chim Bai? Granny Di-Di's beer joint? Brush and flush in the An Lo? You know what I'm saying?"

A slow smile spread across Higgins's features. "The man was there."

"Slope or a friendly, how do you know? Charlie doesn't wear a sign. He doesn't wear black pajamas when he's working a rice paddy. Slope or friendly, you make a gut decision. You look at body language, which way he moves when he sees you, where his hands go, what happens to his eyes when you're toe to toe. Charlie with a rice sack is still VC and that guy in the ranger's uniform is still a sniper. He used the Wall for an ambush and he's using you to cover his escape. Gut decision, who're you going to believe?"

They were wavering now, Keith could see the uncertainty in their faces. Someone said, "Let the police sort it out."

"Sure, let ARVN handle it, you know how much good that does. A man's been shot, where's a Park Ranger going if he's for real?"

"He's right," Higgins said. "Man ought to be here." He turned and pushed his way through the crowd. "Hey, you, Ranger . . ."

Severa had reached the street. Ignoring the shout, he looked for a taxi, saw none. His right hand unbuttoned the raincoat and slid inside to grasp the Deutonics in its shoulder holster. If he had to take a car by force—

A taxi turned onto the street heading east. Severa flagged it down. There were footsteps behind him and someone calling, "Hey, just a minute there . . ." As he moved forward, the man grabbed his arm. Severa spun, slammed his right fist into his solar plexus. As Higgins doubled over, Severa reversed direction and whipped his left elbow into the right temple. Higgins dropped to his knees, stunned. Severa got in the cab, pulled the gun and put it to the driver's head. *"Go."*

The veterans holding Keith had seen the exchange, seen Higgins drop. Angry shouts, Keith was released. He and the others ran after the retreating taxi. The two men went to Higgins but the man was already on his feet, eyes bright with anger.

Traffic was heavy but there were no other taxis in sight. Keith moved in front of a black limousine and raised his hands. The car, with its red, white and blue diplomatic license plates, screeched to a stop. A uniformed driver leaned out of the window. "What the hell you doing? Get out of the—"

"Emergency," Keith said. "Man's been shot."

He yanked open the door, grabbed the man by the coat and pulled him into the street.

"Hey, *hey*—"

Cars behind them had come to a stop, horns sounded. Still in gear, the limo began creeping forward as Keith jumped into the driver's seat. Higgins and two other veterans piled in on the passenger side. In the back a Japanese in a tuxedo leaned forward and waved an identification card. "Diplomat car. Diplomat car." He tumbled backward as Keith hit the accelerator.

A red light stopped Severa's taxi at 17th Street. It was on the inside lane with one car ahead and a row of cars lined up on their left. Severa glanced back, saw the limousine run a light at 19th and said, "Turn right."

"There's a car."

"Over the curb. Go."

He jabbed the Deutonics behind the driver's ear. They eased to the right, then up onto the curb. A family of tourists jumped back, and a moment later they bounded into 17th Street heading south.

Keith saw the maneuver. By the time he reached 17th, the light was green and he fishtailed through the right turn. The Mall was on either side of them now, the reflecting pool to the right, to the left a long grassy hill topped by the Washington Monument. Independence Avenue was the next intersection. The taxi made a skidding left turn just as the light turned red.

Keith yanked the wheel, crossed the empty oncoming traffic lanes and bounced onto the grass. He cut a diagonal across the grass, sounding his horn, scattering a group of college kids tossing a frisbee. The limousine hit a bump, lifted and careened down again. As they reached the street a man selling balloons leaped aside but the fender caught his cart and flipped it, sending a flock of balloons drifting skyward.

The taxi turned north on 14th, and the limousine followed, close enough now so that Severa could see Keith's face when he looked behind. Ahead, the sound of sirens and flash of of blue and white, the police on their way to the scene of the shooting. Traffic was stopped, the road blocked. The taxi driver put on his brakes.

"Run the light," Severa ordered.

"But the police—"

"Run it."

The taxi swerved into the empty lane and accelerated. A police car flashed in front of them, right to left. Keith saw the second police car and braked. The taxi was almost through the intersection when the second squad car struck it, sending both cars spinning out of control. The taxi skidded broadside into a parked car. The police car rammed a streetlight head-on, folding the hood and driving the engine into the passenger compartment. The ornate pole sheared off at the base and toppled across the intersection.

Keith skidded to a stop. He and the others jumped from the limousine, ducked beneath the pole and ran to the taxi. Two of the veterans helped the driver from his cab while Keith and Higgins looked for Severa. The back seat was empty except for the Smokey Bear hat. Keith climbed onto the trunk and above the snarled traffic caught sight of Severa going into the Museum of Natural History.

"Got him," he called out.

With Higgins at his side, they took the broad steps two at a time, pushed through the tall doors and found themselves in a rectangular hall that opened into a huge rotunda. Light from a dome four stories above filtered over an oval pedestal where an elephant was mounted, its trunk raised high, while visitors at the base listened on white phones to a prerecorded tape. Radiating outward from the rotunda were exhibition halls and dioramas, glass-enclosed rooms depicting life in various cultures. To the right was an information booth; to the left were elevators, restrooms and a door marked "No Public Access." Severa glanced back as he disappeared inside.

Keith and Higgins went after him. A uniformed guard caught sight of them and called, "Let's not run." And then, as they reached the door, "Excuse me, gentlemen, that area's closed to the public—"

Closed but not locked. Behind the door was a large well-lit room filled with stacked drawers, four feet square, twelve feet high, arranged in rows. Along the exterior wall were offices. No one was visible but some of the doors were open and Keith could hear voices. There was no sign of Severa.

Keith pointed and they split up, Higgins going one way and Keith the other. He walked the rows, glancing down each empty aisle. It reminded him of driving through farm country where long furrows flicked past like spokes of a wheel. The guard entered, saw Keith and called out, "What are you doing?"

From the next aisle Keith caught the sound of quick footsteps. He motioned the guard to be silent, then ran forward in a low crouch. Severa was in the middle of one of the aisles, pistol in hand, turning toward him. Keith kept moving. A sharp report and wood splintered from one of the drawers. Pressing himself against the wall, Keith wished now that he had retrieved the Army Colt.

"Give it up, Severa," he yelled. "The police have the place surrounded."

Keith glanced back at the guard but the man was gone. From the offices at the other end of the room, a commotion. Keith risked a look around the corner. Severa had disappeared. They were in a rectilinear labyrinth; the man might appear at any aisle at any moment. Keith moved forward, checking each aisle before he crossed it. He reached the far wall and saw a wooden door closing. Keith ran to the door and positioned himself against the wall. As he did, Higgins appeared.

"Here," Keith called as he opened the door and risked a quick look. Inside, dim light and a passageway bounded by walls curving outward, disappearing into darkness and makeshift wood scaffolding. Severa, climbing a ladder, fired a quick shot over his

◀ 329

shoulder. Keith slammed the door but not before he noticed the row of light switches just inside the door.

A museum employee, a small man in slacks, striped shirt, and tie, came toward them. "Who are you people? What are you doing here—?"

"What's in there?"

"I'm asking the questions."

Keith grabbed him beneath the arms, lifted him and shoved him against the wall. "You're answering the questions. What's in there?"

"The . . . the back of the dioramas and exhibition hall."

"Any other entrances?"

"Just access doors to the dioramas."

"Any windows?"

"No, it's . . . it's all interior space."

Keith released him. "Get the police and clear the building." The man took three steps backward, turned and ran.

Pressing himself against the wall, Keith opened the door just wide enough to sneak an arm through. He turned off the lights, shut the door and turned to Higgins. "I can disarm him. You take the door. Don't let anyone turn on the lights. Got it?"

"Yeah."

"The door on my command."

Keith bent low, removed the neutral density contact lenses, and shut his eyes against the glare. He crouched, grabbed the door frame to orient himself. *"Now."*

Higgins yanked the door open. Keith dived inside and rolled against a wall. Two shots as the door slammed shut, and then he was on his feet, running in a crouch. He stopped. So little light seeped through cracks that it took a few moments for his eyes to adjust. The backs of dioramas rose on both sides of him, plaster walls arcing up and away, turning into the roof of dioramas as they disappeared from view. Scaffolding and makeshift ladders crisscrossed the walls; the ceiling was cluttered with ventilation ducts and electrical tubing. The place had a musty odor, and Keith could feel grit on his hands from the floor.

A board creaked. Severa was on the bay above. "Severa?" No answer. "I can get you out of here if you tell me where Gail is."

He heard it again, a sound from the top of the diorama, someone trying to move silently. Then a thump, a grunt of surprise, and a can slid down one of the walls.

"What's the matter, Severa? You can't see?"

"Keep talking, Johnson."

Their voices, sounding disembodied, bounced off the rounded walls.

"You should have spent twenty years in prison, you could read a map in this light."

"I should have killed you in Nam."

Five feet away was a ladder nailed to scaffolding. Keith spoke as he moved to it, hoping to cover the sound of his movement. "I thought you did. I thought you were the one who put heroin in my knife. But you never knew about the plant, did you?"

"I figured it afterward when Wescott got his ticket to Saigon."

"But you didn't plan it." Keith had reached the base of the ladder.

"If I'd wanted to take you out I'd have done it on patrol."

There was a shuffling from above, Severa working his way toward the edge. Keith put his foot on the bottom rung. "I didn't know that. It's why I came after you."

"Your problem, not mine."

"Give it up and I can get you out of here." The rung creaked as he set his weight on it.

"You coming up here, Johnson?"

The room was silent now, both of them alert to the other's movement. The muffled voices of people visiting the museum were audible. Keith pulled off a shoe and lofted it like a grenade, up and over. It landed on the roof of the diorama and a shot rang out. Keith quickly climbed the remaining rungs and stopped as soon as his head cleared the wall. Now he was looking over the roof of the diorama, an area connected by catwalks suspended from the rafters above. It took a moment before he picked out Severa's darker form, kneeling about twenty feet away on the catwalk, his head cocked to one side, gun in both hands. Keith turned his face toward the floor to disguise the direction of his voice. "You pull the trigger again and I'll drop you." Severa's head swiveled, trying to locate him. "I can see you now, Sergeant."

"Bullshit."

"You're on your knees. Raise a hand, I'll tell you which one. Go ahead."

"Okay, there." Severa hadn't moved.

"Nice try. Your hands are still on the gun." A hesitation, then Severa lifted a hand. "Left hand in the air, my gun at your heart. This is daylight to me, Severa. I'll give you a five count. You want to aim at my voice, you'll have one shot before I nail you."

"You don't have the gun."

"I got it back."

"Bullshit."

"Five, four . . ."

"Give me a warning shot."

"Not with one bullet left. Three, two . . ."

"Take me out and your girl dies, I made sure of that."

"Where is she?"

"Remember the Bamboo Reef? Your little trick with the helium? I was more generous. She's got air in her tanks, but not much longer."

"Where?"

"A river, a swimming pool, the Chesapeake Bay—guess."

"A deal, Severa. You give me her location, I'll get you out of here."

"You get me out first, then you get the location."

"All right, give me the gun."

"I don't think so."

"It's the only way. I take you hostage, move you past the guards outside the building—"

"And put a bullet in my head."

"I could have killed you a dozen times since I came to your office. Give me Gail and we're quits."

He could hear Severa breathing, see him outlined in the gloom as he stood up. "Okay, Johnson. This time your way."

But not quite. Severa wasn't taking any chances. There was a click as he removed the ammunition clip and tossed it onto the roof of the diorama. Then he pulled the slide back, ejecting the bullet that rattled its way down some invisible recess to the floor. Severa held up the gun.

"If you can see it, come and get it."

"Hold your position."

Keith climbed onto the catwalk and started forward. There was a commotion from outside, the door banged open and the lights came on. The passageway below was invisible from the roof, but a voice boomed, "This is the police. Throw down your weapons and come out."

"Go *back*," Keith called. "I've got him . . ."

They were fifteen feet apart, facing each other from opposite sides of the diorama roof. Severa had dropped to a half-crouch when the lights came on. His eyes went to Keith's empty hands, saw he was unarmed, then flicked to the ammunition clip lying on the roof. He stepped toward it, off the catwalk, and the plaster ceiling gave way. Severa fell, enveloped in light from below. There was a clatter of debris and the heavier sound as he landed. The boards bounced as Keith ran forward.

Severa scrambled up from the floor of the diorama. A cave man stood over him brandishing a hatchet, and a woman dressed in bear skins crouched by a false fire, two small children beside her. Behind the glass, in the viewing hall, an old woman leaning on a cane and her daughter gasped as Severa retrieved his ammunition clip from the debris. He took two steps toward the window and kicked at the glass, trying to break through it. The women screamed and ran. Two policemen ran into the hall and saw Severa lift his gun.

"Police, drop your gun."

Severa heard nothing through the heavy glass, saw only his own reflection. Unable to break the glass, he fired twice. Huge cracks leaped across its surface. The fussilade of bullets from the other side caught him by surprise and turned the window into a mosaic of falling glass. Severa stumbled backward, toppling the caveman as he fell.

"Unarmed," Keith yelled as he dropped through the hole.

"Freeze."

Keith crouched next to Severa. "Where? Where is she?"

Severa's eyes tried to focus.

◄ 333

"Where's Gail?"

The lips worked, blood trickled from one side of his mouth. "Fairoaks."

"Hand on your head," an officer yelled. "Do it *now.*"

Keith looked up. The two officers were at opposite sides of the viewing window, each pointing a gun at him.

"Forget it," he said. "He's dead."

CHAPTER 42

Crazy Arab bitch. That was the refrain that echoed in Jerry Burke's brain as the taxi sped across the Roosevelt Bridge. Severa's bullet might have hit *him* instead of Wescott. Not until he was half way to National Airport did he put it together and realize that Nexli must have mistaken Severa for a Libyan. She hadn't screwed up—she was trying to save *him*. He was going to miss Nexli.

He pulled the suitcase to his lap and snapped open the latches. He could see the driver in the rearview mirror.

"Hey, cabbie, turn the mirror."

"What?"

"I said turn the rearview mirror. I don't like people watching me."

"Sorry, brother, that's the law."

"Ten dollars says we fuck the law and you turn the mirror."

"Ten says you're right." The man's hand went up and twisted the mirror away. Burke checked both suitcases. Beautiful. The money was stacked and bound in neat piles.

They bypassed the main terminal and stopped at Butler Aviation, a modern white-and-blue building that served business jets and private aircraft. Important politicians and famous faces often

◀ 335

passed through there, but Burke saw none today. The Gulfstream sat in the transient parking area, its door open, stairs extended.

"Udo?" Burke called as he stepped inside. The pilot stuck his head from the cockpit. "Up here."

Burke shoved the suitcases onto the couch and moved to the cockpit. "Let's get out of here."

Udo Lauer was tied to his seat. In the co-pilot's chair an Arab in baggy trousers and a leather coat smiled as he pointed a gun at him. "Just in time, Mr. Burke."

A sound from the cabin. Burke turned and saw a second Arab step out of the bathroom and move to block the exit. He, too, had a gun. He was not smiling.

"Sundown, Mr. Burke," the first Arab said. "Your time is over."

"Who are you?"

"You may call me Yasuf." The gun waved him back. "Back into the cabin, please."

Burke looked at Lauer, strapped to his chair. Yasuf caught the look and turned to the pilot. "You are in much danger of dying. Until we are gone, make no effort to escape, do you understand?"

"Get off my aircraft."

Yasuf made a fist, exposing a ring on his middle finger, the crescent moon of Islam. He placed his fist against Lauer's forehead, then raked it sideways. A line of blood appeared. "Dead pilots have no aircraft."

"Cut it out," Burke said. "The deal's still good. I've got the money—"

The Arab pushed him into the cabin and shut the door. "You say you have the money?"

"Of course. And it's not sundown yet."

Yasuf smiled. "It is in Tripoli." The other Arab spoke sharply and the smile faded. "Where is the money?"

"Right here. I've got it here. You want to transact business like gentlemen, ask questions first, save the hardware for later." Burke lifted a suitcase to the couch and started to open it. Yasuf pushed the gun in front of his face. "No. He will open it."

Burke stepped back and the second Arab opened the suitcase. When they saw the stack of bills, their eyes widened. "This is one million four hundred and fifty thousand dollars?"

"That's a million of it. Tell you what. Why don't you guys take that, the two of you, and disappear? I won't say anything, maybe they'll think you're dead, you live the rest of your life like kings. How's that?"

A brief discussion in Arabic ensued. Burke kept his eyes away from the second suitcase. He hadn't divided the money and didn't like the idea of showing more money than he owed. Not to errand boys with big guns who might get ideas. Maybe they would just take the money from the first suitcase and leave. Instead, Yasuf grabbed the second suitcase and opened it.

"That's another million," Burke said, trying to recover, make the best of it. "Half of it's mine. I'm moving to England. I told Major Hasnid that you guys could pick up your share in London tomorrow, but what the hell, he said you were already on your way."

Yasuf frowned. "You talked to Major Hasnid? When?"

"Half an hour ago. Just to let him know there was no problem, I had the money, I was on my way. We're setting up a deal for M-16s."

Yasuf eyed him, but Burke just smiled. Bastards wouldn't try anything if they thought he was still tight with Hasnid and the Defense Council. This time the conversation in Arabic was brief. Yasuf sat down at the polished wood table. "We will count the money you owe."

Burke sat opposite him and they divided the money from the second suitcase into two piles, one of four hundred and fifty thousand dollars and one of five hundred and fifty thousand.

"Hey, you guys can even have the second suitcase if you want," Burke said, desperate to get rid of them.

Yasuf stood up. "First we trade places." He pulled his gun from his waistband and waved it at Burke. "Move away. Move to the small pile, please."

"Why should I? You've got your money."

"Yes, but we are needing one hundred thousand dollars for our security bond."

"What security bond?"

"When my brother and myself are safely arrived in Tripoli,

Major Hasnid will return to you this security bond. Did he not tell you this?"

They watched him closely. Was this something Hasnid came up with? If so, they would know he hadn't talked to him if he denied it. But if it was their own invention, they would know he hadn't talked to Hasnid if he accepted it. Burke decided to bet they were lying. "He didn't mention it."

The two men exchanged a glance and Burke knew he had guessed right. Yasuf shrugged. "Then this is something you must clear up later."

"Security bond is not part of the deal."

"But we have the guns, so we make the deal. Get back." Burke watched as the second Arab took the large pile of bills and packed it in the suitcase. He was furious.

"I saw a thief get his hand cut off over in your country."

"And a liar," Yasuf said nastily, "will have his tongue cut out."

The Arabs moved to the door, each with a suitcase, tucked their weapons out of sight and were gone. Burke moved to a window and watched them disappear into the Butler Aviation building. He went to the cockpit and untied Udo Lauer. The ridge of blood had already dried but the pilot was ready to go after the Arabs with his fists.

"Forget it," Burke said. "Let's get out of here. We're going to London."

"I have to file a flight plan."

"Do it in the air. Let's just go." He remained in the cockpit and read the takeoff checklist to expedite matters. Not until they were airborne did he relax. Below them he could see the Lincoln Memorial, where less than an hour ago a bullet had passed within six inches of his head. Maybe it was all for the best, the screw-up at the wall. After all, without Severa's share of the money, the Arabs would have killed him.

He unstrapped the seatbelt and went back to the head. The varnished wood walls and expensive fittings gave him a renewed sense of security. He shut the door and lifted the lid of the toilet. A slight resistance, and then he was looking at a plastic-wrapped package taped to a six-volt battery. A moment of comprehension before the explosion ripped the tail from the aircraft. Udo Lauer was still broadcasting MAYDAY when the broken craft exploded into the earth.

"They've found the body," the officer named Trimble said. Chris pressed her face against Keith's arm. They stood on the dock at the quarry in the gathering gloom. Five scuba tanks had been retrieved beneath the dock but there was no sign of Gail. Now, as the divers swam slowly toward them, Keith felt a desolation he hadn't known since his first days in prison.

The dock sank slightly as Trimble pulled out a flashlight and moved forward to help. The body was face down between the two black-suited divers, but in the flashlight's beam Keith saw a Western shirt and vest.

"It's not her," he said.

Chris turned and looked. "Is it . . .?"

"Prem."

Her fingers tightened on his arm as the police lifted the body to the dock. Trimble turned. "You know the victim?"

"Prem Chaduvedi. A friend of mine."

Chris said, "What about Gail?"

The divers climbed onto the dock. One of them pulled off his hood and pushed his hair back. "I'm sorry, m'am. We can't do anything else until morning."

"Can't you keep looking?"

"Too dark now. Can't see a thing down there."

"What about lights?" Keith said.

"Well, if we had the generator and the equipment . . ."

"Get them. I'll pay for equipment, for overtime, whatever it takes. Get the equipment."

"You better talk to Lieutenant Stutz about that."

As they spoke Trimble pulled out a walkie-talkie and radioed the men waiting at the ambulance to bring a body bag. As he tucked the radio back into its holder, the flashlight's beam swept across the water and illuminated something floating, a face—

"Holy Jesus!" Trimble took a quick step back and then laughed. "Scared the hell out of me. I thought it was a stiff, I really did."

Drifting from beneath the dock was a large wooden Indian, its fierce gaze directed at the sky. Trimble's radio crackled. "Two Adam Six, Base."

He lifted it to his lips. "Two Adam Six, go ahead."

"Eddie, we've got a ten ninety-nine on subject Gail Wescott. You can pull the divers."

Chris moved forward. "Is she all right?"

"Where is she, Bill?"

"Fairfax General Hospital. They brought her in about forty-five minutes ago. That's all we know."

Gail was under sedation when they arrived. According to the statement she had given the police, she had used the wooden Indian to swim to the dock. Then she hooked the chain over a stanchion and climbed out. After regaining some strength she moved the wheel in stages until she got to a road where a passing car found her . . . She was suffering from exposure and had cuts and bruises, but would, the doctors said, make a full recovery.

Alex would not. The bullet damaged his spinal cord and left him paralyzed. Keith was with Chris the next day at Columbia Hospital when the doctor explained his condition.

"The bullet struck your husband's spinal column, Mrs. Wescott. He suffered a C-6 fracture with incomplete cord injury. Fragments of the vertebra have impinged the spinal cord. The senator, I'm sorry to tell you, is paralyzed below the neck."

"Can you operate? Remove the fragments?"

"We removed two fragments when he was brought in. Surgery at a later date is a possibility but you should understand that removing them can't repair the damage to the spinal cord. The senator is fortunate that he can breathe without a respirator. That's unusual in cases of this nature."

The police had already taken Alex's statement. Chris went in to see him, Keith waited in the lounge. After a few minutes, she came back looking pale and shaken. "He wants to see you."

"You told him I was here?"

"He asked."

Keith started to go but Chris didn't follow. "Aren't you coming?"

"He wants to see you alone . . ."

Alex lay in bed, his arms outside the sheets, a plastic identification tag around one wrist. He turned his head when Keith entered but his body remained motionless.

"There he is, the victor. You'll forgive me if I don't leap over the net and shake your hand." He paused. "You heard the good news and bad news?"

"What?"

"The good news is I'm still alive. The bad news is I'm still alive."

Keith tried to feel something—remorse, pity, sympathy—for the once handsome man whose body lay lifeless before him, but twenty years in darkness had numbed his emotions as effectively as the bullet had paralyzed Alex's body.

"Hey, old son, why aren't you cheering? You wanted it this way. Wanted me dead. Almost there. Nine tenths, anyway. By weight or volume, I'm nine-tenths dead. You see the left hand? That's what happens when I try to make a fist." His fingers twitched slightly but the hand remained motionless. "Maybe in ten years I can reach my thumb with my forefinger. A miracle of rehabilitation. I can write a book, be a guest on the Today show, talk about the power of faith, patience, determination." The false smile died. "Forget it. Not for me. That's why I called you. Now's your big chance to pull the plug on me. Go ahead, put a pillow over my face, they'll never know. It'll look like cardiac arrest. Don't stare at me, just do it, do it, goddamn you."

His head twisted back and forth. Keith put a hand on his forehead and the motion stopped. Their eyes met. Keith took his hand away. Ask me again in twenty years, he wanted to say. But did them both a favor and said nothing.

He went to the door. Alex's voice followed him across the room. "I took the bullet, it was meant for you. You owe me . . ."

Keith paused. "For what it's worth, Chim Bai is history. No one will know the truth."

The face on the pillow became a mask of hate. "Fuck your forgiveness, Keith. You're too late."

You, too, he thought, and left without a word.

◀ 341

*　*　*

In the lounge Chris stood with her arms around Nick and Bobby. With them was an older couple that Chris introduced as Alex's parents. His mother was a thin woman with an erect bearing and watery eyes. Congressman Wescott was a fleshy version of Alex, lips tucked inward in an expression of permanent impatience.

"You're Alex's friend from Vietnam," he said. "We once talked on the phone."

"You've got a good memory, congressman."

"You caught the assassin. Any idea why he did it? Why he tried to kill my son?"

Keith shook his head. "You'll have to ask Alex."

When the parents left for Alex's room, Chris introduced Nick and Bobby. The boys had blond hair but their features were a mixture of both parents. The youngest, Bobby, had eyes red from crying and held tight to Chris' arm.

"This is Keith Johnson," she said. "Gail's father, and daddy's friend from Vietnam."

Nick put out his hand and said in a stiff voice, "How do you do, sir?" Bobby turned to Chris and whispered, "When can we see daddy?"

"Let grandma and grandpa have a minute, then we'll see him. Come on, let's sit over here."

She led the boys to a couch. Keith felt distant, estranged. He and Chris had spent only a few moments together since the shooting. Watching her with the boys he realized how little was left of the life they had shared all those years ago. Memories, that was all. And a night of love at the Willard that now seemed more like a dream. Like the time in prison.

Keith turned and walked away. Chris caught up to him at the nursing station. "Keith, wait. Where are you going?"

"I don't belong here."

She closed her eyes. "Don't do this. The boys are watching, I can't reach out, I can't touch you, but don't give up. Please . . ."

"I love you Christie. I want you with me. Right now I want to put my arms around you and take you away—"

"We *will*, I know we will . . ."

He glanced over her shoulder to the boys, to the room beyond. "And Alex?"

"I don't love him, you *know* that. But I'm obligated to him. At least until he recovers, until he learns to live with the way he is, until the children can begin to adjust. I can't walk out now, you wouldn't want me to. But we . . . we can still begin a life. We can see each other, do things together, get to *know* each other again. Just give us time . . ."

Congressman Wescott appeared then in the hall behind her. "Chris? He wants to see the boys."

She glanced back. "I'll be right there." She turned to Keith. "Will you wait? *Please?*"

He watched her rejoin her family, then left the hospital and walked down 23rd Street. He went to the same florist shop Gail had visited and bought a white rose. When he got to the memorial he saw that temporary repairs had already been made to the damaged information booth, which was still tied off with strands of yellow ribbon that said "Police Line, Do Not Cross." At the flagpole there was no sign of blood to mark the spot where Alex had fallen.

Keith walked the wall. He wondered how many *indirect* victims of the Vietnam war there were? People like Prem Chaduvedi and Leanne Burke. Or were they also, in part, victims of his own obsessive need for vengeance? He stood before his own name and thought about the man he had become. Maybe the wall was accurate after all. Keith Johnson was dead. Nothing could change the past, nothing could eliminate the twenty years that Chris had been with Alex. He put the flower at the base of the wall, stepped back and saluted the boy who died in Chim Bai.

When he turned around, Gail was there. He could tell from her expression that she knew, that Chris had told her. She came toward him, eyes searching and finding confirmation in his face. "Dad . . .?"

"Gail . . ."

CRUX

She bit her lip to keep back the tears, and then she was in his arms and he was holding her, holding her close, believing he *could* wait, and knowing he was, finally, home.

It was a beginning.